GHOST HEART

LISA HARRIS

LYNNE GENTRY

Cover design: Lisa Harris

For those who cannot speak for themselves.
May your cries for help finally be heard.

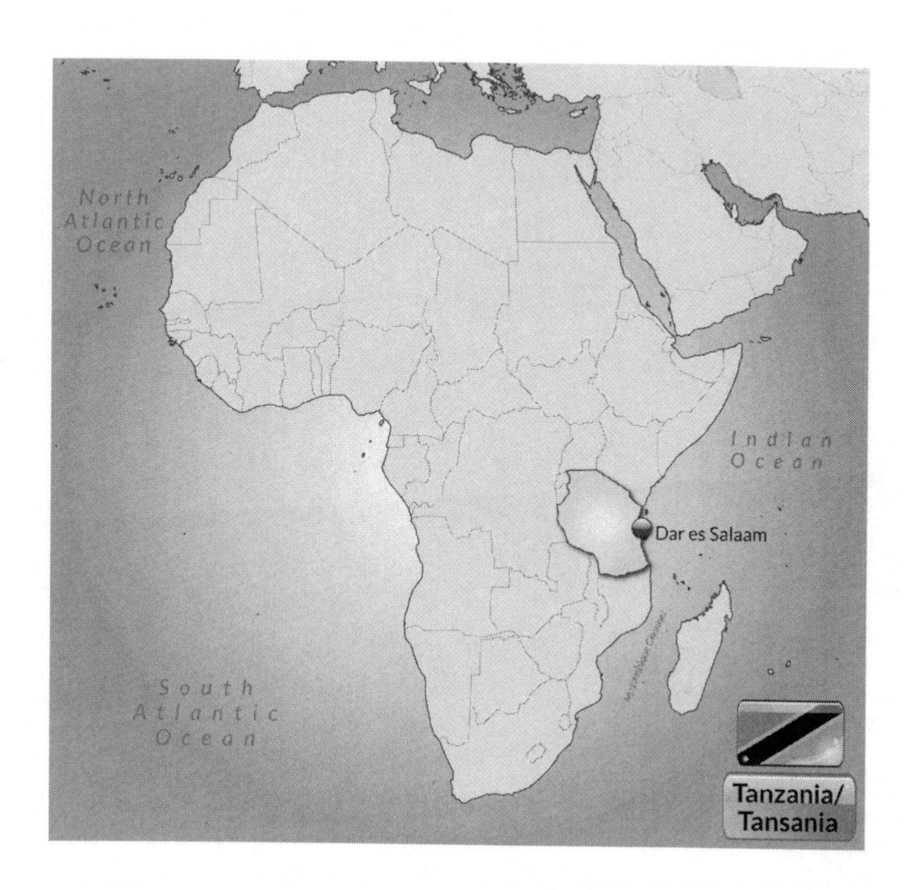
North
Atlantic
Ocean
Indian
Ocean
Dar es Salaam
South
Atlantic
Ocean
Tanzania/
Tansania

GLOSSARY OF TERMS

- *Albino*- A congenital disorder where there is partial or complete absence of pigment in the skin, hair and eyes. People who are albino often have problems with their vision and are susceptible to sunburn and skin cancers.

- *Chipati*- Unleavened flatbread

- *Dala-dala*- mini bus taxis in Tanzania

- *Dar es Salaam*- Tanzania's largest city and major port located on the Indian Ocean coast.

- *Ghost Child or Ghost People*- A term sometimes used for albinos that is connected to the idea that they are ghosts who bring bad luck.

- *Jambo*- A Swahili greeting like Hello.

- *Kanga*- Colorful garment or wrap worn by women and used for a variety of things, including carrying their babies.

- *Karibu-* You're welcome in Swahili

- *Nyama choma-* Roasted meat in Swahili

- *Sangoma-* Traditional healer, witch doctor, or diviner that often calls on the dead ancestors from the spirit world to help with illnesses and spiritual matters.

- *Swahili-* A Bantu language that is used primarily in East Africa, including Tanzania, Kenya, Zanzibar, and Uganda.

- *Tanzania-* Country located in Eastern Africa. Known for the stunning plains of Serengeti National Park and Kilimanjaro National park, Africa's highest mountains. It also includes the island of Zanzibar. Official language is Swahili and English, and it boasts a population of about fifty-three and a half million people.

- *Tetrology of Fallot* - a serious congenital heart defect present at birth. Symptoms include episodes of bluish color to the skin. When affected babies cry, they may develop a "tet spell" where they turn very blue and have difficulty breathing.

- *Ugali-* Traditional dish made from cornmeal or other flours that is made into a stiff dough and eaten with a sauce.

- *UNOS–* United Network for Organ Sharing is the private, nonprofit organization that manages the organ transplant system in America.

- *Wasungu-* Term used to refer to people of European descent.

- *Zeruzeru-* an albino

PROLOGUE

WEDNESDAY, DECEMBER 11TH, 5:52 PM

MAKURU, TANZANIA

According to legend, their kind could never die. When they grew old, they simply vanished from this world, like smoke from the cooking fire that snakes above the spindly baobab trees and slithers away.

But not all legends are true.

Or so Jeme prayed.

Squinting through the shimmering rays of the grueling African sun, Jeme balanced the bowl of dried beans on her head and pressed through the crowded marketplace. A maze of narrow paths twisted around her, each lined with dozens of sellers who sat in cramped wooden shops displaying wares on rickety tables.

The smell of curried meat roasting on the grills mingled with the pungent odor of dried fish baking in the late afternoon heat. Jeme's empty stomach roiled as she hurried past piles of tomatoes, peppers, oranges, and colorful bags of spices. If only she could escape the whispers competing with the buzz of the buyers and sellers. Whispers that spoke of the magical powers of albino blood spilled across the brown earth, and of potions that could bring untold wealth.

She stepped into a puddle left over from the late afternoon rains, barely noticing the mud oozing between her toes. In Makuru, fish and vegetables weren't the only things for sale.

There was a price for human flesh, promising the strongest magic.

A flash of red caught her eye then vanished behind one of the tin-roofed stalls. Jeme jerked around, her breath tangled in the fear that had long ago taken root. Her fingers pressed against the rough wood of the kiosk as her eyes searched for the hunters. If they trailed her to the home she shared with Mbui, Numa, and Zaina, they would uncover her secret.

Jeme willed her heart to stop its frantic pounding and slipped through the back entrance of the market. Without the cover of the pulsing throng, she would be easier to track. Nerves on high alert, she hurried down the dirt path that led to her compound.

Something snapped behind her.

A fleeting look revealed nothing more than a boy watching his herd of goats in the grassy field beyond the market. She fingered the charm around her neck. She couldn't be too careful.

She longed for Mbui's presence and his cunning way of making their path difficult to follow. Not so many months ago, her husband had walked her home from the market each evening to ensure her safety from those who believed in the legend. Then fever attacked him, and Mbui's strength left.

Doctors from the hospital in Dar es Salaam promised her husband a new heart and a new life, but two days ago the fever returned, hotter than ever. He was dying because of the curse. Today she'd called his doctor, begging her to come before she had to bury Mbui beneath the baobab tree.

A quick glance at the setting sun only added to her concern. There was still no sign of Dr. Kendall's plane.

Fifteen minutes passed before Jeme reached the end of the winding path. Uncertain whether or not she'd been followed, she crouched in the shadows edging the compound. She studied the home she'd grown to love. Mbui's once strong hands had built the three huts, with their thick thatched roofs and solid mud walls.

Everything looked the same as when she'd left before the sun had risen from its bed in the sky. Tattered pieces of laundry fluttered in the breeze. Chickens pecked the twig-swept yard. And their goat remained tethered to a sturdy papaya tree. There was no sign of her sister, but Numa rarely ventured into the sunlight.

Glancing over her shoulder, Jeme slipped from the dense foliage. Shooing chickens from her path, she quickly crossed the yard. She passed the hut she and Mbui shared and went straight to her sister's door. She stopped and stared at the crude wooden slab hanging slightly ajar.

She knocked. "Numa?"

Nothing.

Jeme knocked again, panic rising at her failure to rouse her sister's cheery response. She pressed on the door. It creaked open. A beam of light spilled onto the floor. She stepped across the threshold, letting her eyes adjust to the silent darkness.

"Numa?"

Jeme froze.

A skinned body lay in a pool of blood.

"Numa!" Jeme fell to the packed-dirt floor. "No!" Her legs refused to stand, so she crawled the short distance to her sister. Body trembling, she sought Numa's hands, but they were gone. Every limb was gone.

"No!" Her screams rose through the thatched roof.

Jeme pounded the earth, cursing the ancestors who had forsaken her sister. Tears streamed down her cheeks as the sobs shook her chest.

Zaina!

Terror sliced through Jeme with the force of Mbui's sugarcane machete. Where was her daughter?

Jeme jumped up, screaming for the child she'd left in the care of her sister. She tripped over a pile of cooking pots, barely managing to keep her balance as she frantically searched the dark shadows of the room for signs of her baby.

"Zaina!"

Chest heaving, Jeme stopped in the center of the hut. She couldn't breathe. She couldn't think. She couldn't live without her child.

A soft cry broke through the stillness.

She turned to her sister's tiny bed, threw off the thin blanket, and shoved the mattress onto the floor. On top of the wooden bed slats, Zaina lay wrapped tightly in Numa's *kanga*.

Jeme pulled the crying infant toward her pounding chest and quickly quieted her with the offer of her swollen breast. Rocking back and forth, she glanced from the lifeless body of Numa to the door. What should she do? Because it wasn't her own dark skin the albino hunters were after.

Jeme caressed the soft, pale skin of her daughter's pinkish feet. Eventually, the blazing African sun would bake her child's delicate skin until it was thick and leathery. Blemishes would rise and mark Zaina's beautiful face like inky splotches on white paper—like Numa.

Jeme tucked her towheaded daughter deep into the faded cloth and tied her securely onto her back. She would not allow her own flesh and blood to become the hunted.

But if she stayed here, it was only a matter of time before human poachers found this cursed child.

CHAPTER ONE

DECEMBER 11TH, 9:34 AM EST

CINCINNATI, OHIO

Catherine Taylor maneuvered her daughter's stroller around the redheaded toddler squatting amongst the Legos scattered on the gleaming waiting room floor. Although five years of weekly visits to the cardiologist had failed to make the jungle-themed office feel like home, joining other parents in their fight against similar heart defects had spawned a sense of family.

"Look, Kelsey." Catherine peered around the stroller cover. Blonde curls framed the angelic face of the underweight child holding a stuffed monkey in one hand and her soothing blanket in the other. Normal five-year-olds had given up their blankets by now, but the gap between Kelsey and normal children was growing wider by the day. "It's your friend, Timmy."

Kelsey's frail little arm extended the toy she'd requested in her Santa letter. "Want to see my new monkey?" When Kelsey asked why Santa had brought her gifts early and not her brother's, Catherine had told her it was because Santa's sleigh would be too full. The truth was,

Christmas was two weeks away, and she couldn't bear it if Kelsey died before she opened her gifts.

"Let's see if Timmy is feeling better before we share." Catherine quickly wheeled the stroller wide as she eyed the small boy for any signs of last week's runny nose.

Susan, Timmy's mother, left her seat and wrapped a protective arm around her son. "He's not contagious." Desperate eyes, sunken in the haggard shell of former soccer-mom beauty, searched Catherine's for a bit of understanding. Understanding Catherine could no longer afford.

Everything in Dr. Finke's lobby had been specifically chosen so that it could be sterilized on a daily basis. But neither mother could deny what worried them most. The unseen microorganisms. Those microscopic missiles of death that traveled the airwaves seeking to destroy weakened targets like Kelsey and Timmy. Contracting a single germ that normal children shrugged off could kill their babies.

Catherine parked Kelsey in the far corner...just in case. "How did Timmy manage to shake that cold?"

Susan nervously tucked a strand of mahogany hair behind her ear. "Two rounds of antibiotics."

"Whatever it takes, right?" Catherine offered Susan the same hopeful, but useless smile other mothers had once offered her. The clock was ticking and antibiotics wouldn't slow it down.

She removed her fur-lined gloves and dropped them into the giant tote bag she lugged whenever forced to leave the house.

"I want out, Momma."

If only Kelsey could run and play. "Hang on, punkin." Catherine unzipped Kelsey's pink parka and freed her twig-like arms. Ugly purple tracks from endless blood tests scored the tender flesh between her daughter's wrists and elbows. Longing to kiss away the painful bruises, she folded Kelsey's arms across the labored rise and fall of her little chest. How much longer could her child endure this medical poking and prodding?

Kelsey whimpered, but didn't complain. "Can you turn me to the wall?"

All sorts of animals were hidden in the foliage of the wallpaper jungle scene. Kelsey tried to spot a new creature every time they came for a checkup. Last time, she'd found the monkey. His ability to leap from tree to tree had so entranced her, nothing would do until she had one of her own.

"Sure." Catherine checked her watch and felt her own heart lurch. She'd nearly missed the morning meds.

"Punkin, it's time for your special milk." Catherine scooped her daughter into her arms and sank into the nearest chair.

"But I want to show my monkey to the monkey on the wall," Kelsey protested.

"Take a drink for Momma, and I'll help you introduce your monkey to the monkey on the wall." She kissed the nest of curls nuzzled against her chest, drinking in the baby-shampoo scent of her sweet girl.

Digging into her tote bag, Catherine sorted through an assortment of Ziploc bags until she found the one with the Sippy cup. If she could cajole Kelsey into taking half an ounce of the milky supplement, then maybe they'd have a shot at keeping today's meds in her child's distended tummy.

She held the cup to her daughter's clamped lips. "Please. Just one sip."

"I'm tired." A fussy shake of Kelsey's head signaled the start of the cycle of absolute refusal.

Pain, combined with the disgusting taste of the medicine regime, always transformed her child's normally sunny disposition into a full-blown tantrum. Within moments of the exertion, the panting spells would begin. Afraid Kelsey could no longer tolerate the trauma, Catherine withdrew the cup. "Maybe later then." She snatched the night-night from the stroller and offered the silky-edged blanket to her snuffling child.

Kelsey accepted one of the few things that could soothe her and drew herself into a ball around its soft comfort. Seconds later, she drifted off to sleep.

Holding her dormant child tight, Catherine resisted the urge to check for the faint irregular beat of Kelsey's struggling heart.

How long did they have before the deformed organ gave up its battle?

Carefully, she returned her youngest to the stroller, relieved when she saw Kelsey take a breath. She stroked the damp curls away from her daughter's pale, oval face.

Nothing so perfect on the outside could possibly have something so wrong on the inside. A lie, she knew. But easier to swallow than the truth.

Scrubbing the untouched drinking cup with an antibacterial wipe, Catherine refused to give in to the panic knotting her gut. According to Brad, their daughter was a fighter, inheriting her stubborn streak from Catherine. Thank God. If Kelsey had been born with Brad's everything-will-work-out personality, her shriveled blue body would have never made it out of the preemie unit of Cincinnati's NICU.

Catherine sealed the cup in the Ziploc then stuffed it inside Kelsey's bag. Keeping Kelsey hydrated and medicated had become a vicious cycle of trying to stay on the clock. If she delayed forcing Kelsey's morning meds down her, the med schedule would be off for the entire day. She made a mental note to ask Dr. Finke to explain the feeding tube he'd mentioned last week. Maybe if Kelsey's meds could be pumped directly into her frail body, things would turn around. A desperate measure, but one she was more inclined to consider due to Kelsey's continued deterioration.

In an attempt to quiet the butterflies aloft in her stomach, Catherine picked up the same dog-eared parenting magazine she'd read every office visit for the last five years. Flipping the pages without actually reading a word, she watched Timmy quietly press together plastic blocks with older-child precision. Every week, he built imaginary cars he would probably never drive and lopsided castles he would never fill with his own children.

Catherine's eyes slid from the boy to his mother. Susan, perched on the edge of a green-leather seat, stared at Catherine's sleeping daughter. Susan teetered on the brink of a catastrophe similar to Catherine's, and from the pinched look on her face, she knew it. Any moment Susan's son could be lying listless in a stroller while other mothers looked on and thanked their lucky stars he was not their child.

In Susan's fearful gaze, Catherine saw what she'd been telling herself could not be true. Until a few weeks ago, Kelsey's limited play mimicked Timmy's. She'd play quietly with her baby doll, stopping every few minutes to fold herself into the squatting position. The pressure against her chest granted the swollen aorta of her boot-shaped heart a brief reprieve while forcing oxygen-deprived blood into hungry lungs.

Catherine adjusted Kelsey's blanket, her own heart sinking at her inability to rouse her daughter even a little.

Susan reached down and helped Timmy snap two Legos together. Envy, bitter as bile stung Catherine's tongue. Timmy still had a bit of rose in his cheeks. Catherine glanced at Kelsey's sleeping face and grimaced at the total void of color.

Terror clawed at her insides. Kelsey's worsening condition was not Susan's fault. The poor woman would soon have more troubles than any mother should ever have to bear.

"Is it someone's naptime?" Susan's attempt to sound upbeat fell flat.

Catherine stifled the urge to scream, her clenched sigh ruffling her stringy bangs in desperate need of a trim. "Twenty hours out of twenty-four."

Susan nodded, letting the snippy answer go unquestioned.

"Sorry, Susan...I..." Catherine closed the magazine and laid it on the table. Her friend didn't deserve the anger that boiled just below the steely exterior she worked to maintain. But try as she might, she couldn't shake the urge to hit someone. Even on those rare occasions when Brad put forth the extra effort to spell her, she couldn't escape the feeling that any moment she could blow.

Susan dismissed the apology with a wave. "Is she—" Her voice fragile as a brittle leaf. "—going to need a transplant?"

"We find out today."

Susan crossed the room and slipped into the chair beside Catherine. "I've been doing some research. On the Internet." She looked around the room as if it were bugged then quickly removed several printed pages from her purse and handed them to Catherine. "Just in case."

"What is this?"

"You can get a heart. If you have the money."

Trepidation rattled the papers in Catherine's hands. She quickly thumbed through them, trying to make sense of the printed words. She stopped on the page with a red, lopsided heart-shaped map in the upper right hand corner. “What are you talking about?”

“Did your insurance grant preapproval?”

“Brad’s checking on the hold up.” Catherine glanced at the page again. This wasn’t a heart logo. This was a map of Africa. Her stomach cartwheeled. “But we’ve bought a supplemental policy just in case.”

“Good thing, because in the States, a new heart is going to cost over a million dollars.”

“I know. I’ve checked the numbers.”

“Well, in some countries”—Susan scanned the room again—“hearts are more...affordable.”

Catherine stiffened, folded the papers, and handed them back to Susan. “I’m not looking for a clearance rack special to replace my daughter’s heart.”

“How long can you afford to wait?” Susan tilted her head in Kelsey’s direction. When Catherine said nothing, Susan dropped the papers in Catherine’s lap. “I’m just saying, I’d think about it if it were me.” She squeezed Catherine’s arm and then quietly retreated to her side of the waiting room.

Hands trembling, Catherine crammed the papers into her tote. How dare Susan claim to know how much time Kelsey had left. She couldn’t know that any more than she could know about Africa. Just because the woman had googled something on the Internet didn’t make it true.

So why would she believe Susan?

Catherine straightened her blouse. Kelsey had time. Lots of it. She dug around in the tote bag and fished out a Ziploc of bottles and pill canisters. Kelsey had to have those meds.

Catherine blocked the hum of Timmy’s pretend cars, but Susan’s tendered advice continued its assault upon everything she hoped was true. Dr. Finke was the best pediatric heart surgeon in Ohio. He’d fixed Kelsey before...twice. Catherine was counting on him to do it again.

Taking her baby to some dirty, foreign country so some witch doctor could wave a magic potion over her was out of the question.

Who in their right mind would let some quack who probably flunked out of an American med school operate on their child in a primitive, third-world facility?

Catherine fumed while Susan let Timmy drive his Lego car over her face. Susan was crazy. Why hadn't she noticed the woman's desperation before? The truth hit Catherine like cold water in the face. Taking care of a sick child had dried up her own well of common sense.

Think. She had to calm down and think.

From the moment Kelsey was born, Catherine had known something wasn't right. Clear thinking, along with her determination to find the best medical care, had brought them this far. And clear thinking would help her find the cure for her daughter. No frazzled, armchair quarterback could tell her what was best for her baby. She'd think of something. She always did.

Catherine took a deep breath and removed the biggest prescription bottle from the baggie. She shook it well then filled the oral syringe. Lifting Kelsey from the stroller, she worked to rouse her. "Here you go, punkin." She gently pinched Kelsey's cheeks into the formation her stepson Jonathan called "the guppy" and shot the contents into her daughter's mouth.

Holding Kelsey tight, Catherine waited for the retching. She felt the ragged expansion of her daughter's ribcage, bones so fragile they could be easily crushed under her grip. Tears, hot and angry, stung Catherine's eyes. She buried her face in Kelsey's hair, hiding her fear from Susan.

How much time? Did this question haunt every mother? If it didn't, it should. No one was promised more than the present moment, and if Dr. Finke didn't have good news, there would be no future.

She refused to dwell on the possibility. The ventricular septal patch was holding. If she didn't cling to the hope that this advanced prosthetic mesh would keep the hole in Kelsey's heart sealed, her own heart would fail.

CHAPTER TWO

THURSDAY, DECEMBER 12TH, 8:03 AM

MAKURU, TANZANIA

Mia Kendall crouched beside the woven-reed mat of her failing patient, wondering if the source of the putrid smell filling Mbui's dank living quarters had anything to do with the increase in the rejections suffered by her recent heart transplant recipients. She had to find the answer, no matter how many mud huts she had to visit in this rugged continent she now called home.

Scooting forward on her haunches, Mia tried to better her position in the cramped and stuffy quarters. Chickens clucked outside the closed wooden door. The filthy creatures were a nuisance and an infectious risk, but they were not the source of the nauseating smell. She'd witnessed death's onset so many times these past few months, she knew its sickly, sweet odor.

She drew her stethoscope from her bag. If she lost another patient, the experimental training partnership between the government and the nonprofit she worked for would be scrapped, effectively flushing the last of her lofty ideals down the toilet.

Her fingers traced the incision she'd carved through the withering muscles of Mbui's heaving chest only a few weeks earlier. This swelling at the transplant site should have been reported earlier. Were her discharge instructions not clear?

She lifted the cowry-shell amulet tied around Mbui's neck and slid the bell of her stethoscope across the perspiration on his black chest.

Breathing labored. Rhythm uneven. Cough persistent. Mucus greenish. If this young man was to ever outrun the wind again, he'd need more than the magic charms of a *sangoma*.

Mia dropped the stethoscope around her neck, pained that Mbui's obvious deterioration proved modern medicine no more effective than that of the witch doctors. "Jeme, when did the fever start?"

Mbui's wife huddled in the shadows of the far wall, the frightened whites of her eyes darting like fireflies. The pale child she cradled rooted for her mother's breast. Jeme had been unusually skittish since Mia's arrival, hanging back and not saying much. But what wife wouldn't be nervous and distracted by the prospect of losing her husband?

This seventeen-year-old mother, though slight of frame, had impressed Mia as a gritty giant with her fluent English and careful attention to Mbui's care.

Jeme inched from the darkness. "Two days. Maybe three." Her blouse and frayed skirt were stiff with what looked like blood.

What had she missed? Mia wheeled back around and checked Mbui again for bleeding. His legs and ankles were swollen from the retention of fluids, but there was no blood on him that she could see. Her attention shot back to his wife. "Jeme, are you hurt?"

Jeme slid further into the shadows. "I am fine." She gently lifted the tiny albino hand resting against the midnight black of her chest and kissed each little finger.

Mia lowered her eyes, feeling even more the foreign intruder. Maybe she was making more out of Jeme's jumpiness than she should, but telling a woman that her child's father was rejecting his heart and could possibly die was not what she'd signed on for.

Mia felt around in her medical bag and located a flashlight. For now, she needed to focus on Mbui. The presence of a rash would give her another piece in this rejection puzzle. If only this mud hut had electricity or even a lantern, but this family lived at the end of a twisting footpath nearly half a mile from the nearest road.

"Jeme, I need better light. Can you open the door?"

The cool, dry breezes of the higher elevation might lower Mbui's temperature. At the very least, it would sweeten the foul stench of his constant vomiting. Otherwise, the killer combination of unbearable heat and the nauseating smell might cause her to lose the handful of peanuts she'd bought alongside the road before the Med Flight takeoff.

Jeme made no move toward opening the door.

"Can you open the door?" Mia repeated.

"No."

Jeme stood silent, her moist eyes filled with terror. This woman had been through so much, yet never had Mia heard her speak of the fear that surely beat in her own heart after weeks of waiting at the hospital for Mbui to become strong enough for the journey home.

Mia rose from the hard-packed earth, her frustration at Jeme's strange behavior mounting. "The air will help Mbui breathe."

Jeme ran and wedged herself between Mia and the door. "We cannot let evil find us."

Mia sighed at the hold superstition had on these people. "Very well." She returned to her patient's side. "But as soon as my plane comes back, we'll have to take our chances with the door. Mbui has to return to the hospital in Dar es Salaam." She clicked on her flashlight and examined Mbui. "See this rash? It could mean infection. If we change his medicines, maybe I can stop the rejection. But I can't be sure without a biopsy." Mia took a breath, realizing she had once again dumped too much information without waiting to see if her patient's caregiver understood the gravity of the situation.

"We will wait for the plane." Jeme hoisted the drowsy child behind her and secured Zaina against her back with a colorful *kanga* cloth before crossing the packed dirt floor. She stepped around a blanket-covered mound and sheltered the sling-bound child between her and the wall.

Mia nodded, her eyes on the strange heap at Jeme's feet she'd not noticed before. She rose and shined her light on the ratty blanket and then on Jeme and her stained clothes.

Jeme gathered the edge of her shirt into a wad. "No more light."

Mia clicked off the flashlight. It took a moment for her eyes to readjust to the darkness. A slash of sunlight had breached the edges of the poorly-framed door and illuminated large bloodstains on the blanket.

"That's blood on your clothes, isn't it?" Mia asked Jeme. "I just want to help. Please."

Jeme's child was now pressed against the hut's manure-plastered wall. "It is nothing."

Mbui pushed himself up on his elbows. The man had more strength than Mia had first thought. Maybe he wasn't dying. Or maybe he was just desperate. "Jeme, you must tell her."

Mia looked at Jeme then back to Mbui. Something was definitely wrong. "What's going on?"

Jeme shook her head, her eyes darting from the mound to Mbui.

"You must trust the doctor," Mbui gasped.

Jeme shook her head again.

Mia felt her own heartbeat quicken. "One of you needs to tell me what's going on. Now."

Mbui coughed. "Her sister."

"Numa?"

"Numa is dead," Jeme whispered.

"Your sister died? How?" Mia's questions about the young albino woman she'd met on her last trip to Mbui's hut ricocheted off the cracked walls.

"Evil came with machetes when I went to call you." Jeme's lips quivered. She bent and lifted the blood-sodden blanket. "I saved what I could."

Mia clicked on the flashlight and gasped. The dismembered torso of a woman lay in a bloody heap. Butchered like a wild animal. Mia's knees went weak. She retched on the floor. No amount of trauma training had prepared her for such a horror. She swiped the back of her hand across her mouth. "This is...Numa?"

Jeme clapped her hands over her lips and nodded.

Stomach still roiling, Mia shined the light over the mutilated body. Breasts removed. Sternum split. Eyes and tongue removed. Hole in the victim's neck. She shifted the light from the remains to Jeme's horrified face. "Who did this?"

"Human hunters."

Mia clicked off the light, unable to stand the terror in Jeme's eyes. "Why would someone kill your sister and strip her hide?"

"The magic."

"What magic?"

Jeme glanced over her shoulder. "Numa was albino."

"I know, but I don't understand why—"

Zaina cried and poked her blonde head around Jeme's shoulder, and suddenly everything became clear. Mia had heard albino killings had been on the rise throughout the country the past few months, and how these targeted people lived in fear, but she'd never imagined a horror like this.

She turned to Mbui. "Did you see who did this?"

He shook his head. "She was killed in her hut."

"Why. . .did you bring Numa's body here?" Mia choked on the sour words.

Neither of them answered.

Mia clicked on the light. "Why?"

Jeme spoke up. "If I don't bury Numa beneath the floor where my sick husband sleeps, the grave robbers will take all that I have left of her."

"Do the ones who did this know about Zaina?"

Jeme shrugged. "We tried to keep our secret, but people talk." She looked to Mbui. "Our tribe is known for the curse."

"They'll be back, won't they?"

Jeme nodded.

Mia's mind spun in a dozen different directions. "Then I've got to get you out of here."

But how? She'd let Mike, the MFS pilot, drop her off so he could shuttle vaccines to another village over an hour away. MedFlight Services was currently working as a first responder for an outbreak of fever sweeping the northern countryside. But Jeme's husband might not be the only fatality if she didn't get this family to safety.

She had to think, not jump to some paranoid conclusions. She needed to stick to the facts. Her cell phone had no reception here. The road was too far away to run for help. Besides, the odds of encountering the hunters or a corrupt law enforcement officer were too great. The small airstrip was their closest escape.

"We'll carry Mbui to the trees at the edge of the clearing and hide in the tall grass until the plane returns."

Jeme held up her hand for silence. Together, they listened. In the distance, she could hear the hum of a motor.

"My ride's here." Mia covered Numa's body again with the blanket, then threw the flashlight and stethoscope into her bag. "Quick. Help me move Mbui to the door." They each grabbed a corner of Mbui's mat and started dragging him across the dirt floor.

Suddenly, the wooden planks of the door splintered. Blinding light streamed in. Chickens squawked. A silhouetted figure filled the tiny frame. Mia couldn't make out the man's face.

"Mike? Is that you?"

A shot rang out, and a searing force knocked her to the ground, turning daylight into darkness.

CHAPTER THREE

THURSDAY, DECEMBER 12TH, 8:12 AM

MAKURU, TANZANIA

Race Daniels jumped from the cockpit of his Piper J-3 Cub. Small Igloo cooler in one hand, he ran the other hand across the coarse stubble on his face.

He slipped his sunglasses down the bridge of his nose and stared across the field of grass waving in the afternoon breeze alongside Makuru's landing strip located near the small town. Beside the tall grasses, there was no sign of his contact. Nothing more than two large garden plots, a few acacia trees, and a small compound.

So much for his on-time delivery record. Thankfully this hop was fairly short, giving him plenty of time to make the window back to the hospital in Dar es Salaam before the kidneys lost their viability. Flying donated organs across the African savannas might be a far cry from the "Duty, Honor, Country" mantra he'd once held, but it was also a constant reminder that he'd found exactly what he'd been looking for. Tanzania had become the one place where he could escape the country, the ideals, and even the God who'd failed him.

The boom of a gunshot rippled across the savanna.

Years of combat training, thanks to the US military, propelled him automatically into crisis mode. He tossed the organ cooler onto the seat and scooted for cover beneath the plane. Heart pounding, he listened for any sign of fighting or repeated gunfire, but was met with silence. He shoved back the stray lock of hair from his forehead, checked the perimeter, then scrambled toward the direction of the shot.

The compound held three huts and a row of clean laundry, but there were no signs of life other than the dozen or so chickens content to hunt for scraps in the dusty yard. No sign of trouble. No sign of anything.

But he hadn't imagined the gunshot.

The door to one of the huts stood open, splintered and hanging cockeyed on its hinges. Something was definitely off. He approached the wooden frame cautiously, wishing he had his Glock on him.

"Anyone home?"

No answer.

Race stepped inside. As he waited for his eyes to adjust to the darkness of the foul-smelling hut, he had the feeling he wasn't alone. Gradually, his surroundings came into focus.

He assessed the body closest to him first. Young African male, mid-twenties, shallow breathing, no obvious sign of trauma. He turned to the white woman sprawled on the floor, the apparent target of the gunshot. Blood pooled beneath her head. Race ripped off his shirt, wadded it, then pressed it against the injury. She was breathing, but until he cleaned up the wound, he wouldn't be able to tell the extent of her injuries.

A young woman holding a baby cowered in the corner of the hut. "What happened?"

She shrank back as if he were going to strike her.

"I'm not going to hurt you." Race kept his focus on the injured woman in front of him, but in order to assess the danger, he needed information. "Just tell me what happened. I came in on the plane. I want to help you."

"You are Mike?"

"No, my name's Race. Race Daniels."

Her chin jutted toward the bloody woman at his feet. "They shot the doctor."

"Who shot her?"

"I do not know."

Race tried to hide his frustration. Violent crime—including armed robberies—might be on the increase, especially in larger cities, but not out here in the middle of nowhere. It didn't make sense. He pressed on the makeshift bandage that had already turned a bright red. The woman groaned then opened her eyes. At least she was alive. She winced at his touch and groaned as she pulled away.

"Don't move." His gaze searched the hut for something else to bandage her with until he could get help. An open medical kit was lying in the shadows of the darkened room. Untouched and in perfect array. Strange. If this had been a robbery, why hadn't they taken the drugs? He pawed through the bag and scored a pair of latex gloves and a roll of gauze. "What's your name?"

The lanky beauty worked to sit up, pulling her knees toward her chest. "Mia. . .Mia Kendall."

He snapped on the gloves. "I take it you're a doctor."

"Yeah." Mia pressed her hand against the cloth soaked with her blood. "I've got to get that man to the hospital. . ."

"Whoa. Slow down. He's not the only one who needs medical attention."

She sat up and her chestnut hair fell past her shoulders. In any other situation, he'd have taken time to appreciate her full lips, flawless skin, and almond-shaped eyes, but not today. Today, she was a gunshot victim, facing an hour flight to any decent emergency medical help.

Mia's fingers traced the wound the bullet had carved across her temple. "It's nothing more than a superficial wound. I'll be fine."

"Then you had someone looking after you today. Any farther to the left and you wouldn't be talking to me. What are you doing here?"

"I came to check on Mbui, my transplant patient. I need to get him to Dar es Salaam. He's rejecting his heart and needs specialized medical attention."

Race glanced out the door. "How'd you get here?"

"An MSF pilot. He's supposed to return, but not for a couple of hours. We heard the plane, and I thought my ride was early."

"That was my plane."

Wariness furrowed her brows. "Why are you here?"

"Making a pickup."

She rocked onto her knees, balancing herself with her arms. "What kind of pickup?"

"That doesn't matter right now." Race grasped her shoulder to steady her, still not certain she was in any condition to get up. "We need to get out of here in case whoever did this decides to come back."

"Wait." Recognition registered on her face. "I've seen you somewhere."

"I don't think so. I'd remember a girl like you."

"I work at the government hospital. I've seen you flirting with the nurses." Mia pressed the dressing to her head.

"And any other time, I might be flirting with you, but I've got to get you out of here."

She pushed off his attempt to help her stand. "This man is going to die if I don't get him back immediately."

An image of Rachel surfaced. He'd seen enough death in his own life, and if it was within his power, he wasn't going to be responsible for losing anyone else.

He made a snap decision. "I've got room for two."

Mia turned to the girl still hovering in the shadows of the room. "You can't leave them."

"Unless one of you plans to ride on the wing, I don't have space for three. I've got one passenger seat and will risk putting two there, but even that's pushing the weight limit more than I'd like."

"I'll stay." Mia stood then swayed. "Mbui has to go."

Race caught her before she fell against the mud wall. "You've lost a lot of blood. You're coming with me."

"But Jeme and the baby. You've got to take them—"

The African girl held her child close. "We will be fine." Her raspy voice rose barely above a whisper.

Race turned to Jeme. He still had a slew of unanswered question about what had happened in this hut, but for the moment those would have to wait. "Can you find someplace to hide?"

Fear etched the girl's features, the whites of her eyes widened, but she agreed with a nod.

"She has to go. . ." Mia's weight slumped against him. She was out cold. Like it or not, he was going to have to leave the young mother behind.

Race turned to the girl and voiced the only solution he could come up with. "I'll drop your husband and the doctor at the hospital then fly right back for you and your baby. I promise."

CHAPTER FOUR

THURSDAY, DECEMBER 12TH, 8:27 AM

MAKURU, TANZANIA

Jeme stood at the edge of the clearing, holding her breath, as the small plane struggled to lift from the green earth. A moment later, the bright yellow wings rose above the spindly branches of a baobab tree then soared toward the vast blue sky.

He'd promised to come back for her, but how long could she wait in the shadows without being found by the men who'd killed her sister? She'd been lucky the men ran when they realized they'd shot a foreigner, but once they believed it safe to return, they'd come for Numa's remains and her own albino daughter.

Pressing her back against the rough bark of a tree, she cradled Zaina in her arms. The fear that had chased her since she'd given birth to an albino swirled in her head. Her family had been right to cast her and Numa out. Evil came with the curse of pale skin. How else could she explain Mbui's struggle for breath. . .Numa's lifeless body lying on the floor of her hut. . .The deafening sound of gunfire. . .

Zaina wiggled to get down. "No, Zaina." Jeme pulled the *kanga* around her daughter's head to hide the yellow wisps of hair peeking over the top of the cloth. There was no time to grieve. No time to consider what life might be like without the constant threats from those who wanted to take the life of her child.

She had to run.

But where? The pilot had told her to wait here.

Jeme's stomach churned as she tried to grasp her limited options. She knew nothing of the man who had taken Mbui and Dr. Kendall away on the plane. But what other choice was there? She'd seen the fear in the eyes of the doctor before the hunters came. Her husband had little time left. Without medicine he would die.

But what if the pilot did not come back? Or worse, what if he told someone of the child he had seen in this place?

Heart thumping, Jeme fingered the beaded band around her waist through the thin folds of material she wore. Her faith in the amulet, like the cowry-shell necklace Mbui wore, had yet to waver, but that did not change the fact that without the help of a *sangoma* she must rely upon the medicine the white doctor had to offer. It was the only other chance her husband had. Maybe it would turn out to be the salvation that brought life to Mbui and safety to Zaina.

Jeme kept her gaze on the sky, the yellow wings now no more than a tiny dot. A warm summer wind blew against her face, bringing with it the humid air of the afternoon rains. Already, thick clouds had begun to form along the horizon, and she knew it could be hours before the plane returned. If it ever returned. And what reason did the pilot have to keep his promise?

Zaina whimpered in her arms. Jeme offered the child her breast to quiet her. Her father's village lay a long walk north, but the last words he had spoken to her had made his position clear. Numa would have been disposed of at birth if not for the insistent begging of their mother. But even her mother's love for her oldest daughter couldn't change the fact that Numa had become nothing more than a curse to the village, blamed when a crop failed or an unborn child died.

Jeme watched as the plane disappeared, taking with it her last shred of hope. Mbui's fate was now in the hands of the pilot. Zaina's fate was up to her.

Something snapped in the brush.

Jeme ducked further into the shadows of the tall grass then scoured the surrounding vegetation for danger. The persistent chatter of weaverbirds sang above her. A chicken squawked in the yard nearby. A scrawny hen escaped the bushes. Jeme's legs melted in relief. Next time she might not be so lucky. She could not wait.

Before fear shredded her resolve, Jeme ran into the hut she shared with Mbui. The smell of death hovered around her as she rushed to pack a bag with enough food to last a day or two. Her father would forgive her. And even if he didn't, her mother would convince him that she'd had no other escape.

A glance at her sister's body brought her frantic movements to a halt. She couldn't leave Numa. Not here. Not like this. She dropped to her knees and began clawing at the packed dirt floor with her fingernails. Tears spilled down her cheeks. Zaina began to cry. She quickly repositioned the child on her back then continued digging.

Dirt covered her hands. Skin ripped beneath her nails. Zaina's cries intensified, but she ignored the child's legs kicking to be free and started searching for Mbui's metal hoe. She stopped at the edge of their bed. Zaina's wailing increased. A wall of guilt washed over her. Jeme glanced at the door. If the hunters returned now, the doctor would not be here to frighten them away.

She knew what Numa would want her to do. She dragged a thin, woolen blanket from her bed and added it to the bloody one covering the body, praying that their ancestors would forgive her for leaving her sister to be scavenged by hyenas or poachers.

Jeme fled the compound on the dusty path edging the thick outcropping of trees. Stopping to take one last look at the life she had loved, she prayed the evil would not be able to find her. She ran ahead and let the forest swallow her and the child she would protect at all cost.

CHAPTER FIVE

THURSDAY, DECEMBER 12TH, 12:42 AM EST

CINCINNATI, OHIO

Catherine paced in the blue glow of the muted flat screen TV mounted on the bedroom wall. Where in the world was her husband? He'd missed dinner, bath time, and story time. Again. Because she was too worked up to sleep and threatening weather promised the likelihood of school being cancelled, she'd let Jonathan and Kelsey wait up for him. Around midnight the kids had fallen asleep watching a movie in her king-sized bed, and since Brad wasn't here to complain about the kids not sleeping in their own beds, she'd let them stay. The expensive baby monitor cameras they'd installed in Kelsey's ruffled-pink room were no substitute for having her within reach.

Wearing a worn T-shirt and faded pajama bottoms, Catherine perched on the edge of the bed. Her ears attuned to the different sounds of two children breathing. One normally. The other struggling. Salt and Pepper she called them. One dark. The other light. Three years apart. One her biological child. The other her son by choice. Some would call these insurmountable differences, but in her heart,

Jonathan and Kelsey were a matched set, as sure as if they'd been born twins. Living her life without either of them wasn't an option.

A vague awareness of the cartoon characters racing across the TV screen penetrated her thoughts and increased the sense of desperation that had dogged her since her return from the doctor's office. She resumed rubbing the curve of Kelsey's back, her flattened palm a greedy sponge soaking up the faint rise and fall of her daughter's fragile ribcage.

The rumble of the garage door halted her stroke. The irregular beat of Kelsey's heart beneath her touch reminded her that she must wait. Hold back the anger bubbling inside of her. Give Brad a chance to explain why he was becoming more and more distant. For Kelsey's sake, no for the sake of their family, she needed him to come alongside her and help make this decision.

She could hear him fumbling around in the kitchen, running water in the sink, checking the locked doors. Every second counted. Surely even he could see that now. Channeling her fears to that secret place she seldom visited, she forced herself to wait. Her timing must be perfect if she wanted his complete cooperation. And she did. Kelsey's life depended upon an end to this cold war.

From the corner of her eye, she saw Brad stumble into the bedroom, his head down and shoes dangling from his hooked fingers.

"Where have you been?" she asked.

His head shot up, his eyes wide in the light from the TV. "You still up?"

Catherine shot off the bed. "Are you...drunk?"

"Noooo." His inability to let go of his vowels strongly correlated with the smell of alcohol on his breath.

"You are." She clenched her hands to keep from pounding his chest and demanding explanations. "I told you we needed to talk."

"Talk." He waved a limp hand at the kids sleeping snuggled around Kelsey's stuffed monkey. "That's all we ever do anymore."

"Keep your voice down."

"Keep the kids in their own beds."

She caught hold of his rumpled shirt sleeve. "Not here." She grabbed the papers off the nightstand with her free hand and marched him toward the master bath.

For once, he didn't fight her. She didn't have the time or energy to sort through whether that was a good thing or a bad thing. She closed the door and flicked on the light.

Brad's hands flew up to shield his eyes. "Okay. I get it. You're mad." His shirt was untucked and his hair standing on end like he'd raked it again and again. "Look, Cat...I'm sorry..." His eyes were so bloodshot he had no business driving a car let alone deciding their daughter's medical fate. But the clock was ticking and she needed his signature now.

"Your excuses can wait. Our daughter cannot." She presented him with the thick stack of papers the United Network of Organ Sharing had faxed over after Dr. Finke arranged Kelsey's referral. "The UNOS coordinator wants our financial info completed before we arrive at the transplant center."

His dark eyes narrowed, he took the papers but did not look at them. He surveyed her face, a pinprick reminder of how far she'd let her own personal appearance go. "Can't this wait until morning, Cat?" He handed her the papers and started to leave.

"It is morning, Brad." She pointed to the red numbers on the clock on the vanity. "She's had two spells in twelve hours. Her lips are still blue. I want Kelsey on the list today."

He removed his watch. "I've got to be at the courthouse by eight." He threw his keys in the pewter bowl next to the sink, stepped around her, and started for their walk-in closet, unbuttoning his shirt as he went. "I'm going to bed."

"Bed?" She wheeled and marched after him. "I haven't slept in five years. I spend my nights folding *our* daughter into an accordion so she can breathe. The least you can do is take a minute to help me sort through the medical costs."

He stiffened and turned, his eyes seeking the fastest exit. "I'd rather not discuss this in front of the kids." He cocked his head toward the opening door.

Jonathan pushed the door open. His curly dark hair was as tangled as Brad's and his ever-present Batman cape had twisted over his almost-too-small Batman pajamas. "Why's Mommy mad?"

"See." Brad shot her his I-can't-believe-you've-done-this-again look then bent over and playfully knuckle-scrubbed Jonathan's head. "Mommy's not mad." His retreat into the closet left her to settle Jonathan. Worse, Brad's refusal to deal with anything had left her to explain.

Catherine stood motionless, staring at the dark-haired, mocha-latte-skinned version of Brad, furious that the men in her life always assumed she was hormonal. Not sure what to say to fix Jonathan's assessment of his parents' relationship, she smiled. "Go back to bed, buddy."

The boy didn't blink. Instead, his alert, toffee-brown eyes assessed hers. "You sound mad."

He hadn't bought the smile. She'd been a fool to think he would. Jonathan had demonstrated a dolphin-like ability to hone in on family disharmony long before Brad decided to fight the little guy's drug-addicted mother for full custody. Would her stepson lump his new mommy's actions in with his nightmares? The possibility yanked Catherine's belly into a guilty knot. She wouldn't lie to him or make promises she couldn't keep.

She laid the papers on the bathroom vanity and took Jonathan back to the bed and pulled him into her lap. "Mommy's worried. That's all."

"Is Kelsey...dying?"

Catherine shuddered at the sad understanding stewing in those innocent, dark eyes. How could she teach him to trust when she herself wondered how their world could ever be secured? "Kelsey's very sick. That's why Mommy and Daddy have to decide what to do. You understand?"

He nodded, the flicker of belief shortening the strings tying him to her heart.

She spotted the half-eaten Pop-Tart sitting on the nightstand. "Hungry? It's your favorite."

He obediently held out his hand. "Want me to share the rest with Sissy?"

"No. Let her sleep." She kissed his cheek and set him beside his sister. "Keep an eye on her for me, will you? I've got to finish talking to

Daddy." Catherine lifted Jonathan's chin with her finger, willing his eyes to lock with hers. "You're a good big brother." She carefully tucked Kelsey's night-night under her chin. "I'll check on you once you're asleep." She left Jonathan chomping a dry pastry.

Catherine slipped into the bathroom expecting to find Brad finishing up at the sink, but he had completely disappeared. She checked the walk-in closet. He was threading a belt through the loops of a different pair of slacks.

Catherine braced her hand on the doorframe. "Thanks for making me look bad."

A flash of rare remorse crossed his face. "Sorry. For everything." He leaned over and dropped a kiss on the top of her head. "I just don't want to scare him, okay?"

"He's already terrified. He's smart. He knows something's not right. We've got to talk about this."

He scooted around her and escaped to the bathroom. "I'm leaving."

"Wait. Where are you going?" She scrambled after him, tripping over the pink tote bag she'd left on the floor after Kelsey's last round of meds.

"To the office."

"Now?"

"Our bed is full. Remember?"

So he wasn't as drunk as she'd originally thought. The arrow he'd just delivered hit her heart with sober accuracy. "Brad, please."

"I don't want to fight anymore, Cat." He started for the door.

"Did you know that every day eighty people receive an organ?"

He stopped and turned slowly. "Cat, why can't this wait?"

"Why?" Her voice rose in strength. "Because every day, twenty-two people *die* waiting. It could take months to find a heart Kelsey's size." She snatched the papers from the bathroom vanity. "I know you don't want our daughter added to the list that didn't make it."

He looked from Catherine's face to her outstretched hand and back again. Without a word, he closed the bathroom door.

"Show me what you've got." Seeming to slump under the weight of the packet, he exhaled slowly then began flipping through the pages.

He stopped about a third of the way through. "Here we go. Average Transplant Costs."

The word *costs* hung in the air as heavy as a Cincinnati snow cloud. Catherine shifted under the weight of the financial significance, but said nothing.

Brad regarded her as if he knew what he'd find, took a breath, and then read on. "Heart procurement, 90K. Doctor, sixty-five thousand plus. Hospital..." His voice dropped off. In silence, his eyes finished scanning the page. He lifted his head, his face gray. "We're looking at a million dollars, Cat. Minimum. That doesn't include the cost of her anti-rejection regime and the possibility of more surgeries as she grows."

The serious-edge tone sliced open every fear she'd managed to seal away. "But you talked to the insurance company, right?"

"They're not going to approve the transplant." He swallowed, his chin quivering slightly.

"Why?"

"They want her to undergo another round of less invasive and less expensive tests."

"She doesn't have the time or the stamina for a bunch of tests that will only prove what we already know. She needs a heart. Now."

"They're within their rights. Kelsey's specialist and the transplant hospital where he has privileges are out of network."

"What does that mean?"

"It means they'll both send us a big fat bill that we can't pay." He tossed the papers onto the vanity, the thud burying his brief revelation of vulnerability. "We're screwed, Cat."

"Who gave some stodgy old men in some far away New York office the right to decide our daughter's medical care? Dr. Finke is the best."

"It's the law."

"Then fight them, Brad. You're a lawyer."

"Winning takes time and money...lots of it...and we're short of both."

She locked her knees in an effort to stop the melting of her legs. "We bought the supplemental policy to cover any gaps."

The color drained from Brad's face. "I had to let it lapse."

A trembling rage ignited every nerve ending in Catherine's body. "Kelsey's not covered? She's supposed to be covered."

The shake of his head was small and pained. "Not if our primary doesn't preauthorize the transplant."

She'd gotten used to her husband's distance, even the occasional glower, but this browbeaten defeat was something new. Something she couldn't take. What was going on? What happened to the man who'd leapt tall buildings in a single bound?

Catherine reined in her reeling mind and the horrible accusations burning a hole in her tongue. "If the insurance won't pay, we'll just have to raid our savings."

"We cleaned that out to pay the deductible for her last surgery."

No savings? They'd never been without a cushion to fall back on for those unexpected expenses. She doused the embers of fear beginning to burn a hole through her insides.

"So we'll sell some stock from our portfolio," she declared.

"Gone." Brad kicked at the assortment of Batman and Barbie toys scattered on the tiled floor. A plastic Batmobile sailed across the marble and crashed into the tub. "Along with the boat, the jet skis, and that flat screen TV on our bedroom wall as soon as those lucky Facebook bidders come pick them up."

Catherine's knees buckled. She grabbed the vanity, grateful for its solid support. "You're selling stuff?"

"How do you think we make this house payment each month?" His question hung in the cold air then fell with a sinking thump upon her heart.

She didn't know. Had no idea how they paid the bills. She'd convinced herself that between the occasional art lessons she gave and his Assistant District Attorney's salary, it was enough. "Why didn't you tell me about the savings and the stocks?"

Embarrassment, or loss of pride, she couldn't be sure which, flushed his cheeks. "Because juggling the money is the only thing I *can* do to help."

They stood for a silent moment, their eyes riveted on each other. Catherine's stilled voice sought that place of common ground that had existed before Kelsey's chronic illness. But for once, she had nothing to say. The hard reality of daily life had transformed their domestic bliss into nothing more than a hazy memory.

"And look where that got us," she said.

She felt Brad's large hands clasp her shoulders. "There's not enough money in the world to fix the real problem here."

"What are you talking about?"

"As long as you keep blaming yourself, there's no room for anything or anyone else in there." He lightly poked her aching heart. "Kelsey's heart condition was nobody's fault. It just happened."

With a flick of her chin, Catherine shook off his justification, a dispensation she didn't deserve. "Every time she can't breathe, I wonder what I did wrong during my pregnancy to cause the hole in our little girl's heart."

"How many doctors have to tell you that it wasn't your fault before you can let it go?"

She stiffened and pulled away. "Let's sell the house."

"You think I haven't considered that?" He raked his fingers through his hair. "If it sold today, we'd barely clear enough to pay off the second mortgage. We could put every nickel we have on the table, and it wouldn't be enough to offer the hospital a small down payment on a heart."

"Other people do this, Brad. There's got to be a way." She paced the gray square tiles, her mind combing through pieces of obscure information she'd read over the past five years, but never planned to need. "What if we check with some of those organizations that provide crisis funding for transplants?"

"I've done that. We make too much money for assistance programs."

That he would take such a demeaning initiative sent a fearful ripple down her spine. She paused, struggling to wrap her mind around the humiliation he'd endured. They were in deep trouble.

She pushed back the guilt, unwilling to permit a shred of wounded pride to derail their purpose. She had one more card, an ace up her sleeve. A far-fetched idea she'd hidden away like a spare house key. Brad wouldn't like it any more than she did, but it had to be played.

"What about a GoFundMe campaign? People do it all the time now—"

"For a million dollars? Catherine, if all of our friends gave, we couldn't come close to raising that kind of money."

"A public fundraiser event then?"

"No." His voice, more angry than wounded, bounced off the tiles. "Don't even go there."

"You know he'd do it."

"We're not asking that jerk for one red cent." Brad's nostrils flared, and she could see that she'd been mistaken. The hurt she thought was one-sided ran both ways, far deeper than she'd imagined.

"His radio station helps people all the time."

"Tom Bruce wrote you off the minute you decided to marry a guy with a bi-racial kid. What makes you think he'd help us now?"

She didn't know for sure. She raised her chin, the cartoon melody from the old show the kids had watched earlier now running through her head. After all these years of not speaking to the man, she was a Looney Tune to even consider asking now. But she would...even if it meant crawling back to him on her belly.

Catherine swallowed the fear creeping up the back of her throat. "Because he's my father."

"Some father. He wouldn't even come to the wedding to walk his daughter down the aisle." Brad held up his hands to stop her protest. "Let's pretend the old goat has softened. Let's say he agrees to give you two hundred thousand. That's still eight hundred thousand short of a million. We can't pay for a transplant, Cat. And I don't care how rich and famous Bruce the Deuce is, or how bad he might feel about disowning you, I'm not borrowing the money from him."

Catherine scanned the bathroom as if the answer was hidden under the dirty clothes strung across the floor. Her eyes lighted on the papers sticking out of the pink tote. Her heart lurched.

"There is one more option."

She quickly retrieved the information from the tote's side pocket. Information she'd read last night after she had Kelsey settled. Information that had scared her to death. Information she'd dismissed as sheer lunacy.

Catherine held the pages out to Brad. "Susan gave me this stuff yesterday."

He surveyed her cautiously and then took the crumpled stack. "Medical Value Travel?" A scowl spread over his stunned face. "Transplant tourism?"

"I know it sounds crazy. I thought the same thing myself when I first read it. But I checked it out. This seems legit. Many Americans go overseas every year to get an organ because the wait is too long here."

"So?"

"So, it must be safe."

"It might be legal, but safe? Are you kidding me? Listen to this." He scanned through the pages. "Need a kidney? Buy one for $20K in Russia. Need a liver? Visit the Philippines. Cost only $129K. Need a heart? Africa has them for the bargain basement price of only a hundred and fifty thousand." He stared at her like she was some stranger he'd never seen before. "Have you lost your mind?" He tossed the papers on the counter alongside the discarded financial forms.

"Yes!" She frantically scooped up the loose pages. "Every time I look at our kids and what this is doing to our family, I go a little bit more crazy."

"You need some sleep."

Sleep? She hadn't slept since the night they cut Kelsey's umbilical cord. Until her baby could function without her, she would never sleep again.

"Do you see your children? I mean really see Jonathan and Kelsey?" She knew this conversation treaded dangerously close to war. But she didn't care. Too much was at stake. "We have a second-grader turning into an old man because he's up half the night fretting over his dying sister. Kelsey's hands are beginning to club, and she's not growing. Our children are failing to thrive, Brad. Doesn't that make *you* crazy?" She picked up Susan's papers and thrust them under his nose. "If Jonathan needed a heart, you'd already be on this plane."

Brad's eyebrows shot up.

"I'm sorry." The apology flew from her mouth while her mind sought to destroy the unwelcome demon that had possessed her and seared those inexcusable words on her tongue.

She took a step back, as if she could retrace the origin of her wrong turn, correct her misstep, and banish the intense feeling of shame sucking the breath from her lungs. Thank God Brad had closed the door and hopefully eliminated the possibility Jonathan had overheard.

The one thing she and Jonathan had in common was an understanding of what it felt like to want a mother. How could she have said something so incredibly stupid? She knew Brad loved both Jonathan and Kelsey. And as long as Jonathan called her Mommy and Kelsey had a pulse, she had a shot at being the mother she'd always wanted.

She tucked the papers under her arm and reached for Brad. "Please, you know I didn't mean—"

He stiffened under her touch and stepped away. "What's happened to you, Cat? The girl I married had fairytale dreams, but she lived in the real world." His disappointment drilled a hole straight through her. He didn't wait for her answer. "Just because I'm not falling for this flaky Internet scheme doesn't mean I don't love our daughter. What else do you want me to do?"

"This." Catherine snatched the papers from him. "Africa will be good for all of us."

Jaw clenched, he shook his head. "Explain to me how taking our child to Africa could possibly be *good* for us, because I'm not seeing it."

"I'm just asking you to consider it a viable option." She pressed the papers back into his hands. "Please."

"A third-world heart is not an option. It's a death sentence."

"America doesn't sell hearts at Target, Brad. What do you suggest we do?"

"We'll figure out something." He snatched the rest of the financial forms from the counter. "We'll enroll Kelsey on the list and worry about the money later."

"Kelsey doesn't have that kind of time. She needs a transplant now. And you said we don't have a way to get that kind of money. Dad can give us enough for Africa."

"No."

"Brad, listen to me. For a fraction of the cost, we can take Kelsey to Africa now."

"No."

"No?" Catherine felt heat rising from the coals she'd doused earlier. "Why do you get to say no? Are you the one who sits in the hospital for days after one of Kelsey's surgeries, or lugs her to all those doctors' appointments, or tries to coax a teaspoon of nourishment down her throat every morning? No. I am. So, tell me, Mister Hot-Shot Lawyer, what gives you the right to say what's best for our daughter?"

"Because you're so close to the situation you can't see straight."

"I'm close because you stay as far away as possible." She watched hurt flash across his eyes, gratified that the arrow had hit its mark.

"Kelsey can barely stand the trips to the med center. She's hasn't had the strength to say two words since her last visit. What makes you think she can fly to Africa?"

"These people are medical professionals. They know what they're doing."

"You actually believe that?"

"I want my daughter to live."

The sound of Kelsey's arousal cry drifted in from the bedroom. They both froze.

Papers fell from Brad's hands and fluttered to the floor. "She's awake."

Catherine nodded, every muscle tensed as she listened for the grating wail. "I'll check on her."

She stepped to the door and opened it slowly.

Jonathan hovered over Kelsey, trying to entice her to take her night-night. Catherine blinked back a wave of tears along with the urge to rush to his aid, knowing if she showed panic, her attitude could immediately set the TET spell, Kelsey's inability to breathe, in motion. She watched, willing herself to stay put as Jonathan gently coerced Kelsey to take the blanket. Catherine chafed at the unfairness of an eight-year-old carrying the burden of helping his parents keep his sister alive. A few tender pats from Jonathan, and slowly Kelsey settled, her breathing labored, but at last marginally effective.

Jonathan caught her staring at him. "Sissy's better now." His smile revealed front teeth that would one day need braces.

Catherine smiled back, the pressure slowly draining from her chest. "Good job, buddy. Thanks."

She stepped back into the bathroom and closed the door. Brad stood in the middle of financial forms and Internet pages, his expression hopeless.

"You want me to go back to work, Brad?"

He shook his head. "Hiring specialized care for Kelsey would eat any extra income you could make."

"Then that just leaves Dad...and Africa."

"No."

A piercing cry rattled the door. A brother's love had only delayed the spells. Dread swooped down on Catherine. "We don't have a choice."

Anger flared in Brad's eyes and jolted him from his frozen position. "You think you're going to do this no matter what I say, don't you" He leaned in close, his breath hot on her face. "But you try taking my daughter to that hell hole on your father's dime, and I'll—"

"You'll what? Drag me through court like you did Jonathan's mother?" Catherine squared her shoulders. She wasn't an anesthesiologist with a drug problem who had everything to lose if she didn't concede to the courts demands. "I'm going to get my daughter a heart...even if I have to give her my own!"

"You already have."

The flat of her hand whipped across Brad's cheek. "How dare you." Surging adrenaline expelled a spray of venom at his stunned face. "With or without you, I'm going to—"

The bathroom door flew open. Catherine wheeled, the sting just beginning to register on her hand.

Jonathan stood in the doorway, the beautiful cocao color drained from his face, his eyes wide and panicked.

"Mommy! Kelsey's blue!"

CHAPTER SIX

THURSDAY, DECEMBER 12TH, 9:43 AM

SHINWANGA REGIONAL HOSPITAL

"Dr. Kendall, can you hear me?"

A worried voice prodded Mia from her fitful dreams of gunshots and crying babies. She forced her gritty eyelids open. A naked bulb dangled over her bed. Yellow light pierced her gray fog and knifed the back of her skull. She flinched then slowly released her squint.

Beside her bed, her head surgical nurse fiddled with the tubes that ran from her arm to a monitor teetering on a pole.

"Shadrach." Mia's voice scratched across the surface of her parched lips.

A smile ripped a broad white seam through the middle of his midnight-black face. "Welcome back, Dr. Kendall."

She scanned the room. Cracked cement walls were lined with metal beds occupied by bare-breasted women nursing small infants and keeping a curious eye on the lone white woman in their midst.

"Why am I in the maternity ward, Shadrach?"

"We had no other beds."

Mia lifted a heavy hand to staunch the pain at her temple. "What happened?"

"You must not bother your sutures." He gently lowered her hand. "You were shot."

Comprehension pushed through her muddled thinking and propelled Mia upright as she searched her foggy memory. "What?"

Why couldn't she remember?

Shadrach hushed her with the shake of his head. "Someone shot you, but this happened far away in the mountains. There is no reason to fear here." He gently threaded a blood pressure cuff around her arm. "The bullet grazed your cranium, but did not penetrate the inner table. You are very lucky." His toothy grin revealed his pleasure at having a captive audience to impress with his mastery of the medical jargon he'd picked up since his escape from the Congo.

"If you can count an elephant-sized headache as luck." Mia fingered the row of neat little stitches. "What's my prognosis?"

"Your CT scan indicates you should expect no serious or long-term effects." His twinkling onyx eyes awaited her approval.

She rubbed the throb at her temple. "I appreciate all you've done, but I still don't understand. Who would want to shoot me?"

The nurse eased her back onto a stack of pillows. "That's what the pilot asked." Shadrach cinched the pressure cuff.

"Mike. . .no. . .Mike wasn't there."

She searched her memories, but came up blank. If Mike wasn't there, then who was? She needed answers.

"Race Daniels brought you here." Shadrach pumped the bulb at the end of the black cuff's tubing, his eyes glued to the gauge.

Snippets of memory slowly began to surface. She'd flown out early this morning to check on a patient.

"Who?"

"The man who sometimes brings the hearts you transplant."

"Where's Mbui?" Clarification would put an end to the panicky thoughts racing through her mind. "Where's Jeme and the baby?"

"Mbui is being prepped for a biopsy." Shadrach raised his head. "His wife and child did not come."

The image of Numa's hacked torso flashed in Mia's mind. "She has to be here. It's not safe for her there. Someone murdered her sister because she was an albino. And now her baby is in—"

A warning flashed in Shadrach's eyes. Mia visually cast about the room for a clue, but failed to locate the sacred line she'd crossed.

"What did I say?" she whispered.

Shadrach's gaze scoured the room then dove low as if to hoping to escape the subject. "You should not speak of these things, Dr. Kendall."

"What things?"

"No one speaks of the cursed," he whispered.

"Cursed?" She frowned at his words, wishing he trusted her enough to speak openly. But she didn't want to be like her mother, assigning motives to people where there might not be any. Trust was a two-way road she was still learning to navigate. "Zaina is just a baby. She is not cursed."

His darting eyes conveyed his continued reluctance to agree, but always anxious to please her, he gave in. "It is no secret that the albinos are being slaughtered mercilessly for their power to make people rich."

"Presumed power," Mia corrected.

Shadrach put his index finger to his lips. He leaned in close and removed the blood pressure cuff. "Many in this country believe the magic of the black man in white skin is very powerful."

"But that doesn't make it true." The thought of a terrified Jeme covering the remains of her sister brought bile to the back of Mia's throat.

Shadrach lowered his eyes and busied himself with cranking the bed until she was a bit more upright. From the set of his jaw, she could tell she would make no more progress into understanding his world today. Which was just as well. She didn't want to understand how such evil could be dismissed as the way things were. She was in no condition to address this barbaric practice at the moment, but that didn't mean she wouldn't revisit the subject.

She pushed herself up in the bed and scanned the row of cots. She was going to need to talk to this organ pilot who'd brought her here and find out exactly what had happened, but in the meantime, she needed to know about her patient. "Who's doing Mbui's biopsy?"

"Dr. Amandi was called."

Although she would have preferred to work more closely with the chief specialty surgeon in the region, Amandi had kept her at arm's length. He preferred doing his surgeries at the better equipped and privately funded Kaboni Hospital. He only graced her poorly funded government facility with his presence when heads needed to roll. She had, however, recently heard him speak at a medical conference in Johannesburg. In his keynote address, Amandi claimed to be the pioneer of the ventricular assist device—a mechanical aid capable of keeping failing transplant patients alive while awaiting their organ match. Mia's father would not be pleased if he knew another doctor had commandeered the credit for his prized invention. She would have confronted Dr. Amandi, but his folly was no more her business than her connection to Baltimore's top cardiovascular surgeon was his.

"Why did you call in Amandi?" Mia flung the covers from her bed. Not only was Mbui her patient, she was currently one of only three surgeons in Tanzania qualified to perform this procedure. "Help me up."

Shadrach shook his head. "You were unconscious. Dr. Amandi was already here for a meeting, and Mbui could not wait."

Her head swimming, Mia clutched the edge of the bed. Her patient's health came before her personal prejudices. "You were right to call Amandi, but Mbui is my patient, and I've got to get to him." She tried to stand.

"You must not leave your bed."

"Listen to me, Shadrach." The urgency in her voice shook them both, even though she kept her voice barely above a whisper. "Mbui shouldn't be in this condition. I need to know why my patients are dying, because Mbui isn't the only one. What's causing the higher rejection rate over the past few months? Is it faulty organ procurement? The method of transport? Possibly some unidentified infection in the organ supply line? I've done everything I know to do to identify what's wrong, but now. . .now I need your help."

His brow furrowed. "You need rest."

"I rest and Mbui may die," she said, grabbing on to the metal bed frame. "Is that what you want?"

Shadrach appeared to weigh the looks her raised voice had garnered then shook his head.

Blinding pain shot through Mia's skull. She slumped onto the bed.

"Dr. Kendall?"

"I'm fine." She lowered her voice once again to a whisper. "But after today, I need you to do something I should have already done. I need patient files for the past six months. All of them. Go to records. Be discreet. You know how fast gossip travels in the hospital. I don't want anyone else, especially administration, to catch wind of my questions just yet, but I've got to figure out what's going on."

Shadrach gave her a wary look then turned to follow her orders. Thank God he was as faithful and prompt on the floor as he was in her operating room. Shadrach would have made a wonderful doctor had life given him a fraction of the opportunities so many Americans took for granted, including her.

A charmed life. That's what her colleagues had called her journey through the medical ranks. Maybe so, but they hadn't grown up in her house. Or stood beside her at a young cheerleader's grave. Perfect families had no room for failures. Mia reached for her shoes lying at the side of the bed. She could not fail again.

CHAPTER SEVEN

THURSDAY, DECEMBER 12TH, 9:48 AM

SHINWANGA REGIONAL HOSPITAL, DAR ES SALAAM

Race crammed a stick of spearmint gum into his mouth and tried to curb the mounting guilt squeezing his insides tight. Today's emergency pickup hadn't been his first experience in transporting patients to remote areas across the vast Tanzania landscape, but it had been different from all the others.

This morning, he'd left someone behind.

He pushed his way through the crowded corridors of the government hospital where patients sat against chipped blue walls, waiting to be treated. Life in these halls might move in slow motion, but he was running out of time. He'd already spent twenty minutes on the ground tending to Dr. Kendall and Mbui. Another hour flight back to the landing strip in Makuru wouldn't put him on the ground until at least eleven, adding more than two hours since he'd left Jeme. He might not have had a choice, but that hadn't stopped his conscience from debating the wisdom of his judgment.

He noticed a young mother sitting on one of the long, narrow benches. She held a dark child with a swollen abdomen and a glistening forehead. The woman's haunted expression reminded him of the fear he'd seen in Jeme's eyes as he'd carried her husband toward the plane. The mountain of guilt and disconcerting questions refused to loosen their iron grip. What if the frightened girl had run, or worse, what if her fears had been realized and the men who'd shot Dr. Kendall returned?

His parents would have told him it was time he started praying for the young girl, but praying to a God who'd failed him one too many times didn't come easy, nor did it bring any peace. Assurances from Shinwanga Regional's head nurse that his quick return to Dar and the newly opened heart wing had probably saved two lives did little to ease his conscience about the two he'd left behind. Who was he to choose one life over another?

He slipped past the nurses' station, with its long wooden counter, undetected. On a typical day, he'd drop off an organ or a patient then waste fifteen minutes drinking chai with the nurses during their break before heading out. But not today. Because Jeme's situation wasn't the only thing he was worried about. Not only had his split-second decision left a young mother and her baby at risk, he'd also missed his contact in Makuru.

A call to the Kaboni Private Hospital where the organs had been scheduled to be delivered had failed to give him any updated information on the location of the donated organ or the patient. Acid gnawed at his stomach as he scurried to avoid an orderly pushing a metal cart. He knew the risks his job entailed. And his failure to pick up and deliver that organ in a timely manner could mean more than the loss of his job. It could mean the loss of a patient's life.

Stepping outside the main entrance into the bright sunlight, he felt in his shirt pocket for his sunglasses and slipped them on. For now, he'd have to deal with one problem at a time. He'd return to Makuru, find Jeme, then try to locate his contact on the ground.

A loud voice boomed from the other side of the well-manicured shrubs. Race looked past the young man raking flowerbeds to the familiar face of Dr. Jacob Amandi. Pausing midstride, he considered the fact that the head surgeon of Dar es Salaam's leading hospital might have the information on the missing organ he needed. While he'd only met the doctor once, he knew this man was behind the expansion of the country's organ donor program. Amandi's work had ushered into Tanzania modern medical advances unheard of ten years ago, including a united push by the government to help change the negative views most people in the country held toward organ donation. Since Dr. Amandi was usually involved in every aspect of the program, he should know who could help Race find the information he needed.

Crossing the cement pathway flanked by multi-colored blooms that ran along the front of the hospital, Race rushed to catch up with the doctor, who was talking on his cell phone. "Dr. Amandi." He cut him off at the side entrance.

The doctor held up his palm, indicating for Race to wait while he finished his conversation.

Race took in the doctor's expensive watch and gold necklace. He'd heard the rumors that the doctor spent the majority of his fat paycheck on women and booze—a potentially deadly combination in the medical field—but whether or not they were true, no one could argue that the flashy doctor had made tremendous inroads in advancing medical care in the country.

After a few terse words in Swahili, the doctor ended his call.

Race took the opportunity to jump in before the doctor moved on. "Dr. Amandi?" He stuck out his hand. "Race Daniels."

The doctor just looked at him, his face irritated that he'd been slowed down.

"I'm one of the pilots who transports organs for your hospital."

"Ahh, yes. . .Mr. . ."

"Daniels. I wondered if I could have a quick word with you."

Dr. Amandi dropped his cell phone into his pocket and pushed through the double doors. "If you want to talk, you'll have to walk with me. I was here for a meeting with the director and was just called back in to do an emergency heart biopsy."

Race matched the pudgy man's stride. "On a patient from Makuru?"

Dr. Amandi slowed enough to toss him a speculative gaze. "How do you know about my patient?"

"I just flew in from a compound outside Makuru where I was

supposed to pick up a pair of kidneys for transport. Instead I ended up bringing in a heart transplant patient, Mbui Kinyori, and Dr. Kendall."

"Kinyori is not my patient, but something happened to his doctor, and I must pick up the slack." Amandi continued down the narrow corridor.

"Dr. Kendall was shot."

"I heard."

Race ignored the doctor's seeming lack of concern for Dr. Kendall's well-being and glanced at his watch. He really didn't have time for these territorial games doctors played, but if this guy helped him locate the missing organs, he could pick them up when he went back for Jeme. He followed Amandi past the maternity ward and toward the new heart wing.

"There was no sign of my contact in Makuru," Race continued. "And when I checked in with the hospital after landing, they told me they hadn't heard from the contact."

"Mr. Daniels, I don't mean to sound indifferent, but they are waiting for me in the surgical ward. And besides that, I'm afraid I can't help you. My secretary typically makes the arrangements for all organ transports." Dr. Amandi stopped in front of the double doors leading into the new heart patient wing. "You picked up Dr. Kendall. What in the world happened out there?"

Race took a deep breath. The offensive stench of the hut still lingered in his nostrils. "To be honest, I'm not sure, but I assume Dr. Kendall will be able to answer some of those questions once she's conscious."

"Did you see the shooters?"

Race shook his head. "They were gone by the time I got to the huts. I think my plane scared them off. Dr. Kendall's the one you should talk to."

"Perhaps I'll stop by her room later and assure her that I'll look into the situation. The last thing we need is for our doctors to be in harm's way when on a simple mission of mercy into the bush."

"I'm sure Dr. Kendall would agree." Race moved aside to let one of the nurses pass through the doorway. "I'm leaving for Makuru right now."

"To look for the missing organs?"

Race started to tell him about Jeme, but something stopped him. "No kidneys. No paycheck."

Retracing his steps, Race hurried toward the hospital's south entrance. A woman brushed past him then paused, bracing her arm against the wall for support. Chestnut brown hair tumbled loose around her shoulders. Large green eyes stared up at him. What in the world was she doing out of bed?

"Dr. Kendall?" He gripped her shoulders to steady her. "I don't know where you think you're headed, but you're obviously in no condition to be up yet."

"I'm fine." She touched the neat row of sutures on her temple. "The wound is only

superficial."

"Superficial?" With his hands still steadying her, he started steering her back

into the room. "You took a bullet to the head."

She blinked her eyes as if searching for a memory. "You're the pilot. The man who flew us here, aren't you?"

"Name's Race Daniels—" He stopped midsentence in the doorway she'd just come out of. A dozen women rested on metal-framed beds. A baby cried. He felt his Adam's apple bob. "They put you up in the maternity ward?"

"This is a government hospital. There is always a shortage of beds."

Race reached out to steady her, conscious of the multiple pairs of female eyes trained on him. Spotting the one empty bed, he led Mia to it then sat her on the thin mattress. He glanced at the half empty IV bag and loose IV line lying on the sheet. "I might not be a doctor, but I'd bet my dog tags you were told to stay off your feet for a couple of days."

"I don't have a couple of days. Mbui is my patient, and sitting here isn't helping anyone."

She attempted to stand again, but he stopped her. "Stay put. I'm going to find one of the nurses."

"You can't tell me what to do—"

"You've just been shot."

"And I've got to figure out why another patient of mine's rejecting his heart." Her tight grip on his forearm made him hesitate. "Please. . .I need to see Mbui. I know his case better than anyone, and besides that, I'm going to go crazy just lying here."

"Mbui's in good hands, I promise. They called in Dr. Amandi, who's one of the best transplant surgeons in the country."

She shook her head. "You don't understand. It's not just Mbui I'm worried about. Jeme doesn't have any family in the city. I want to see if I can find a place for her to stay where she'll be safe."

"Jeme's not here." Race's brow furrowed. "Remember?"

Her head jerked up, her eyes darting as if she was having trouble connecting the dots, keeping things straight. "She has to be here. Mbui. . .Jeme. . .little Zaina. . ."

His arm brushed hers as he sat beside her. "You don't remember what happened, do you?"

"I remember bits and pieces. The gunshot. . .Jeme's sister. . .Mbui's fever." Panic registered in her eyes. "If she's not here, then where is she?"

"I'm on my way to get her."

"You left her?"

"If I'd known what I was going to be transporting, I would have flown in on one of our larger Cessnas. But the plane I was flying only holds one passenger. I was pushing the weight limit bringing you and Mbui. But Mbui was dying, you'd been shot. . .I had to make a choice."

She looked up and caught his gaze. "Jeme's sister. She was in that hut, murdered because she was an...albino. And Jeme's daughter—"

"—is an albino." Guilt raged afresh as all the pieces came together. *But there hadn't been a choice. Or had there?* His mind flashed to Rachel. "I didn't have a choice."

"You did. But you chose the wrong one." Mia's voice rose and her breathing quickened. "You should have left me. I've got to go find her."

"Dr. Kendall." Several of the women glanced their way, unable to decipher what they were saying but able to tell something was wrong. Race lowered his voice in an effort to bring some sanity to this woman climbing out of bed. "I'm sorry, but I didn't know about the girl's sister. I didn't have time to weigh all the consequences."

"If they find that baby, they'll kill her."

"Tell me what I can do to help, and I'll do it, but you need to stay here. I promised Jeme I'd come for her, and I will."

"I'm the one who's sorry." She shook her head as she reached for her black medical bag beside the bed. "You were right. Mbui is in good hands for now. But if you want to help, take me with you to Makuru."

"You're in no shape to leave the room."

"I'm coming."

"There's no room, and it will take too much time to switch planes."

"She and Zaina together weigh less than Mbui." Mia lifted her chin. "You managed before. You can manage again."

He could tell by her furrowed brow that there was no use arguing. "Fine. But don't blame me if we go down on the savanna."

CHAPTER EIGHT

THURSDAY, DECEMBER 12TH, 10:01 AM

SHINWANGA REGIONAL HOSPITAL

"Wait." Mia rose from the floppy mattress, as Race headed toward the door.

Lightning bolts of pain shot straight to her bullet-grazed head. The force nearly doubled her over. "You're not leaving without me, Mr. Daniels."

"You better keep up then."

Hand against the edge of the bed frame, she steadied herself and willed the dizziness to pass. Lugging her medical bag, she followed him out of the ward.

Ten minutes later, they stood beside a small bush plane parked at the far end of the private airstrip.

"Had her refueled, but I'm gonna have to zip through the preflight checklist. Board at your own risk." Race circled the plane. In one fluid motion, he lifted his muscular body from the sandy soil and folded his impressive frame into the pilot's seat.

Mia yanked open the passenger door. The pungent odor of potato chips and rotten produce assaulted her nose. A blackened banana peel fell at her feet. "You live in this heap?"

"Let's just say things have been a bit hectic lately."

She reached in and cleared the seat of candy wrappers, wadded papers, and a couple of old word-search paperbacks. "Here's some weight we can cut."

"I'm guessing you're more of a private jet kind of girl?"

Mia crushed the trash in her hands. "How would you know what kind of girl I am?"

"Not hard to figure," he said, going through his pre-flight check. "The charter service I work for organizes fly-in safaris and private charter flights to generate funds for its nonprofit side. I'm thinking you probably have a rich daddy back in the States footing your little African safari."

"Not even close." She shot him a wry smile. Two could play at this game. "Let *me* guess. You're the frustrated son of some retired military general who was never home."

Race laughed. "Traveling with you was a lot easier when you were knocked out."

"Thanks for the compliment."

Race started the plane. Burning fuel mingled with the stuffiness of the cockpit.

Mia scanned the area for a trash bin. When she didn't find one she snatched a crumpled plastic bag lying on top of an odd assortment of five-pound rice sacks and new blankets crammed in the tight space behind the seat. "What's all this?"

"Part of my work."

"Are you feeding these people?"

He squared his shoulders. "Look, Doc—" Anger flared his nostrils and narrowed his killer-blue eyes. "I don't tell you who to operate on. You don't tell me what to haul in my plane."

"So you're a closet humanitarian. And a humble one at that. I'm impressed. Up until now, I thought you just transported tourists and organs on occasion."

She eyed his lean profile. Makuru was a hard day's drive inland, assuming the rains had not made the roads impassable. Even in the dry season, it would take much too long to reach Jeme with a jeep. And, once again, it seemed circumstances beyond her control had forced her to give in to the judgment of this rough-and-tumble chauffeur.

She scooped the last of the trash into the plastic sack. Any guy that passed out food and medical supplies to starving people couldn't be all bad. Maybe she should have given him the benefit of the doubt. Trust he had his reasons for leaving Jeme behind. After all, regretting a snap decision was a feeling she could understand. She tossed the sack of trash behind the seat to be disposed of later.

But bellies filled with rice wouldn't protect the albinos from ruthless killers with high-powered assault weapons and sharp machetes. Someone, most likely a neighbor or maybe even a friend, had betrayed Jeme's family to the albino hunters.

Mia tamped the memory of Numa's mutilated body hidden beneath a sodden blanket. If the human poachers returned for Jeme and her albino child before she could get to Makuru, there wouldn't be much left to cover.

Mia hoisted herself into the cockpit. Her shoulder brushed Race's. The solid strength of him sent a jolt through her body. The man was a strange and disconcerting mixture of grit and compassion.

Who also happened to transport human organs.

A disturbing thought shot through her still fuzzy brain.

If Race had been in Makuru to pick up organs for the hospital, was it possible someone had harvested Numa's organs to sell? No. That wasn't possible. There were strict regulations and rules governing the procurement and distribution of transplant organs. Even with high corruption in the country, albino hunters would never be able to circumvent that process.

Or would they?

Legs drawn, knees nearly to her chin, she searched for a place to put her feet as well as her ridiculous paranoid thoughts. "We'll have to strap Jeme and Zaina to the wing when we find them."

"We'll make it work," he shouted as he donned his headset. "As long as you can move that Igloo and let me get this plane in the air."

She glanced at the load behind her. "Where do you suggest I put it?"

"If you're as smart as they say, you'll figure it out." He winked.

Was he flirting with her? Now that she knew who he was, she knew better than to be sucked in by this show of charm. Word of Race Daniels' magnetism was legendary around the hospital. Nurses lined up when the handsome pilot was scheduled to deliver an organ. But why try to win her over? Maybe he was just trying to keep her as off balance as her spinning head already made her feel. "Who are *they*?"

"The hospital's a small world. People talk." Race cut his eyes away quickly. "It's a joke, Doc."

"I knew that." She tried to sound nonchalant, but Mr. Daniels had no idea how seriously close to the truth he'd come. Making friends had never been her strong suit, even though she'd tried especially hard to start over here. She lifted the empty cooler and changed the subject. "Is this what you use to transport organs?"

"Yep."

She frowned at the admission.

"Look," he said, as if reading her mind. "I ensure that my flight times give an organ the chance it needs to remain viable. You can turn your nose up at me or my plane all you want, but my coolers are clean and my organ procurement and delivery times well within the viability time limits. There's too much at stake to have it any other way."

"But are all the delivery boys as careful as you?"

She turned and jammed the cooler behind the seat, in between some blankets and her medical bag, hoping he was right. In the meantime, she'd take extra care not to touch anything in his slimy cockpit and to keep her bacteria-tainted hands away from her face. The propeller was whirling when she swiveled around. How far could she trust this bucket of bolts and this guy who flew it? She ventured a sideways glance at her pilot.

One thing she could be certain of—her knight wore armor that was far from shiny. The guy needed a shave, and running a comb through that thick mop of hair would improve his appearance considerably. And while she'd admit there was a certain charm to his rugged persona, his whole setup screamed germs and trouble. But for now, this pilot and his junky plane was her only choice.

Race pumped the throttle and thumped gauges. “Here, wear these.” He tossed her a vintage headset that matched the pair over his ears.

Mia adjusted the earpieces, trying not to think about how many unwashed heads had worn these relics of the Korean War.

“Might want to strap in as well.” He snapped his seat belt into place and she did the same.

He revved the throttle. The plane taxied to the top of the beach-front runway, the engine gaining power and rattling Mia’s teeth. She sucked in her breath and clenched her jaw. Race threw her a cocky smile then sped toward the sparkling ocean. Right before they collided with the surf, he pulled back hard on the yoke and the plane’s nose rose skyward.

“You can breathe now.” He shouted into the headphone mic.

The excruciating drone of the engine throbbed inside Mia’s head, making her painfully aware of all six-foot-four inches of raw power wedged into the pilot’s seat. The sooner this guy landed this crop duster, the sooner she’d escaped the discomfort of being sandwiched next to a guy who kept her equilibrium off balance. Her hand went to her stitches. “Are you always such a show-off?”

Race grinned. “Only for beautiful docs.” He cranked the control yoke slowly and the plane banked right. “But I can slow down some if you’d like.”

“There’s a baby out there who might die if you ease off because of me.”

“Then you better hang on, doc.”

CHAPTER NINE

THURSDAY, DECEMBER 12TH, 10:32 AM

OVER DAR ES SALAAM

Race made a tight U-turn over the clear, calm ocean, leveled out the plane, then headed west. He gave the woman beside him a quick once-over. It had been a rough day, but he was clearly in it up to his ears now. No sense being enemies when they were about to land in a place where there were guys with guns. He decided to give starting over a try.

"Listen. . ." he said. "Don't worry. We're going to find your friends and bring them back."

"I hope so."

"Why did you insist on coming?"

"I promised I'd help her." She turned her face to the window and shut the door on further conversation.

They rode in silence as the plane skimmed the swollen Ruvu River. The muddy waters of Dar es Salaam's main water supply cut a wide, snaking path through the lush forests of the Uluguru Mountains. Smoky plumes rose from the woodcutters' fires and obscured the horizon, all familiar territory he knew as well as the small Nebraska town where he'd grown up.

Race pulled back on the yoke, and they climbed through the choking clouds. Within seconds, they broke free of the haze and burst into dazzling sunlight. East Africa's second-busiest port evaporated below the azure sky, leaving nothing but the breathtaking beauty of acres of palm trees and verdant rice paddies. If all suffering could be so easily transformed—his own included—he'd never come back down to earth.

Once they reached the plain, Race flew low over the vast grasslands where cattle and goats grazed between villages and small towns.

"They call this airplane terrain." Race pointed at the spidery roads crisscrossing long stretches of uninhabited land. "Barely more than cattle paths. Drop into one of those ruts and never be seen again, though you don't have to worry about that happening to us today."

Mia laughed then caught herself, as if she'd suddenly remembered they weren't friends.

"Ah, not only does she risk her life for strangers, she smiles too." Race adjusted a knob on the dash. "Can I ask you something?"

Her wary glance warned him to tread carefully. "I suppose."

"You said something at the hospital that implied Mbui wasn't the first patient you'd had recently to reject his heart?"

"What if I told you I had a theory it might have to do with organs being transported in unsterilized conditions?"

"I told you I always follow protocol." He cranked the control yoke a sharp left. The wings tipped and she slammed into him. He could be just as stubborn as she was. "And I can ride like this all day. How about you?"

She pushed against him, but as he'd known, couldn't break the powerful g-force gluing her shoulder to his.

"I might be able to help, but if you continue to give me the cold shoulder. . ."

Mia, rigor-mortis-stiff, yelled, "Okay. I give."

"Now we're getting somewhere." He leveled the wings, and she popped free.

He chuckled as she scooted toward the opposite door, though

where she thought she was going, he had no idea. Apparently, anywhere, as long as there was distance between them.

She pressed her full lips together, which highlighted her flawless skin and strong cheekbones. He glanced away. The last thing he needed right now was a distraction.

"Mbui isn't the only one. Over all I've had a higher number of patients experiencing acute rejection over the past few months," she admitted into the mic.

His brow arched. "Isn't rejection the constant threat for any transplant patient?"

Mia plastered her nose against the window, while he waited for her answer in silence.

Finally, she turned to him. "Transplant recipients battle chronic rejection all the time. The gradual loss of organ function comes with the territory. That's why patients must agree to a lifetime regimen of immunosuppressant drugs. But the immediate rejection of a viable organ transplanted into an otherwise healthy individual raises all sorts of red flags." She let her voice trail off. "Let's just say, having several acute rejections in a row is not making the governmental program look very good."

"Or you." He turned his attention back to the sky. "Sorry, cheap jab. I honestly didn't mean it that way."

"What people think of me is the least of my worries. You said you might be able to help? I need to see the private hospital's transplant records so I can compare them to mine. You have access there."

"How would their records help?"

"My hospital receives all of its organs from Kaboni Private. Comparing my graft survival rates with theirs will give me numbers to support the length of time an organ functions after the transplant. The comparison could tell me if my increased rejections are the result of organ preservation or organ procurement. If something is happening to the organs before they arrive at Kaboni, the rejection rate should be the same. But if our rejection rates are different, then I'm worried the organ failures could be caused by something that happens after the transplant."

"Like what?"

She shrugged. "Our patient care protocols could need tweaking. Maybe it's an issue with the anti-rejection drugs. Or..." An unsettled look crossed her face.

"Or?"

"Something may be wrong with my technique." The idea had clearly shaken her.

Resisting the urge to take her hand, he said, "You don't strike me as a person who makes mistakes."

Her quivering hand went to the stitches above her temple. "Maybe I should have stayed in bed."

"There's a frightened little mother out there who'll be glad you didn't."

She let out a frustrated snort at his attempt to cheer her up. "The bottom line is that something's not right, and I've got to find out if the same thing is happening at Kaboni."

"You ever consider the problem could be the living conditions of your patients?"

"Every day." Mia scanned the horizon as if the answer to her problem was hiding in the distance. "Most of my patients are poor and lack access to certain aspects of basic hygiene like running water. Which means while I can educate them, I can't protect them from all of the risks. But I still believe we're dealing with something more than just that."

"So basically, even if they follow your instructions, you're still looking at an unexplained risk factor you can't qualify."

She raised her brow. "You might just be the pilot, but it sounds like you know a few things about the process."

He winked at her. "Transported a surgeon's brain once. Guess some of that gray matter rubbed off on me." He pointed at the rugged mountain rising majestically from the flatlands and put both hands on the yoke. "Mt. Meru's to the right of us, but where we're setting down there's not much of a landing strip. You might want to hang on again."

Wanting to make sure no unwanted visitors were still hanging around Mbui's compound, Race made a quick pass over the huts. The glint of silver could have been nothing more than an abandoned hubcap used for a chicken feeder. He pointed the plane's nose toward the tracks his last visit had left at the base of the rugged southern slope. The wheels hit the ground. Mia clung to her seat beside him as the plane bounced uphill and finally coasted to a stop. Eight-foot-high elephant grass bordered the black-clay ruts. Mia reached for the door handle.

Something shiny caught Race's attention beneath the shadow of a mango tree. "Wait."

"I can't. I don't want that terrified girl alone another minute."

Mia started to leave the plane, but he reached across the seat and grabbed her arm. "Let me take a look first."

Not waiting for her to argue, Race opened the cockpit door and let his lungs fill with the wild scent of Africa. Losing himself in this forgotten part of the world had been easier than he'd ever imagined. Unfortunately, losing himself and forgetting what he'd left behind were two different things.

He slid around the nose of the plane then crouched down, weighing his options. If there was going to be trouble, he was going to have to keep the pretty doc out of it. No matter how determined she was to save the world, she was in no condition to confront a group of gun-slinging murderers.

Tall grass blocked his view of the compound, making it impossible to see what was going on from this distance. If the glint of silver he'd seen from the air had been a vehicle, he could be walking into a hornet's nest. And because his landing wouldn't have gone unnoticed, the bad guys had just scored the advantage. Signaling the doctor to stay put, he crept toward the compound. With Jeme's life at stake, going in blind was a chance he was going to have to take.

Halfway across the field, the sound of a motor broke through the relative quiet of the afternoon.

"No!" Mia sprinted past him, too fast for him to yank her back to the safety of the plane.

"Get down!" He chased her into the compound then charged across the rubble-strewn yard painted with bird dung. The tail end of a jeep disappeared into the thick bush.

"Jeme!" Mia flung open the broken door of the hut where he'd first seen the young girl. "Jeme!" She proceeded to the next structure as she continued her search of the compound. Thirty seconds later, she whirled, accusation in her eyes. “She’s not here.”

The familiar torment of losing Rachel and the baby ripped through him like a fresh wound. And now he’d failed again. He’d left Jeme alone to fend for herself and now there was a good chance those butchers had her. He searched the perimeter. There was no trace of the perpetrators, only the heavy smell of death lingering in the breeze.

Mia stood frozen in the doorway of the darkened hut as he walked back to her, empty-handed. “They’re all gone. Jeme. . .Zaina. . .Numa’s body. . .”

“We need to leave,” he panted. “There’s nothing more we can do here.”

“You’re wrong. She’s got to be here somewhere.”

Mia’s hand went to the trickle of blood coming from her stitches. She stumbled toward him then collapsed against his chest.

His arms automatically wrapped her in a steadying embrace. Unsure of what to do next, he held Mia tight and scanned the compound again for any sign of Jeme. “We’re going to find her.”

She looked up at him, her eyes leaking tears. “Don’t promise me something you can’t deliver.”

He caught the deep compassion in her eyes and wished he could make everything right again. But against the circulating evil, he knew compassion would not be enough.

CHAPTER TEN

THURSDAY, DECEMBER 12TH, 8:23 PM

JEME'S FATHER'S VILLAGE

Beneath the cover of the African night sky, Jeme slipped through the tall grasses of the savanna and approached her father's village. The fear that had chased her across the flat terrain now wrapped its greedy fingers around her soul and tormented the dark corners of her mind. Numa was dead. Mbui dying. And her child was being hunted.

Pulling Zaina closer, she stopped at the edge of the clearing filled with a dozen thatched huts. Yellow flames flickered beneath iron pots where the women cooked the nightly *ugali* and sauce. The aroma of simmering goat stew stirred the hunger that had been gnawing at her empty belly for miles.

Where was her mother?

Jeme dared to inch closer. Her gaze searched the doorways of the candlelit huts for the short, plump woman who'd given birth to her seventeen years ago. Laughter from her father's wives and their children competed with the occasional shrill cry of a bush baby. She'd once sat at her father's fire and laughed with her siblings, but now she was filled with the heavy uncertainty that her father would even receive her.

Zaina whimpered in her arms, and the fingers of fear squeezed Jeme harder. When Zaina was born pale-skinned like Numa, her father claimed curses had come to the village. Numa and the child would have to go. So, he sent Numa, Jeme, and her family away. Now, she could only pray to the ancestors that time had softened her father's heart. Surely, once he knew she and Zaina were being hunted, he'd welcome her—and his granddaughter—back into the safety of the village.

Jeme pulled Zaina to her breast to quiet her then padded through the darkness. She crouched out of sight in the tall grass, watching her older sister's small hut at the far edge of the compound.

Patience had been the only one in the village, besides her mother, who'd ever dared defend Jeme from their father. The first time Patience stood between their father's walking stick and Jeme was when Jeme refused to marry the old man her father had chosen. The second was when Jeme gave birth to Zaina. But that day, none of Patience's persuasive words had been enough to change their father's mind about the ghost child. And when Jeme refused to leave her daughter to die in the forest, citing her father's unwillingness to do the same to Numa, he ordered the villagers to drive Numa, Jeme, Mbui, and Zaina from their home. As they ran into the thick foliage, Jeme heard her father shout, "Never come back."

Heart beating against her chest, Jeme crept from the shadows and eased toward the candlelight glow spilling from the hut's open door. "Patience?"

A moment later her sister pulled her across the threshold. "Jeme?" Patience's belly was swollen with new life.

"Patience." Jeme reached out and grasped her sister's hand. "No one must know I am here. Not yet."

Patience glanced at Zaina, who lay nestled against Jeme's chest. Her expression softened. "You look exhausted. Wait here." She poked her head out the door and surveyed the compound. Satisfied Jeme had arrived unnoticed, she closed the door. "I have some food left over from my dinner if you're hungry."

Jeme glanced at the red dust clinging to her callused feet. She picked at Numa's crusty blood that stained her kanga, along with her dream of returning to her village triumphant. She and Mbui had failed to make a good life for Zaina and Numa. Desperation had forced her to return in shame.

Patience filled a bowl with *ugali* and sauce and offered Jeme a seat at the wooden table. "It's not much."

Jeme shook her head. "You have welcomed me. That is enough."

"You must have your strength, for there are those who will not welcome your return."

Jeme sank onto the little stool and scooped up a handful of food. Fear soured the doughy maize ball crammed in her mouth. She swallowed hard. "Surely my mother will speak up for me. I had hoped, given time, that she would be able to convince our father that Zaina isn't a curse."

Patience's gaze dipped. "Your mother is dead."

"Dead?" Jeme's hands shook as she absorbed the news. Without Mbui. . .without her mother. . .

"I'm sorry." Patience skirted the table then pulled two tin cups from a narrow shelf. "Truly, I am."

Zaina stirred in Jeme's trembling arms. Her smile reached all the way to her pudgy cheeks, blissfully unaware of the pain her birth had brought with it. Or the deep despair Jeme felt. Her mother would never know her grandchild. Jeme kissed her baby's soft neck then nuzzled against her face.

"When did my mother die?"

Patience poured some steamy chai into the cups. "Six months ago."

Hot tears cut trails through the dust on Jeme's cheeks. "No one sent word to me."

"Father would not allow it."

Her father was right. Pale skin was a curse. It had caused her family to hate. Any lingering hope that her father might have changed his mind began to dissolve. As did her confidence that she'd made the right decision to return to her family.

Jeme sipped the hot tea, praying it would calm her nerves. "Is he here?"

"He will be back by daybreak. I'll talk to him, if you'd like." Patience stroked Zaina's blonde head. "But you must understand there are no guarantees Father will allow you to stay."

Jeme set the cup on the table. "I have nowhere else to go. My husband is dying. Numa is dead. . ."

Horror filled Patience's expression. "Numa is dead?"

Jeme pushed the hot drink away from Zaina's groping hands and clutched her tighter. "Murdered. By those who believe albino flesh can bring them good luck." Jeme leaned forward. "But what if the curse is a lie, Patience?"

Her sister strode to the window then spun around to face her. "Lies or not, you shouldn't have brought your albino child here. Two months ago, one of our father's children drowned in the lake. We have lost acres of maize because of army worms, and our cattle have been continually raided, which has only fueled the fears of many that this village is cursed because of Numa and Zaina."

"I don't understand. Albinos are murdered for good luck then blamed because they are cursed?" Jeme untied the kanga and thrust Zaina into her sister's arms. Zaina tugged on Patience's long, black braids then giggled in delight. "Look at her, Patience. Look at her. She is a child no different from any of your children."

"She is a ghost child, Jeme. A zeruzeru—"

"No. Zaina means beautiful, and that is how I see her. Why should she be hated because of the color of her skin?"

"Jeme, you must understand—"

"No!" Jeme fought to breathe. "You are a mother of four and now there is yet another life within you. Surely *you* understand the bond of the children you have borne and who have suckled at your breast. You know there is no truth to what many would have us believe. This child brings no curse to our people."

Patience thrust Zaina back into Jeme's arms. "It does not matter what I think. There are those who wish to gain from the rumors of such superstitions."

The child began to cry. Jeme silenced her by offering a small piece of her ugali. "You mean lies. Tell me you honestly believe that this innocent child can curse a village."

"It is not I you need to convince." Patience glanced again at Zaina's chubby face then turned away. "You may stay here tonight, but tomorrow, whether or not you stay will be up to our father."

CHAPTER ELEVEN

THURSDAY, DECEMBER 12TH, 7:20 PM

BPH TECHNOLOGY LAB, BALTIMORE, MARYLAND

Axton Blade's fingers gripped the edge of the cliff. With his legs dangling beneath him, he strained to find a foothold on the treacherous surface of the sea ledge. Digging his right foot into the rock face, he found a toehold then slipped again. Muscles burned as he caught himself. His lungs threatened to burst. He glanced down at the black waters crashing against the rocky shoreline. The thousand-foot drop guaranteed death by drowning or being dashed to pieces against the jagged cliff, neither of which appealed to him.

A scream echoed through the trees of the thick forest above him. Nausea ripped through him. If Dryden found Paige...

Using every last ounce of strength he could muster, Axton hauled himself onto the rocky ledge above. Fighting a wave of dizziness from the deep gash on the side of his head, he forced himself to stand and study his surroundings. He had to find Dryden. Because if he didn't, no one on Blackwell Isle would survive.

"Dr. Spence?"

Harry Spence jumped as the tangled forest of Blackwell faded into the stark white walls of his lab. Valerie Pippin, his assistant, stood over him, silky red hair dusting her shoulders, blue eyes glaring at him impatiently, and the strong scent of gardenias bringing him squarely back into the real world.

She dropped a file onto his desk. “You were daydreaming again.”

“I wasn’t daydreaming. I was. . .”

He swallowed his explanation. She’d laugh if he told her about the five-hundred-page handwritten manuscript currently sitting on his desk at home. Or the fact that Axton Blade had become as real to him as the drug he was researching for BPH Technologies. Or that Paige Cruz just happened to look exactly like the beautiful Miss Pippin.

He took a deep breath of her perfume then sneezed.

Valerie dangled the keys to the lab between her fingers. “Well, whatever you’re doing, it’s seven thirty and I’m going home.”

He shoved the thick rims of his glasses up the bridge of his nose and looked over the computer screen. “I just need another five minutes.”

“You said that five minutes ago. And five minutes before that.”

He grabbed a Cheeto from the open bag on his desk and popped it into his mouth. He needed to focus. Something was still wrong with the formula, but he’d yet to put a finger on the problem in his calculation. “I’m close to a breakthrough. I can feel it.”

Harry sneezed again then glanced up at Valerie. She slid off her lab jacket, revealing subtle curves he’d memorized the first day they met. He swallowed hard. If only he had the guts to ask her out, instead of doing what he always did. Return home to an empty apartment, pull out a microwave dinner, and work on his novel. It was the same thing he’d done every night for as long as he could remember.

Unless. . .

He cleared his throat. He turned forty in two weeks. Maybe it was time to live it up. “Valerie.”

She pulled on her coat then grabbed her purse from her desk. “What?”

“I was wondering if you. . .if you’d. . .” His mouth went dry. He crunched down on another Cheeto. What did he think he was doing asking a coworker out on a date? And besides that, she’d never say yes.

“What?” she repeated.

He glanced back at his computer screen. "Would you mind taking a look at something?"

"Not tonight. I have a date."

"A date?"

She shot him an exasperated look. "It's what men and women do when they like each other. They go grab a drink or dinner, and get to know each other. You should try it sometime."

Right.

"Oh, and one other thing," she continued. "Dr. Billings called and he wants a time confirmed for when you're going to be ready to start the human trials. He sounded impatient."

"I told him two days ago, perfecting a miracle isn't a process that can be rushed." Harry pushed up his glasses again. "There are still months of research left until the drug is ready for human testing."

Valerie applied a luscious coat of pink lipstick. "He said to let you know that you have until the end of the month."

"The end of the month? You and I both know that's not enough time." Sweat beaded across Harry's forehead. He tugged on the collar of his shirt. "Do you think it's hot in here?"

"No."

"You'll have to convince him to give me another six months." Just because he wasn't starting from scratch didn't mean he could whip up a revolutionary anti-rejection drug overnight.

She tossed the lipstick into her bag. "Call him yourself."

"Me?"

"I'm tired of fielding your calls."

Harry lowered his brow. Valerie had never raised her voice at him before. "But that's. . .that's what assistants do."

"Assistants assist in research and help with lab experiments. I spend my time answering your phone, putting Billings off, making sure your lunch doesn't contain any traces of gluten, and ensuring your supply of Cheetos never runs out."

He shook his head. "I. . .I don't understand—"

"Which is precisely the problem." Valerie yanked her scarf off the hook on the back of the door then swung it around her neck. "You're not glucose intolerant. You're— "

"Cautious," he countered.

"Intolerable." She tossed him the key. "I'm not staying late tonight. You can lock things up. And in the morning, I'm requesting a transfer to another department. Maybe there I'll be appreciated."

"But Valerie. . ."

"Good night, Dr. Spence."

The door slammed behind her, stopping any further conversation. Harry frowned. Paige Cruz would never have walked out on Axton Blade. He dropped the half empty bag of Cheetos into his desk drawer. He might as well go home too. He wouldn't be able to work anymore tonight. He shut down the computer then checked to make sure everything was put away. Just because Valerie had a date didn't mean she couldn't have finished cleaning.

He took an extra thirty seconds to count the vials through the locked glass door. Sixteen. . .seventeen. . .eighteen. . .Nineteen? His palms grew sweaty. He had to have miscounted. A vial had gone missing once before. Billings had told him he was working too hard and had somehow misplaced it. But he knew that wasn't possible. He rubbed his eyes then started counting again. Obviously, the sixty-hour work weeks were starting to catch up with him. Why would anyone want to steal his unfinished drug?

He counted again. Nineteen vials. He'd been right. One was missing. He squeezed his eyes shut, unbuttoned the top button of his shirt, then reached into his pocket for his handkerchief. Blotting his forehead, he paced.

The missing vials could be deadly in the wrong hands.

CHAPTER TWELVE

FRIDAY, DECEMBER 13TH, 5:19 AM

JEME'S FATHER'S VILLAGE

Blinding light ripped Jeme from the escape of sleep. The smell of smoke burned her throat. Blistering heat enveloped her. Hungry flames licked the dry thatch above her. Sparks fell onto the thin blanket covering her. Jeme threw back a sheet of flames. She choked at the thick smoke filling the cramped hut.

Fire!

Zaina's wails competed with the roar of the flames. With fiery hot embers falling from the ceiling, Jeme groped for the child. She covered Zaina's face with a kanga and stumbled for the door. Patience grasped her arm and shoved her across the threshold. By now, the entire village had emerged from their homes to witness the catastrophe. Flames jumped to the next hut then quickly devoured the feed bin where piles of dried corn lay stored for the coming winter.

The few buckets of water, still full from last night's trip to the well, were useless against the fire. When the crackling flames died down, three huts had been charred and months of food destroyed.

Jeme gasped for breath with smoke-filled lungs. Her father

emerged from the center of the chaos, barking orders at several of the young boys to watch and ensure the fire didn't erupt again. Turning toward the sound of her cough, he stopped. Surprise flickered in his eyes then burst into flames of anger. "You?"

Zaina started crying again as Jeme's father quickly bridged the gap between them and thrust them toward the center of the encroaching throng. "You dare return to the village to bring more curses upon our family?"

Jeme jostled Zaina, desperately trying to quiet her. "I had nothing to do with this."

His gnarled finger pointed at Zaina. "She is *your* ghost child."

"This was not her fault!"

"You are both cursed."

Fear seeped through Jeme like a poison, completely choking out any remaining seeds of hope. There was nowhere left to run. She gathered the last of her courage. "Then you are cursed as well. Do you see the dried blood on my clothes? It's from the cursed child *you* spawned. Numa's dead. Butchered in broad daylight for her skin and hair—"

"Enough. How dare you blame me. None of this would have happened if you had allowed this child to be killed when she was born, as I ordered."

Clutching Zaina tighter, Jeme took a step back. "Zaina is my child, and I'll give my own life before allowing you or anyone else to harm her."

He gripped Jeme's forearm and thrust her toward the smoldering huts. "Then explain this damage. Someone is to blame, and someone will pay."

Jeme stumbled in front of the accusing stares that had lined up to judge her. Brothers and sisters. Her father's wives, women who had once treated her as a daughter. Their faces were now masked with suspicion. Her hand moved to an inflamed spot on her shoulder where a fallen ember had burned her skin.

Her father spat. "We will have nothing to do with those who are cursed."

Jeme's heart pounded, as fear gave way to defeat. What if she really was cursed? Mbui was dying. Numa lay butchered. And she had nothing left with which to help Zaina. Not even Jeme's own death would save her child.

"You must both die." Her father grabbed them, but Jeme pulled away.

"Patience, please. Help."

"It's too late, Jeme. I'm sorry." Patience's chin dipped, but not before Jeme caught the look of guilt registered in her eyes.

Jeme jerked free. Clutching Zaina tight, she bolted for the forest.

Her father shouted at her. "You can run, Jeme, but you carry the curse."

CHAPTER THIRTEEN

FRIDAY, DECEMBER 13TH, 7:14 AM

SHINWANGA REGIONAL HOSPITAL

Race waltzed into Dr. Kendall's office unannounced and dropped a two-inch-thick folder onto the desktop neatly piled with papers, a computer, and a collection of plastic puzzle cubes. A quick glance around the small room clashed with his first impressions of her. The classy woman belonged in a front-window office, and yet she'd chosen to work from a janitor's closet filled with a couple of file cabinets, a desk, and an orchid.

She peeked up from behind the cup of coffee she held between her hands and stared at the file. "Most people make an appointment, or at the very least knock before they come barging into the private office of the chief transplant surgeon."

"I'm not most people." He fiddled with the packet of gum in his pocket, wishing he could erase his other impression of her. That of holding a brown-haired beauty with long legs and full lips who also happened to be smart, self-assured, and driven. "Nice office."

She wasn't smiling. "Try again."

"Did you sleep okay last night?"

"When I wasn't worrying about Jeme and her baby."

"Me too." He glanced back at her coffee mug. "You wouldn't happen to have more coffee, would you?"

"Normally, yes. I have a friend in the States who supplies my one vice."

"Only one?" He caught her faint smile and scanned the rest of the room, looking for the source of the brew. Instead he discovered a handful of photos hanging on her wall—but no coffeepot. The lingering scent of vanilla and maple made him crave a stack of buttermilk pancakes and a fresh pot of decaf from the local diner he'd eaten at a hundred times back in Lincoln. He couldn't even remember the last time he'd had a decent cup of coffee.

She emptied the mug then set it on the desk. "Unfortunately, that was the last of it."

"Then I suppose that's my cue to jump into why I'm here." He picked up the Sudoku cube from her desk and rolled it between his fingers. "I brought you something."

"I see that." She lifted the cube from his hand, dropped it back in the exact spot on the desk where he'd found it, then turned and opened her laptop. "But unless it's word on Jeme's whereabouts, I'm not interested."

"Oh, I think you'll be interested in this." Apparently, he wasn't the only one who tended to be a bit irritable before his second cup of coffee. And he'd missed his first one this morning. "Are you always this crabby in the morning?"

Her expression softened, giving him another quick glimpse behind the iron façade she wore. He wondered if her somewhat icy exterior was because of the high-risk profession she'd chosen, or the difficult place she'd elected to practice. "I just can't stop worrying about Jeme."

He sat in the rickety chair facing her desk. "We'll find her."

"How?" Mia pulled her hair into a ponytail and secured it with an elastic holder she snatched from her wrist. "Either the poachers took her when they came back for the rest of Numa's body, or she's hiding."

"Have you talked to Mbui? More than likely she went back to her home village. If we knew where it was I could fly us there."

"I thought of that, but Mbui's been in and out of consciousness.

Unless we can get his vitals stabilized, he won't be going home. But she has my number. I'm just praying now that she'll call me." She shut the laptop, her gaze communicating a deep sadness at the possibility she could lose another patient. "So what did you bring me?"

"Files on every heart transplant done at Kaboni Private in the past six months."

"Files on their transplants? You weren't kidding when you said you might be able to help." She crossed the room and shut the door. "You didn't actually go in there and steal patient files."

He picked up the folder. "If you don't want them—"

She snatched the folder from him. "Of course I want them. I just wasn't sure you'd actually be able to get your hands on them."

"You do know it's a bit too late for second thoughts, don't you?"

"Yes." She looked up at him. "And I know how much trouble you—and I—could get into if someone finds out about this."

Race tapped the edge of the folder. "Like I said, if you don't want them—"

She moved so her desk was between them. "I really do want them, but seriously. You didn't steal these files, did you?"

"Does it matter?"

"Yes, it matters."

He flashed his best smile. "You'd be amazed at how far a little charm goes. You should try it sometime."

The tips of her ears turned red. "Oh, I've heard plenty about your charm."

"Then you know there's nothing to worry about. These are copies, and my source has sworn herself to secrecy."

"But I still don't know—"

"A simple 'thank you' will do."

Her jaw tensed. "Thank you."

"You're welcome."

"But if you're trying to make up for losing Jeme, you've still got a long way to go."

He leaned back in the chair, stretched out his legs, and crossed his ankles. "Maybe, maybe not." He nodded at the folder. "Better wait till you see what's in there."

"Have you read these?"

He shrugged. "May have glanced through them."

She flipped open the folder then paused. "Why would you risk your job to do this for me?"

"You told me people are dying, and I knew I had a way to get the information you needed."

"I don't buy that. Not completely, anyway. There's got to be more to it."

For a moment he was back in the Persian Gulf. He'd trained tirelessly for that mission, but nothing could have prepared him for what he'd ended up losing in those eleven months.

"Let's just leave it at that for now."

Mia started reading the files. Within seconds she was jotting notes on a yellow legal pad then pulling out a small calculator. "This doesn't make sense."

He picked up the Sudoku cube again and started trying to solve the math puzzle. Normally playing with puzzles calmed him. Sitting so close to this woman, he wasn't sure anything would. "What doesn't make sense?"

She glanced up at him through the longest lashes he'd ever seen. Man, he hated the way she messed with him. "Why do I get the feeling you already know the answer to that?"

He held up his hands. She didn't have to know that he'd spent the last hour pouring over the files in the relative safety of his jeep. He had his own questions he wanted answered. "Like I said—"

"You're just the delivery boy." She tapped her pen against the pad. "I'm going to have to take some time to look at these numbers in greater detail, but from what I can tell right off, there's been no change in the organ rejection rate of patients at Kaboni Private over the past few months. But what are they doing that I'm not?"

"What if you factor in your patients' poorer lifestyle? Would your rejection rate be about the same?"

"Within a margin of error, yes. But not this much."

Her secretary opened the door. "I'm sorry, Dr. Kendall. . .I didn't know you were in the middle of a consultation. You have a patient waiting."

"It's fine, Sarah. Mr. Daniels was just leaving." She nodded as the older woman stepped back out of the room. "I'll be ready in just a minute."

Race stood as the door shut. "Why don't you call me Race? No one calls me Mr. Daniels."

"Race. Where in the world did you get that name, by the way?"

"How about we leave that story for another day, Dr. Kendall."

"Mia."

He grinned at her reluctant concession. "Mia."

She picked up the folder. "What if I'm not doing something they are?"

He dropped the Sudoku game back on the desk, careful to place it exactly where he'd gotten it, and she smiled. He wondered if he should interpret her softened expression as appreciation for his attention to detail or as a truce between them. "Only one way to find out."

"You're right." Mia shoved the folder into the top drawer of her desk before locking it. "I think it's time I paid Dr. Amandi a visit."

CHAPTER FOURTEEN

FRIDAY, DECEMBER 13TH, 11:38 AM

DAR ES SALAAM

Mia slammed on the brakes. Her fishtailing vehicle slung mud onto the rail-thin cattleman prodding a cow into her path. Heart racing, she aimed for the ruts that separated Africa's two distinctly unequal worlds—those with enough money for cars and decent healthcare, and those who had to walk and pray they never became seriously ill. Brake pedal pressed to the floor, she managed to stop just a few inches short of the animal's wasted hindquarters.

She released her white-knuckled grip on the steering wheel. Keeping one foot on the brake, she worked to gather the contents of the file folder now strewn across the floorboard. Explaining to the Kaboni's head of cardiology how she'd come into possession of his confidential stats didn't worry her near as much as her growing stack of unanswered questions.

Why was her rejection rate so much higher than his? Why were her patients dying and his weren't? What if the problem was her fault? That was the question that scared her the most.

As much as she hated to admit it, her theories about organ procurement, preservation, or even transportation didn't hold water when she ran the numbers. Amandi was not losing patients. Did he have some new procedure she didn't know about? Doubtful. She'd trained under the best and completed her fellowship at one of the world's most prestigious transplant hospitals. But she'd been out of the loop for over a year. New developments occurred in medicine all the time. She had to know what Amandi knew.

A horn blast jarred Mia from her futile sorting of conjecture from fact. She waved the dilapidated truck around then crammed the papers back into the folder. She tossed the folder onto the passenger seat, confident once Dr. Amandi learned the seriousness of the rejection mystery, his partnership with her government-sponsored teaching program would demand that her losses become his concern. Her problem could quickly become his problem as well if the cause was not pinpointed soon. Hopefully, his realization of the tragic consequences would diminish any disciplinary repercussions her illicit procurement of his records deserved.

She scanned the now empty road then stomped the accelerator. Bouncing over the ruts, she hooked a right at Pugu Highway and headed for the bay on the better side of town.

In the chaotic heart of the city, she navigated the crowded streets, her progress slowed by the thick black smoke of the *dala-dalas*. The packed minibuses were stalled by an army of street peddlers. Despite the stifling heat, she rolled up her window to block the smell of exhaust, then flipped on the deficient air conditioner.

She turned onto a recently repaved road entering the area of town the government had renovated to attract tourists. She sped past the bungalow-type houses and mansions of the expatriates, noting the high-walled security fences crowned with barbed wire or broken glass.

As the fairly new, eighty-bed hospital building came into view, a pang of jealousy prickled Mia's clammy skin. Funny how spending several months operating and teaching in the public government-run hospital made this 1960's facility with its small, but adequate research lab, seem state-of-the-art. She wheeled into the parking lot and was reminded again how Tanzania's developing health system still lagged behind the rest of the world. The American Embassy's reluctance to vouch for this country's medical care was justified.

She jumped out of her jeep and slammed the door. Following the covered sidewalk, she pushed the discouraging realities of her limitations from her mind. She didn't have to save the world today, but she did have to direct her energy toward solving this problem.

Compared to the multistory hospital complexes she'd had to learn her way around in her former life, this complex was easy to navigate. All she had to do was march down the hall of the main building and around the corner. Amandi's office was located next to a cozy lobby filled with a handful of patients and a receptionist's desk. Mia approached the familiar dark-skinned woman pecking at a computer keyboard surrounded by mounds of papers.

The woman pushed her glasses up the bridge of her nose as she glanced up. "Dr. Kendall?"

Mia nodded her greeting. "I need to see Dr. Amandi. It's urgent."

The secretary glanced at her computer, looking caught off guard at the unexpected visit. "I am sorry, but I was not aware you were planning to stop by, and unfortunately Dr. Amandi won't be available for the rest of the day."

Mia held up the manila folder that had been tucked under her arm. Mbui might not still be alive tomorrow. "Like I said, it's urgent. I believe he'll want to know what I discovered from this file. I promise I won't need much of his time, but if I could speak to him in private, I could explain everything. Is he doing a transplant?"

The secretary's back straightened. "He's in a series of meetings today."

"Please. I need you to understand the seriousness of this situation." Mia pulled out the piece of paper where she'd written down her findings from the folder and thrust it across the desk, then lowered her voice so the patients on the other side of the room couldn't hear her. "Our hospital is seeing a high number of rejections with our transplant patients. I thought it best to speak to him in person, but all my calls to him over the past couple weeks have gone to voice mail, and he's yet to return my call."

"You must understand that Dr. Amandi is a very busy man."

Mia bit her lip in an attempt to control her temper. "My patients are dying because something is wrong with either his donor organs or my procedure. And Dr. Amandi is the only one who can help me sort this out."

The woman glanced out across the lobby to ensure that none of the patients were listening in on their conversation. "Perhaps you could write out your concerns and I could pass them along to the doctor as soon as he becomes available."

Mia stuffed the paper back into the folder, still forcing herself to keep her voice at a whisper. Why was the woman putting her off? Just like Amandi. She didn't have time for delays and politics. "You know what, you're right. I think I'll skip Dr. Amandi and take my findings directly to the private funders of this hospital—"

"Please. . ." The woman pushed back in her chair and scurried around her desk. "Wait here."

"Thank you," Mia called after the secretary disappearing down the hall.

She hated wielding impertinent threats, but no hospital could afford to lose funding. Mia paced the tiled floor, flipping open the folder and sifting the facts through the strainer of the secretary's frosty reception.

"Dr. Kendall?" A minute later, a uniformed security guard walked into the room behind the secretary. "I'm going to have to ask you to leave."

"Wait a minute." Mia looked back at the secretary. "You can't be serious."

"I'm sorry." The secretary nodded toward the door. "But like the security guard said, you are going to need to leave. I'll make sure the doctor contacts you, but we can't afford to upset our patients."

Even if there were a possibility those patients could die?

Mia fumed as the guard escorted her back down the hall of the main building, then felt his eyes boring into the back of her head as she walked across the parking lot, furious at how she'd been brushed off. She opened her car door and dumped the folder onto the passenger seat. She was obviously going to have to come up with a different plan.

She paused. A piece of paper attached to the windshield wiper flapped in the wind. Mia tugged the scrap of paper loose then read the hand scrawled letters.

BPH Technologies

CHAPTER FIFTEEN

FRIDAY, DECEMBER 13TH, 4:20 AM EST

CINCINNATI, OHIO

The minivan's wipers scraped against the ice-glazed windshield. Catherine wheeled into the radio station's parking garage. Traffic had been light on the slick drive in from the suburbs, so she'd made good time. And time was precious. With every passing second, Kelsey's health deteriorated a little bit more. She couldn't wait on Brad. Her headlights swept the dark cement cavern, empty except for a red Beamer and a shiny news van.

She tightened her grip on the steering wheel then whipped into a visitor space. Six years of dead air, and still her grisly memories of reporting those breaking news stories for her father could claw their way to the front of her mind and rattle her to the core. She swallowed the pain that always accompanied the recollection of those horrible sights and smells of being first on a tragic accident scene.

Catherine was glad when a big network snapped up her father's independent station and made him a rich man. If it weren't for ABC's restructuring of her family's mom-and-pop news shop, she never would have escaped The Deuce's expectation that she become an ace reporter in a major market. Someday, when her life settled down, she'd write the network's acquisition suits a thank-you note.

Catherine threw the gearshift into park. Hurting her father, the man some claimed had been gifted with more talent than God, had never been her intention. She had to believe love was the sole reason she'd jumped ship when Brad offered her the picket fence, two kids, and a dog. Because admitting she'd simply wanted a normal life would make it impossible to deal with the irony that the stress of Kelsey's illness had shot that fairytale all to pieces.

What was "normal"? She turned off the van and sat tapping the wheel. She'd lived at such a fast pace for so long, she doubted she could ever be a fair judge. Surely waiting for someone else's child to die so that her little girl could live wasn't even close to the quiet existence she'd craved.

Cold seeped through her clearance-rack dress pants and crawled up her spine. She picked at the dried protein-drink stain Kelsey's three o'clock feeding had left on her thigh. No matter how professional she tried to look, her father would never accept the fact that Brad Taylor provided everything she needed...everything but Kelsey's health.

The orange numbers on the dashboard clock glowed 4:25 a.m. Almost thirty minutes before The Deuce took to the airwaves. She could sit here and idle her fuel tank empty, or go in and confront her father. Only the hard choice would help her daughter.

Catherine sucked in frosty air, the knife-like pang to her lungs spurring her into action. She yanked the keys from the ignition. Last year's Santa photo dangled from the chain. Planting a kiss on the sweet-cheeked boy and the golden-haired girl, she dismissed the nagging fear that this Christmas would be Kelsey's last. She stuffed her children's picture into the small purse she'd dug from the rubble at the bottom of her closet then bolted into the frigid darkness.

She entered the high-rise building through a side door, crossed the deserted lobby, and took the elevator. Christmas music proclaimed this the most wonderful season of all. Obviously, the musician didn't have a dying child and only one last option. At the tenth floor, the elevator doors opened. She took a deep breath and exited. A dozen steps later she stood outside a locked door. Nose pressed to the glass, she peered around the etched network call letters.

At the opposite end of the station's small lobby was the large viewing window of the soundproof control room. Her father, his back to the plate glass, was hunched over one of three computer screens that surrounded the large microphone at the soundboard. Vinnie, The Deuce's best friend and long-time producer, leaned against the opposite counter, sipping coffee and scanning his phone for what she assumed was the latest news.

Pulse racing, hands clammy, Catherine considered the best way to catch the attention of the squatty Italian without alerting her father. She decided to forgo the knock, pulled off her gloves, and rallied a tentative wave.

Just as Vinnie noticed her, The Deuce turned.

Catherine froze. Condensation from her jagged breaths clouded the network logo. Thundering adrenaline heated her body. Taking a step back, she tugged at the zipper of her parka. Why hadn't she taken the time to replace the missing button on her worn, black-wool overcoat instead of wearing this ratty parka? Hoping to disguise her growing apprehension, she willed a tight smile to her lips and let her hands fall to her side.

Her father's surprised head-to-toe perusal of her quickly morphed into cold indifference. He mouthed something to Vinnie she wished she'd been unable to make out, then he turned and stalked from the control room.

Tears forming in her eyes, Catherine watched Vinnie fly after him, shaking a finger. What would she do if her father refused to see her? She throttled the panic racing through her veins. If she had to, she'd camp on this doorstep until The Deuce's fast-food habit drove him from his lair.

With the flat of her hand, she pounded the glass. "Dad. It's not about me."

A few seconds later, Vinnie appeared before her, his quick black eyes apologetic. He pushed a button and she burst past him.

"Where is he, Vin?"

He grabbed her arm and reined her to him. "Hey, Cat. Long time, no see." He elevated himself on tiptoes and kissed her cheek. "You look good."

"I look like crap, but thanks for putting a good spin on it." She'd forgotten how much she missed the smell of stale coffee and strong cologne. "He won't see me, will he?"

"He's still growling, but he won't pass up an exclusive on what brought you back." Vinnie scanned her face with the same intensity he trolled the Internet for anything trending.

She lowered her eyes, desperate to keep the purpose of her mission to herself.

Vinnie clicked on her shifty response like he'd hit pay dirt. "How's our girl?"

Unexpected hope lifted Catherine's head. "So he read the cards and letters I sent?"

Sometimes, when she didn't think she could take it another minute, she imagined her father secretly pouring over those annual scraps of information she sent until every detail of her life had been investigated, including Kelsey's illness. Surely if he knew her pain, he'd regret the acidity of their parting words as much as she. Why had she let her wounded pride keep her from picking up the phone and investigating the possibility?

Vinnie shrugged. "Found them in the trash."

Catherine stiffened, damning the years she'd spent nursing her foolish guilt, and denied the tears provoked by such a waste. Crying would not change her past or her daughter's future. "I only need a minute with him."

"Give him a story he can't resist, kid." Vinnie squeezed her hand then ushered her straight into the den of The Deuce.

Her father sat at his desk. His hair a bit thinner, his face a tad fuller, he drummed his fingers on a stack of CDs. Behind him, autographed photos of her and a younger Deuce bookending famous athletes, actors, singers, and politicians covered the yellowed walls.

Catherine planted her feet on the worn carpet. "Hi...Tom, uh... Dad." An overwhelming desire to take back the butchered greeting, jump into his arms, and rewind the clock thirty years washed over her, but her feet refused to be uprooted. "It's good to see you. You look great."

"You don't."

The trademark silky-bass of The Deuce's lower register had not changed, but the timbre, the rich, loving tone she associated with her childhood, had turned as dry and brittle as his collection of signed rock star posters.

"Thanks, Dad."

He looked past her, most likely assessing the clock on the wall behind her. "I air in fifteen minutes."

Catherine fought the urge to turn around and rip the idol he worshipped from the wall. She knew better than to waste time trying to reconnect the severed strings of his hardened heart. A man who spent four hours a day tied to an on-air clock listened to others in the same kind of sound-bite increments. She had about a minute and a half to make her case before his brain cut to commercial.

She gulped a quick breath then blurted, "Kelsey's dying."

The muscle that ran along the side of his jaw twitched.

She followed his gaze to a bulletin board. Among the scheduling notes was the wedding photo she'd sent of her and Brad standing alone on a Caribbean beach. Wedged in behind that snapshot was last year's Christmas photo of their family, a thumbtack stuck right between Brad's eyes. Apparently, not all of her correspondence had been trashed.

"And I need money." In one simple sentence, she'd admitted he was right. She'd failed.

He flinched. A tiny flicker of darkness clouded his hazel eyes, and she knew his keen ears had not missed the quiver in her voice. "You have something to sell?"

"My soul, if I have to."

"Think you've already punched that card." He rose from his desk and went to the coffeepot on the sidebar. "What does she need?"

"A heart transplant."

He filled an oversized mug to the brim. "When?"

"Yesterday."

He took a long sip, his gaze over the rim of his cup boring into her. "How much?"

"A hundred and fifty thousand, plus the cost of a medivac plane." Catherine paused, letting him calculate the cost before she offered the punch line. "I'm taking her to Africa."

If he was surprised, his face didn't allow the folly of her plan to register. Instead, he pulled the cup down and studied her intensely—the way he used to when she made preposterous claims of having finished her homework in record time.

"Africa?" His scowl pulled his brows together. "A dirty, third-world country is the best plan that bozo you married could come up with?"

"We can't afford to do the surgery stateside."

"Why not?"

"Insurance bureaucracy." She'd thought about what it meant to have no financial security. Saying it out loud drained the starch from her knees. She clutched her purse strap and continued. "It would cost over a million dollars at Children's."

"You're telling me Bozo's willing to put a dollar limit on your daughter's life?"

"His name's Brad." Catherine ground the consonants for emphasis. "And he's spent every cent we had trying to save her. He'll pay back whatever it takes...if we can get a loan from you."

His brows shot up and he chuckled. "So Bozo thinks the father he convinced you to have no part of will simply write out a check for a couple hundred thousand dollars?"

"He didn't want me to come here." She knew her father had tripled his investments from the sale of the station, but even that wasn't enough to cover the high cost of surgery in America. Unless he'd guzzled away everything, he could afford Africa. She took a breath and stepped toward him. "I was hoping you could—"

"Do what, Catherine?" Hearing him speak her name stopped her cold. "You waltz in here after all these years and what? Expect me to launch an on-air fundraiser?"

"No! Brad would never agree to...besides, there's not enough time."

"Now you're telling me the illustrious *Assistant* DA wouldn't think of giving up his son, but he'd let his daughter die?"

"Dad, this isn't about Brad, his ex-wife, or even Jonathon." She ripped their family photo from the wall. The thumbtack flew across the room. "The transplant list Kelsey is on could take weeks, maybe even months." She thrust the picture as close to his face as she dared. "This little girl doesn't have days."

The tick of the wall clock's second hand echoed in the silence. Her father's eyes flashed from her to the Christmas postcard.

"Daddy, please. Help me help my daughter," Catherine begged.

He took a step back. He ran his hands through his hair. "I want to see her."

So was he going to do it? If they could put the past behind them and become a family again, it would go a long way toward healing her own heart.

"Sure." Catherine crammed her gloves into the pockets of the coat she had not removed. She'd deal with Brad's protest later. "We'd like that."

"You've made all of the arrangements?"

She shook her head. "I've clicked around on the Internet, but no one will talk to me without the money."

"I'll do it." He rubbed his temples and let out a long, deep sigh. He dropped his arms, giving her a glimpse into his rarely-exposed compassionate side. "I know a transplant specialist in Baltimore." He fished his cell phone from the holster on his belt. "If anybody can pull strings, it's this guy."

"We have a doctor."

"But he's not pushing Africa, is he?" His laser stare sealed the breach her plea had made in his hard-as-nails armor and rendered her speechless. "I didn't think so." He started scrolling through his contacts. "I emceed a fundraiser for this guy. Made a killing for his little charity. He'll take my call."

"At four-forty-five in the morning?"

"He owes me."

Feeling like a ten-year-old being told exactly what to do, Catherine dropped into a chair and watched her father commandeer the helm of her life. She should defend his implication that she and Brad had failed their daughter, but she couldn't. Shifting the life-and-death weight of

Kelsey's future onto her father's broad shoulders, for even a few seconds, made breathing possible. While he dialed, she filled her lungs for the first time in weeks.

"Hastings? Tom Bruce...Sorry to get you out of bed, old man... Enjoy those Orioles' press passes?. . .Yeah, there's nothing like being in the locker room after a win. . .Say, I've got a little situation here that could use your attention. . .I need to buy a heart. . .No, not for me. . .I need a pint-sized one. Good and healthy. . .The recipient is *my* business. . .Listen, I've got limited funds, so I'm looking to going abroad. Any suggestions?"

Catherine watched her father's face as he listened to the prestigious voice on the other end. What was this doctor saying? Dare she hope he could help her daughter? The second hand on the wall clock, jumpy as her own heart, ticked off valuable seconds. Catherine dragged her gaze from her father's furrowed brow to the sagging leather couch, rumpled blanket, and the heap of wrinkled clothes in the corner, then back to the unflappable Deuce.

"So, I send the money to you, and she goes to the top of your list?" Her father rubbed his stubbled jaw. "No, call this number, and I'll relay the pertinent info. I owe you, Hastings." He lowered his phone and grabbed a post-it note. "Fax Kelsey's medical records to this number." He handed the note to Catherine. "Putting everything in place shouldn't take long. Pack a bag and stay by your phone."

Catherine felt her heart still. She could have her Kelsey healthy in a few days? Barely daring to hope, she struggled to free the gratitude stuck in her throat, her eyes searching his for the reason he'd had a change of heart. Maybe restoring their relationship wasn't as farfetched as she'd thought.

Before she could explore the possibility further, her father ducked behind the desk and sank into the oversized chair, leaving her emotionally out in the cold again.

She scooted to the edge of her seat. "You sleep here now?" She pointed at the couch.

He ignored her question and opened the desk drawer. "Here's the deal." He tossed a checkbook on the desk.

Catherine's heart lurched. "Deal?"

"I'll pay for everything." He removed the pen from his pocket and clicked it. "The transplant. The doctor. The hospital. The transportation." He opened the leather holder and started scribbling on the pale-green paper. "Everything."

"And the catch?"

"The house has been empty since your mother died."

"I know, I've—" Catherine stuttered at his suddenly raised brows. "Driven by."

Vinnie poked his head in the door. "Deuce, we're live in five."

With a wave of his hand, her father dismissed Vinnie and any attempt on Catherine's part to bring up how much they both missed the woman who'd been the family glue. "I want you and Kelsey moved in with me."

"Me and Kelsey?" Catherine searched the steely depths of her father's eyes, the photo crumpling within her clasp. "What about Brad and Jonathan?"

His expression did not soften. "You want Kelsey fixed?"

Catherine's befuddled thoughts turned liquid, spilled down her cheeks, and splattered the photo. Did he hate her husband that much? "I can't leave them."

"You move home, I'll send you to Africa. All expenses paid." He folded the check along the perforation. "When you get back, I'll hire full-time nursing care. My house will be full again. The station gains an ace co-host." He ripped the check from the book then shoved it across the desk. "And everyone's happy."

Catherine let her eyes slide from his unruffled stare to the five-thousand dollar figure scrawled across the line. "What's this?"

"You'll need money over there. Make sure you go cash it this morning."

She stiffened. "And if I refuse your terms?"

"You won't." He rose from his chair, came around the desk, and removed the photo from Catherine's shaky hand. "This beautiful little girl looks too much like her mother."

CHAPTER SIXTEEN

FRIDAY, DECEMBER 13TH, 1:14 PM

OYSTER BAY

Race stepped into the air-conditioned restaurant Friday afternoon and was immediately drawn to the stunning panoramic view of the Indian Ocean spilling across Oyster Bay. While most of the city was an eclectic mixture of Swahili, German, and Asian architecture, the Mafala Grill had settled for a contemporary decor with the subtle Arabian influence of the Swahili coastline, dark-wood furnishings, and recessed lighting.

But the coastline was the lure that kept tourists and locals alike coming back for the succulent catch of the day. And it was the one hint that the God he once worshiped was still in control. While days off were rare, he still took every early morning he could to spend an hour along Dar's endless shoreline, watching the traditional Arab dhows masterfully sail beneath the bows of cargo ships as they returned to shore with the night's catch. Somehow, the mesmerizing mixture of the gray-blue ocean and swaying green palms always managed to fill the deep chasm in his heart he seldom acknowledged.

Halfway across the carpeted dining room, he spotted Mia. He

hadn't expected to see the busy doctor again any time soon. He'd arrived back in the city from his morning safari transfer of a group of tourists to a text asking him to meet her as soon as possible. Apparently, the good doctor had become quite proficient in giving orders. For now, he was too interested in her dilemma to argue.

Mia sat at a table beside the picture windows that ran the length of the restaurant, wearing a turquoise dress that showed off her slender frame. She was chewing on the corner of her lip. Except for the tiny row of stitches, she was a picture nearly as perfect and enticing as his early morning ocean meditations.

She looked up as he approached. "I was afraid you weren't going to make it."

"I promised I'd come. Traffic was bad." He slid into the seat across from her. "Any word yet from Jeme?"

She shook her head, worry clear in her expression. "Nothing."

"I'm sorry."

"Me too."

"The view at this place is incredible," he said, changing the subject as the guilt resurfaced.

"It is, isn't it?" She stared out the window.

"Though perhaps a bit out of the way." While he hadn't minded the drive, he was curious why she hadn't simply asked him to meet her at the hospital.

"I needed somewhere private to sort through what's happened the past twenty-four hours."

"Then I can assume that you asking me here is strictly business?"

She turned and caught his gaze. "What were you expecting?"

He bit back the quick comeback that threatened to roll off his tongue. While he was used to flirting with women without a hint of expectation involved, Mia Kendall didn't seem the type who played that game.

She pushed a plate of fried somosas across the table toward him. "Help yourself. They're fantastic sprinkled with a bit of lime juice."

"Thanks." He hadn't thought he was hungry, but the spicy scent of Indian cuisine changed his mind. "What are you drinking?"

"A Malawi shandy." She stirred the drink with a long straw while he debated between the lemonade and ginger ale mixture and his usual Coke standby.

He signaled for the waiter. Once he had his attention, he asked him for a Coke with ice then he turned back to Mia. "I have to admit, I was surprised to get your call."

"I didn't know who else to talk to." She stared out the window at a pair of boats sailing in the afternoon breeze.

Race frowned. He wasn't used to being someone's last choice. But the cocky, self-assured woman intrigued him, making him wonder what she had to say. "Have you thought about talking with a counselor? Because face it. You're having to deal with a lot. You were shot, discovered a murdered corpse, Jeme is missing—"

"You're telling me I should go see a shrink?" He had her attention now, but she looked anything but pleased.

He busied himself with one of the somosas. Apparently, Dr. Kendall didn't like taking advice. "Just a suggestion. Forget I brought it up. Tell me why I'm here."

"I went to see Dr. Amandi at Kaboni Private this morning." She squeezed a wedge of lime over one of the triangular fried meat pies.

"And?"

"Let's just say his secretary wasn't happy with my questions. She became even more unhappy when I threatened to take my findings to the private funders of the hospital."

He couldn't help but chuckle at the image her description invoked. "You went for the jugular?"

"I just want to know why my patients are dying, and I'm tired of being ignored."

Her answer sobered him. "What happened?"

"I was told to leave, then escorted outside the building."

"Ouch."

"But that's not all," she said.

"What do you mean?"

Mia slid the note she'd been given across the table. "I found this on my windshield as I was leaving."

Race picked up the note and read the message out loud. "BPH Technologies? What's that?"

"They're a pharmaceutical lab back in Baltimore."

"And you have no idea who left it there?"

"No." Mia took a sip of her drink. "All I can figure is that someone overheard my conversation at the hospital."

The uniformed server set a bottle of Coke and a glass of ice in front of him, "Anything else?"

"We're fine, thank you." She waved the young man off. "The bottom line is I still don't know what specifically is causing the rejections, but now not only is Dr. Amandi's office acting strange, someone seems to be hinting that BPH is involved." She leaned forward and caught his gaze. "Tell me I'm not just being paranoid."

"No." He could think of a dozen other descriptive words that fit her. Stubborn, obstinate, tenacious, gorgeous. . .but not paranoid. "Though threatening the head of an expensive transplant program with the prospect of losing his financial backing might not have been the best way to handle things."

She frowned. "And you thought you were the impulsive one."

Race poured his Coke. Like it or not, she had a point. "Where do I fit into all of this?"

"Until I know for sure what's causing my rejections, everything's on the table. Like where you get your organs."

The implied accusation that he was part of the problem stung. He did what he did to save lives. "Like I told you, I occasionally transport organs for Kaboni Private and fly them directly to the hospital. That's it. No one tells me where they came from or who's getting them."

"I'm not going to let this go." Sparks of determination glinted in her emerald eyes. "Just because my patients are poor doesn't mean they're any less deserving of quality medical care and a chance at a quality life than those who can afford the private hospital."

"I agree, and never meant to imply you should let it go."

Her phone rang and she fished it out of her bag and answered the call instead of him.

A second later Race's phone vibrated in his pocket. He pulled it out and saw a familiar name on the text.

"Listen. . .I'm sorry, but I'm going to have to cut this short," he said once she'd hung up. "An emergency transport."

“Me too. I’m needed back at the hospital A.S.A.P.” She dropped a couple bills on the table. “Will you help me?”

“What do you want me to do?”

Mia leaned forward and cornered him with her gaze. “Help me find out why my patients are dying.”

CHAPTER SEVENTEEN

FRIDAY, DECEMBER 13TH, 4:43 PM

KABONI PRIVATE HOSPITAL

Dr. Amandi slid off his lab coat then flung it onto the brass coatrack inside his office door. The clattering blades of his ceiling fan ground like nails into his pounding skull while doing little to relieve the heaviness of the afternoon air. Dropping into the leather chair behind his desk, he reached in his drawer and removed the flask he kept tucked away for days such as this. He took a long swig, reveling in the burn. Once relief began to pump through his veins, he picked up the pile of messages that had come in while he was out.

He'd hated every minute of the all-day board meeting where he'd been required to give a full update on the financial status of the heart program he'd implemented two years ago. Thankfully, the numbers spoke for themselves, and the program continued to be a viable asset to the hospital—even if there were several details he'd conveniently left out of his hour-long report.

Like Hastings.

He scanned the note his secretary, Asha, had left on his desk and labeled as urgent and smiled. The previous nine months of their business relationship had lined both their bank accounts with healthy sums. Hopefully, today's request would turn out to be yet another step forward in their very lucrative relationship.

"Welcome back, Doctor." Asha appeared in the doorway. "Your wife is on the phone. She said it is urgent."

Isn't it always? "She can wait. I want you to hold all calls for the next thirty minutes."

"Certainly, but there is one matter that cannot wait." She took a quick breath and straightened herself. "Dr. Kendall came by this morning, and—"

Dr. Amandi waved his hand. "Not now, Asha. I've got an important call to make."

"But. . ." Asha pressed her lips together. "Yes, sir."

Dr. Kendall would have to wait, along with Silvia and her never-ending problems. No doubt his wife was upset because he hadn't been home in the past three days, but just because she'd chosen to be unfaithful didn't mean he should sleep alone.

As soon as Asha shut the door behind her, he picked up the phone and dialed the long-distance number scrawled at the bottom of the urgent message. Today's technology never ceased to amaze him. Two decades ago, communication from across the ocean would have come over on a slow boat or plane. Today, he could contact a person directly, a necessity his latest business venture demanded.

In less than a minute, Hastings was on the line.

Amandi smoothed his tie over his pudgy belly. "Hastings, it is nice to hear from you. I just returned to my office and received your message."

"Are we good to go with the girl?"

Amandi forced himself to excuse the blunt response. In all his years spent abroad at Harvard, he'd never accepted the Americans' inability to find time for the expected round of small talk before delving into business. "As soon as your patient arrives, I will be ready."

"And you're sure there won't be any complications?" Hastings pressed. "We're both well aware of your love for women and liquor."

Amandi clicked his tongue at the man's blatant lack of confidence.

"I know as well as you do that if I want to compete in this market, I have to uphold the highest of standards."

"You'd better keep it that way, because I can only continue sending American referrals as long as you maintain an exemplary performance record." There was a slight pause on the line. "And I'd hate to have to withdraw my generous financial support."

Amandi restrained a cutting remark that flew to the tip of his tongue. Theirs was a mutually beneficial relationship, but he knew he needed Hastings far more than Hastings needed him. "All I need to know is your patient's arrival time."

"Travel arrangements are being taken care of as we speak. She'll be on a flight to Dar es Salaam this evening. At your hospital tomorrow afternoon."

"And the money?'

"You'll get your percentage."

A minute later, Amandi hung up the phone then sat down in his chair with a satisfied smile on his lips. He fingered the albino charm hidden beneath his lab coat. The witch doctor had been right. The charm had helped him tap into a gold mine.

He no longer noticed the heavy afternoon air nor cared that his wife stayed with him for reasons of status only. He held the heart of Africa in his very capable hands. Nothing else mattered.

CHAPTER EIGHTEEN

FRIDAY, DECEMBER 13TH, 9:03 AM EST

BPH TECHNOLOGY LAB, BALTIMORE, MARYLAND

Axton raced through the thick jungle of Blackwell Isle with the devil on his tail. Dryden and his renegade army would be stopped, but first he had to ensure Paige was safe. He'd last seen her on the outskirts of the settlement moments after Dryden's men struck, forcing him to send her, along with a dozen of the villagers, to one of the underground camps. But spies were a common threat on the island lowlands, and their lives were still in danger.

Five minutes later, Axton found her on the road to Zarfor, tied to a willow tree, scared but unharmed. Breathing heavily, he quickly unfastened the ropes and pulled her against him. "I feared your life had been taken."

Tears pooled in her eyes. "Not mine, but my father's. Dryden killed him then brought me here where he knew you'd find me. He gave me a message for you."

Raw determination surfaced as he realized that yet another good man's life had been sacrificed by Dryden's hand. "What kind of message?"

"He knows where our people are hidden." Her fingers toyed with the golden locket encircling her neck. "He said you must leave the island by nightfall or he'll wipe out every village from Zarfor to Kingsport."

"I would never let that happen—"

"He has the vials."

"And I have the serum that will neutralize the virus."

"But what if you can't stop him?" She grabbed his arm and pulled him toward her. "There's enough of the virus to wipe out the entire island. You must do as he bids."

"I won't leave." Axton searched Paige's face for the innocent girl he once knew, before Dryden had brought them into the time of darkness. "I will find a way to stop him. If we can neutralize the formula—"

"You'd be a fool to go after Dryden. He'll kill you—kill all of us—before you have a chance to stop him."

"No." He pressed his finger against her lips to hush her. "For your father, I am deeply sorry, but Dryden hasn't won yet. Find Lord Longfellow and tell him what has happened then go to the crystal caves. It is the one place you should be safe. I will meet you there when it's over."

"And if we find that Lord Longfellow is one of Dryden's spies?"

"That is a chance we will both have to take."

The blaring ring of a cell phone rocketed Harry away from Paige and the grove of willow trees, and back to his lab. Valerie sat at her desk, seemingly oblivious to the offending object vibrating next to her.

"Would you please answer that phone?" Harry sat back in his chair, feeling the beginnings of a migraine coming on. He rubbed his temples. "How in the world am I supposed to work with that incessant noise?"

She glared at him, but didn't move to answer the phone. "Sorry, I didn't realize you'd been working. You've been staring at your computer—again—for the past thirty minutes."

"I was thinking." Frustration had driven him back to Blackwell Isle, the one place in his life he still had control. Valerie might never agree to go on a date with him, but he could choose to shoot Dryden in the heart with a poisoned arrow or end the villain's life with the swift draw of a sword. Not that Valerie deserved that explanation. The ringing stopped then started again.

"Answer the phone," he repeated.

Valerie dropped the ringing cell phone into her purse then snapped it shut, only partially muting the sound. "I'm sorry, but I can't answer it."

"Why not?"

"Because it's Bert."

"Who's Bert?" Harry flicked his pen against the desk and stared at the computer screen, no further along in his investigation into the missing vials and no closer to finding the problem with his formula than he had been four hours ago.

"Bert was my date from last night. We've been. . .going out for a few months."

Harry grabbed a Cheeto from the ever-present bag on his lap and tried to ignore the stab of jealousy. "And the two of you have a problem?"

Valerie picked up a stack of file folders from her desk. "He thinks I'm cheating on him."

"Why would he think that?"

"Because he's Bert."

Harry crunched down on the chip, uncomfortable talking about Valerie's love life. "If you hadn't noticed, we have a crisis far more pressing than a quarrel with your boyfriend."

"Ex-boyfriend." She shot him a look of irritation then dropped the files in front of him. "I have everything you asked for right here. Log books for the past three months, research notes, and printed data."

"Any discrepancies?"

"I've marked anything questionable with a sticky note. One thing that did stand out was that Peterson logged in three times in the past two months."

Harry's brow rose. "Peterson's not on the list of those with access to the lab."

"Which is why his name stood out. Dr. Billings approved him."

Someone swept through the glass door of the lab. So much for Billings's promises of high security. Harry might as well move his lab into the cafeteria so he could be near the vending machines, not hidden away in a basement laboratory working on a drug potentially worth millions.

Valerie's face paled. "Bert?"

Her ex-boyfriend, presumably, plunged into the room, picked up the purse containing the still ringing phone, and dumped the contents onto the desk. "I've been calling all morning."

"How'd you get in here?" Valerie grabbed for her things, but Bert pushed her against the edge of a file cabinet.

"Hey!" Harry scrambled from his chair. The bag of Cheetos dropped, scattering chips across the floor. "What do you think you're doing?"

"You sit down." Bert pulled a gun from his back pocket and waved it in the air.

Harry dropped back into his chair. Mr. Ex-boyfriend was bald, skinny, and dressed like a used car salesman. And he'd been the one afraid to ask Valerie out.

Harry managed to find his voice. "Valerie, what's going on?"

"You be quiet. This is between Valerie and me." Bert's gaze flashed at Valerie. "It's him, isn't it?"

"Who?"

Bert waved the gun toward Harry, whose lungs constricted. He'd never been good at confrontations, let alone clashes that involved a man with a gun.

Bert grabbed Valerie's arm.

"Dr. Spence?" Her voice squeaked.

Harry shoved his glasses up the bridge of his nose then stood. Surely he could talk some reason into the man. "I. . .I." He glanced at Valerie then at the gun. Even an IQ of 140 couldn't make him an expert hostage negotiator. "What exactly do you want me to do? The man has a gun."

"Tell him we're not having an affair."

"Of course, we're not." He turned to Bert. "I've never even worked up my courage to ask her out."

Valerie caught his gaze. "You wanted to ask me out?"

"I wanted to, but—"

"You're lying," Bert spouted.

Harry swallowed hard at Bert's unbelief. He'd earned three PhD's and an M.D., but no one would ever put hero after his name. Axton was the man who could save the world while winning the heart of the leading lady. Harry Spence was stuck dealing with high cholesterol and half a dozen phobias.

Bert closed the gap between them before Harry could react and swung his fist, slicing Harry's cheek with the edge of his ring. Harry fought to stay on his feet. He dabbed at the pool of blood. A jabbing pain seared through his chest and his vision blurred. He was bleeding. Dropping onto his chair, he gulped and tried to fill his lungs with air. The room spun and suddenly two attackers stood in front of him. Or was that Valerie?

"I. . .can't. . .breathe."

Someone grabbed Harry's arm.

"What's wrong with him?" Bert shouted.

"He has. . .issues."

"Issues?"

"Phobias. Like dust, nature, heat strokes, gluten, and blood."

Harry's mind swam. *And crazy men waving loaded guns at me.*

He could smell Valerie's perfume beside him as his eyes came back into focus.

"Harry, I want you to put your head between your legs and breathe slowly."

Harry took off his glasses and dropped them onto the table. Axton would have taken the man down with the swift swing of his sword and won the girl. Harry tried not to vomit.

"Maybe we should call an ambulance."

"Why, so you can scare them with your toy gun too?"

Toy gun? Harry looked up as Valerie grabbed the gun.

"Do you know how much trouble you're in?" She waved the gun at Bert. "What were you thinking?"

The security alarm blared.

Bert dragged Valerie toward the door. "What is that?"

"Security. This lab's supposed to be off limits, which means the alarm goes off whenever they discover an unauthorized person on the video cams."

Two guards entered the room, their guns raised—no doubt real and fully loaded.

"Release the girl and raise your hands."

Bert obeyed immediately. "I wasn't going to hurt anyone. You've got to believe me. Look for yourselves. It's not even a real gun. I just thought. . ."

"Whatever you thought was wrong." The security guard slapped a pair of cuffs on Bert and hauled him out the door.

Harry watched from behind his desk as if he had front row tickets at the cinema. But his throbbing face told him this wasn't Hollywood. Still, the little weasel was nothing but a coward like himself.

Dr. Billings walked in as the guards exited the lab. "What happened to you?"

Harry dropped his bloody tissue into the trash and stood up. "He punched me." He looked to Valerie for some sign of remorse, but she turned and stormed from the room.

"I can have you checked out in the infirmary," Dr. Billings said.

"I'll be fine." Harry shoved his shoulders back. "I've left a dozen messages with your secretary. One of my vials is missing. And it's not the first time."

"That's why I'm here." Dr. Billings tugged on his expensive tie. "Forget about the missing vials for now. Just get that formula right. Our funding isn't going to last forever."

"Don't worry about the missing vials?"

"Funding trumps your neglect."

"I didn't...we've got to find out who has them. They're not ready to be used. They haven't even been tested."

"I told you, we have more important concerns."

"You're acting as if this is inconsequential, yet this isn't the first time I've reported missing property to security."

Dr. Billings eyed Harry's desk. "For all we know, the missing vials are buried beneath that mass of folders and. . .Cheetos."

Harry clenched his fists, wondering what would happen if he took Bert's approach and knocked the man out. "Dr. Billings—"

"I told you I'd take care of things. Your only job is to get this new formula right."

CHAPTER NINETEEN

FRIDAY, DECEMBER 13TH, 5:16 PM

KABONI PRIVATE HOSPITAL

Dr. Amandi felt the familiar gnaw of acid eating away at the lining of his stomach. He patted his white coat pocket in search of his flask. Remembering he'd drained the rum earlier, he popped two more antacid tablets into his mouth. He'd worked too long and too hard to lose everything because of the unverified accusations of an interfering American. He had a reputation to uphold. An epidemic of failing organs at the government hospital, which was also under his jurisdiction, would leave damaging marks that even he wouldn't be able to erase.

He turned to face Asha, unwilling to let her forget that she was as much involved in this as he. "I want you to tell me exactly what Dr. Kendall said. Both our jobs are at stake here."

Her gaze swept the floor while her knuckles whitened against the file folder she clutched. She knew too much for him to fire her, but he also wasn't beneath throwing out a few subtle threats to keep her in submission.

"She. . .Dr. Kendall wanted to see you." Asha tugged on the lacy hem of her jacket. "She kept saying something about organ failure and contacting the hospital's financial backers."

Dr. Amandi raised his voice. "And *you* threw her out?"

"You were in the board meeting. . .I didn't know what else to do."

"Does she have proof something is wrong?"

"I don't know."

"You stupid woman." He raised his hand then pulled back before striking her. Taking out his anger on Asha would do nothing to help his cause. He needed her on his side. Rubbing his pounding temple, he contemplated his options. There had to be a way out of this. All he had to do was find it.

He lowered his voice. "The last thing I need is accusations of suspicious organ failure on my watch—whether or not she has evidence—the authorities can have this place shut down before either of us have time to pack up the office."

"I am sorry, Doctor. I thought. . ."

"No, you did not think. That is the problem. We cannot afford for someone to start asking questions."

"You are right."

Of course, he was right. He sat down at his desk and tried to sort through the situation. "We need to know exactly what she knows, and where she got her information."

He scribbled notes on a pad of paper. *Dr. Kendall. . .organs. . .*What did that woman know?

He had to talk to her.

He dropped his pen on the desk. "I want you to track down Dr. Kendall then transfer the call to me."

Confusion wrinkled her brow. "Why?"

"Because I happen to know she's been trying to get ahold of me. If I say nothing now, she is more likely to believe that whatever information she has is true."

"I will put the call through right now."

Five minutes later, he had her on the line. "Dr. Kendall, I regret I missed an opportunity to speak with you this morning. My secretary just informed me of the...unfortunate misunderstanding."

"Unfortunate misunderstanding?" He could hear the anger in her voice. "I've been trying to reach you for days, and instead I was escorted by security from your office without any guarantees of your cooperation."

"Let me assure you that I am calling to correct that erroneous impression." Amandi worked to keep his voice calm. "My secretary overreacted, and I apologize for that, but you know as well as I do the negative attitude toward organ donation we face in my country. It is something I have worked hard to change, but change does not come easy. We cannot risk any of my patients overhearing concerns and drawing wrong conclusions about Kaboni's transplant program."

For many, giving away a part of your body—even after death—meant giving up a part of your soul.

"I am aware of the stigma of organ donations," Dr. Kendall said, "but issues with the program is the reason I have been trying to get ahold of you. Something clearly neither of us want. I'm not looking for apologies. I need answers."

"I understand. My secretary mentioned that you are concerned with a higher number of rejections with your transplant patients."

"Yes."

"You know the procedure then. You are going to have to start verifying all the controls and procedures from the moment the organs arrive at your hospital through the surgical prep and actual placement of the organ. You will also need to consider a possible deficiency in your own technique." He hurried on, hoping to deflect any blame back on her. "Your pump time could be too long. Or your anastomoses too weak. . ."

"While no surgeon can claim perfection, I feel my skill level is more than adequate. And I can assure you, I've gone over all the points you've mentioned but still haven't been able to pinpoint the source of the higher rate of rejections."

He paused briefly. "There is also the reality that many of your patients live in difficult. . .financial situations which has been clearly documented to increase the chances of poor health."

Mia let out a short breath. "I agree, but I'm concerned this rash of recent rejections my patients have been experiencing over the past six months could be result of a deeper problem."

"Such as?"

"Your organ procurement, for one, is a natural place to start looking. That, or perhaps there is an issue with the anti-rejection drug."

"Have you been able to come up with any actual stats?" he asked.

"My patients have been experiencing kidney failure which could point to the anti-rejection drug."

Did she have evidence, or was she merely fishing? He couldn't tell.

"If you have information substantiating these allegations, it would serve us both if I had access to that information," he said. "And I assure you, if there is any validity to your claims, I will be the first person to enforce a full investigation."

"I'm glad we agree that this situation merits immediate action."

He let out a slow breath. What he'd feared was happening. Dr. Kendall had stuck her nose where it didn't belong. But proving the organs he sent her were viable wasn't going to be the difficult part. The difficult part was going to be convincing her to back off and let him handle things. "I am sure you understand as well as I do the delicacy of the situation. We are both involved in life-saving efforts. Any rumors to the contrary will only hurt the progress of our work."

"I understand, but I have information that allowed me to compare the two hospitals' rejection rates. My patients are rejecting at a far greater rate, and I need to know why."

The acid in his gut burned. What information had she obtained and how had she gotten her hands on his private records? He glanced through the open doorway of his office to the desk where Asha worked. For now, he wouldn't accuse the American doctor of illegal activity, but he would make certain Dr. Kendall would not be able to use the information to hamper the business he'd so carefully nursed into a profitable enterprise.

"Why don't you send me everything you've got, including a detailed description of your current procedure? I will begin my own investigation into the discrepancies, though I have a feeling, Dr. Kendall, that the differences in the rejection rate can be readily explained."

"Meaning the problem is either me or my patients?"

"Like I said earlier, we both know, whether it is fair or not, that my patients have a marked advantage. Most of your patients come from disadvantaged backgrounds. They typically are malnourished and have weaker immune systems. As we both know, these factors alone can lessen the body's natural ability to fight off infection."

"That might be the case, Dr. Amandi, but—"

"Please let me go on to say that neither of us wishes to lose the funding we receive."

"Of course not."

"Then let me help you find the truth. If it is something as simple as decreasing your pump times, wouldn't that be better than torpedoing our whole program?"

"I...yes."

"I promise to get back to you as soon as I know something."

He hung up without allowing her further protest. He popped two more antacids and reached for the bottle of rum he'd stashed behind some medical books.

Mia Kendall was persistent. Though perhaps she was about to discover she was too persistent for her own good.

CHAPTER TWENTY

FRIDAY, DECEMBER 13TH, 5:45 PM

SHINWANGA REGIONAL HOSPITAL

Race picked up the Sudoku cube and waited for the info he'd googled on Mia's computer to load. Propping his boots on the edge of Mia's neat and tidy desk, he started twisting the colored squares. Nine. . .seven. . .five. . .eight. . .Sweat beaded across his forehead despite the metal fan clanking above him. He'd texted Mia and told her he was coming by, though part of him wasn't sure why he'd agreed to help her.

He tossed the game back onto the desk and gulped down the rest of his Coke. He'd spent five years serving his country and making what he'd once thought to be a difference in the world. His heroism had earned him a Bronze Star. But while he was off saving the world, he'd failed to protect the thing that mattered most: his wife and unborn child. What made him think he was going to make a difference this time?

He rubbed his thumb across the top of the Coke can. It was funny the things he remembered about Rachel. They'd argued via email about their baby's name. He'd wanted something classic like John or Anne. She preferred the more modern names like Chloe and Aiden.

The truth was, he hadn't cared which name was chosen as long as both Rachel and the baby were healthy.

He crushed the can between his fingers then tossed it at the metal wastebasket. It hit with an empty *thunk*. He despised the man he'd become since losing his wife. His parents had been the ones who'd tried to persuade him not to distance himself by moving to Africa—and who'd prayed for him day and night since Rachel died. He'd thought that moving halfway around the world would still their persistent requests, but even here their concerned voices refused to lie dormant. His father faithfully emailed him twice a week with news from the farm, updates on the community, and the ever-present reminder they were praying for him.

Prayer hadn't changed anything. And he wasn't sure helping Dr. Mia Kendall would either.

The search page finally loaded. He plopped his boots onto the floor and typed in the biotech facility's name. BPH Technologies. If Amandi ever learned what he was doing—including the fact he'd already snatched a bunch of files—the doctor would have him kicked out of the country faster than he could fly from here to Arusha.

But his gut told him it was a risk worth taking.

Because this entire situation had him worried. If he were honest, he had his own doubts about what was going on. He'd never questioned where the hospital's donor program procured their organs because he didn't want to find out that concerns that had worried him from time to time were true. He'd simply held onto the fact that saving a life somehow covered a multitude of sins.

Now he wasn't so sure.

A moment later, the lab's homepage filled the screen, complete with a full-color architect's rendition of their multistory state-of-the-art facility. He scanned the page. BPH boasted a large staff of researchers and chemists. Even he knew that the global sales of biotechnology drugs were a lucrative business, but from the looks of that shiny building on the screen, lots of money was flowing into someone's pocket.

He scanned page after page of the lab's services, prices, commitment, and qualifications then started digging deeper through the long list of online articles wherever BPH was mentioned. There had to be something here that would help Mia. He clicked on another link, then stopped at an article discussing an anti-rejection drug for heart transplant patients called Tryoxylate.

ACCORDING TO A RELIABLE SOURCE, THE FOOD AND DRUG ADMINISTRATION IS LOOKING INTO SEVERAL DEATHS SUSPECTED TO BE LINKED TO THE ANTI-REJECTION DRUG, TRYOXYLATE. THE FDA'S CONCERNS WERE FIRST EXPRESSED THIS SUMMER WHEN THE FEDERAL REGULATORY AGENCY RESPONDED TO THREE LAWSUITS—

Someone clearing their throat drew his gaze upward.

Mia stood in the doorway, arms folded across her chest. "I see you've made yourself at home in *my* office."

He shot her a grin. "The battery on my laptop died this afternoon."

"Buried alive under all that rubble in your plane, no doubt." Her expression remained solemn, but her eyes were smiling.

"In my defense, not only did I tell you I was coming by, I was also told that you'd be back any minute and that I was welcome to wait right here."

She returned the Sudoku cube to the exact spot where he'd found it. "So you could play with things that aren't yours and surf the net?"

"You should really set a password."

"I did."

"'Mia Kendall'? Original."

"So you are surfing the net?"

"I'm not surfing for pleasure, scout's honor." He gave her a three-fingered salute, but despite the lighthearted banter between them, he didn't miss the fatigue in her expression and the weariness in her shoulders. "Is everything okay?"

"Mbui's rejecting his heart."

He frowned at the news. "Can you do something?"

"I'm doing everything I can. I just don't know if it will be enough." She leaned against the desk. "I also received a phone call from Dr. Amandi."

"And. . ."

"He promised to help me get to the bottom of this."

"Do you believe him?"

"Honestly. . .I don't know. What I do know is that with another patient rejecting his heart, I can't just wait around for hospital bureaucracy to figure things out."

"I agree. Which was why, knowing you were tied up, I thought I'd do a bit of research on BPH Technologies."

"That was my next move." She glanced across the desk at the screen. "Did you find something?"

"A fairly recent report that the FDA is considering pulling one of their anti-rejection drugs formulated specifically for heart transplant patients. Several people have died, and they are trying to link their deaths back to the drug."

"What's the drug called?" she asked.

He scrolled to the top of the article. Call it male ego, but he enjoyed finally knowing something she didn't. "Tryoxylate. Have you heard of it?"

"That's the anti-rejection drug we use. Both here at our hospital and Kaboni Private."

"Well, it seems as if this little medical wonder is losing favor in the medical community."

Mia shook her head. "This can't be a coincidence."

"What do you mean?" he asked.

"An issue with the anti-rejection drug would explain my patients' kidney damage." She came around the desk and leaned in. "Does anything you've found point to specific side-effects the FDA is questioning?"

"Not yet, but I can keep looking." He scrolled through an article. "From what I've read it looks as if the FDA is still combing through postmarking surveillance data before drawing any conclusions and releasing their findings. Do you know anything about the company?"

"Not much." Mia paced the office, the wheels in her brain clearly in overdrive. "But I don't see how Tryoxylate could be the source of the rejections. If there's an issue with the drug, the ratio of rejection between the two hospitals should be fairly similar. Instead, my patients are the ones dying."

"Maybe Amandi's skewing the results somehow." Race threw out.

"I can't see him putting his patients at risk. That would destroy his career if anyone found out, and while I may not like the man, he's worked too hard to get to where he is." Mia leaned back against the edge of the desk. "Besides, all we really know is that the FDA *might* pull Tryoxylate from the market because of safety issues. It's not enough to start handing out accusations."

"There is one other thing we know. There's huge competition from pharmaceutical companies for a piece of the market and a lot of money at stake if they fail." Race glanced back at the computer screen, trying to determine what BPH's next step would be if the drug was banned. "If the FDA ends up pulling Tryoxylate, BPH will need a new drug already in the queue."

"It is logical that they would start working on a replacement," Mia said, "but drug trials take time."

"From what I've read so far on their website, BPH works with a number of foreign countries where they are involved in human drug-testing trials in West Africa, China, and Mexico."

"That's standard procedure. Once a drug has been cleared by an ethics board, it has to go through laboratory and animal tests before it even gets to human drug testing. Then they have to pass a review by the FDA proving that the benefits outweigh any known risks."

"All before it can be approved and marketed in the US?" he asked.

"Yes." She studied his face. "What are you thinking, Race?"

"Would they do testing in this country?"

"It's possible."

"This is going to sound crazy, but what if someone's doing drug testing on your patients?"

She shook her head. "That's not possible. A new drug would mean a new name, not to mention a well-verified and highly controlled paper trail of consents and response data the pharmaceutical company would need from me and my patients."

"Maybe," he said, working out the details like a Sudoku puzzle. He planted both palms on the desk. "But what if someone decided to do an illegal test on a new drug and speed things up in case the original drug is pulled?"

"What do you mean?" He had her complete attention now. "Secretly switching Tryoxylate with a new, untested drug?"

Race nodded. "It would explain the differences between the two hospitals."

"I don't know." She stood up and started pacing. "The logistics alone would make something like that almost impossible."

"But not *totally* impossible."

She hesitated before responding. "I suppose not. So, what you're suggesting is that someone decided to do a bit of testing on an uncleared drug in a little off-the-map country where it would be easier to keep things under the radar while pushing it through faster."

"You're catching on," he said. "You just might be as smart as you are beautiful."

She leaned in closer, not the least bit intimidated. "Let's skip the flattery and make sure we stick to my rejection problem."

He raised both hands as if in defeat and grinned. "Absolutely."

She gave a little nod and let out a long, slow breath, the only sign that she'd had to regroup. "What you're suggesting is a huge stretch. I still can't be a hundred percent sure as to why my patients are dying, and on top of that I have zero evidence that anything illegal is going on here."

"All that is true, but I still think it's worth looking into further."

"How do you suggest we do that?"

"For starters, you might want to take your patients off Tryoxylate for the time being. Secondly, we need to find out who owns BPH." He clicked on the staff listings and scrolled through the list. "There's a list of the directors, technical managers, finance operators, and other key people. Of course, if there's something illegal going on here, it's not going to be mentioned on their website. Do you recognize any of these guys?"

Mia dragged a chair around the desk so she was sitting beside him, the heat of her proximity adding to the heat melting the ice around his heart.

"I recognize a couple of names as friends of my father."

"Your father's a doctor?"

"I'll save that saga for another day." She angled toward the computer, the scent of vanilla inciting his nostrils. Race took a deep breath and focused on the screen. Apparently, he wasn't the only one with secrets.

"If there is something going on with the drug," she said, "then there's a chance that somebody there knows something."

"You think the suits at BPH are going to give us any damaging info that might get back to the FDA?"

"No, but it's a place to start."

Race turned back to the screen. "Where's this lab located?"

"Baltimore." She dipped her chin, but not before he caught the flicker of concern that registered across her face. "If there's a telephone number for the lab director that might be the best place to start."

"What are we waiting for?" Race punched the number into his cell phone, hoping they'd find someone even though it was the weekend.

Thirty minutes later, he had a new friend at the switchboard and the cell phone number of the head cardiovascular researcher. Race punched in the number and prayed Dr. Harry Spence was easier to win over than the beautiful transplant surgeon.

CHAPTER TWENTY-ONE

FRIDAY, DECEMBER 13TH, 11:26 AM EST

CINCINNATI, OHIO

Catherine sprinkled cheese over a bowl of spaghetti and set the gooey concoction on Jonathan's laminated Batman placemat. She'd worked hard to master his favorite dishes. Even harder to become his perfect mother. But who was she kidding? Years from now, his memories of extra cheese, doctored boo-boos, and cuddly bedtime stories would never fill the hole her abandonment would carve in his heart. Or hers.

Resentment twirled like pasta noodles on a fork in Catherine's upset stomach. She turned from the four place settings, unwilling to consider a table set for only two. Her father could not have meant his harsh stipulations to be permanent. Despite Bruce the Deuce's tough-guy persona, this morning she'd caught a brief glimpse of the man she'd grown up calling Daddy. She just had to come up with a plan to jump-start his stalled heart.

Maybe when they got back from Africa, she could move in with him and stay until Kelsey's health returned. A daily dose of exposure to her family could lessen the emotional distance between them. The

Deuce would think he'd gotten his money's worth, her kids would acquire a grandfather, and her marriage would remain intact.

She glanced across the open kitchen bar into the large family room. Discussing the particulars with Brad and convincing him that they had no choice but to play along would be no small hurdle.

White lights twinkled on the Christmas tree she'd had yet to find the time to finish decorating. Cartoons played on the TV. Kelsey slept, curled on a pallet in front of the glowing fireplace, weak as a kitten from her last TET spell. Jonathan hovered close by, driving a Batmobile over a mountain of couch pillows without making a sound, his eyes alert to every one of his sister's labored breaths. Maybe not most people's idea of a Hallmark-perfect moment, but she'd learned to appreciate even the briefest respite from her storm.

An aching pain shot through her. Who was she kidding? This quiet was the eye of the hurricane. What kind of a mother justifies breaking one child's heart to make another child whole? Leaving Jonathan, even for a few months, would shatter the trust she'd worked so hard to build. She blinked, and the Christmas-card serenity evaporated, taking with it the deluded thoughts that accepting her father's terms would be the best solution for anyone. She swiped at the lone tear trickling down her cheek. She couldn't do this...or could she? If the call her little girl had been waiting on for years finally came, she couldn't deny Kelsey her only shot at a viable heart.

"Come eat your lunch, buddy."

Jonathan stopped his Batmobile's silent descent of the pillow mountain. He shot his full focus in her direction. His double-barrel gaze was loaded with the expectation that sooner or later she'd finally answer the questions he'd been asking all morning. Why were the suitcases out, and where were they going?

Catherine squirmed under Jonathan's scrutiny, praying her face wouldn't give away the ugly truth. Jonathan's knowing that her father did not want any part of becoming her stepson's grandfather would not build the bridge she hoped these two would cross once things settled down.

"Today, Jonathan."

"Okay." He rose and padded sock-footed over to Kelsey and carefully parked his black plastic car beside the blanket and monkey she clutched. "Want me to wake Sissy?"

His constant vigilance brought a lump to her throat. "Let's let her sleep."

His brow furrowed.

Catherine smiled at his ability to communicate his disagreement about what was best for Kelsey without uttering a word. "I'll feed her after her nap," she reassured him, then reached into the cupboard for another plate and a believable excuse to redirect the conversation. "Daddy still looking for his files?"

Jonathan shrugged off his obvious disappointment. "I guess so." He skated across the kitchen floor then hoisted a hip and wiggled onto his chair. "Yipee. Bsketti and cheese."

Was it her imagination or had her boy's shoulders grown broader and his face wiser as Kelsey's seemed to shrink? Catherine poured a glass of milk then slid it toward the ebony-haired boy, the light in her dark tunnel. "You go ahead. We'll pray when Daddy gets to the table."

Her eyes left the boy with a milky moustache and cased the far side of the family room. The door to the master bedroom remained closed tight. Brad had come home unexpectedly a few minutes ago, with nothing more than an announcement that he'd forgotten some files for the case he was working on. Unlike Jonathan, Brad hadn't asked her a single question about her early morning trip to the radio station. Nor had he come out to ask about the suitcases on the bed.

She knew him well enough to know this silent treatment could go on for days. How could she tell him they didn't have that kind of time? How could they work this out if he wouldn't even talk to her? Sorting through the heart-rending ramifications of her father's terms was too much to handle alone. She needed his help and, once again, he'd stubbornly withheld his support. Anger, bubbly as the red sauce she'd ladled over a pile of noodles, simmered inside her.

"Brad," she called out. "Lunch is ready if you want to eat."

Her cell phone rang.

Startled, Catherine fumbled the plate, the mound of spaghetti slipping into her outstretched hand. She'd given her father every possible number, from her cell to Brad's office. Surely the Deuce's doctor hadn't found a heart already? She dumped the hot spaghetti into the sink and ran a quick burst of cold water over the burn.

"Want me to get it, Mommy?"

She dried her trembling hands on her sweatshirt and lunged for the phone on the counter. "Better let me."

She checked the name on the screen, quickly answered, then balanced the phone between her ear and shoulder. "Dad?"

"Hastings just called."

Her heart lurched. "How is that possible? It's only been a few hours."

"I thought you were the one in such a hell-fired hurry, and money speaks."

"I am in a hurry, but—"

"An ambulance will arrive at your house in less than an hour. I'll meet you at the charter hanger. Bring the papers."

Click.

"Papers?" Catherine shouted into the receiver. "What papers?" The disconnect silence blared in her ear.

The doorbell rang.

Jonathan shot out of his chair. "I'll get it."

Rooted to the tile floor and unable to breathe, Catherine stared at the phone in her shaking hands. Her mind spun in the muck of impossibility. Was she really on her way to making Kelsey a healthy little girl? Dare she allow herself to risk hope when she hadn't even talked to Brad? She'd started down that path so many times before, only to encounter one roadblock after another. Could she go there again without collapsing into an emotional heap if things didn't work out?

She grabbed the counter as her thoughts whisked toward the image of a little girl with golden curls bouncing across a playground. She could hear the laughter of her exquisite child running and playing like the other children. Tears seeped from under Catherine's lashes and seared her cheeks. This moment had been so long in coming, it didn't seem real. She pressed the phone to her heart as if its erratic thumping would summon her father back on the line to hear her thanks.

"Mommy, the man said you have to sign for the package."

Jonathan's tug on the hem of her shirt jerked Catherine from her daze. "What man?" She set her phone on the counter.

"The man at the door."

"Not now, Jonathan." She bent and held his face between her hands. "Kelsey's going to Africa." She kissed his forehead. "Our girl is going to be well."

"But the man said I needed to get my mommy."

Jonathan's words penetrated her excitement and finally registered. She looked at his face. The serious narrowing of his dark eyes prickled her skin. She released him and dashed through the living room. At the entry hall, she was met by a blast of cold air. Standing just outside the wide-open door was a uniformed man stomping snow from his boots, a large express delivery envelope in his gloved hand.

"Catherine Taylor?"

"Yes." She stepped cautiously to the threshold. Her stockinged feet soaked up the tiny ice puddles left from melting snow. A chill scampered up her spine. She shuddered and rubbed her arms. She pointed at the parcel. "That for me?"

"Yes, ma'am."

She snatched the envelope then threw her arms around his neck. "It's true. We're going to Africa."

He quickly pried himself from her embrace and pushed her back inside. "Lady, I just need a signature." Face flushed, he thrust a clipboard at her then retreated a safe distance.

A huge smile cracked the frozen façade she'd worn for so long, and with the commencement of the thaw, she felt the glacier of doubt and fear break free and slowly drift away. "My daughter's getting a heart."

"In that package?"

"No." She laughed at his horrified expression. "In Africa." She tucked the envelope under her arm and scribbled her name on the delivery confirmation. "Bet you don't get that kind of reaction every day."

The shaken courier's uncomfortable gaze shot behind her. "Never when a woman's husband is home." He snatched the clipboard and sprinted off the porch.

"Africa?" The ice in Brad's voice froze her in place. "When were you going to tell me, Catherine?"

She whirled around. "I just found out."

Heat radiated from his silent stare and melted holes in her flimsy justification. She should have told him earlier. Why hadn't she stormed the barricade he'd erected between them and explained that they simply had no other option but to play by her father's rules?

They stood facing each other, the package suddenly hot and heavy in her hands despite the chilly wind trespassing the open door.

"I just got the call. They've got a heart for our girl." She held the envelope out to him. "Look, everything's all arranged. Kelsey and I have got less than an hour to catch the transport."

Brad kept his arms crossed over his chest. "How did this happen?"

She pulled the envelope back and fingered the flap, weighing how much to tell. The urgent phone call had changed everything. She couldn't afford to waste time debating the gory details. Until they could sit down and she could reassure him of her intentions, the less he knew the better. She'd be in a much stronger negotiating position once she had a healthy Kelsey back on American soil. By then, the money would be spent, Kelsey would be well, and what father would argue with that? Neither of them, she hoped.

"The Deuce," she finally croaked. "He's got connections."

Brad flinched then instantly regained his ramrod-straight stance. "So you went crying to Daddy, and he bought into your cockamamie plan, no questions asked?"

"He set us up with a doctor in Baltimore who deals with this stuff all the time."

"And that's supposed to make me feel better how?"

"This is not about how *you* feel, Brad. This is about making Kelsey feel better. I'm not jumping a plane to Africa and getting out at the first hut I come to." She reached for the front door and slammed it shut. "I've got a world-renowned transplant surgeon who is part of some charity foundation making all the connections and arrangements. He helps people like us. Like Kelsey. All we have to do is get her to the airport on time." She stormed past him and bumped into Jonathan, wide-eyed and lower lip quivering.

"Can I go?" The terror in her son's gaze stopped her heart.

Catherine squatted, tucked the envelope under her arm, and clasped his shoulders. "Not this time, buddy. I need you to stay here and take care of Daddy. Can you do that for me?"

"No. He can't. And you shouldn't ask him to." Brad yanked the envelope from Catherine. "What is this?"

"Brad, stop yelling. You're scaring Jonathan." She opened her arms and Jonathan leapt into them. "I'm assuming it's our flight arrangements."

"When did Schuster and Stern become travel agents?"

Her brow wrinkled in confusion. "Schuster and Stern are Dad's lawyers." She released Jonathan and stood to get a better look at the return address.

"I know who they are, Catherine. They wouldn't hire me after your father had me black-balled, remember?" Brad tore open the seal and withdrew a thin stack of legal-sized papers. "In the matter of Taylor vs. Taylor." He stopped reading and glared at her, hurt crashing against the rocky ledge of anger in his eyes.

"What does that mean?" she demanded.

"You're divorcing me."

She grabbed the papers. "No. That can't be." She read the yellow sticky note attached under the Divorce Petition title.

Don't bother coming to the airport without Bozo's signature. Dad

Catherine slumped to the floor. "Oh, God."

He jerked her up. "What have you done, Catherine?" He shook her. "Answer me!"

"Sold our souls to the devil."

CHAPTER TWENTY-TWO

FRIDAY, DECEMBER 13TH, 12:06 PM EST

CINCINNATI, OHIO

Catherine kept her back to Jonathan as she ransacked her closet for some equator-friendly clothing. She felt the heat of his worried stare searing a hole in her sweatshirt. Saving her daughter didn't mean that she could ever stop loving her son. Brad had been wrong to hurl such ugly accusations in front of the boy. Did he really believe she would do something this drastic without considering the risks? Her husband could try to saddle her with his guilt, but his justification would not make up for his refusal to consider Africa their only choice.

She kicked at Brad's size-eleven shoes strewn across the closet floor. Why couldn't the man swallow that enormous pride of his and make peace with her father? If he did, there wouldn't be a nasty envelope on the kitchen counter and she wouldn't be sandwiched in the middle of a male turf war.

The wail of an ambulance interrupted Catherine's internal lament. She stopped her frantic packing and sought her son's questioning eyes. When Jonathan became aware of her troubled gaze, he froze, as if any movement on his part might give her the reason she needed to justify leaving him behind.

Unwilling to add her fears to his obvious distress, Catherine summoned a smile. "Come on, buddy. I could use your help." She grabbed a couple of T-shirts, a pair of shorts from a shelf, and two faded summer dresses tucked behind her winter sweaters. She left the closet and headed for the bedroom.

Jonathan followed her to the small suitcase she'd left spread open on her bed. While she folded clothes, he silently picked up a pair of pink pajamas and carefully laid them on top of the jumbled items.

She choked back tears and ruffled his hair. "Sounds like Kelsey's ride is here."

"I'll get Daddy."

"Wait, buddy." Catherine sat on the edge of the bed and beckoned Jonathan into her open arms.

He leapt into her grasp and wrapped his arms around her neck. "Take me with you."

She squeezed him tight. "Mommy loves you. Don't ever forget that." She released him and took his face in her hands. Confusion and doubt swam in his eyes. "I'm coming back. Soon as Kelsey's well. We'll work this out." She kissed his cheek, drinking in the spaghetti-and-cheese smell of him like a hungry Italian. "I promise."

"Don't make promises you can't keep, Catherine." Brad stalked across the room and snatched Jonathan from her arms. "Come on, son. Let's go tell your sister good-bye."

The boy nodded and followed his father. He stopped and gave Catherine one last pleading glance. He padded from the room, taking with him a huge piece of her breaking heart. Had he believed her? How could he? She was leaving them. Brad knew it. Jonathan knew it. And so did she.

Catherine wrestled with the suitcase, tugging at the zipper. Why, God? Why must she choose one child over another? The moment she and Kelsey returned from Africa, she'd find a way to restore order to her crumbling world.

The buzz of the doorbell jarred Catherine back to the immediacy of her situation. For now, getting Kelsey to Africa, no matter the long-term costs of that action, had to be her first priority.

She rummaged through the dresser drawers until she found the passports they'd gotten two summers ago for a short family cruise. She tossed the books with Brad and Jonathan's pictures back into the drawer and shoved it closed with her hip.

The doorbell rang again. She crammed her passport, along with Kelsey's, into the bulging tote bag then flung the strap over her shoulder. She grabbed the suitcase and sprinted toward the living room.

Brad sat in the recliner, his face buried in his sleeping daughter's curls. Jonathan stood sentinel-still beside them.

Catherine set her luggage beside the leather chair. "We have to go, Brad."

He refused to look at her, burying his nose deeper into Kelsey's hair. Jonathan hovered over them, rubbing his daddy's arm.

Anguish thrashed Catherine's soul, shredding any hope that once this crisis was behind them, everything would work out. She reached for the clingy trio, longing to reclaim her place at the center of their little huddle. Just before she touched the dark waves of Brad's head, the doorbell rang again.

She withdrew her empty hand, the weight of loss dragging it limply to her side. "I'll let them in." Catherine went to the foyer and opened the door. A woman with short gray hair smiled at her.

"I'm Margo Stinson, your flight doctor." She extended her hand, her grip warm and sure. "May we come in?"

Catherine nodded.

The woman gave the two attendants flanking either side of a small gurney a go-ahead signal. They lifted the white-sheeted bed effortlessly onto the porch.

Catherine backed into the foyer, her heart racing as she turned and led the surreal little parade into her living room. "So, what kind of a doctor are you?"

Margo smiled. "Pediatric cardiologist." She whisked into the living room like she was used to not wasting precious time. "Mr. Taylor?" The doctor's gentle, but firm tone brought Brad's head from its bowed position. "I'm here to help you get your little girl to Africa." She reached for Kelsey. "Mr. Taylor? Can I have a look at our patient, please?"

Brad, tears streaming down his face, obeyed, and mechanically held a limp Kelsey out to the uniformed strangers. They took her from him and gently placed her on the stretcher. With seasoned precision, Margo took Kelsey's vitals, attached her to some oxygen leads, and had the attendants wheel her out the door.

Margo remained behind. "Mrs. Taylor?" She held a pen poised over a clipboard.

"Yes."

"Do you have your passports?"

"Yes."

She made a checkmark on her list.

"Driver's license?"

Catherine nodded.

Another check. "All shot records? Medical records? And any medications?"

"Yes."

Check. Check. Check. "Is this your only suitcase?"

"Yes."

She looked up from her list. "Each family member can take two small bags. Where's Mr. Taylor's luggage?"

Catherine looked at Brad, then turned her attention from his hardened features back to Margo. "He's not coming with us."

Margo's trained eyes darted between them, assessing the situation. "I see." She tucked her clipboard under her arm and gathered the luggage. "I'll give you two a minute, but time is of the essence, Mrs. Taylor." She whirled around and headed for the door.

"Sissy!" Jonathan bolted past Catherine and zipped around the woman pulling the small carry-on. "I want my Sissy!" He flew out the front door.

Catherine touched Brad's arm, her tears refusing to comply any longer with her efforts to hold them back. "Brad, please."

Brad wiped his eyes with the back of his hand then slowly pushed himself up from his chair. Silently, he followed her out to the ambulance.

Jonathan had climbed inside and planted himself beside Kelsey's stretcher.

"Don't let them take my sister." He threaded his wire arms through the railing.

Margo squatted beside Jonathan but aimed her gaze at Catherine and Brad. "Mommy and Daddy, why don't you explain to Kelsey's brother that we're going to take good care of his sister?"

Catherine felt the intent of the woman's calm, heated stare. Yet she remained frozen, completely unable to navigate the treacherous sidewalk.

"Mr. Taylor, could you give us a hand here?" Margo's lifted brow and stern voice prodded Brad into action.

He glared at Catherine, but a mammoth glacier had slid into place and iced her rippling emotions. He shook his head then moved stiffly toward the ambulance and hoisted himself inside.

"Come on, buddy." Brad pried Jonathan's clenched fingers then scooped the sobbing boy into his arms. "The only way we can help Sissy is to stay home." Patting Jonathan's heaving back, he bent and kissed Kelsey's forehead. "Daddy loves you, Angel."

"It hurts, Daddy." Kelsey's hand reached for Brad.

"She's talking." Brad wheeled. "See, we've got time."

"Hurts," Kelsey whispered. "Fix it."

Brad's face scrunched in pain. "Mommy's going to make it better." He bent and kissed her again. "Daddy loves you."

With Jonathan's arms entwined around his neck, Brad stepped carefully onto the glassy sidewalk and stopped in front of Catherine. "Happy now?" Anger swirled in his vaporous breath. He pulled the rolled-up special delivery envelope from his back pocket. "Go get your heart." He dropped the envelope into her trembling hands. "And your divorce."

"Brad, I—"

"Save your strength, Catherine. You're gonna need it."

Brad turned and tromped through the snow.

Jonathan screamed over his father's shoulder. "Take me, Mommy!" His hands reached for her. "Pleeeeze!"

Brad whisked Jonathan inside the house and slammed the door, officially cutting her off from the family she'd dreamed of having her whole life. Catherine fell to her knees.

Strong arms lifted her to her feet. "Mrs. Taylor, we've got a plane to catch."

Catherine allowed Margo to help her into the back of the ambulance and drop her into the little jump seat across from Kelsey's stretcher.

"Buckle up, Mrs. Taylor."

Oh, God. What have I done? Hands shaking, she obediently fumbled with the seat belt.

"Mrs. Taylor?" Margo offered her best professional-comfort smile and helped her secure the clasp. "I know this isn't easy for you, but if we work together, this trip will be a whole lot easier on Kelsey."

"Sure." Catherine heard voiced agreement leave her lips, but it sounded muffled, like the drowning woman in her nightmares, the one unable to defeat the drag of the current.

The ambulance lurched over the mound of snow piled at the curb, jostling Catherine's head against the metal wall. The driver cranked the siren and she cringed. She was doing this. She was actually going to a third-world country to get her daughter a heart. What was she thinking? Catherine struggled to tamp the panic making her want to cry out for the driver to circle the cul-de-sac and take her home.

"Why don't you start by giving me a little history?" Margo waved her hand in front of Catherine's face. "Mrs. Taylor, are you listening?"

The beat of Catherine's heart pulsed loud in her head, the noise drowning out the weak peep of Kelsey's rhythm flashing across the monitor.

"Mrs. Taylor, are you all right?"

No, she wasn't all right. Her soul was dying. She'd never be well again. Catherine blinked, compelling her mind to decode the repeating message on Margo's moving lips. "Didn't you get a copy of her records?"

"Yes, but the more you and I can work together, the better prepared we'll be in case ..." Her trailing voice indicated she'd caught wind of Catherine's increasing anxiety and decided to change tactics. "Have you ridden on a Lear jet before, Mrs. Taylor?"

"No."

"Well, perhaps if you know how a medflight works, you'll feel a little more at ease." The doctor took a quick breath and then launched into her sales spiel. "We're a premiere evac company. Every possible arrangement has been made for you. We pick the patient up at their door, care for their every need along the way, arrange refueling stops, and deliver the patient to the waiting hospital."

"I only agreed to this *arrangement* so Kelsey could have a new heart beating in her chest. So, unless you can ensure that outcome, nothing you can say about this trip will make me feel better."

Margo gave a slow, deliberate nod. "I understand."

"You don't understand anything." Catherine clamped her lips, wishing she'd done so before spewing bitterness and lack of appreciation all over this wonderfully kind woman. Dr. Stinson wasn't to blame for the mess Catherine had gotten everyone into, and she certainly didn't deserve the angry attack of some stranger's very personal war.

But someone did. Catherine's mind ran over the list of possibilities. Brad? Her father? God? She shuddered. Here she was getting the very thing she'd prayed for, and where was her faith now? She was a fake. A fraud. She'd always said she'd be happy if only Kelsey could be healed, knowing all along her happiness was conditional. If God could not meet all of her requirements—a healthy child, a happy family, her relationship with her father restored—then He need not bother. She'd lied to God and now she had hell to pay. Just having Kelsey well wasn't enough. She wanted more. Much more.

"I'm sorry. I'm just—"

"Scared." Margo slipped the clipboard out of sight. "You've had a sick little girl on your hands for a long time. But I can see that she's been well cared for and very loved. Why don't I give you a moment for the reality of this long-anticipated day to sink in. We'll work through any questions on our flight."

Catherine nodded, words to express her gratitude failing her.

She battled the feeling of falling off a cliff as the ambulance left her subdivision and sped away from the security she'd known. As they tore down the interstate, Catherine silently watched as strangers ministered to her dying daughter. She twisted the envelope in her hands, not the least bit tempted to peek at the finality of Brad's name scrawled across the signature line. Nothing in this world was certain. The sooner she came to grips with that fact, the better prepared she'd be for whatever awaited her and Kelsey in Africa—life or death.

Thirty minutes later, the ambulance screeched to a halt. The driver jumped out and opened the double doors, chilling Catherine with a blast of cold air and her first glimpse of the sleek jet taking them abroad. Envelope in one hand, she hefted Kelsey's bag onto her shoulder with the other and followed the stretcher out onto the tarmac.

Her father's red Beamer was parked between them and the plane. He was leaning against the hood, his arms crossed over his chest, his breath forming a dragon-like cloud around the grave features of his face.

Catherine trailed Kelsey's gurney, tucking blankets around her frail frame as they wheeled her across the tarmac.

"Wait." Her father began a hurried navigation of the icy patches between them.

Catherine stopped, but waved the doctor and Kelsey's attendants on. She turned and faced her father. "Is this what you're looking for?" She handed him the envelope.

He reached for her. "Catherine—"

She jerked free of his hold. "Don't."

The Deuce slipped the envelope inside his black overcoat. "I want to see her."

"Make it quick."

Catherine watched him bound the steps and duck inside the plane. She stood on the frozen tarmac, jet engines revving overhead. Her father's money had bought her this opportunity. A grateful daughter would thank him. A loving father wouldn't have put a price on his love.

She gave one last glance toward home, the life she'd left behind swallowed up by the darkness. Icy winds tore open her coat, but she could make no effort to button herself against the assault. She deserved the needle-like flogging that beat her aching chest.

"Mrs. Taylor?" Margo's voice rose above the swirling tumult with urgency that picked up Catherine's heavy feet and pointed them toward the plane. "Come quick. That man is agitating Kelsey."

Catherine stood at the bottom of the metal stairs, her numb mind struggling to interpret Margo's summons. Suddenly the doctor's frantic words and actions chopped through the crust that had formed over Catherine's heart. Alarm, as inciting as a fire drill, rattled her consciousness. Every muscle awakened in her body. She barreled up the steps at mother-bear speed.

CHAPTER TWENTY-THREE

FRIDAY, DECEMBER 13TH, 1:31 PM EST

CINCINNATI, OHIO

Fear and anger propelled Catherine up the jet steps two at a time. She burst through the narrow cabin door, her eyes sorting through the bedlam surrounding her daughter's tiny stretcher. Her father was trying to pick up Kelsey.

She elbowed her way past him. "Dad, she can't take this." She reached over the rails of the gurney and folded Kelsey into a squat.

"I'm sorry...I didn't mean to upset her...I'll go." He backed away, dismay at the seriousness of Kelsey's situation written all over his face. "I didn't know."

"Welcome to my world." Catherine lowered her gaze. It wasn't her fault he didn't know his own granddaughter, and she wasn't going to let him dump his guilt on her.

Kelsey jerked then went limp. The dead weight instantly yanked Catherine from any regret her father had stirred within her. She flipped Kelsey over and discovered her daughter's purple lips. She pulled Kelsey's knees to her chest. No sign of breath.

"Dr. Stinson!" Panic swelled in her chest as her father backed out of the plane. She shook Kelsey. No response. "Help! The fold's not working."

The doctor grabbed an oxygen mask. "Let's try this." She ripped the nasal cannula from Kelsey's nose and slipped the strap of the mask over Kelsey's head. "If this doesn't do it, we'll try some morphine." She held out her arms. "Give her to me."

Catherine squeezed Kelsey tight, loath to admit the real weight she could no longer shoulder was failure. Saving her daughter had passed into a realm far beyond the limited expertise she'd acquired these past five years. She shifted the burden of her child's care into the doctor's capable hands, then sank into the nearest seat.

Margo hurtled herself into multi-tasking mode. She adjusted machines and ordered the flight nurse to inject morphine into the saline lock of Kelsey's intravenous access tube. Within seconds, the drugs and the oxygen nudged the bruised-looking tint from Kelsey's face. The doctor placed the sleeping girl on the stretcher, careful to keep her on her side. She checked Kelsey's vitals then let out a slow breath.

"She's stable—for now."

"Thank you." Catherine kneaded the knots from the base of her neck. "Do you think she can make the trip?"

The doctor pulled a blanket out of the overhead bin. "I'll be honest. Flying a little girl in this condition halfway around the world is—"

"Crazy. Right?"

"A first for me. And gutsy for you." She tossed the blanket to Catherine. "You'll be glad you slept."

"You want me to sleep?" Catherine clutched the blanket. "I haven't slept since she was born."

"There's only room for one on that gurney," the doctor said. "You're about to drop."

Catherine peered around the doctor. The adrenaline draining from her body had left her weak and shaky. "You'll wake me, right?"

"When we stop in Frankfurt to refuel."

"Will Kelsey have to be taken off the plane?"

The doctor shook her head. "We'll request concurrent servicing.

Customs will come aboard." She spread the blanket over Catherine's legs and slipped a bottle of water into a nearby cup holder. "You need something to help you sleep?"

"No thanks."

The thrust of the jet's takeoff pressed Catherine's head into the leather seat. She clutched the blanket to her chest and closed her eyes. She *was* crazy, and she didn't need a professional giving her the once-over to arrive at that diagnosis. She'd gambled everything for this one last chance to save her daughter. Win or lose, someone would pay. She just prayed it would not be Kelsey. Or Jonathan. Or Brad.

The jet leveled out. Catherine opened her eyes and turned her head to the window. Far below the gray void, life continued. Parents with perfect children and their perfect lives going on in perfect normalcy. A heavy sadness settled in her gut. What was happening in the home she'd left behind? The man and boy she loved so much every muscle in her body ached with it? She snapped the shade closed.

Rehashing the what-ifs of this whole situation would give her nothing but pain. For the sake of that little girl on the stretcher, she had to stop thinking like a wounded wife and prodigal daughter and start acting like a mother. Second-guessing herself was no longer an option. Africa wasn't just the fastest way to save Kelsey. It was the only way.

Catherine's eyes roamed the cabin. Blinking monitors and the steady hum of medical devices were her reality. Modern technology had kept her daughter alive since birth, and under this flight doctor's watchful eye, every medical device would continue to be employed until Kelsey got that new heart.

What would she have done without the long list of dedicated medical professionals who'd helped them? Gratitude nudged at her thoughts. The idea startled her. How could anyone be grateful their daughter lay tethered to a machine? Tears slid down her cheeks. Having so many struggles was not the picture she'd have painted for her life, but hindsight made it impossible to decide which trial to eliminate. The years working beside her father? Falling in love with Brad? Caring for a stepson? Comforting her precious daughter when no one else could? Life struggles had reshaped her relationship-deformed heart and taught her how to love. What fool would give up a chance to love?

Catherine swiped at the tears. *God forgive me, I owe much to pain and sorrow.* Peace enveloped her. The din of turmoil faded and she slept—her first real rest in five years.

"Mrs. Taylor?" Margo jostled her shoulder. "We need you to talk to Kelsey. Keep her with us until we can get her to that heart."

Catherine sprang from her seat. She maneuvered around the machines surrounding the small stretcher where Kelsey flailed about, her face an icy blue. Margo worked to secure the loosened EKG leads.

"Fold her." Automatically, Catherine flipped Kelsey onto her side, slid her hand under the bony knees, and pressed them tight against the faint movement of her daughter's chest. "How much longer to our refueling stop?"

"We're a few minutes outside Dar es Salaam." Margo studied the tape spitting out of the EKG machine.

"You promised you'd wake me," Catherine scolded.

"Prepare for a rough landing." The captain's voice came over the intercom, interrupting the doctor's opportunity to explain. "It's stormy out there."

Catherine put her lips to Kelsey's ear. "Hang on, punkin. Mommy's gonna make it all better."

Margo upped Kelsey's oxygen level as the plane sliced through the torrents. The wings tipped and an overhead bin popped open. Boxes of rubber gloves, IV tubing, and other medical paraphernalia flew through the cabin. Catherine shielded Kelsey, pulling her tighter. When she looked up, the color had drained from the faces of the crew. Everyone grabbed something to hold on to. Dr. Stinson was mouthing what looked like a prayer.

Seconds ticked by as the plane bucked against the wind. Lower and lower. Ground lights flashed out the windows on the left. The plane tilted and then lights flashed out the windows on the right. Catherine's breath had frozen in her chest. With a jarring thump the landing gear hit solid ground. The plane's engines screamed as the jet ground to a halt on the rain-slick runway.

"Welcome to Africa," the doctor gasped.

In the time it took for the captain to leave his seat and open the door, the rain had stopped. Margo hustled them out onto the steamy tarmac and into intense heat. A wet, unfamiliar stench churned Catherine's stomach.

The doctor took hold of the stretcher. "Let's go."

Catherine started toward the waiting ambulance then hesitated. Surely they weren't transporting Kelsey in a faded and dented heap which most Americans would have sold for scrap a decade ago.

Margo helped the wiry driver hoist Kelsey's stretcher and shove it inside. "Move it, Mrs. Taylor."

The doctor's command jarred Catherine into action. She splashed through the puddles, threw the tote bag and little suitcase on wheels under the stretcher, squeezed in beside Margo, and braced herself for a whirlwind ride.

They left the airport at a snail's pace.

"Faster." Catherine pounded the mesh wire between them and the driver. "Why don't you go faster?" She pressed her foot to the floor, but only the speed of her pulse increased. "Margo, tell me I haven't screwed up."

"Keep talking to her, Mrs. Taylor."

Catherine stroked Kelsey's wet curls, then pulled the monkey from her bag. "Guess what, punkin? They have real monkeys in Africa. And as soon as you're feeling better, we'll find one. I promise."

Kelsey's eyes didn't open. The one-hundred-degree temperature of this poorly air-conditioned vehicle was sapping the last of her strength.

"She needs air." Catherine jiggled the latch of the dirt-smudged window as the ambulance slogged toward the city.

The ambulance bounced onto a paved road lined with makeshift houses. Small children drove blocks of wood as if they were homemade cars over a pile of old tires. Older boys kicked a ball made from string in a makeshift game of soccer. Even surrounded by poverty, these children were playing. All except her child.

Street vendors suddenly mobbed the ambulance. Gaunt, black

faces peered in the windows, begging them to stop long enough to buy their withered fruits or fake Rolex watches.

Catherine gathered Kelsey's hand into hers. Cold. The child's body temperature was dropping, despite the sweltering heat. Fingers trembling, she traced the tiny blue veins visible beneath Kelsey's translucent skin.

What had she done? Her daughter was dying, and the noose of blame belonged on her neck and no one else's. Expecting an impoverished land that struggled to keep its own children alive to heal her child was utter foolishness. Brad and Margo were right. She would need every ounce of strength she could muster.

Oh, God. Help us.

A horn blared. Their ambulance made a sharp turn at the light, pitching Catherine against the wall. As their vehicle picked up speed, Catherine scrambled back to the stretcher. They rattled through the crowded city. Sweat trickled down her back, her sweatshirt melting onto her frame. Desperate for a breath of air, she fumbled once again with the window latch. A hard elbow jab popped the window open.

The strong, nasty smell of fish swamped the ambulance and immediately upended Catherine's stomach. The contents splattered all over Margo's sensible shoes.

"Try to breathe, Mrs. Taylor." The doctor ignored the mess at her feet. "We must be getting close. According to the flight plan, the private hospital is situated on the bay."

Wiping her mouth on her sleeve, Catherine prayed Kelsey would live long enough to see this ocean halfway around the world. The ambulance rumbled past several blocks of grandiose Arab-inspired architecture, decaying from years of neglect, then squealed to a sudden stop.

Catherine raised her head and peered out the window. Three stories of chipped cinder blocks crumbled the last of her expectations. She just thought she'd lived in hell the past five years. But she'd been wrong. Apparently, eternal flames have many degrees of torment. From the looks of this place, bringing her daughter here might prove to be her most soul-blistering decision yet. She deserved the burn in her chest.

Margo shouted through the mesh divider between them and the driver sitting idly behind the wheel. "We need to hurry."

The driver cast an unappreciative look over his shoulder then hopped out of the ambulance. He sauntered to the back of their vehicle and yanked open the door. The sticky coastal breeze hit Catherine and fanned the guilt singeing her heart.

A very dark-faced man in a very white coat appeared at the foot of the lowered stretcher. He offered his hand. "*Karibu.* Welcome. I'm Dr. Amandi. Head of Cardiology."

Dr. Stinson leapt from the ambulance. "We have a stat situation."

"That is why you're here, is it not?" He buttoned his coat over his round belly, his gold tooth sparkling at the corner of his forced smile. "I shall make everything better." He motioned for Kelsey to be lowered. Once the stretcher was unloaded, he leaned over the gurney and put his stethoscope to Kelsey's chest, then straightened immediately. "Come. We must hurry."

Dr. Stinson began rattling off Kelsey's current stats and medical history as Dr. Amandi redirected his healthy girth toward the hospital with a remarkable agility. As he led the frantic parade through the dingy corridors, curious staff parted for the stretcher flanked by two Americans. Dr. Stinson manned one side holding an IV, Catherine the other, desperately trying to hold her quivering emotions together.

At the swinging, double doors, Dr. Amandi stopped. "I know you are worried, but be assured that your daughter is in excellent hands. You can go no further." He dismissed Catherine with his sharp turn toward the nurses' station. "Send me that heart the moment it arrives." Without another word, he followed Margo into the operating room.

The doors swung shut in Catherine's face. "Dr. Stinson?" Catherine pressed her nose to the cloudy glass. "Margo!"

In her tear-filled periphery, Catherine noticed the uniformed people behind the nurses' station. They stared at her, their black faces silent and frozen, as if they'd never witnessed the startling sight of a white woman melting into a puddle on their pitted linoleum floors. She stepped away from the operating room doors and slumped against the gray walls.

Air. She needed air and a private place to throw up again.

Head down, she sprinted toward the corridor opening that had sucked her into this nightmare. She crashed into something solid and stumbled back.

"Whoa." A man grabbed her arm to steady her. "You okay?" Kind blue eyes examined her face. "You don't look so good. Let's find you a chair." Supporting her weight, he guided her down the hall a few feet and eased her into a chair. "Look, I gotta make this delivery pronto. It'll only take me a minute. When I'm through, we'll get you some help. You gonna be okay?"

Catherine nodded, although the blood thumping in her temples had blurred most of what he was saying into gibberish.

"Good girl." He picked up a red cooler box he must have set aside to help her. "I'll be right back."

Delivery? The word broke through Catherine's haze. "Wait." She leapt from her seat and latched onto him, her head spinning. "Is that a heart for Taylor?"

He shrugged. "I just make the delivery. I never open the package." He took hold of the hand she had clamped around his arm. "I'm a little late. Dr. Amandi frowns on tardiness." He gently sloughed her hold then jogged toward the nurses' station. "Hey, girls. Order's up."

Stunned, Catherine watched him smile and flirt with the swarming nurses like he was delivering a pizza. Didn't he know he carried life?

And death.

The thought hit Catherine like an unexpected slap. She stumbled back, missing the chair and hitting the floor with a jolting thump. Somewhere in this godforsaken country, a child had died so that her child could live.

A child...dead.

Grief-laden tremors shook her body. Questions of how, when, and where twisted like a brewing storm in her mind. Black-and-white images of the dirty-faced street children swirled in raw and mortified speculation.

She'd come to Africa without giving a single thought about where the doctor would get her daughter's heart. Was she really so stupid to think that they sold children's hearts on the street peddlers' carts?

Catherine clamped her hand over her mouth, the churning remains in her stomach demanding an exit. Even when she enrolled Kelsey on the UNOS list, she hadn't allowed the answer to the question of where the heart would come from to take on a human shape. In America, Kelsey was an anonymous blood-typed number on a list that would be matched with an anonymous compatible heart. The viable organ could come from any number of circumstances, accidental death being her justifiable and palatable reason of choice.

Surely that was the case here as well. Somewhere some African parent had selflessly signed off on a mortally injured child so that an American child could live. No matter how Catherine tried to spin the tragic scenario in her mind—traffic accident, lion attack, third-world poverty—the brutal reality finally reached her heart—a dark-skinned child had died in her white-skinned daughter's place.

She heaved, and bile pushed past her hold and soiled the floor.

Sobs, wrenching and deep, racked Catherine's body. She slid down the wall and dropped next to the mess of her own making. The image of an African mother wandering the streets alone because her child's heart now resided inside an American child clawed at her empty belly.

How could she live with what she'd done? But Kelsey would have died if she'd waited in America.

Catherine drew her knees to her chest and hugged them tight. The fold forced guilt into every chamber of her aching heart. She curled herself around the futile wish that she could have been the one to die.

CHAPTER TWENTY-FOUR

SATURDAY, DECEMBER 14TH, 1:04 PM

KABONI PRIVATE HOSPITAL

Strong arms lifted Catherine from the floor and gently put her in a chair. A cool, wet cloth dabbed at her lips, but the foul taste of guilt remained in her mouth. Someone's child had died so her child could live. She opened her eyes to see who was attempting to salvage the mess she'd made of so many lives, her own included.

Two black nurses hovered beside her, muttering in a language she couldn't understand. One took her pulse while the other rinsed a soiled rag in a metal basin. Behind them stood the tall man with the Igloo cooler.

He pointed at her sweatshirt. "You a Buckeye?"

She tugged at the heavy fabric clinging to her torso and baking her like a potato. "My husband went to Ohio State."

He thumped the big red N on his hat. "I'm a Husker. Born and bred." The combination of his easy-going smile and idle banter calmed her. "Your husband's surgery should be a go now."

Recalling Brad's hardened face banished her shaky peace. "Not my husband. My daughter."

The smile slid from his face. "A kid?" The news had noticeably set him back, but he quickly gathered his composure. "Well, these girls will take care of you both. They're the best." He winked at the nurses. They giggled and ducked their heads. He tipped the brim of his hat and started to leave.

Catherine scrambled to her feet, upsetting the water basin. "Wait." She grabbed his arm. "I have to know. Where did you get that heart?"

"Ma'am..." His free hand rubbed the back of his tanned neck. "What's your name?"

"Catherine."

He lowered his hand, his eyes searching hers. Why was he stalling? Couldn't he see how desperately she needed this information?

"Catherine, I just make the emergency deliveries."

She nodded, relieved his reluctance hadn't been because he expected or wanted justifications, because she didn't have them.

His phone beeped. "Excuse me, Catherine." He pulled it out of his pocket and checked the message. "Gotta go." He did a military-style pivot toward the nurses. "Girls, I'd appreciate it if you could find my friend Catherine a place to wait this one out."

As his long legs carried him toward what must be another urgent pickup, Catherine fought the need to run after him, to beg him not to leave her. How could she bear being alone, not knowing what was happening to Kelsey? Why hadn't she refused to comply with her father's demand that she leave Brad behind? She swallowed the panic crushing her chest. She wasn't alone. Margo was in the operating room, and that would have to suffice.

Flanked by foreign nurses, Catherine allowed herself to be guided to an out-of-the-way private waiting room with a row of chairs.

A few minutes later, someone tapped her on the shoulder. "Mrs. Taylor?"

Catherine turned to see Margo, her scrubs blood-splattered, standing beside her. "Dr. Stinson. . .tell me what's going on."

"Kelsey's been prepped. The organ appears a viable match. Looks like everything's a go." She offered a weary smile. "I hate to leave you, but my medical authority actually stops at the hospital door. I've got a plane to catch."

Heart sinking to her knees, Catherine asked, "You can't help Dr. Amandi?"

"Too much liability." She offered a tight smile. "He seems skilled enough. He's not a pediatric surgeon, but I'm sure Kelsey's in good hands."

How could anyone be sure? What had she been thinking to blindly place her confidence in an African doctor's competence with no way to check his credentials? She muzzled the panic demanding that she beg Margo to take the risk. It was too late now to ask this woman for anything more. Catherine gulped down the wedge of fear lodged in her throat and thanked Dr. Stinson for the reassurances. They hugged, then Margo reluctantly pulled away. Catherine turned her back, unable to watch the exit of the last of her supporters. She listened with every taut muscle in her body until the squeak of the doctor's sensible shoes no longer echoed in the empty hallway.

The next four hours, Catherine paced between the row of plastic chairs, a small coffee table with a healthy plant, and a bank of windows that looked out over a neat and tidy garden. This African version of a surgical waiting room was surprisingly clean, but it didn't stop her from repeating her plea that God guide the hands of the surgeon operating on her daughter.

Just as the evening began to settle on the well-tended flowerbeds, Dr. Amandi appeared in the doorway. "Mrs. Taylor? Would you like to see your daughter?"

She bolted from her chair. "How is she?"

"The surgery went well."

Catherine's relief swooshed out in one huge breath. "The heart was compatible?"

"Everything looks good, but of course, even with a perfect organ match there is always the risk of rejection."

"Can I see her?"

"Be prepared. She is hooked up to many machines." He led her to a small glass room with the letters ICU written on the door. He paused, his dark features drawn in serious caution. "She is still unconscious."

Catherine shot around him, unwilling to waste another minute apart from her baby. She burst through the door and froze. Kelsey slept in the middle of a twin-sized bed. She was still as death, but pink. Not pasty gray. Pink. Glowing with the color of life. Her little chest rose up and down in an easy rhythm. Not even a trace of blue lined her tiny perfectly-formed, cherry-colored lips.

My baby is well.

Catherine clapped a trembling hand over her mouth to keep from shouting and waking Kelsey. Tears of joy sprang from her eyes and cascaded over her fingers. "Can I touch her?"

Dr. Amandi nodded and stepped aside.

Catherine eased forward, stopping short of the bed long enough to take in the beauty of this incredible sight, a sight she'd feared she would never see. She reached over the rail and gently dragged her finger along Kelsey's relaxed hand. "Her body temp feels so...normal." Laughter split the shell into which she had retreated and bubbled forth like a mountain spring.

Dr. Amandi smiled. "We've started the anti-rejection drugs." He scooted past her, his girth taking up a sizable amount of the space, and began checking Kelsey's many lines. "This little one will be up and around in no time." He pushed a plastic chair beside the bed. "Stay with her. Talk to her. I will check on her progress in the morning."

"Dr. Amandi—" She clasped his large ebony hand in hers. "Thank you."

He nodded and left the room.

Catherine sank into the chair. She gently lifted Kelsey's hand. Warmth pulsing through the tiny veins infused her with hope and an intense desire to call Brad to celebrate their victory.

CHAPTER TWENTY-FIVE

SATURDAY, DECEMBER 14TH, 5:42 PM

SHINWANGA REGIONAL HOSPITAL

Mia leaned over Mbui's hospital bed. Using the bell of her stethoscope, she slowly traced the red-hot zipper scar in the center of his heaving chest. Listening to the runaway rhythm of his distressed organ, she prayed for answers. Race had been unable to get a hold of the head cardiovascular researcher Dr. Harry Spence, which in her opinion had left them with nothing more than an unsubstantiated theory that could very likely have no validity at all. Every time she prescribed an anti-rejection drug, she had to consider the patient's risk. Every medication came with its own set of side effects. And just because the FDA was taking a closer look at Tryoxylate didn't mean the drug wasn't still a viable option.

Still, she'd personally sent Shadrach over to the private hospital to procure the drug directly from their pharmacy as an extra precaution. Any theories Race had come up with that someone might be using her hospital to test a replacement drug were worthless without evidence, but that didn't mean she was willing to take any extra risks until she knew what was going on.

She straightened and raised the rail. If the hospital couldn't find another heart, or if she couldn't somehow with certainty pinpoint the reason for another acute rejection, this young father would die.

Letting the bedrail support the weight of her weary body and baffled mind, Mia mentally retraced every step of Mbui's transplant procedure like she'd done over and over the past forty-eight hours. From the donor organ's apparent viability to the moment she took him off the by-pass machine. Contrary to Amandi's insinuations of below par skills, everything had gone by the book. Her father would have been proud.

Mia shoved the recollection of her father's image from her mind. He had been forgiving. She was the one who could not forgive or forget her mistake. Coming to Africa had been the only way she could blot her failure from her record and protect her father's good name. If she helped enough people who couldn't help themselves, maybe then she'd earn back the level of respect the doctors in her family commanded in the medical profession. But, for now, her patient's problems took priority over her own.

Returning her attention to Mbui, she reached for his chart and rescanned every entry on his records. His recuperation had progressed so nicely that she'd confidently sent him home after only three weeks of hospitalization. Now, not only was he rejecting his heart, but there were signs of kidney failure. Had she placed too much faith in a bag full of drugs and Mbui's renewed sense of hope? She closed the file and returned it to the holder at the foot of the bed.

She lifted the sheets and checked Mbui's legs. His swollen ankles indicated the heart's inability to deal with the fluids collecting in his body. Since Mbui's return to the hospital, she'd pumped him full of the highest dosage of every rejection and infection-fighting drug she thought his immune system could take. And yet, Mbui was slowly drowning in his own body fluids. What would her father do if Mbui was his patient?

Shadrach burst into the room and startled her upright.

"Dr. Kendall. God has sent us a miracle." He motioned Mia outside the room.

It took her a few seconds to take in the sodden and road-worn woman who stood in the hallway.

"Jeme!" Mia threw her arms around the small woman. "Thank God, you're alive." She released her for a quick examination. "How did you get here?"

Jeme, who smelled of sweat and the tang of the grassy savannas, shook her head and lowered her eyes.

Mia followed her gaze and gasped at Jeme's tattered bare feet. "You walked?"

"Part of the way. A family picked me up once I made it to the road."

"Let's get you cleaned up." Mia herded Jeme into a small room with a sink and eased the woman into a chair. "How's Zaina?"

Jeme stroked the bulge in the kanga tied across one shoulder. "She is safe." She lifted her tear-filled eyes. "My Mbui lives, yes?"

Mia swallowed, filling the sink with warm, soapy water. "I'll take you to him, once I have you fixed up." She dipped a clean cloth in the suds.

"Please, I must know about my husband."

Mia hesitated, gently washing the dirt from Jeme's feet. "Do you remember when I talked about the possibility of Mbui's body rejecting his new heart?" Mia rinsed the rag, taking a moment to think of a better way to explain the seriousness of Mbui's situation without adding blame to the terror in Jeme's eyes. She dried her hands and gently put them on Jeme's trembling shoulders. "Sometimes the body thinks a new heart doesn't belong there. Which means its defense system will try to...kill it."

"Like the albino hunters."

"Yes, like the albino hunters," Mia whispered as she bent to apply an antibiotic ointment to the gash on Jeme's foot.

Mia wrapped gauze around Jeme's foot. How she wished she could remove the weight of the world's evils from this exhausted girl's stooped shoulders. For now, she'd have to settle for dressing the traumatized mother's feet and getting some food into her.

"Mbui will be glad to see you. I'll not make you wait." Mia turned to Shadrach. "Bring her something to eat, please." She took Jeme by the hand and ushered her toward Mbui's room. She stopped outside the door. "Remember, your husband is very sick."

Jeme nodded.

Mia opened the door. The distinctive stench of encroaching death hovered in the room. Mbui's body was shutting down. Jeme limped past Mia and padded silently to Mbui's bed. Mia trailed close behind, ready to catch Jeme once the realization of the seriousness of her husband's illness sank in.

Jeme ran her hand across Mbui's sweat-beaded brow. His eyes fluttered open. A small smile of recognition tugged at the corner of his lip. She picked up his limp hand and placed it on the bundle at her breast. "No worries, Mbui. The witch doctors will never peddle your daughter's remains under the shade of a mango tree." She lightly dragged her finger over his tight, chapped lips. Her touch, ancient as this land itself, infused Mbui's smile with a strength none of Mia's modern medications had managed.

Mia edged toward the door, this private moment making her feel even more out of place than she did when she shopped the local markets. Jeme was right. Being the only white face in a sea of black was very disconcerting. She'd been reluctant to distinguish between the pain of ostracism she'd felt every time she walked Dar's crowded backstreets and the pain of no longer belonging in Maryland.

Prejudice came in many forms. Some thinking they were better at a particular technique than another. Some having an educational advantage that another lacked. Others certain they'd never make the mistake that had sent another into hiding. Shame clenched her stomach.

Whatever form prejudice took, it divided and separated like a murderous sword.

Shadrach bustled through the door with a small tray of food. "This is all that was left in the kitchen."

"Thank you, Shadrach." Mia quietly carried a chair across the room. "Sit, Jeme. Eat." She handed Jeme the *chapati* Shadrach had brought. "Eat...for Zaina's sake."

Jeme eyed the flatbread then reluctantly broke off pieces and began shoving them into her mouth, one after another, hardly taking the time to chew. "I hope it was all right for me to come. I was afraid the pilot would not come back so I went to my family. . ."

"We did come back for you, but you were gone. I've been so worried." Mia squatted beside the young woman. "Tell me what happened, Jeme."

Jeme wiped her mouth with the back of her hand, appearing a bit embarrassed she'd devoured even the crumbs. "My family sent me away."

"Why?"

"My sister told me that in a village not far from my hut, an albino man was eating dinner in his home a few days ago." She swallowed hard as if she could barely stand to tell the rest. "Four strangers burst in and hacked off his arms and legs with machetes." She reached for Mbui. "His wife was helpless to save him." Jeme knew her husband was dying, yet she sat ramrod straight, as if this added assault would not get the best of her.

Her resilience pricked Mia's heart. She wanted to shout out, how do you do it? How can you take it? Instead, she whispered, "Did anyone tell the police?"

Jeme shook her head, her thumb rubbing Mbui's hand.

"Why not?" Mia stood. Someone had to take a stand. "Jeme, these horrible crimes cannot go unreported."

"The police have given out cell phones and even escorted registered albinos to school, but they cannot be everywhere or help those who will not sign the rolls." Horror swept across Jeme's face. "Where we live, albinos must hide. That is just the way it is."

"But why?" Mia snatched a towel from the shelf. "Why does it have to be that way?"

"They are cursed in this life. Valued in the next."

Mia dried her hands. "I don't care how long I live here I will never understand the power given to these superstitions."

"It makes no difference. Your understanding will not change the truth." Jeme slowly withdrew her grip of Mbui. "When Numa was born my father ordered his cursed child killed, but my mother hid her for two years in her sister's village. By the time he discovered he'd been tricked, Numa was old enough to find her way back home every time she was left in the forest to die." Jeme raised her chin. "Someone told the witch doctors where my sister lived."

"You think a family member turned Zaina in for money as well?"

Jeme shrugged, but the pain in her eyes did not escape Mia's notice. Family secrets and betrayal were hurts she knew well.

Zaina stirred and began to cry.

Jeme freed the child from the *kanga*, her pale little legs kicking at the freedom. She kissed her baby's cheek then settled the child against her torso, quieting her with the offer to nurse. She looked up at Mia.

"I'm not leaving my Zaina. Not ever. She is the daughter of a great man." Jeme glanced at Mbui. "There is no better luck than to have the love of a child."

Mia stepped toward the mismatched pair and stroked the top of Zaina's downy head.

Jeme snuggled her baby closer. "We are safe here?"

Were they? Mia's mind raced through the maze of dangers harboring this child in the hospital could bring. "Does anyone know where you are?"

Jeme shrugged. "Does it matter? My father wants nothing to do with an albino." Sadness and fear filled her eyes. "He said I could run, but I could not hide from the curse."

"He's wrong, Jeme. I'm going to make sure you're safe."

Mia turned away, praying her words were true as she quickly gathered up the evidence of treating Jeme's wound. Maybe she was simply being paranoid, but even Shadrach had whispered his concerns to her that a place as public as the hospital might not be safe for the pair. A statement that had only managed to catapult her senses to high alert.

Her gaze flicked back to Jeme. "As soon as I'm done working, I'll take you somewhere safe for the night."

CHAPTER TWENTY-SIX

SATURDAY, DECEMBER 14TH, 7:56 PM

MIA'S APARTMENT

Mia checked the chain lock on her apartment door for the tenth time in the last thirty minutes. Even though the sun had set well over an hour ago, the only light in the living room was a couple candles sitting on the table. Despite Shadrach's continued concerns, she'd reminded him that Jeme would be safer hidden away with her than sitting in a public hospital. Unfortunately, she was having second thoughts.

A banging noise sent a chill scampering up her spine. She moved across the room to peek through a dime-sized hole in the drawn curtain. By the light of the rising moon, she could see a man knocking at a neighbor's home across the apartment complex's small parking area.

She let out a relieved sigh and backed away from the window. Adding the weight of preventing another horrible albino murder to her heart rejection concerns had put her on edge and left her sitting paranoid in the darkened apartment. Since moving to Africa, she'd spent many evenings alone in the dark. Power outages were common, and not once had anything bad happened. Tonight should be no different, especially since she'd paid extra to live in a place surrounded by a high security fence and a couple of armed patrols.

Besides, she and Shadrach had been very careful to keep Jeme's arrival quiet until they could leave the hospital without detection. The fact that Jeme's husband lay dying in Shinwanga Regional didn't mean that whoever shot her could track them down here.

Mia squared her shoulders and grabbed the plate of food she'd bought from a street vendor for Jeme on their way home. Cowering in the dark was silly, but she couldn't bring herself to turn on the lights. She backed away from the paper-thin curtains and grabbed her emergency candles and matches. She'd take a shower by candlelight and pretend this precautionary blackout was normal.

Navigating the sparse furnishings, she made her way to the closed bathroom door where she'd offered Jeme a shower. She stopped and put her ear to the rough wood, listening for the sound of running water. "Jeme, do you need anything?" She waited for a moment then tapped. "Jeme?"

The door slowly opened. Jeme stepped out in a cloud of fragrant steam, dressed in the shirt and skirt Mia had offered her earlier. Except for the whites of her eyes, her ebony features receded into the darkness. "I am a coward for leaving my husband."

Unfortunately, the best way to pry a woman from her husband's deathbed had not been taught in med school. "You're brave for saving his child. It's what Mbui would have wanted."

Armed with the plate of rice and fish sauce, Mia followed Jeme's soft footfalls to the bedroom.

God, show me what to do for her.

The clock by the bed ticked in the silence as Jeme quietly dropped beside the ghostly-white child sleeping on a pallet. Moonlight seeped around the edges of the closed shade and bathed Zaina's glistening skin in a silvery glow.

"Are you hungry?" Mia asked, handing her the plate of food.

Jeme nodded her thanks, then placed the plate on the nightstand. "I'll eat later. Right now, all I want to do is sleep."

"Okay. You sleep then. I'll be right outside this door if you need me."

Jeme curled herself around Zaina and closed her eyes.

Mia grabbed an old sorority tank top and a pair of running shorts from the drawer. She backed out of the bedroom and closed the door.

Ten minutes later, Mia emerged from the shower, exhausted but too keyed up to go to bed this early. She cracked the door to the bedroom, the sounds of her guests' heavy slumber a welcome relief, knowing how exhausted Jeme must be from her long trip to Dar.

Mia grabbed her laptop then sat down on her couch. A couple of clicks later and Google popped up. She skipped a cursory check of her email and typed in *Albinos*. The discovery that losing her husband wasn't the only thing Jeme had to fear haunted Mia. She clicked on a website. Curiosity, and then horror at what she was saw, nudged her from one site to the next as she continued reading about the brutal machete attacks and black market trade in albino body parts.

She leaned back and closed her eyes, trying to comprehend the evil involved in this horrifying trade. She already knew some about the problems of organ trafficking. Brokers who took advantage of the high demand of viable organs and made huge profits from selling body parts on the black market. There were countless stories from around the world of the poor selling their organs to the rich. Of people kidnapped and killed in order to harvest their organs. Poverty and the lack of laws governing the practice all played a part in the increasing rise of these crimes.

And while these scenarios of the black market organ trade sickened her, what they were doing to the albinos—if it were possible—seemed even more horrific. The frenzy over these *ghost people* was fueled from a belief that charms and potions made from those body parts could bring riches, power, and good luck. But how could anyone believe that the blood of an albino contained magical powers that could line one's pockets with wealth?

A knock at her front door startled her. Mia left her computer. Heart racing, she sneaked across the room and peeked out the window.

"Mia? It's Race." He knocked again. "You home?"

She let out a relieved sigh and opened the door, but did not remove the chain. "What are you doing here?"

"I promised to help, didn't I?" He flashed a hopeful grin then held up a brown paper sack. "Chinese takeout seemed the best place to start. I figured even if you were home you probably hadn't had time to eat a proper dinner."

She freed the chain.

He brushed past her. "Electricity out?" He stood there, with two big bags that smelled of sweet and sour chicken and egg rolls. At least she hoped that's what it was.

"I'm. . .saving money."

From the expression on his face, her flimsy excuse had fallen flat. "Good thing dinner's on me then."

He reached around her, his arm brushing hers, and flipped the light switch. The tingle of his touch ignited the room's single bulb and something warm in her. His piercing blue eyes quickly took in her damp hair and bare legs, making her wish she'd taken time to run a comb through the mop on her head.

She glanced at the light switch, deciding to leave it on for now. "I was planning to call you. Jeme's here."

"Here?" His eyes widened. "How?"

"She hitchhiked, toting nothing but Zaina on her back."

"That's a killer journey." The concern on his face was surprisingly attractive. "Are they okay?"

"Scared and worried." Mia reined in her galloping emotions. "Shadrach and I decided they'd be safe here. She and the baby are sleeping."

He carried dinner to the small table where her computer sat. "Have you talked with her about what happened back in Makuru?"

"What do you mean?"

"Maybe she has an idea of who tried to kill you."

"I gave my statement to the police today. They're convinced that the shooter wasn't gunning for me, and I think I agree. I kept Zaina out of the conversation, but the authorities found Numa. I think the shooter returned in hopes of taking the rest of her body. And if they knew about Zaina, taking her as well."

"We may never know the entire truth, but I'm just glad they're safe."

For now.

"Wanna clear a spot?" he asked.

Mia closed the lid to her laptop and scooted it out of the way. "Whatever is in that bag smells fantastic." Whether or not someone was after Zaina for the same reason they'd killed Numa was just a theory. But it was also one she was finding easier to believe. Armed criminals didn't waste their time robbing mud huts. It was far more profitable to target the wealthy.

Thankfully, Race didn't call her on the subject change as he set the food on the table then blew out the candles. "I discovered Ming Ling's Happy Takeaway about three months ago. Serves the best Chinese food in all of Dar in my opinion. You'll love it, I promise."

She breathed in the scent of his aftershave that mingled seductively with the food spices then quickly forced aside any romantic inklings of relighting the pair of candles on the table and turning off the overhead light. No doubt she wasn't the first doorstep on which he'd shown up with an armload of Chinese takeout and his Midwestern charm. He removed the lids of the containers. Intoxicating aromas filled the room. Her stomach grumbled. Sweet and sour pork, egg rolls, fried rice, and two ice cold Cokes.

Once he had everything laid out, he rubbed his hands together. "Now all we need are some chopsticks."

Mia's stomach protested the butterflies his steady gaze had incited. "Will a fork do?" She gathered the utensils from the holder sitting in the center of the table.

"If you promise not to stab me with it."

"Don't worry." She grabbed two plates from the tiny kitchen adjacent to the living room and handed them to him, fighting any attraction with a smug smile. "I know a good surgeon."

"Then I just might have to let you hurt me." He started dishing up dinner. "If you're the one who'll be putting me back together."

She swallowed hard as she turned to her plate, ignoring his wide grin. Her mouth watered at the first bite. Why did food always taste better when you had someone to share it with? Most nights she ate alone, picking through the leftovers in her semi-empty refrigerator.

Mia glanced up at him. Forget the food. Why did her pulse pick up every time his lopsided grin activated his parenthetical dimples?

She took a bite of egg roll. Gratitude, most likely, caused the spike in her blood pressure. He'd saved her life. The one-time heroic act deserved her admiration. She didn't need—nor did she want—to be rescued on a daily basis. Growing up with country clubs, tennis lessons, and the elite social events her mother hosted had not only taught her that she wanted her life to count for something more, but it had given her a sense of self-sufficiency.

Besides that, she knew his type. Race Daniels was nothing more than a flirt, and right now, she was acting like a shallow sorority sister on the prowl. Which couldn't be further from the truth. Jeme and Zaina were in her extra bedroom, afraid for their lives while Mbui was in the hospital fighting for every breath. Keeping this struggling family together was all she needed to be thinking about at the moment.

"I delivered another heart to Kaboni Private tonight," he said between bites.

Mia stopped mid-chew. "Really?"

"It was for an American."

"That's rare, isn't it?"

"Happens more than you think."

"Must have been an emergency."

"Or they had the money."

"Where did you get it?"

He dug into a container of noodles. "A mobile clinic a hundred miles north of here."

"And?"

"And I made sure procurement was done exactly by the book."

"How did the child die?"

"I wasn't told." His brows furrowed at her interrogation. "What are you getting at?"

Mia's appetite suddenly waned. "I can't stop thinking about Mbui dying, Numa's murder, albino hunters, and yes, even your crazy theory about the drug testing."

"You think I could be on to something?"

She couldn't help but smile. "Let's just say I haven't dismissed the idea. But I also remembered you mentioning the huge amount of money at stake with drug companies."

"Okay."

"Well, we both know that the trail of corruption is often discovered by following the money. And there's another practice that could very well be connected to all of this."

"What's that?" he asked.

"Human organ trafficking."

Race's frown deepened. "What do you mean exactly?"

"You, of all people, have to know that the black market for organs is alive and well."

"Of course I do."

She was stepping on his toes, and she knew it. "It's a growing multimillion dollar industry found in almost every country in the world. Even in the US there are broker friendly hospitals with doctors who never ask where the organ they're putting in someone came from."

He looked up and caught her gaze. "Like me."

"I'm not accusing you of anything, Race. I know that the nonprofit you work for transports all types of supplies and humanitarian goods—not simply organs. But the bottom line is that profits can be huge on the black market, which makes temptation hard to resist, for medical staff in particular. Add to that, we live on a continent where you have cultures that shun organ donations, meaning the *need* has become exponentially greater than the *amount* of organs actually donated."

He dropped his fork onto his plate. "What have you found?"

She moved the computer in front of them and flipped up the lid, hating that he felt she was accusing him. As far as she knew Race did what he did simply to save lives and nothing more. Hopefully nothing would ever change that opinion.

"I'll start with the albino connection," she said. "Maybe it's just another crazy theory—like yours—that can't be proven right now, but I haven't been able to stop thinking about Numa and Zaina. I did some more research on the ghost people, or the *zeruzeru* as they call them in Swahili."

"Okay." Caution laced his voice.

"The historic mistreatment of albinos is chilling."

He dabbed a piece of chicken in the red sauce. "I'm listening."

She clicked open the article she'd been reading when he arrived. "Less than a century ago, most albinos born here would have been killed at birth—viewed as proof of a woman's adultery with a European man. Because the gene for albinism is recessive, parents can both carry it and pass it on to their child, even if they look normal." She glanced up at him. "What many people don't understand is that albinism is a genetic condition, not a curse."

"I'm not taking sides, or anything, but that's easy for you, a doctor to understand. Africans see a black man in white skin. Someone cursed by the gods."

"But being born with a lack of skin pigment doesn't justify their annihilation. People are being murdered because of a genetic condition."

Race's expression sobered. "They're being murdered because of greed."

CHAPTER TWENTY-SEVEN

SATURDAY, DECEMBER 14TH, 8:41 PM

MIA'S APARTMENT

Eyes wide, lips pursed. . .Mia definitely had his attention. In more ways than one. The woman had a lethal combination of brains, spunk, and beauty. Something he knew he'd be wise to avoid. The situation they faced was explosive enough without the added complications of falling for someone this passionate.

"Race?"

Her impatience snapped his thoughts where they needed to be. He'd come because she'd asked for help. And if this was true, she was going to need an army.

"Sorry."

"Look at this." She pointed to a BBC article. "The incident of albino killings across the country has been on the increase the last six months. And six months ago, my recovery rate for heart transplant patients started dropping."

"That could be nothing more than a coincidence, Mia."

"True, but that's not all." She pointed to a picture of a murdered albino man. "A year ago the poachers were primarily only taking hair, eyes, skin—the trademark features of the albino. Sometimes they'd also take limbs."

"This is sick."

"Yes, but those are the body parts the witch doctors use to make their *magic* amulets. In Numa's case...they did something even more frightening. They took her organs. And it wasn't the first time. I also don't think it was a coincidence that you got a call to make an organ run only hours after Numa's death." She shifted her gaze back to Race. "What organs were you called in to transport?"

He paused a moment to think. "Kidneys and corneas."

"That fits."

"Fits what?"

"Numa was killed late in the day. What if your contact knew you wouldn't have been able to make a pickup until early the next morning. Her kidneys and corneas—as long as they were kept chilled in a preservation solution—would have been fine."

Race felt his Chinese food rebel. "What about the heart?"

She shook her head. "It wouldn't have been viable for that long."

"Spell it out for me. Exactly what are you getting at?"

"I'm still trying to connect the dots, but what if all of this is somehow related? We know there's big money in transplants." She took a breath. "What if there's a connection between the increase in albino murders and organ procurement?"

"Who would do a fool thing like that?"

"Someone whose demand couldn't keep up with the supply. Maybe someone who needed to fast track a new drug. Because it makes sense that one would fuel the other. In order to test the drug, they would need more organ donor patients."

"And in the process, it would line someone's pockets from both ends." A sick feeling settled in Race's gut. Rachel's death might have turned him into a cynic, but he'd never wanted his theory to be right. "Someone at Kaboni Private?"

"I didn't say that."

"Good. Because that's quite an accusation."

"And one I'm not ready to make yet." Her pensive face said the whole idea hadn't done much for her stomach either. "But I know this:

beneath the color of our skin, we're all alike. I couldn't look at a heart and tell you whether it came from someone with red, yellow, black, or white skin."

He still wasn't convinced. "The government doesn't condone murder. This may be Africa, but even I know they'd frown on someone going around and yanking out organs and selling them on the street. There are checks in place. . .even here."

"What if superstition isn't the only reason albinos are being slaughtered. Seventy-five thousand dollars is the going rate for a body."

"Whoa. I knew greed was involved, but not that kind of money."

"In the last few years, there have been over seventy documented killings in Tanzania alone. And those are just the reported murders. That doesn't include the abductions, mutilations, and the killings never reported."

"There could be more if people are too frightened to say anything."

"Exactly." She pointed her fork at the BBC headlines glaring at him from the screen. "Think about it. When money's involved, people find ways around the law. Organs that come from non-regulated donors would have to be passed under the board's radar, but the profit would be enough motivation for someone to risk prosecution." She dropped her fork onto her plate. "Have you seen anything that seemed out of the ordinary with your transport runs?"

He fiddled with the crisp brown edge of his eggroll, but his appetite had vanished at the mention of human poachers. He'd told her the truth when he said he didn't know where the organs came from, but if he were honest, he'd have to admit there were times when he'd questioned the hospital contacts. But he'd never found a shred of evidence to back up that annoying gut feeling he'd so far chosen to ignore. It was simply too easy to squelch concerns when lives were being saved.

Green eyes stared him down. He squirmed under her examination and decided to come clean. "I'll admit there have been a few times when I've wondered if all the organs I've transported were from legitimate donors, but only because you can't get away completely from the corruption."

Judgment veiled her expression. "And you've never questioned your sources?"

"I don't know that organs *are* being harvested illegally." He refused to let his eyes return to the computer image of a hacked albino corpse. "But what I do know is that there are lots of people, like Mbui, whose lives are being saved every day because of your program. So no, I don't ask questions."

"The end justifies the means?"

He slammed his hands against the table. "Of course not." He escaped to the other side of the room, as far from her judgment as he could get.

"Shh. You'll wake the baby." She nodded toward the bedroom door. Her defensive body posture softened. She got up from the table and took a step toward him. "This isn't just a job to you, is it?"

He glanced around the room at the closed curtains and candles. How was her hiding in this tiny apartment any different than what he'd been doing the past year? He'd come to Africa to lose himself in the wilds of this dark continent, but no matter how hard he tried, even here he couldn't escape the past.

"Someone I knew. . ."

Mia reached out and grasped his hand. "What happened?"

"It's nothing." Race pulled away from her fiery touch. Rachel had nothing to do with this. "Do you have anything else to drink?"

She pointed to the fridge. "You're welcome to whatever you can find."

Race opened the fridge and snagged the last can of Coke sitting on an empty shelf. "I'm afraid this'll clean you out."

She closed her computer, clearly distracted. "Someone needs to find out what's really going on and put a stop to this."

He popped the soda tab. "That someone wouldn't happen to be tall, brunette, and gorgeous, would she?"

CHAPTER TWENTY-EIGHT

SATURDAY, DECEMBER 14TH, 10:48 PM EST

BALTIMORE, MARYLAND

Axton searched for the two crystal vials hidden in the midst of the hundreds of lit candles then stopped. He glanced around the shadowy entrance of the cathedral. The last rays of sunlight streamed through the stained glass, leaving a puddle of color on the stone flooring. The only sound he could hear was the faint music coming from the monastery.

He turned to the yellow glow of the candles. He'd been told by one of Lord Longfellow's aides that Dryden had hidden the vials among the church's prayer candles, but as he replayed the brief encounter in his mind, he suddenly questioned his source. The informant's gaze had dropped, his feet shifted.

Axton touched the handle of his sword. What if the aide had been another of Dryden's spies, and Axton's impatience to save his people had blinded him to the truth? Finding the hiding place of the vials had been easy. Too easy.

The thick, carved door squeaked open and an old woman entered the room, her head covered with a dark veil. As she smiled up at him, the flicker of the candles caught the glint of the blade hidden in the folds of her long robe.

Axton ripped off the old woman's cape.

Dryden.

Their swords clashed midair.

"So we meet again." Dryden's smile sent an eerie chill up Axton's spine.

His opponent lunged forward, but was still too slow for Axton. Months of training beside the Zoren Sea had toned his muscles and quickened his reaction time, making him a worthy opponent to the enemy of all enemies. Courage swelled in his chest as he swung his blade.

The steel edge of his opponent's sword nicked Axton's cheek. Axton swept his weapon in a tight circle, adrenaline making him oblivious to the pain. His only thought was that he would defeat Dryden. He took a step back at the revelation. If he was to win against the darkness, he must never succumb to pride. Pride would only serve to accelerate his demise.

"You are well-versed in the ways of the sword." Dryden quickened his steps. "But are you skilled enough to defeat a master?"

Axton concentrated on the man's movements and not his empty words. "That we shall see in due time."

"A man wise in the ways of the sword, but who dares protest my rule?"

"I have not come to merely protest, but to win."

"Then I hope you're ready, because this time it will be to the death."

The bright lights of oncoming traffic tore through the interior of Harry's Subaru and transformed the magical Blackwell Isle into the empty-stretch of Interstate 695. Harry wiped his brow with his sleeve then clutched the steering wheel. The past forty-eight hours had turned his monotonous existence into a battle scene straight out of Blackwell Isle. All he'd ever wanted was to research drugs that saved lives and to get his adventure novel published.

Thank goodness Billings said he'd take care of everything. Not having to worry about what happened to the missing vial was a huge weight off his shoulders. Instead of trying to piece together a growing list of questions with no plausible answers, he could spend his time finishing up his research and his novel. Billings could sort through the small shreds of evidence that didn't add up. Things like a couple of unauthorized visits to the lab and those two missing vials of an untested anti-rejection drug.

Harry sped past a slow-moving SUV with one taillight out and a license plate from New York, anxious to get home and put this day behind him.

His mind returned to Valerie and the Bert character who'd held him hostage with a toy gun. How humiliating. Axton Blade would have known what to do, and he certainly wouldn't have cowered behind his desk at the first sign of trouble. But even if he had managed to come to Valerie's aid in some valiant move, it would have no doubt fallen far short of impressing her.

In elementary school, he'd been the loner with asthma no one wanted on their team. In high school and college, things had improved slightly, but only because he'd freely offered his brains in exchange for not being bullied.

Twenty years later, he was still the shy, nerdy type who spent Friday nights—every night for that matter—stuck in a lab doing research. Not that he craved the fanfare of recognition hanging beside his framed degrees, but he hadn't spent the past fourteen months working on his latest formula to see his name vanish completely off the lists of research credits.

He thrust his hand into the open bag of Cheetos beside him and pulled out a handful. Bright headlights came up behind him. Chips flew everywhere as he flipped his rearview mirror to the night-vision mode and sped up, but the vehicle behind him stayed on his tail.

"What the—"

Harry tapped his brake. The vehicle cut around him and zoomed past. He breathed a sigh of relief. His claustrophobia couldn't tolerate tailgaters. He watched as the offender, a big guy with a thick neck, flew down the road. Suddenly the speeding SUV changed lanes directly in front of him then slowed.

Harry slammed on the brakes. Was that the vehicle he'd passed earlier? He pulled into the left lane, out of the way. He had no desire to get involved in some foolish game of road rage. He reached up automatically and touched his bruised cheek. He'd seen enough violence with Valerie's ex-boyfriend.

Half a mile later, the SUV swerved again into the lane in front of him and hit the brakes. Harry slammed on his brakes. He cranked the wheel to avoid hitting the car. His Subaru spun toward the highway barrier at sixty-five miles per hour. Adrenaline punched him in the gut then seared through his extremities. He felt the impact of metal upon metal. The exploding airbag drove his glasses into his face. Darkness overcame him.

CHAPTER TWENTY-NINE

SUNDAY, DECEMBER 15TH, 7:31 AM

DAR ES SALAAM

Mia wondered why she even bothered to shower in this tropical humidity. She dusted herself with powder and wiggled her sticky arms into the peasant-style cotton blouse that complimented her ankle-length skirt. Staring into the bathroom mirror, she cringed at the dark circles under her eyes. Until way past midnight, she and Race had scoured article after article they could find on BPH, organ trafficking, and the albino crisis. After he left, she worried every time Zaina awoke during the night. She didn't want the neighbors complaining to the police about her houseguests. Some of the articles said no one could be trusted.

That's why she'd awakened the fugitives camped on her bedroom floor and insisted that they accompany her to church this morning. She felt certain Pastor Scott and his wife, American missionaries based in Dar, could offer Jeme and Zaina the same safe haven she'd experienced the first time she stumbled upon their eclectic little house church.

Careful to avoid the railroad-track stitches across her temple, Mia used her hands to slick her wet hair into a ponytail and secure it with a holder. She'd given up makeup her first week in this humidity. The ringing of her cell phone interrupted her final look into the mirror.

Lord, don't let it be the hospital calling with bad news for Jeme.

Mia ran to retrieve her cell from the charger. The number on the screen was that of the private hospital, not hers. Amandi? Had he found something in the files she'd sent? Something that could possibly support her anti-rejection drug theory? She took the call. "Dr. Kendall here."

"Doctor, I'm the chief surgical nurse at Kaboni—"

"Yes?" Mia could not hide her curiosity.

"We have an emergent situation and request your assistance."

Ambulance sirens and emergencies always raised her heart rate, and even though the private hospital rarely requested surgeons from the government hospital, stat was stat. "What happened?"

"We have a transplant patient suffering possible acute rejection with signs of kidney failure."

A rejection? With kidney failure? And this one at Kaboni Private? Mia squelched the urge to phone Amandi directly. "Why are you calling me?"

"Dr. Amandi is...unavailable."

"Where is he?" In Mia's mind, the nurse's hesitation infused truth into the vague rumors she'd heard about the pretentious doctor. "He's drunk, isn't he?"

"Dr. Kendall, I am not at liberty to discuss Dr. Amandi's whereabouts."

She had no desire to cover for the man, but if a patient's life was at stake. . ."Last time I came to your hospital, I got kicked out. I'm not driving clear across town to have that happen again."

"Dr. Kendall, our patient is five years old."

Mia's breath caught in her throat. "A child?"

"An American child. She arrived yesterday from the States with her mother."

Phone wedged between her ear and shoulder, Mia snatched her

purse and began digging for her keys. Race had mentioned he'd delivered a heart for an American, but it never occurred to her to ask the age of the recipient. Nor could she imagine in her wildest dreams why an American woman would purposely come to Africa for a heart. "That's one desperate mother to bring a kid here."

"Desperation often drives us to do things we might not otherwise do."

"Like calling a surgeon like me?" Mia instantly regretted snapping at a woman who probably had nothing to do with this reoccurring theme of rejection. "I'm on my way. Have her prepped for biopsy by the time I get there." Mia hung up and rushed to the bedroom where Zaina was playing contentedly on the floor. "Jeme, grab Zaina and come with me."

Terror flashed in Jeme's eyes. "Is it Mbui?"

"No. Another patient. An American child."

Ten minutes later, Mia spun into the parking lot of Shinwanga Regional and dropped a wide-eyed Jeme and her baby at the door. She shouted at Shadrach who was waiting outside. "Take her straight to Mbui's room."

"But you said my child is not safe here." Jeme had covered Zaina as well as she could.

"Stay close to her, Shadrach." Mia sped off, hating that her hurried explanation to Jeme probably seemed that she'd left them to fend for themselves so she could go rescue an American family. But what other choice did she have? A child might be dying, and she could not let that happen again.

Twenty minutes later, Mia's jeep squealed into the private hospital's bayside parking lot. She jumped from the vehicle and hurried up the covered walk.

The sweet smell of Betadyne met her at the door. A surgical nurse thrust a medical chart into her hands then turned and quickly led her down a corridor to the closed door of the ICU and the glassed-off rooms. Mia took a moment to flip through the scanty records for names and a brief overview of the child's medical history, including Dr. Amandi's prescription of Tryoxylate. Once she had her bearings, she stepped into the room.

A frazzled blonde paced the length of the small metal bed. She stopped and looked up. "Who are you?"

"Dr. Kendall." Mia offered her hand.

The woman snatched hold of Mia's hand like she'd been tossed a life preserver. "Why isn't it working?" She pointed at the little girl lying motionless in the tiny bed. "A new heart was supposed to make my baby well." Terror lined the woman's face.

Mia's knees weakened. She gripped the chart as if by some small chance it contained potential answers. If this child was a victim of the rejection problem, she didn't have a good explanation for this mother. "Mind if I examine her?"

The woman shook her head and stepped aside, allowing Mia a closer look at what was obviously a very sick child. The girl's below-the-growth-chart size, coupled with clubbed fingers sporting bone enlargements around each fingernail, told her that if she'd been the first to open this child's tiny chest, she probably would have been looking at a boot-shaped congenital defect present from birth.

"Tetrology of Fallot?"

"Yes," the mother whispered.

"Most Americans wouldn't be comfortable flying to a third-world country for medical treatment, let alone for an organ transplant. Why did you come here for a heart, Mrs. Taylor?"

The young mother didn't flinch. Instead, she straightened her back and cast an I-will-not-be-intimidated gaze directly at Mia. "You have kids, doctor?"

"No."

"Then you wouldn't understand what it's like to hold your newborn for the first time, counting her fingers and toes and thinking everything's fine, and then—" The mother paused, collecting herself. "One minute you're on top of the world. The next, a doctor swoops in and tells you that your baby will die if she doesn't have emergency heart surgery. What he didn't tell me was that one surgery wouldn't cure her. That reality took several operations to sink in."

"I'm sorry. I'm sure this has been trying."

The mother stroked her child's hand. "Not long ago, the doctors replaced the outflow patch on the outflow tract of her right ventricle.

It held for a bit, but then it leaked, causing her right ventricle to become weak and..." She swallowed, like the word had gotten stuck in her throat.

"Fail." Mia quietly finished the sentence, ashamed that she'd allowed the physical demands of day-to-day medicine to harden her to people's mental suffering. The realization rocked her to the core.

"Yes."

She'd been wrong to make assumptions without getting all the facts. This child might not have survived the American UNOS wait-list. Taking that chance was a risk she wouldn't have taken either if this golden-haired cherub had been hers. "Mrs. Taylor, I'm sorry if I sounded judgmental. I need you to tell me everything you know about the transplant."

"Not much." The starchiness left Mrs. Taylor's shoulders. "All I know is that after the guy arrived with Kelsey's heart, the actual transplant only took about four hours." Her gaze locked with Mia's, and Mia prayed she wouldn't have to defend Race or his delivery service. Instead Mrs. Taylor asked, "Doctor, where did that man get my daughter's heart?"

"Honestly, I don't know." Mia's chest tightened at the question. Sooner or later this self-condemning query surfaced in nearly every transplant recipient or their guardians. Back home, she had a staff of trained counselors to help families deal with the guilt of taking a healthy organ to replace a failing one. Back home she could say with confidence that heart had not been stolen. Here she was on her own. "Mrs. Taylor, do you have anyone with you?"

"No."

"Well, while I have Kelsey in surgery, why don't you spend the time calling your family? It'll take your mind off what's happening here."

"I doubt it."

Mia considered the woman's flat-line reply. So many times she'd seen the burden of caring for critically ill children destroy marriages and families. What had this mother gone through and given up to get here? From the exhausted look of her, she hadn't had her own life in years. "It'll be best if you stay in the hospital. Be available in case we need you."

A haunting sadness flashed across the mother's face. "I have nowhere else to go." She caught Mia's arm. "I have no one else." Eyes moist, pleading for understanding, she went on, "I've read that transplant patients have better odds of surviving and a lower risk of rejection, if they get organs from donors of the same sex. Did my little girl get a boy's heart?"

"I'm sorry, but I don't know."

The helpless churning Mia felt when that young cheerleader had died on her operating table in Baltimore returned to her stomach with a vengeance. She gritted her teeth to keep from doubling over. What could she say to make this woman, who'd obviously educated herself on every aspect of her daughter's condition, feel better? Kids with these life-threatening abnormalities could die in the best of circumstances. Deciding to have a transplant in a third-world hospital had not stacked the odds in this child's favor. Especially if the cause of Kelsey's heart rejection and kidney failure was somehow linked to the mysterious demise of Mia's patients.

Mia stalled, struggling for a way to reassure this frightened mother that the risks didn't apply to her baby.

She forced a smile, hoping to bring the woman a modicum of peace. "Men generally have bigger hearts, while women have greater pumping capacity. Some research even suggests that hormones come into play, but the truth is, necessity dictates that we take the first matching organ that's available."

"So you really don't know anything about the heart she got?"

Mia shook her head, careful to mask her mounting fears. What good would it do to let this mother know her concerns about the origin of the African organs being transplanted? Right now, nothing.

Mrs. Taylor squeezed Mia's arm tighter. "Dr. Kendall, don't let my baby die."

"I'll do everything I can. I promise." She gently pried herself free of the woman's iron grip and quickly exited the room.

Safely out of Mrs. Taylor's sight, Mia collapsed against the hallway wall, her legs as rubbery as the IV tubing running from Kelsey's bag of meds to her tiny body. She'd concluded that the issue with the anti-rejection drug was limited to her hospital, but what if she was wrong?

Changing Mbui's medicine to Tryoxylate she'd obtained from the pharmacy of Kaboni Private hadn't helped him. So how was she going to keep this child alive when she couldn't be sure what was killing her?

CHAPTER THIRTY

SUNDAY, DECEMBER 15TH, 6:52 AM EST

BALTIMORE, MARYLAND

Sunlight peeked through the thick branches of the forest, compelling Axton forward. He'd barely escaped Dryden's sword and now that the tyrant knew he'd refused to leave, Dryden's last words had promised him that death would be his only escape. Axton's only consolation was that he'd left a deep gash across Dryden's forearm, but he knew that the mere flesh wound wasn't enough to stop his foe—nor the promised release of the virus.

Axton's chest heaved as it filled with air, the effort bringing with it a stab of pain to his ribcage where Dryden's sword had sliced through the rough fibers of his coat and pierced his side. Lungs burning, he stopped to catch his breath in the cover of a grove of trees. His tongue stuck to the roof of his mouth. His belly stirred with hunger. He'd been on the move for hours, but the detour into the forbidden magic guarri copse had been his only choice. Malkkin and Lorn would meet him at midday on the far side of the island to plot the rescue of the hundreds of vulnerable inhabitants who counted on him to rid their world of Dryden's evil.

Drawing in another deep breath, Axton started running again. A ray of light pierced through the thick treetops. Voices surrounded him. . .but from where? He searched the trees for movement until a familiar figure appeared above him.

"Paige?"

"Harry." Someone poked his shoulder. "Harry, are you awake?"

Harry opened his eyes then squinted as the bright light breaking through the trees rushed toward him. He gasped for air.

"Breathe slowly, Harry. You've been in an accident."

The blurred figures morphed into a beauty wearing jeans and a purple sweater. He blinked. Valerie?

"Harry, can you hear me?"

"Yes, I. . ." Why was his throat so dry and his lips so chapped? "Water, please. I need water."

Valerie pressed a straw to his lips. "Don't talk."

"Where am I?"

"You were in an accident. I've been so worried."

He searched his memory, but found nothing beyond the dark forest of Blackwell Isle. "I don't understand."

Her hand grasped his. "Your car flipped on the interstate. It's a miracle you're even alive."

"No." He closed his eyes and tried to pull himself back into the dream where he was once again Axton, and he could control his own destiny. Axton would find the vials, destroy Dryden, and save Paige and her people. Here, he was nothing more than a coward.

He wiggled his fingers and toes then strained to sit up. Pain shoved him against the bed.

"You've got a broken nose from the airbag and you're a bit beat up." Valerie answered his unspoken question then applied a coat of lip gloss. "The doctor decided to keep you overnight for observation."

Bert's unannounced visit to the lab had caused Harry to question any interest he had in his fiery redheaded lab assistant, but not enough to dismiss his misplaced feelings. If only playing the role of hero didn't involve high-speed chases in real life.

"Do you want me to call someone and let them know where you are?" Valerie asked.

He frowned. Besides Billings, who was probably in a rage because Harry wasn't working over the weekend, he didn't even have a pet goldfish that needed him. "There isn't anyone."

She plopped down beside him, shaking the bed and jarring every aching muscle in his bruised body. "Everyone has somebody."

Not everyone. He glanced up and caught her gaze. "Why are you here?"

"The lab received a phone call that you'd been in an accident and the switchboard called me."

A cell phone rang. "And you simply dropped everything and came?"

"Of course I came. I wanted to make sure you were all right." Valerie picked up his phone. "It's yours. Do you mind if I answer it?"

He shook his head then lay back with his eyes closed, wondering who in the world might miss him on a Sunday morning.

"Harry." Valerie covered the phone and turned back to him. "You need to take this call."

"Why?"

"It's a doctor who has questions about Tryoxylate."

"At seven o'clock on a Sunday morning?" He didn't have to look far for an excuse. His head pounded, his wrist and side ached, and he still wasn't thinking straight. "I don't think I can."

Valerie thrust the phone into his hands, her attitude leaving no room for negotiation.

He cleared his throat and shakily brought the phone to his ear. "Hello?"

"Dr. Spence. Thank you so much for taking my call. I've been trying to reach you. My name is Mia Kendall. I'm a heart transplant surgeon working in Dar es Salaam. Africa."

His mind spun like a rusty wheel trying to keep up with the information she'd rattled off. Dar es Salaam. . .Indian Ocean. . .Tanzania. . .wild jungles.

"Africa?"

"Yes. I understand you're recovering from an accident. I'm sorry my timing is bad, but I need to ask you a couple very important questions."

Harry worked to control the vertigo thrusting his once safe world toward destruction. If someone from the FDA found out that two vials were missing, his entire career could be over. "No, it's fine. I'm just a bit groggy."

"I understand that you're the lead cardiovascular researcher who helped refine the anti-rejection drug, Tryoxylate."

His stomach lurched. "No, I was actually hired by the company a year and a half after Tryoxylate was put on the market. I'm currently working on a second-generation version." Harry's heart pounded. He hated conflict, and he hoped that his telling more than he should have didn't get back to his boss. "Is there a problem?"

"Potentially. I'm calling because there's been a spike in the number of deaths in my transplant patients and one of the possible connections is the Tryoxylate. I need to narrow down the possible source of rejection, which is why I'm calling you. I understand that the FDA is looking into a number of cases where patient deaths have been rumored to be linked to the drug."

"Yes, though I believe that is common knowledge."

"Do you know when the drug was approved in Africa?"

Harry groaned, wishing the room didn't feel as if it were spinning. "I. . .I would assume approval was granted shortly after the FDA put their stamp on it."

"Do you know of any differences in the batches?"

"I'm sorry, but I really can't help you, Dr. Kendall. I'm a researcher. That's it—"

"But if I could find out when BPH Technologies shipped this last batch of Tryoxylate to my hospital and possibly Kaboni Private, then I would know if the arrival of that particular drug correlates with the spike in rejections."

"Like I said, I can't help you."

"Wait. Don't hang up, Dr. Spence." She sounded a little desperate. "Do you have any further information on the specifics of these unexplained death accusations against Tryoxylate?"

"No." Harry picked up his glasses from the bedside table, wondering if this woman was an FDA spy out to frame him, then remembered his broken nose. He clutched his glasses. Doctor or FDA plant? Either way, she wouldn't get anything out of him that would let her tack his hide to the wall for letting those vials out of his sight. "As I'm sure you know, all drugs have side effects, but I don't have any input into the FDA parameters of mandated drug removal from the market. Nor do I have any connection to the regulation of drugs in Africa." There. An elusive answer Axton Blade would have been proud of.

The line crackled. "And this new drug you're working on. What can you tell me about its testing patterns?"

"Nothing. ZAR242 hasn't been approved for human testing and won't be for several months."

There was a pause on the line. "If I send you the records on my rejection cases, would you at least look at them?"

"I'm a busy man, but. . ." Harry glanced at Valerie, the flicker of expectation on her face spurring him on. Giving this doctor's files a cursory glance might give him a clue as to who this woman really was. "Email me everything you've got, including patient histories and drug regimens. I'll see what I can do."

He hung up after giving her his email address, wondering if he'd just cooked his own goose.

"What did she want?"

"Information. She claims there's been a marked increase of rejection in her patients using Tryoxylate."

"You think she's onto something, don't you?"

Harry pulled the white sheet further up over his hospital gown and added medical facilities to his list of phobias. "The rejections her patients are experiencing could be caused by a number of reasons. Anything from tainted organs to unsanitary surgical process, to—"

"BPH hired you to save the company, Harry."

He squeezed his eyes shut.

"We both know about the deaths linked to the Tryoxylate and what will happen if the FDA pulls the drug," Valerie continued. "The BPH suits need you to develop a new, super-selling version that will save them financially, which must mean that someone at the top believes there's truth behind the accusations."

"No." He refused to believe he'd been hired to assist in a cover-up.

"BPH would never condone human trial testing in a third-world country."

Valerie tugged at a strand of her hair, surveying the room like his monitors were outfitted with hidden cameras. She leaned in close—close enough that the scent of gardenias sent Harry's heart racing. "We both know the possibility that BPH's involvement in questionable practices is real."

"*I* don't know that." Harry gritted his teeth. All he'd ever wanted was his own lab and maybe a shot at the Nobel Prize. He'd devoted his life to helping others, not to being exploited by someone else's quest for financial gain.

"I found your notes."

"You what?"

"It was an accident. Honest," Valerie rushed on. "I was looking for a file you wanted and found what you've been gathering on Hastings and Billings."

"You had no right. . ." Harry's defenses dropped. Realizing he'd spent the last fourteen months working to protect a company that might be pushing a potentially fatal drug knotted his belly.

Valerie grasped his hand. "I read about how when Tryoxylate was evaluated, the FDA originally rejected the drug because of possible life-threatening side effects, but when Hastings complained, the veteran medical officer originally assigned to the case was removed from the review."

"All of that is rumor. Unsubstantiated rumors."

She pressed in so close he could have kissed her, if he'd had the guts. "And how eight months later, Tryoxylate was approved. Months ahead of time."

Harry pressed his lips together. Valerie's astute conclusion gave weight to something he had convinced himself was nothing more than a vague and faulty theory. "If I can produce a super-anti-rejection drug without side effects, I'll be saving lives."

"Yes, but maybe it's time you found out what's taking lives." Valerie's persistence could wear out a man as determined as Axton Blade. "BPH has been cutting corners, and they're willing to do whatever it takes to guarantee a payoff—even at the price of human life."

"What do you want me to do?"

"You could go to Africa yourself and see what's going on."

"Africa?" Visions of cannibals and poachers and voodoo dolls sent a chill through his body. He was far better off staying in his lab and working his formula in an environment he could control. At least to some degree. "I'm not flying halfway around the world on some ridiculous quest to prove something I don't even think is true."

"I'll tell you what's true." Valerie snapped her fingers. "The FDA is about to pull Tryoxylate. People are dying. Vials of your new super drug are missing. You told me once that you did this work because you wanted to save lives and to make this world a better place."

Acid rose in his throat. "If I go to Africa to prove there's something wrong, they'll ruin me."

"Which is why no one has spoken up so far. I'm an underpaid lab assistant, meaning no one who could do anything about this will listen to me. But people will listen to you, Dr. Harry Spence. You're one of the best researchers in the business." When he didn't respond, Valerie dropped his cell phone onto the bedside table. She grabbed her coat from the end of the bed, her face etched with disappointment. "You know, after dating dozens of men like Bert the Jerk, I thought you were different."

"Me?" Harry squirmed at the tidbit. "Different."

"Different. In spite of your long list of quirks and phobias, I've always thought you were a good man." Valerie stuffed her arms into the sleeves of her coat. "I've worked with plenty of people, and most of them are looking at the profits, but you are looking at the people who are going to benefit from your super-drug. Real people like your mother."

Anger seared through his chest. He never should have told her about his mother. Dorothy Spence had died due to severe left-ventricular dysfunction after a heart transplant at the age of thirty-two, three days after his fifth birthday.

Valerie's voice ripped him back to the present. "You know, the funny thing is that if you'd have asked me out, I would have said yes. Maybe it's time you took a chance, Harry."

"Valerie." He reached for her, but she was already out the door.

His jaw tensed. If going to Africa to search for the truth was what she wanted, then she could go. Nothing he did would make him worth something in Valerie's eyes. Because unlike Axton, even exposing the truth didn't guarantee he'd win the girl. At least not in his world.

CHAPTER THIRTY-ONE

SUNDAY, DECEMBER 15TH, 5:23 PM

KABONI PRIVATE HOSPITAL

Catherine stared at her cell phone, debating whether or not she was ready to hear Brad say I told you so. Jerk or not, he had a right to know that his daughter was in the process of rejecting the foreign heart. After the biopsy, the American doctor immediately ordered massive doses of IV steroids and offered several hopeful reassurances. But Dr. Kendall's upbeat pep talk hadn't fooled either one of them. They both knew Kelsey wouldn't last long without another heart.

When the doctor suggested they pray for God's provision, she'd balked at first. How could she ask God for a second heart when there were others, as sick as Kelsey, waiting for their first? She knew the doctor had made the suggestion in good faith, but to her it smacked of greed at its worst. But she'd give her own heart if it meant Kelsey could live. So even though expecting another heart was more than she deserved, she didn't care. Because if she ever had to come to grips with the fact that she'd gambled everything on this long shot and lost, she'd have to start dealing with the reality of losing Kelsey.

Catherine jammed the phone into her pocket. Who was she

kidding? That kind of courage would have to come from a higher power.

She leaned over Kelsey's bed rails and straightened the shimmery pink gown Jonathan had insisted she bring. Careful to avoid Kelsey's red and swollen scar, she lightly traced the smiling lips on the Barbie logo covering her daughter's laboring torso.

At her touch, Kelsey's eyelids fluttered. Catherine waited, longing to hear Kelsey say Momma one more time. But the exhausted child had only enough energy to fuss briefly at the pain and pull at the tube in her arm. Catherine grasped her daughter's clumsy fingers. Kelsey's tiny hand was even hotter than it had been an hour ago.

Catherine swiped a tear and worked to bring calm to her voice. "It's all right, punkin." She eased herself into the bed and snuggled next to her child's feverish body. "Momma's here."

Kelsey moaned but then quickly settled into a fitful sleep against Catherine's breast. The dismal walls seemed to be closing in on Catherine's dreams of raising her child. She buried her nose in Kelsey's curls and wept until she drifted off to sleep.

Sometime later, a hand touched her shoulder. "Mrs. Taylor?"

Memory could give her back nothing as she searched her dream for the source of the soothing voice. She opened her gritty eyes, not sure how long she'd been asleep. "Dr. Kendall?" Catherine slid her arm out from under Kelsey and pushed herself up in the bed. "Have you found my baby another heart?"

"Not yet."

A flash of mottled color behind the doctor drew Catherine's attention. "Who's that?"

The doctor motioned forward a young black woman toting a ghostly white child on her hip. "This is Jeme." She guided the cautious pair closer to the bed. "And this little cutie is her daughter, Zaina." Dr. Kendall stroked the tiny fist that clenched some kind of trinket hanging from a beaded cord around the mother's sinewy neck.

Catherine drew herself erect and aimed a rigid gaze at the doctor so that her fellow American would not miss her meaning. "We're not up to company."

Dr. Kendall's brow raised, but she made no effort to clear these unwanted spectators from the room. "Jeme's husband is a transplant recipient." She came around the bed, leaving the unnerving natives uncomfortably close. "He's also rejecting." She lifted the stethoscope from around her neck and plugged the earpieces into her ears. "I wanted to check Kelsey and hated to leave Jeme alone." She indicated she wanted to listen to Kelsey's chest. "May I?"

The doctor's staccato reply brought on a mixture of shame and empathy that knocked the sharp angles of haughtiness from Catherine's shoulders. She searched Jeme's flawless ebony face for any indication of a similar prejudice. If the woman's emotions had been stirred against her, she had not allowed them to register. Catherine eyed the pale baby, curious about why this very black woman had given birth to this very white child.

"Does Jeme speak English?" Catherine asked the doctor.

Jeme's chin raised, her eyes taking on the glow of pride. "I do." She released Zaina's hand from the charm and shifted her to the hip closest to Catherine. "My mother cooked for an American family. I attended the missionary school until I was eight."

So, this woman had the advantage. A tiny insight into her world, while she had little to no knowledge of hers. "I'm sorry about your husband." Pangs of missing Brad cut Catherine to the quick. "Caring for someone who is very sick is never easy."

Understanding lit Jeme's onyx eyes. Zaina smiled and suddenly lunged for Catherine. Catherine's hands instinctively shot out to catch the child trying to wiggle free of her mother. Jeme reeled Zaina back in. Catherine felt every fiber of her being gravitating toward those tiny outstretched arms and the snaggle-toothed smile that dimpled those surprisingly chubby cheeks.

"Can I hold her?"

Jeme's eyes darted between Catherine and the doctor.

The doctor nodded her approval. Without a word the African mother released her child in a trusting way that unlatched Catherine's heart. She gathered Zaina into her arms and impulsively kissed her cheek. Zaina giggled and Catherine wrapped her hands around the tiny waist and held the child at arm's length for a better look.

"She's adorable." Catherine laughed as Zaina planted her bare little feet against her thighs and pushed herself erect, a show of strength Kelsey had never managed. "And strong."

Jeme smiled. "Very."

But Catherine noticed that, like any mother would when someone unknown handled their child, she made an almost imperceptible move closer. Although she seemed content to allow Catherine this pleasure, Jeme's hands remained open and ready to snatch back her most valuable treasure, should the need arise.

Such animation. So much energy. Catherine clung to Zaina's tiny hands. "How old is she?"

"Almost a year." Jeme peered around Catherine and pointed at Kelsey. "And your child?"

The kindness with which this soft-spoken woman gazed upon Kelsey touched Catherine, tugging at every one of her mothering instincts. "Kelsey's five."

"She is very beautiful."

Catherine smiled. "Like your daughter."

Zaina's fingers gripped Catherine's thumbs, the vitality to her giggle-induced bounce a painful contrast to Kelsey's difficult breathing. Up and down Zaina propelled her body, until she finally tired and plopped down on Catherine's lap, her huge smile indicating pride at her performance. Catherine released her hold and clapped, wishing Kelsey was awake to enjoy this real-life baby doll and precious distraction. Zaina twisted in Catherine's lap, snatched Kelsey's blanket, and rubbed it against her face.

"Zaina, no," Jeme scolded.

"It's all right." Catherine gently removed the blanket from Zaina's tight little fist, tucked it beside Kelsey, then returned her attention to Zaina. "Her eyes are so blue."

Jeme's features sobered. She plucked Zaina from Catherine's lap and backed away from the bed. The baby fussed to be returned. Jeme held her tight, refusing to give in to her squirming.

What cultural faux pas had she just committed? Had her question evoked prejudices she didn't understand? "Did I say something wrong?"

"Zaina is albino." Dr. Kendall rushed around the bed like she was the cavalry. "Your admiration of Zaina's unique features makes Jeme a little jumpy."

"I'm not sure I understand."

"Right now, things in this country are unsafe for albinos."

"Why?"

Jeme receded against the wall. "Some say albinos are cursed."

The doctor put her arm around Jeme and eased her forward. "God does not curse children. He has a plan for this child, just as I'm certain He has a plan for yours, Mrs. Taylor."

Catherine's eyes darted between Zaina and Kelsey. So different. Yet the same. Each child born to hardships they didn't ask for or deserve. How unfair was that? Could a loving God really be so cruel? Her gaze met Jeme's. "I'm so sorry. I didn't know."

Understanding, stronger than before, passed between them. They were mothers backed into a corner. Their troubles different. Their sentences the same. Neither had been offered a way out.

Dr. Kendall looped her stethoscope around her neck. She picked up Kelsey's chart and started scribbling. "Do you have a phone you can use here, Mrs. Taylor?"

"Yes."

"Kelsey's rejection seems to be progressing."

Catherine swallowed. "I can see that."

"I've left a message for Dr. Amandi to contact me the moment he returns, but I'm going to give you my cell number too. I'm a pediatric specialist and I want to help, however I can."

They exchanged numbers. Dr. Kendall closed the chart as if she'd done all she could then herded Jeme and Zaina toward the door.

"Wait." Catherine stood and grabbed Kelsey's pink blanket. "Here, Jeme. Take this."

Jeme looked at the blanket and then at Kelsey. She shook her head. "We cannot."

"It's all right. We have others. I never go anywhere without a couple of spares." Ashamed about how excessive that explanation must have sounded, she handed Zaina the blanket. The baby immediately buried her face in the soft fabric. Catherine couldn't help laughing. "That's exactly how Kelsey does it."

Jeme reached behind her neck and undid her necklace with one hand. She held it out to Catherine, the dangling charm beautiful in the late afternoon light. "For Kelsey."

Tears stung Catherine's eyes. She held out her hand, humbled by the gift.

Jeme dropped the beaded necklace into Catherine's palm then folded Catherine's hand shut as if forever sealing their kindred suffering. "To protect Kelsey in this life and in the next." She turned and silently left the room.

Catherine stood rooted to the floor, unable to move, as two absolute strangers walked off with a part of her heart. The door closed. The antiquated ceiling fan whirled above, moving the sticky air she could not breathe. She opened her hand then gently slid the necklace over Kelsey's head. She watched the charm rise and fall with each of Kelsey's gasping breaths, knowing only one more thing remained to be done—call Brad.

CHAPTER THIRTY-TWO

SUNDAY, DECEMBER 15TH, 10:01 AM EST

DOWNTOWN BALTIMORE

Maybe it's time you took a chance, Harry Spence.

Harry lifted his good arm and hung his jacket on the coatrack. Every muscle in his body still aching, he shuffled to the kitchen of his downtown apartment. Of all the ridiculous ideas, Africa had to be Valerie's most nerve-racking yet. Like he would actually fly across the ocean on some wild goose chase. Surely Valerie knew him well enough to know that traveling halfway around the world to some godforsaken continent full of malaria-carrying mosquitoes and wild animals was something he'd never consider. Ever.

Take a chance, Harry Spence.

He dumped the stack of papers from Dr. Kendall onto the kitchen bar and groaned at the grating sound of Valerie's broken recording playing in his head. Axton Blade was a man who took chances. He, on the other hand, had stayed inside most of his growing-up life because he had asthma, which was why he still feared dust, animals, and nature in general.

He swallowed the pain tablets the doctor had prescribed with a swig of water from a bottle in the fridge then opened the pantry. A conglomerate of canned soups, gluten-free snack bars, and Cheetos stared back at him. He slammed the door shut and glanced at the file. The information the doctor had sent was inconclusive, but it was enough to convince him that her spiked increase of rejections was somehow related to the Tryoxylate. And there was definitely something in a trip to Africa for him. If he could determine the cause of rejection in this drug, it might help him finally solve the problem in his calculations for ZAR242.

The doorbell rang. Harry froze. He'd mulled over one scenario all morning. If Billings thought Harry was going to expose him, it wouldn't take much for the weasel to plant evidence that would have the FBI pounding down Harry's door. All Billings would have to do was accuse him of stealing key ingredients in the experiment and paint him as some dirty information pirate selling patented technologies overseas.

The doorbell rang again.

"Harry?"

Valerie. He blew out a sigh of relief.

A second later, he opened the door and Valerie bustled into the entryway loaded with two large takeout boxes. "I've been feeling guilty all morning about what I said to you at the hospital, so I decided to bring a peace offering."

Harry's stomach growled as he eyed the offering. Anything beat canned soup. "Smells like pizza."

"Even better. Two gluten-free pizzas." Valerie slid the boxes onto the bar. "Grilled chicken, bacon, and soy-based mozzarella cheese for you, and sun-dried tomatoes and artichokes for me."

Harry bit his lip. He couldn't remember the last time a woman had been in his apartment. "You really didn't have to."

Valerie spun to face him. "I shucked out forty bucks for these pizzas and subway fare to get here, and all you have to say is *you really didn't have to*?"

"Well, I. . .you didn't. . ." Any snippets of intelligent conversation evaporated into the black hole of his social skills.

"Of course I didn't have to." Her fists pressed against her hips.

"You know, you really can be exasperating. What I said at the hospital might not have been the nicest thing, but it was true."

"I'm sorry."

"Forget it. Do you want to eat?" Valerie lifted up the lid of the first box, filling the apartment with the aroma of grilled meat, tomato sauce, and melted cheese. Maybe he was hungry after all.

"Yeah."

She began opening cabinets, pulling out plates and glasses, and looking completely at home in his kitchen.

His kitchen? He'd never found the nerve to ask her out for dinner let alone up to his apartment.

He cleared his throat. "Can I help?"

"You're the patient. Go sit on the couch."

He complied and a minute later she appeared, balancing two plates of pizza and a couple cold sodas. "I've always pictured you living in a one-room bachelor flat strewn with empty takeout boxes and Cheetos bags. But this—while simple—this isn't bad." She set the food on the coffee table in front of him then moved to the window that overlooked the view of the city, costing him an extra couple hundred dollars a month.

He tried to see the room through her eyes. A mix of traditional and modern furniture including a roll-top desk and a 55-inch flat-screen TV. On the walls, a few pieces of art he'd found at a garage sale, though he'd never tell her that. Then there was yesterday's half-empty coffee mug, and a stack of unread newspapers. Too much brown. Too little color.

She moved to his desk and the printed manuscript sitting on top. "What's this?"

He choked on his first bite of pizza. "Nothing. I—"

She'd picked up the top page and started reading before he had time to move. *"In the next moment, Axton was lost in the sweetness of Paige's kiss. Every fear that had tried to overcome him the last few weeks disappeared into the breeze. He brushed back a strand of her red hair—"*

Harry leapt from the couch and grabbed the page from her hand, wincing from the sudden movement. He dropped the wrinkled paper onto the printed stack and shoved the whole thing into the top drawer of his desk.

Her eyes widened, obviously amused. "Axton, Paige. . .you're writing a novel, aren't you?"

"It's nothing." Maybe if the day ever came when a publisher took him seriously and published the story, he might consider giving her an autographed copy, but until then, he planned to keep his pastime a secret. Along with the fact that Paige's red hair was no coincidence.

He moved away from her and sat, his adrenaline waning. "What are you doing here, Valerie?"

She stared out the window, arms folded across her chest, jaw tense. "Like I told you. I left in a huff and wanted to say I'm sorry. Besides, the idea of you going to Africa *is* crazy."

Harry's resolve to run wavered. He'd never win the girl this way. Lack of respect and confidence would only get him pity, not admiration. "The idea of me going to Africa is not so preposterous."

She let out an exasperated *humph*. "You want me to list your phobias? I could start with snakes, malaria, and—"

"People are dying, Valerie, and I think I might be able to help."

Her arms dropped to her sides and her mouth fell open. For a full ten seconds, she actually had nothing to say. A rather pleasant state in which he'd never seen Valerie before. "You're actually thinking about going?"

"Maybe."

He was nothing more than a science geek who spent his free time writing a novel about a hero who saves the world. But if Mia Kendall was right, and any version of Tryoxylate was causing people to die, he wasn't involved in something that was saving lives.

"Valerie, sit down."

She hesitated then sank onto the leather sofa across from him.

He pointed to his broken nose. "This wasn't an accident."

"What are you talking about?"

"I don't know what's going on, but I think someone wants me out of the way."

Valerie's eyes widened. "Which means. . ."

"I have to go to Africa." He didn't miss the fear in her baby blues. "They know I'm onto them."

Valerie's eyes narrowed. "Two hours ago you told me you'd never leave on some ridiculous quest to prove something you didn't think was true."

"That doesn't matter. You were right. It's time I took a chance."

He shoved aside the stack of notes on his desk and logged onto the Internet. Three minutes later, he'd found what he was looking for. "There's a flight leaving at two thirty today and arriving tomorrow in Dar es Salaam."

"You're serious about this, aren't you?"

Harry turned to her, breathing in the familiar scent of gardenias. He sneezed. "Completely."

She reached up and brushed a strand of hair from his eyes. "Do it, Harry Spence."

Before he had a chance to consider the consequences of trying to save the world—and winning the girl— Harry clicked his mouse and booked the flight.

CHAPTER THIRTY-THREE

SUNDAY, DECEMBER 15TH, 7:19 PM

DAR ES SALAAM

The rhythmic slap of the jeep's windshield wipers was no match for the rain slowing Mia's progress as she left the hospital and headed back to her apartment. She gripped the wheel and listened to Zaina cooing in Jeme's lap beside her. She'd never get used to seeing kids out of car seats, but it wasn't as if she could just run to Babies R Us and pick one up. In this culture, no one here thought twice about piling people in cars, seat belts or not.

Mia shifted her thoughts back to Mbui and Kelsey and tried to settle her fears at the same time. Tracking down the answers for them was where she should focus her attention. That was the only way to steer clear of the possibility she might fail again.

She'd tried everything she knew to do for her dying patients, yet her efforts had been totally ineffective. On top of that, she'd yet to hear from Amandi with any help on her rejection rate. She swerved around a pothole then forced her jeep back into the ruts. If this cardiovascular researcher that Race dug up on the Internet wouldn't cough up the proof she needed to convince Amandi that Tryoxylate might be killing his young patient too, she'd have to call someone who could.

Her father.

Dread seeped into Mia's heart. Contacting him to ask for help with another blot on her record was the last thing she wanted to do. But her father had connections. Important ones. Getting a drug that could potentially be worth millions pulled off the FDA's test list would require the help of every one of his high-ranking influencers. Even though she'd abandoned their lucrative practice, her father wouldn't deny that their Hippocratic Oath demanded they do everything within their power to save lives.

The sucking sound of Zaina pulling free of Jeme's breast drew Mia's attention from the road. Milk dribbled from the corner of Zaina's puckered lips. Only a few minutes earlier, she'd been howling at the top of her lungs. Now she slept contentedly.

"Will that woman's child live?" Jeme dabbed at Zaina's face with a corner of the blanket. "There must be another medicine you can give her."

"I am. Just like I did for Mbui."

But like Mbui, Mia was afraid it might already be too late. Kelsey's condition had begun deteriorating before she arrived in Africa. And even if she hadn't been given a tainted drug, the odds of her tiny body rejecting a heart were still higher than normal.

Mia yanked her gaze back to the road and turned onto the paved street. She knew what the frightened woman was really asking. Would *her* husband live? While Kelsey's rapid deterioration could simply be the result of procuring an organ too late, her symptoms were nearly identical to Mbui's. And the common denominator was both had been on Tryoxylate.

Even a poorly educated layman could see that a bad prognosis for one most likely meant a similar outcome for the other. Until she could get her father on the phone, erring on the side of caution had demanded that she take Mbui off Tryoxylate. She just wasn't sure what Amandi would say when he found out she'd done the same thing for Kelsey.

"I'm doing everything in my power to save them." Mia glanced at Zaina. "We can't let our new friends down, can we?"

"What are you going to do?"

She didn't have an answer to Jeme's question. But she wouldn't quit and leave the futures of two children hanging in the balance. Not this time.

"I don't know. I think something may be wrong with the medicine."

The panic on Jeme's face was the very reason she'd been reluctant to say this out loud. But the rapidity of the onset of acute rejection in each patient coupled with the damaging reports about the drug Race had found on the Internet made her sure of it. But if Mbui and Kelsey's rejections were both caused by Tryoxylate, why had she started losing patients long before Amandi? Had both hospitals received a bad batch, but she'd been first to use it?

Without lot numbers to compare, she couldn't take an unsubstantiated theory to the government officials and expect to have Tryoxylate officially pulled. Amandi would never voluntarily pull this supposed miracle drug on the say-so of a doctor he'd practically accused of being incompetent. To protect his treatment regime, he might not even give her the lot numbers to compare. Saddest of all, without a definitive explanation as to why Mbui and Kelsey were rejecting, she had no way to facilitate their recovery.

There had to be a way to find out what was really going on.

Mia slammed on the brakes to avoid a goat that had wandered into traffic. Realization screeched through her brain. It would take more than one bad batch of Tryoxylate for the FDA to threaten to pull it. If Amandi was as up-to-date on the latest in transplants as he claimed, he had to have heard about the recent accusations against Tryoxylate. So why risk giving it to Kelsey?

Her mind searched for another explanation.

What if the files Race had trafficked into her possession had been sterilized as he'd suggested? Cleaned up so the truth would be harder to track down? Amandi had tried to pass off her ejection from the hospital as nothing more than the actions of a distraught secretary. He'd seemed evasive. Insisting he'd take care of it, as if he didn't want her involved. As if he was hiding something.

Bad drugs. Sketchy organ procurement. . .She hadn't wanted to make accusations, but there was only one person who could pull this off.

Amandi.

If she could just get inside Kaboni Private's lab, maybe she could dig up the answers that would save Mbui and Kelsey. That was it. She had to get inside that lab.

And she knew just the guy to help her do it.

"Hang on, Jeme." Mia stepped on the gas. "We'll pick up something to eat, then I'll take you back to my apartment. I've got to make a couple phone calls."

Thirty minutes later, Mia had Zaina tucked in for the night on her pallet and Jeme settled in front of a plate of *nyama choma*. The smell of grilled meat and pepper sauce filled the entire apartment. Mia's stomach growled, but she was too anxious to eat.

She needed proof and the cunning of Race Daniels to get it. Now all she had to do was convince him. She kicked off her sandals and grabbed her phone.

He answered on the third ring. "Missing me already?"

"Funny." Mia picked up one of her tennis shoes. "I need your help."

"You know, you're running up a pretty steep tab."

Mia crammed her foot into the shoe, preparing for action. "I think it's time we tested your theory. How much do you charge to break into a secure research lab?"

CHAPTER THIRTY-FOUR

SUNDAY, DECEMBER 15TH, 8:04 PM

DAR ES SALAAM

"You've got to be kidding." Race spewed a mouthful of Coke across the steering wheel of his 4X4 then swerved to miss a pothole, almost dropping his cell phone. He should have known the moment he caught Mia Kendall sneaking out of the hospital that the good doctor was going to be nothing but trouble. Maybe the situation she'd stumbled onto wasn't her fault, but how had she managed to talk him into stealing patient files and tracking down a purportedly tainted drug? He wasn't sure this was a game he wanted to be involved in any longer. Especially if it included the criminal offense of breaking and entering Amandi's lab.

"I'm dead serious." She obviously wasn't finished pleading her case. "You've got connections at the private hospital, and I need to know what's going on in that lab. If Amandi's doing something illegal, I need proof, and there's got to be a paper trail somewhere."

Race maneuvered his way onto the side of the tar road, grabbed a wad of toilet paper from the glove compartment, and sopped up the sticky drink. "It's going to take a lot to pay off this kind of tab."

"You got me the files the last time without breaking a sweat," she countered.

He was going to end up getting arrested by the end of the day if she got her way. "I had connections with someone who had a few extra photocopies of patient files lying around, which isn't the same as breaking into a secured lab."

"If I can get my hands on some positive proof for what's causing the discrepancies between the two hospitals, then I can call my dad and—"

"What in the world does your dad have to do with all of this?" His brow furrowed. Mia didn't seem the type to run home to Daddy when things got tough.

"He's a. . .let's just say he's got a lot of influence in the world of medicine and transplants."

"A lot of influence. Great. And your daddy's influence is supposed to be my motivation to shrug aside the last remaining shreds of my ethics?"

"What happened to the brave guy who vowed to help me find out why my patients are dying?"

An image of Rachel surrounded by a classroom full of children flashed before him, drowning out some of his irritation. Being vulnerable wasn't a feeling he was used to, yet it had haunted him the past twenty-four hours.

"I thought you were with me on this," she continued.

"I was. . .I am. But I agreed to keep my ears open for information, not to break into Amandi's lab. I think it's time we go to the authorities."

"With what?" Impatience rose in her voice. "We still don't have anything solid. That's why I need to do this."

Race rubbed the two-day stubble on his chin. Surely there was another way to the truth. "I don't know if—"

"Race, I'm doing this with or without you. The files were telling, but not conclusive. Amandi's ignoring me again, and Harry Spence is a dead end, but people are dying, and I'm out of options. The hospital's lab is the next logical place to look."

Race weighed the logistical issues of getting into the lab. No one would question his presence at the hospital, but getting inside a secured area without getting caught was a whole other issue.

"Listen, I've got to go," she snapped. "Forget I asked."

"Mia, wait." He slammed his hand against the steering wheel then cut out onto the busy street. "Where are you?"

"At my apartment."

"I'll be there in ten minutes."

He made it in seven, still uncertain that the risk of getting caught was worth looking for something she wasn't even certain existed. Another twenty minutes put them in Kaboni Private's parking lot.

Mia grasped the door handle as he shut off the motor. "So what's your plan?"

He glanced at her, wishing she wasn't so doggone gorgeous. "Who said I had a plan?"

Her eyes widened. "You don't have a plan?"

He leaned over and opened the glove compartment, pulled out the two small flashlights he kept for emergencies, and shoved them into his back pocket. "It's not like you gave me a lot of time to come up with some daring heist."

From the look that crossed her face, she wasn't impressed with his flippant answer. "Don't you want to know if you're carrying illegally obtained organs or if it's the drug?"

"Of course." He combed his fingers through his hair. "It's just that if we get caught—"

"How hard can it be? It's not as if we're trying to steal the crown jewels. How much security do you think they'll actually have in place?"

"We should find out in about thirty seconds."

A security guard stopped them at the outside rear entrance. Race recognized his old friend, Innocent, and breathed out a quick sigh of relief. If anyone could get him in, it was this knobby-kneed elderly man.

Innocent's smile widened. "Mr. Daniels. You are here later than usual."

Race shook the uniformed guard's hand. "I'm hardly one to keep regular hours."

Innocent laughed, revealing a wide, white grin. "True."

"How are your kids, Innocent?"

"They are well."

"And little Precious?"

"You would never know she was sick, thanks to you."

Race cleared his throat. "Innocent, this is a friend of mine. Her name's Mia."

She shot Race a strange look then shook the guard's outstretched hand. "It's nice to meet you, Innocent."

"I hate to put you on the spot," Race continued, "but I've got a favor to ask."

"You know I would do anything for you, Mr. Daniels."

"I need to get into the lab."

"The lab?" Innocent's smile faded. "I am only allowed to open it in an emergency—"

"This is an emergency, Innocent." Mia took a step forward. "Medical business. Please."

"Medical business? I don't know. . ." Innocent looked to Race.

"You're going to have to trust me on this one," Race added. "It's very important. As important as it was when I helped Precious." Race hated calling in a favor he'd never expected to be repaid.

Innocent glanced at his watch. "I go off duty in twenty minutes, and if I do not hand over the keys to the night guard. . ."

"We'll be out in fifteen, I promise." Mia sounded a tad too eager in Race's estimation, but he let it pass.

Innocent hesitated a few seconds longer then slipped the key from his chain. "Fifteen minutes."

Race grasped the key in his palm and hurried into the hospital behind Mia. Shadows formed along the walls of the darkened hallway. The only light illuminating the passage was from the full moon and occasional spotlights filtering through the windows.

"I thought it prudent not to announce that Dr. Kendall was involved in this," he whispered.

"I suppose that's a good idea, but what about you?"

"Innocent will keep our secret."

"How many more guards are we going to run into?"

"None, if we're lucky." He took the corner then quickened his steps.

Race snapped off his flashlight and moved down the hall. He'd never taken compliments well. Paying Precious's remaining hospital bill seemed little compared to the great need he saw every day.

The lab lay twenty feet ahead. "You're not having second thoughts, are you?" Race whispered.

"No, but I can't help but think if we get caught, your friend will lose his job and our careers will be over."

"It's a little late for what-ifs now." Race flipped on his flashlight. "There's a little girl who needs her father and a mother who needs her little girl." He tossed her a flashlight then opened the door.

Stark white counters, a couple file cabinets, lab equipment, and computers that seemed fairly high-tech for a third-world country. In spite of Amandi's numerous bad habits, he'd done a lot of good for this hospital. "Where do we start?"

"Honestly, I'm not sure." She shrugged then headed for the nearest file cabinet. "I know the lab is set up to do a limited amount of testing for the hospital, but that's not what we're concerned about. If they're doing something illegal, there will still have to be some sort of paper trail in order to track the results. Look for anything that has to do with Tryoxylate's lot numbers, organ donors, or BPH Technologies."

"How about I start with the desk." Race slid into the padded chair, feeling completely out of his element. Winning a dogfight in the Persian Gulf seemed more likely than finding this needle in a haystack.

But there wasn't time to question his actions. A clock on the wall ticked off the seconds behind him. Thirteen and a half minutes left and counting.

Mia thumbed through a stack of files. "Never thought your humanitarian side would come in handy."

"Bleeding hearts don't last long in prison." Race rummaged through the top drawer filled with office supplies then moved to the next one. A shadow crossed the opaque window and paused.

"Race?"

He held up his hand and motioned for her to be still. Her light clicked off. Race's heart pounded until the footsteps finally faded down the hall.

She clicked her light back on and tugged on the top drawer of the next file cabinet. "This one's locked."

"You keep searching the open files. I'll try and find a key."

Race crossed the room then felt around the top of the file cabinet. Heavy security didn't seem a priority, which meant it had to be here somewhere. He kept searching until he pulled a silver key from a small metal box, slipped it into the keyhole, and opened the drawer.

Mia smiled for the first time all evening. "Guess I was right when I decided you'd come in useful."

He leaned in close. "You haven't seen useful until you see how I can crack a safe."

Her light nearly blinded him. "You're useful. . .not James Bond."

He raised his hands in surrender, returned to the desk and flipped through three more drawers of files, but found nothing even remotely tied to organ transplants. Whatever they were doing in this lab, none of it seemed to have anything to do with their quest.

He glanced again at the clock. They were down to five minutes. "We're running out of time."

Mia dumped a pile of files onto the cluttered desk beside him. Maybe his conclusion had been premature. "Race."

"What is it?"

Even in the dim light, he could see her face had paled. "Files tracking my patients' reactions to an experimental anti-rejection drug."

An uneasy feeling filled his gut. "An experimental drug?"

"Dr. Spence's ZAR242."

"I don't understand. Dr. Spence said that drug's not ready for testing. And why would Amandi have your patient files?"

She held up a thin file, anger flashing in her eyes. "Because you were right. Someone's using my patients as lab rats."

CHAPTER THIRTY-FIVE

SUNDAY, DECEMBER 15TH, 10:30 PM

KABONI PRIVATE HOSPITAL

Catherine checked her watch. Taking into account the eight-hour time difference, she calculated it was two-thirty Sunday afternoon in Cincinnati. Brad was probably working on his computer while Jonathan sat in front of the flat-screen for his weekly dose of buttery popcorn and his choice of any episode of the 1960s Batman TV series in Brad's DVD collection.

She kissed Kelsey's forehead. Burning hot. Hotter than she was when Dr. Kendall started the new meds a few hours ago. The regimen of mono-whatevers was not working. Where was Dr. Amandi? Despair knifed Catherine's gut.

She forced herself to pull away from the sickly, sweet smell of Kelsey's fevered body. She dug her cell phone from her pants pocket and slipped into the hall. Calling Brad could not be put off any longer. He probably couldn't get here before Kelsey was gone, but at least if she held the phone up to Kelsey's ear he could say good-bye.

She owed him closure with his daughter.

Propping herself against the wall, she punched his cell number.

Thoughts of what to say churned in her mind. Exactly how did one tell her husband that his wife's stupid decision had cost their daughter her life? She waited for the call to connect.

Ring.

Ring.

Ring.

Where were they? Brad had worked in his home office every Sunday afternoon for as long as she could remember. Maybe they'd gone to a movie and he had his phone on silent. Maybe she'd dialed the wrong number. Maybe Brad really meant that they were finished and he would never speak to her again.

Just as she was about to hang up and redial, Jonathan's missing-teeth voice, the one Brad had recorded the day he got his new phone, announced that his dad couldn't come to the phone.

"Brad, I know you're there. Please pick up. It's me."

Nothing. . .Nothing but the empty sound of separation.

She waited for a second then jumped in with the rest of her message before her time ran out.

"Kelsey's dying. Please come."

CHAPTER THIRTY-SIX

MONDAY, DECEMBER 16TH, 4:54 AM EST

CINCINNATI, OHIO

Brad crossed the deserted lobby, ducked into the empty elevator, and stabbed the number ten. Casting a quick visual retrace of his steps, he mashed the button again with a caffeine-induced strength.

The coast seemed clear enough, despite the fact that two vehicles had been in the parking garage when he'd expected only one. But he hadn't stayed up all night researching everything he could find on his father-in-law to shrink at the possibility of witnesses. According to Catherine's message, he couldn't put off settling the score with Tom Bruce any longer.

The stainless steel doors clanged shut.

He reached for the leather case in his pocket, flipped it open, and checked the time on his phone.

Five minutes to air. Concluding his business with The Deuce wouldn't take two.

As the elevator lumbered toward the radio station, he scrolled through his unread emails.

Nothing new from Catherine since she'd left a voice message that his daughter was dying.

Ding.

Brad crammed his phone into his pocket. Had they really expected him to swallow all of this with no questions asked? He stepped out of the elevator, his eyes seeking his target destination.

To his left, the darkened doors of a mortgage company. To his right, two fluorescent back-lit glass doors with a huge network logo.

This was the place.

He stormed the station's doors. Locked. Now what? He peered around the etched call letters and into the small lobby. At the far end was a large window that showcased a room decked out with several large microphones, three flat screens, and five or six computers. Two men stood with their backs to the window.

Brad's heart thumped with pleasure at the thought of breaching the ivory tower that had held Catherine's heart captive, despite the fact that she'd left it for him. Pacing the width of the double doors, he contemplated whether to knock and give his enemy an opportunity to formulate a plan, or go for the surprise and kick his way in. He glanced toward the control room once again and stopped midstride.

Both men remained behind the slab of plate glass, but now they faced the front door, their lips pursed, their displeased gazes fixed on him.

So much for the element of surprise. Brad squared his shoulders and eyeballed them defiantly. He pointed at the door handle. "Let me in."

The greasy-haired short guy shook his head. The tall man said nothing, seemingly intent upon keeping Brad within the cross-hairs of his dead-eye glare.

The scrutiny ignited the frayed nerves in Brad's body and sparked recognition in his mind. He knew the face of the tall man. He'd seen it plastered on several billboards around the city, on the radio station's website, and in his dreams when he recalled the dinner meeting when he'd shoved Tom Bruce's offer back in his face.

"Deuce," he mouthed as he dragged the blade of his gaze over the father that Catherine had tried so hard to please. Not quite the bigger-than-life specimen he remembered, but imposing nonetheless.

"Bozo," the man mouthed back confidently.

Fists clenched, Brad raised both hands and pounded the glass. "Open this door, you miserable piece of—"

The Deuce said something undecipherable to his sawed-off sidekick. His directive elicited an immediate frown and adamant disagreement from the short guy, but The Deuce repeated himself and his employee shot from the room. Within seconds, the errand boy slid to a halt before Brad.

"Tom doesn't have time for visitors," he shouted through the glass.

Brad diverted his attention from the man he'd intended to speak to for the past six years to this short guy sizing him up from behind the office suite's locked doors. "Open up."

"No way."

He pounded the glass again. "Open the door, you little—"

Tom Bruce appeared beside the short guy. "It's okay, Vinnie." He cocked his head toward the entry. "This conversation has been a long time coming."

"It's your funeral, Deuce." Vinnie pushed the button.

Brad heard the click and burst through the doors.

Vinnie grabbed Brad's arm and whirled him around. "Whoa, slow down there, boy."

Brad tried to knock the little guy's crushing grip from his elbow. "I understand I owe my father-in-law for what he's done for my little girl."

Vinnie's eyes darted from Brad to Tom then back to Brad.

"Let me go," Brad growled.

"This is the most gumption he's displayed in years, but trust me, Vinnie, I'm sure Bozo here is harmless."

The short guy scowled at The Deuce, but reluctantly released his hold.

Brad charged forward. "I'm here to settle my account."

A smug smile crawled across The Deuce's face. "Bozo, you're in too deep for that." He crossed his arms over his chest.

Brad drew back his right arm. "I always find a way to pay my debts." He tightened his fist. "Here's the interest." He swung through, the full force of his upper-cut connecting hard with The Deuce's chin. Then, before his father-in-law could recover, he balled his left hand and drove it straight into the man's stomach. "And here's the down payment on the principal."

Heart racing, Brad stepped away from the man doubled over and dripping blood onto his alligator shoes. "Did you really think I'd let you kill my daughter and do nothing?"

"What?" the Deuce gasped.

"She's rejecting that cheap heart you bought."

Before the gasping man could defend his defenseless actions, Brad stalked from the station and then from the building, relishing the throb in his hand. Once in the parking garage, he strode toward his weathered Tahoe parked beside the red Beamer with *Deuce* on the license plate. He eased between the two vehicles and yanked open his driver's side door.

Metal scraped metal.

The grating sound brought a smile to Brad's face. He freed the door of his SUV from the side of the shiny sports car then climbed in behind the wheel.

He surveyed the damage, pleased at the ugly wrinkle he'd made in the paint the color of Kelsey's blood.

"Paid in full." A smile tugged at his lips. "But I'm not done yet."

CHAPTER THIRTY-SEVEN

MONDAY, DECEMBER 16TH, 2:17 PM

SHINWANGA REGIONAL HOSPITAL

Mia finished her afternoon rounds and returned to her office. Still fuming about the horrific discovery she and Race had made during their previous night of crime, she slammed the door. She needed a moment alone to calm down. To plan her next move. Not only had someone contaminated her drug supply with an unapproved deadly anti-rejection drug, someone was passing her patient files to Amandi's office. And she had no plans of stopping until she could prove who was sabotaging her work.

She'd taken a few of the files from Amandi's lab so she could double-check her own statistics against the replicas they'd found. If she was going to accuse Tanzania's leading heart surgeon of conducting secret drug trials on his unsuspecting countrymen, she'd better be sure she was right. Hurling accusations of murder by unethical drug testing at a top medical official was serious business. Serious enough to get her kicked out of the country, another failure to add to her list.

She dropped into the wobbly desk chair. The ancient ceiling fan rattled overhead without making a dent in the suffocating heat rising up within her. Refusing to succumb to the fatigue, she dragged herself upright and listened carefully for footsteps in the hall.

Convinced she was safe to proceed without interruption, she retrieved the files that she'd hidden in her locked filing cabinet. Race had protested her insistence that she take the files to work with her, but she didn't want to leave the information in her apartment. Until she knew more about what was really going on and who was feeding her patients' information to Amandi, the files stayed with her.

She flipped open the first file and fought back a yawn. Her on-call residency years hadn't worn her out as much as this battle. But had fatigue played a part in her putting her trust in the wrong person? Was Race's concern for her a ruse to slow her down and cover up things Amandi didn't want discovered? If Race was part of this scheme, he stood to gain exponentially if this exploitation of Tanzanians proved successful. The more organs he transported, the more he got paid.

Maybe she was being overly paranoid, but even if Amandi was behind this, he had to have help. She just had to figure out who.

Mia rubbed the back of her neck, unable to accept the possibility of Race's involvement, but the scenario ran all too familiar. Memories of her mother claiming that things between herself and Mia's father might not be as perfect as they seemed ran through her head. She loved her father. Had left because she'd disappointed him. But her mother's continual complaints about Mia's father had left her skittish around men, never letting them close.

She stared at the open file. It couldn't be him. Besides, if she couldn't trust Race to help her find out the truth, then who could she trust? Panic slithered from the recesses of her mind and coiled around her heart. *Think*. She had to think. Who else could be involved? The hard-to-pronounce names of her own staff paraded through her troubled thoughts.

Shadrach stood to her right at every surgery, offering his able assistance. His position gave him access to privileged information on every transplant and rejection that had come through her operating room. He had access to all of her files. And he was hungry for success. But was his ambition enough to entice him to take shortcuts? She didn't think so.

Desperate for proof that her fears of such treachery were unfounded, she flipped through Amandi's lab files. The signature on the bottom of every T-cell report connected to her patients was as undecipherable as a doctor's prescription. On the shipping invoices, the sender's address information had been blacked out or torn from the paper. Someone wanted their tracks very difficult to trace and had gone to a great deal of effort to ensure anyone involved in switching Tryoxylate for ZAR242 remained anonymous.

She needed to talk to someone. Even with her questions, Race was still her first choice, but he'd flown a group of tourists up to their safari outpost at the foot of Mount Kilimanjaro and wasn't back yet. Who else could she trust? Someone who might care enough about drug testing to wonder along with her how an unapproved drug could make its way across the ocean.

Dr. Harry Spence?

The circled name of the researcher from America leapt from the piece of paper Race had stuck on her bulletin board when they'd tracked down BPH Technologies. While Dr. Spence hadn't offered much in the way of actual help when she contacted him earlier, the fact that he hadn't hung up on her gave her hope that he could be convinced to care. Especially now that she was pretty certain what was behind her patients' deaths.

Mia ripped the note free. Maybe if she could get Dr. Spence on the phone again, she could wheedle the information out of him she needed. She understood the scientist's hesitancy to release industry secrets, but lives were at stake here. If he continued this resistance, she'd be forced to resort to stalking Amandi. She grabbed her phone, hating to think how messy taking on one of the best transplant surgeons in Africa could get. She punched in the number and prayed the scientist would pick up.

"You've reached the voice mailbox of Dr. Harry Spence. I'm up to my pocket protector in T-cells. Leave a message."

Frustrated, she tucked her hopes away and waited for the tone.

"Dr. Spence. This is Dr. Mia Kendall, the transplant surgeon who called earlier. It's about the emergent organ rejection problem here in

Africa...it's a child, an American child. Your anti-rejection drug expertise is required, stat." Mia clicked off her phone.

If that part about the rejection being an American child didn't get to him, what would?

She gathered her sweaty hair into a thick ponytail and secured it with the elastic holder she slipped off her wrist.

What now? If she couldn't be certain of the traitor in her ranks, the only thing left to do was...question Amandi. Maybe if she could confront him with the truth of her findings, she could back him into a corner and make him cry *uncle*.

But how?

Her earlier attempts to question the slippery doctor had gotten her nowhere. She'd left a dozen messages and couldn't even get him to return her calls. Maybe she should skip him altogether and take her information straight to the authorities. But could she count on them to help? Amandi was African. She was American. All Amandi had to do was slip money into the right officials' palms and an African's word against an American's would win every time.

Maybe her patients would have rejected and died on their own, but Amandi was going to explain to her face-to-face why he was willing to treat people like lab rats. All she had to do was figure out how to facilitate a showdown.

She drummed her fingers on the desk, staring at the orderly array of notes and reminders tacked to her bulletin board. She thought she would have run into Amandi when she went to check on Kelsey's progress this morning. The young American was still in critical condition, but her doctor was AWOL. Where was he? When she'd asked his secretary at the front desk, she'd said he was getting fitted for his party tux.

Mia's eyes landed on the gold-embossed edges of the Embassy Christmas party invitation. That's it. *Have I missed it?* She snatched the card and checked the date. The gala was tonight. Formal attire required. Everybody who was anybody, including the major funders of the private hospital, would be at this glitzy shindig. Amandi would never miss this opportunity to rub his oversized shoulders against anyone who could throw money his way.

She had to go, even though the thought of dressing up and schmoozing like her father made her physically ill. She fingered the invitation, weighing her options. If she had any hope of saving Mbui and Kelsey, she must take this opportunity no matter how unpalatable it was.

What if her little black cocktail dress didn't even fit? She'd lost fifteen pounds since moving to this tropical sauna. And she'd need a date. But who?

Race.

His name hit her afresh with the force of a defibrillator. And she'd need one. Another night of conquering the world with a man she still wasn't sure she could fully trust might very well put her heart into cardiac arrest.

CHAPTER THIRTY-EIGHT

MONDAY, DECEMBER 16TH, 7:25 PM

DAR ES SALAAM

Race tugged on the hem of his rented monkey-suit and frowned. The last time he'd donned a tuxedo had been at his cousin's wedding four years ago. This one's quality was poor and it smelled like a goat, but it was either this penguin ensemble or his normal bush-wrangler look. Something he had a feeling Mia wouldn't approve of. And while he should have said no to her last-minute invitation, scavenging through Amandi's lab had convinced him that his crazy theory was right.

His cell phone rang as he stuffed his wallet into his back pocket. If Mia had come up with another harebrained idea to add to the one she'd already suckered him into. . .

His mother. Race thought about letting the call go to his voicemail, then thought again. "Hi, Mom."

"Race, it's good to hear your voice. I didn't think I'd get a hold of you, you stay so busy."

Fear punched through his gut at the unexpected call. "Is everything alright? Is Dad—"

"Your father and I are fine, but I'm the one who's supposed to be asking you that question. You know I worry about you living in such a dangerous place. And lately, I confess, I've had such overwhelming urges to pray for you."

He reached down to slip on one of the rented shoes. "It's not that dangerous here, Mom."

"So you're all right?"

Race paused for a moment, knowing he could never tell her about Amandi's lab experiments, or the possibility that he'd spent the past eighteen months of his life possibly trafficking in illegally obtained organs. "I'm fine. Really. I was just on my way out."

"On a date?"

Race pressed his lips together. Wouldn't Mia love that question. "No, Mom. It's a Christmas party at the Embassy. I'm escorting an American doctor who lives here. She's just a friend. Nothing more."

"It's okay to be happy, you know."

If he closed his eyes, he could almost see Elizabeth Daniels sitting in her favorite worn chair in the living room that was always cluttered with his father's books, catalogues, and piles of out-of-date newspapers. "I know, Mom."

"Rachel would hate knowing how you've pushed yourself away from everyone who loves you."

Just like she'd hate knowing that he was still running away from losing her. And how his rogue behavior had distanced him from his parents. And how he still wondered if it was possible to get even with a God who'd failed him.

He picked up the black-and-white wedding photo of him and Rachel that he kept on the bedside table of his one-bedroom apartment. They'd had their whole lives ahead of them until fate stole her away in an instant. And just because Mia Kendall happened to stir something inside him he hadn't felt since he lost Rachel, it didn't mean he was ready to throw away his past. He dropped the picture onto the table.

"Listen, Mom, I hate to have to run, but I'm already late."

"Just know that your father and I love you. . .and we're praying for you."

"Thanks." The past few days flickered through his mind like a bad news reel. "Truth is, I could use a few extra prayers right now."

He hung up the phone a moment later, popped a piece of gum into his mouth, then glanced into the bedroom mirror. It was going to take the prayers of somebody with better connections than he had to get him out of this one.

Twenty minutes later, he stood at the door of Mia's apartment, feeling more like an adolescent prom date than a grown man. Except he wasn't sixteen, and no matter what his mom had said, this wasn't a date. Mia simply needed an escort, as she'd put it on the phone. Someone to help her wrestle the truth from the meaty fists of Amandi.

The door of her apartment swung open. Mia stood in front of him wearing a little black dress and heels which showed off those long tanned legs he hadn't failed to miss before.

Race swallowed his gum. "Wow. You look. . .beautiful."

"You don't have to sound so surprised."

"I didn't. . . I'm not. . ." Mia had already become a distraction he didn't mind. He needed to take care that she didn't become more.

She shot him a grin. "You don't look so bad yourself."

"Thanks." He yanked on one of his sleeves and hoped his new cologne masked the goat smell. "What about Jeme and Zaina?"

"The pastor from my church and his wife offered to stay with them. Zaina's loving the attention."

"Good. Then you're ready?"

"Ready as I'll ever be. And you?"

"Besides the fact that we're completely in over our heads and are about to confront the private hospital's head of cardiology on charges that could end his career and possibly our lives? Why not?" He held out his arm and nodded toward his jeep. "Your carriage awaits, Miss Mia Kendall."

CHAPTER THIRTY-NINE

MONDAY, DECEMBER 16TH, 8:14 PM

AMERICAN EMBASSY, DAR ES SALAAM

Mia swung her bare legs out of the jeep and planted her stilettos firmly on the steamy asphalt. Trusting her balance to the glitzy trappings of her past was nearly as risky as trusting her handsome date. But she didn't have a choice. Her patients were worth the gamble she was taking tonight.

A salty breeze fluttered the gauzy fabric of her dress while the coastal humidity draped her bare shoulders like the full-length mink her father insisted she wear to his many Christmas soirées. Hands trembling, she tucked in the stray strands of hair escaping her self-styled updo. Her attempts to get Amandi's help hadn't worked, which meant he'd left her no choice but to confront him in person. She could do this. For the sake of the patients she'd lost, those in peril now, and those in the future, she would do this.

She poked her head into the jeep's cab. "Ready?"

"Do I have a choice?" Race unfolded his well-dressed form from the driver's side and came around to her. "You sure you want Amandi to know we've been nosing around in his top-secret business?"

Her mind flitted back to the text Race had received the day he met her at the restaurant. He'd acted strange after he read it. Why? Had he already reported back to Amandi everything she'd discovered? She netted the suspicions fluttering in her stomach. She would do what she came to do and deal with Race Daniels later. "I doubt Amandi's lab techs have noticed they're short five secret drug files. So, unless your friend Innocent isn't so innocent and gives us away, I'm not so stupid to announce that we took anything."

"Then how are you going to explain knowing about his secret drug tests?"

"I won't."

"Then why are we here?"

Good question. What was she thinking? One wrong move and her work in Africa could be finished, maybe even her medical career. What good would she be to her patients then? "I just want to look him in the eye. Prime the pump. Find out how deep he is in this, and if the government is involved. All I need from you is help obtaining a moment alone with the good doctor."

Race quirked a brow. "From the fire in your eyes, I'm thinking better Amandi than me." He placed his hand on the small of her back. "After you, Sherlock."

Making their way from the visitor's parking lot, Mia tried to ignore the heat of Race's hand against her spine. Foolishly believing he was on her side—if he was guilty—could be her undoing. She caught herself. She sounded as paranoid as her mother. She coerced her stiffened body to yield to the firm pressure of his touch, becoming putty in his hands.

Ankles wobbly, she followed the maze of sidewalks that wove through the lush vegetation. She felt like an inept secret agent—in way over her head. Maybe if she focused on the Embassy compound's layout instead of the rugged scent of Race's cologne, she'd be better prepared if her probing touched raw nerves and prompted the need for a quick exit.

Dar es Salaam's old Embassy building had been destroyed years ago by a bomb. Both African and American government officials touted this new facility, set on a large, trapezoidal acreage, as one of the most secure in the world. She prayed that claim wasn't the usual political hype and hogwash.

By the time they neared the well-lit portico of the Chancery building, her shoes had rubbed blisters on her feet and Race's touch had sparked a disconcerting ping in her heart valves. Uncomfortable on every front, she allowed him to steer her past the machine-gun-toting guards, surly dogs, and two airport-sized metal detectors. Once she cleared the no-nonsense American soldier with a security wand, she gathered her lipstick and cell phone from the plastic bin and crammed them into her purse. She waited for Race to finish stuffing his wallet into his back pocket.

He offered his arm. "Madam?"

She rested her hand in the crook of his arm, and they followed the crowd heading into an impressive chancery atrium.

Men wearing spotless white coats and shiny shoes greeted them formally then funneled them down a wide tiled hall that led into the grand atrium. Sparkling lights hung from the high ceiling. The festive air crackled with music and the aroma of grilled meats, fresh breads, and the heavy-handed perfumes of the rich. The extravagance rivaled her family's Baltimore country club and certainly trumped anything she'd seen since arriving in Africa.

Race's arm hooked her waist. "Hope you didn't have your heart set on turkey and dressing." His minty breath warmed her neck. "White Christmas is a unique choice of music, don't you think, considering the temperature is probably eighty degrees?"

"A snowflake wouldn't stand a chance in here. Doesn't anybody in this country believe in cranking up the air conditioning?"

"Tanzania makes every effort to conserve its power resources." He nodded in the direction of a jovial man in the center of a cluster of attentive admirers. "Speaking of conserving power, shall we start with our tubby Ambassador?"

While his touch made her weak in the knees, Race's rock-solid presence offered support for her wavering backbone. "What would he know?"

"Doc, you may think I'm just a hayseed in a monkey suit, but you start messin' with somebody's gravy train, and I'm pretty sure you're going to need friends in high places."

Mia turned her gaze to the balding man holding court with a few of his cronies and a uniformed man who appeared to be in local law enforcement. "Our esteemed Ambassador doesn't look like he'd know a T-cell from a tee time."

"Our American tax dollars at work." Race clutched her elbow. "Come on, I'll help you win him over." He led her across the room.

A few feet short of their target, she stopped. "I'll take it from here."

He shot her a wary gaze. "Remember, we're trolling for information, so don't go in with both guns blazing." He pulled her close and whispered in her ear, "I'll see if I can't round up Amandi and steer him your way." Then he said loud enough for everyone to hear, "You thirsty, sweet potato?"

"No." She tried to pull away. "Why are you talking like a deranged southerner?"

"You'll see." He winked and planted a kiss on her cheek. "You mingle, darlin', while I scare us up something to wet our whistles." With a smug grin, he wheeled and blended into the resplendent crowd, his wavy brown hair head and shoulders above anyone in the room.

Mia stood motionless, an annoying tingle leaping from one nerve ending to the next. No doubt, her flustered cheeks now matched her strappy red heels. She squashed the feeling of naked vulnerability Race had roused in her and reeled her attention back to the stubby little man smoking a very large cigar.

"Ambassador Thompson." She flashed her most bewitching smile. "I'm Dr. Kendall."

"Ah, yes." His gaze approving, he continued, "Amandi was right, you are too beautiful to be a doctor." His southern accent hung between them as he turned to address his admirers, and Mia immediately understood the purpose of Race's Rhett Butler impersonation. "Gentlemen, may I present one of Tanzania's finest cardiothoracic surgeons."

Mia ignored their murmured approval and leveled her gaze on the Ambassador. "One of only a very few cardio surgeons for the country."

"Change takes time, doctor." He tamped the ashes of his cigar into his empty champagne glass. "But we *are* making progress. I was just telling the chief ...you have met our esteemed local official chief of police, have you not?"

"No. I can't say as I have." Mia extended her hand and had it greedily swallowed up in the chief's firm grip. Race's words of how she would need support in high places paralleled her observation that this man reminded her of an African version of Wyatt Earp minus the handlebar moustache. Corruption would be hard pressed to have its way with such a self-assured man. "It's good to know that Dar es Salaam's well-being is in such good hands."

The officer nodded and flashed a brilliant white smile that split his pock-scarred face.

"Dr. Kendall, I was telling these gentlemen about my aunt's recent kidney transplant."

Mia turned her full attention back to the ambassador, grateful his determination to impress her with his medical interest might inadvertently provide her with another piece of information. "In the States?"

"No. Here in Dar. At Kaboni Private."

"Your aunt is an expatriate?"

He laughed and snagged another glass of champagne from a waiter. "Oh my, no. Aunt Lilly's as southern as fried chicken. She's from Atlanta."

"Then why..." She caught herself, allowing her mind a moment to frantically sift through the questions pelting her thoughts.

She could think of only two reasons why Americans would risk below-par treatment in a third-world country...fear and money. Fear they couldn't outlast the UNOS wait-list time, and money if they were unable to pay for the expensive procedure if, by chance, they were lucky enough to beat the odds of getting an organ in America.

Kelsey's little African safari wasn't simply the last-ditch attempt of a desperate American mother. Insurance problems had forced Catherine Taylor to scrape together the money to buy what her daughter had been denied in America. And she clearly wasn't the only one.

But what these medical tourists didn't know was that in many countries some of those precious organs had likely been harvested from the impoverished. People whose own desperation had left them no choice but to sell their body parts or the parts of their loved ones.

Or perhaps some donors weren't given a choice. Like Numa?

A chill raced down Mia's spine. She checked the chief's face to see if he'd picked up on any of this, but one of the ambassador's friends had him sidetracked and, as far as she could tell, she was on her own. Tempting as it was to start hurling questions, she decided Race had a point. Maybe she could catch more flies with honey.

Working to infuse calm into her voice, she asked, "So tell me, Ambassador, how is your aunt's recuperation going?"

He took a long drag on his cigar and exhaled the smoke slowly as if the answer to her question pained him. "The old girl's touch and go at the moment." He winked. "But nothing Amandi says he can't handle."

"Dr. Amandi?"

"Of course. I wouldn't trust Aunt Lily to my hairdresser." His friends joined his laughter.

One of the ambassador's colleagues jumped into the conversation, the ice rattling in his empty scotch glass. "Thompson here was telling us that the World Health Organization estimates kidneys are the most sought after organ around the world. I hear that in India's slums many are willing to exchange an extra kidney for a small handful of cash. Poor fellows."

The ambassador clapped the man on the back. "Howard, no point in boring our beautiful doctor. I'm sure she, of all people, understands the global need for organs."

Mia raised her chin. "I understand how those in poverty could be coerced or even exploited to meet that need."

"Doctor, the poor we will have with us always." He downed his champagne.

Her tongue coiled to strike. "Surely you aren't advocating that Africa hang out a transplant tourism shingle to the world?"

"Dr. Kendall, I think you are getting ahead of yourself."

"It's bad enough that a possible shortage of human organs for transplantation in America is enticing people to risk an arduous and dangerous trip abroad. But if a world-wide trend develops that allows the wealthy, in search of their own survival, to seek organs from the poor—the results could be disastrous. Without strict regulation and cross-governmental agreements, who would control the procurement of organs? The poor would never be safe again." She snatched a quick breath. "And not just the poor. The rich could have no guarantees of the organ's quality from unscreened or illegally-obtained source. My operating table would become a crap shoot."

The ambassador took a long, slow sip from another glass of champagne. "My, my. Beauty and brains. A lethal combination, Dr. Kendall. Lethal."

She snatched an offered shrimp skewer. "As international organ demands increase, I suspect so does the local profit?"

Thompson smiled. "Buying and selling organs is illegal in this country, Dr. Kendall. And shall remain so."

"But soaring demand could open a window for an enterprising middleman capable of providing the service of linking those desperately in need of organs with, let's say, private hospitals keen for revenues. Wouldn't you agree, Ambassador?"

"My understanding of transplantation is that, while risky, the procedure is increasingly seen as the best solution to end-stage organ failure and therefore the only option for. . ."

"People like *your* Aunt Lily." She dropped her empty shrimp skewer on the tray of a passing server.

Thompson smiled again. "Absolutely." He lifted his empty glass and immediately a waiter replaced it with another full one.

He had successfully evaded her question with the skill of a seasoned politician, but what more could she say? If she wanted to continue working in this country, she needed to take special care not to stir up trouble with her own countrymen. Ambassador Thompson might prefer to delude himself, but she had no plans to ignore what was happening. Mia wrestled with the dilemma of how much more to press her point.

She dug her heels into the grout between the tiles and locked her knees. "I would hate to see Africa's official American presence encourage a situation that would limit a patient's ability to know whether their transplanted organ came from a destitute mother, an executed prisoner, or a criminal source." Mia squared her shoulders. "Traceability of and accountability for human organs is paramount to achieving an impeccable standard of care for Africa. Wouldn't you agree, Mr. Thompson?"

"There you are, sweet potato!" Race appeared at her side with a cup of red liquid and Kaboni Hospital's head of cardiology in tow. "Punch?" He thrust the glass in her direction, along with a look that said *Settle down*. "I believe you know Dr. Amandi, don't you, darlin'?"

Mia forced a tight smile. "We're colleagues. Working together for the good of medicine in Tanzania." She took the cup, her anger probably turning her face the color of the fruity liquid. "But I fear the chief of the country's transplant program has been avoiding me."

"What fool would avoid such a beauty?" Amandi extended his hand. Nearly every finger sported gold, his breath sporting more than champagne. "Dr. Kendall, please accept my deepest appreciation for the little biopsy you performed on the American child."

"It was an emergency situation." She didn't even want to think about how the tipsy doctor managed to get a paw of that magnitude inside Kelsey's tiny chest cavity. "Keeping people alive is what we do. Which is why I want to discuss—"

"Now, darlin'." Race stepped between her and the doctor. "Don't you think that if you and the good doctor are going to talk bloody hearts that maybe you should step outside?" He smiled over her head at the ambassador. "I'm sure these fine gentlemen wouldn't want their fancy dinner ruined."

For someone who loved to give an uneducated impression, this bush pilot could be brilliant.

Mia reined in her galloping blood pressure and offered Dr. Amandi her most stunning smile. "Care to get some air, doctor?"

He gave a gracious nod. "I relish any opportunity that allows me to delve further into the concerns of my colleagues."

Dr. Amandi followed her through the double doors that led to a small covered patio. Beautiful exotic birds called from their roosts in the largest baobab tree in Dar es Salaam.

He cleared his throat. "Once again, let me thank you for offering your invaluable surgical services, despite the rude treatment you received from my staff. As you know, Dr. Kendall, good help is hard to find. I also wanted to assure you that I have begun looking into the issue we discussed on the phone."

"I'm glad you brought that up." She opened her purse and pulled out a sheet she'd ripped from one of his lab's files. "Because I've been looking into the matter as well, and I need to ask you a question."

"Of course. Anything."

"Why are you using *my* patients as *your* guinea pigs?"

His eyes scanned her and then the paper. "What are you talking about?"

She smacked the name scribbled across the bottom of the page. "This is proof that Tryoxylate at my hospital was ordered to be replaced with the yet approved drug ZAR242."

He grabbed the paper out of her hand. The deer-in-the-headlights look in his bloodshot eyes was all the confirmation she needed to know she'd just hit a nerve. "Why would you accuse me of this? These papers are from Shinwanga Regional which is your responsibility. Not mine."

"This came from your hospital." She didn't wait for him to respond. "You're running drug trials on *my* patients."

"That is a serious allegation, Dr. Kendall. One you would be hard pressed to prove, because your claims are completely bogus."

"Maybe, except you made a mistake." She pulled a vial of Tryoxylate she'd taken from Kelsey's room out of her purse. "This vial came from the American girl's room. Your patient is now dying with all the same symptoms as Mbui, who instead of Tryoxylate—like I prescribed—was intentionally given ZAR242."

"That is not true."

"Really? Because we both know that all it would take is one clerical error. One vial meant for Shinwanga Regional to end up in one of your patient's room at Kaboni. . .a patient like little Kelsey Taylor." She paused for emphasis. "Any reputable chemist will be able to verify which drug is in this tube."

His cocky expression sobered. "I find your accusations insulting, Dr. Kendall. Here in Africa, when people come to a hospital, most of them believe they come to die. It is an attitude we have worked hard to change. And yet now you come to me throwing out false accusations that have the potential to spread like wildfire and destroy everything I have worked for in building up in this hospital and its transplant program. Are you prepared for people to die while you chase after these rumors and risk setting medical progress here in Tanzania back thirty years?"

"People *are* already dying," she said, unconvinced by his arguments. "And I won't stop looking until I get enough info on your connection to BPH's human drug testing to cut your heart out and lay it on the medical review board's table."

His lips slithered into a slow grin, the light of the tiki torches reflecting off his gold incisor. "How much?"

"What?"

"This is Africa, Dr. Kendall. Money is a great reliever of the struggle."

"Are you kidding me? If you think you can bribe me, you don't get it." Mia jammed her hands on her hips and leaned in close. "If you don't come clean and put an end to all of this, when I get through with you, *you'll* need a heart transplant."

"Don't think for a moment that I am confessing guilt with my offer. I don't know what your motivation is, but I am willing to do anything needed to protect the hospital and the good name I have created."

"Well, let's just go ask Ambassador Thompson what he thinks about what I know." She whirled and started for the door, realizing he'd just matched her bluff.

Amandi grabbed her arm. "You need to stay out of this, Dr. Kendall." He squeezed until his knuckles whitened.

"Take your hand off me—"

"You have no idea to what lengths someone might go to stop you from interfering."

CHAPTER FORTY

MONDAY, DECEMBER 16TH, 9:23 PM

JULIUS NYERERE INTERNATIONAL AIRPORT

Harry felt his lungs constrict as he stepped off the plane into the humid night air. He fumbled for his asthma pump, took in a deep breath, then dropped the device back into his shirt pocket. While thirty thousand feet in the air, he'd been able to convince himself he was flying to Los Angeles or maybe Seattle. The airport terminal now looming before him, a series of reinforced concrete overhangs built to resemble a jungle canopy, was enough to convince him he'd landed in some parallel universe. Further removed from his lab in Baltimore than Blackwell Isle. Even Axton Blade would feel out of place here.

Crossing the tarmac with the rest of the passengers, Harry squeezed his fingers around the pouch containing his passport, three hundred dollars in cash, and the thin travel book on East Africa Valerie had bought for him at Baltimore Washington International. In the twenty-odd hours since his departure, he'd memorized everything from where to stay, to how to avoid crime, to the best tourist spots. Except he wasn't here on holiday.

Or to think about Valerie.

Which meant he'd have to deal with the possibility that her lingering good-bye kiss was exactly that—good-bye. He swallowed the lump of fear in his throat and tried to breathe. For now, all he had to do was concentrate on navigating the throng of passengers on their way through customs and the fact that something at BPH was very wrong.

Harry pulled a handkerchief from his pants pocket and wiped the sweat beads that had formed across his brow. Night had long fallen across the city, but even at this late hour, the temperature, with its high humidity, felt like it hovered in the high nineties. A significant spike from Baltimore's current frigid weather. He wiped his forehead again then shed his coat as he stood at the end of the line that snaked through immigration.

Forty-five minutes later, with a visa, stamped passport, and a wallet full of shillings from the ATM, he finally grabbed his suitcase off the squeaky luggage carousel. Toting enough instant soup, gluten-free breakfast bars, and Cheetos from his pantry to last him at least a week, he followed the signs to the exits. A crowd of smiling faces held cardboard signs and waited for their passengers. His last-minute hotel arrangements had promised him a direct shuttle connection outside the airport terminal. He swallowed a growing lump of fear and pressed through the crowd.

"*Jambo*." A dark-faced man brushed up beside him.

Harry tried to ignore the smoky, earthy scents of Africa permeating his pores and the stranger invading his personal space.

"I can get you the best safari packages in all of Tanzania. Or if you need a—"

"Thanks, but I don't need anything." Harry turned away only to collide with another eager seller, anxious to peddle his wares.

"If you are looking for a tour package, taxis, city guides, hotels—"

"No." Harry cut off the tall, slender man before he had a chance to finish his spiel. Along with warnings not to walk along any isolated areas of the city or on the beach after dark, his travel book had cautioned travelers to beware of the dozens of scams played out in the crowded airports and throughout the city. Baltimore's west side suddenly seemed tame compared to the unfamiliar jungle he'd just stepped into.

The man introduced himself as George then followed Harry through the terminal. "Please, I have had bad luck and did not earn any money today. Anything you need, I can get it. And at the best price. Just tell me what you want."

"What do I want?" Harry shoved his glasses up the bridge of his nose then winced. "I don't need anything. I'm fine."

"There must be something. If you are hungry, I know a restaurant not far from here. I can take you there."

Already, the smell of perspiration mingled with fried fare from a food stand had Harry's stomach roiling. Taking Valerie up on taking a chance had better be worth it.

"I can get you a hotel," George continued. "Or a—"

"Fine." Harry's patience snapped. "I need to make a phone call. I was told I could buy a sim card for my phone outside the arrivals terminal."

"Three thousand shillings," George said with a grin. "It is the best deal in the city."

"Three thousand?" Harry hesitated.

George's gaze dropped. "Okay, I will give you a discount—twenty-five hundred—but I will not eat tonight at such a ridiculously low price."

Feeling the sting of guilt, Harry slapped the money in the man's hand then waited for him to return with his purchase. If he'd been a fool to give the man his money, it was only a couple dollars, but he would not be fooled twice. To his relief, the man returned, big smile on his face, sim card in hand.

Not sure his cell phone would work even with the proper sim card, Harry had written Dr. Kendall's cell phone number, along with that of his hotel, the American Embassy, and the direct number to his health insurance agent, and stuck the list into his passport holder as an added precaution. A man could not be too careful.

The doctor's voicemail picked up on the fifth ring. "You've reached Dr. Mia Kendall. If this is an emergency, please call the hospital directly. Otherwise, leave a number, and I'll return your call as soon as possible."

Harry swallowed his disappointment then waited for the beep. "Dr. Kendall, this is Harry Spence. It's urgent that you call me as soon as you get this message. I'm here in Dar es Salaam, and we. . .we need to talk."

Harry carefully rattled off his cell number as well as the number of his hotel. He hung up feeling deflated. Saving the world was going to be even harder than he'd originally thought.

"You need a taxi now?" George flashed a toothless, eager smile.

Harry waved away George's question. "I'm taking the hotel's shuttle."

"Ah, but my way is quicker." The man's smile brightened. "And I will get you the best deal in the city."

CHAPTER FORTY-ONE

MONDAY, DECEMBER 16TH, 9:40 PM

AMERICAN EMBASSY, DAR ES SALAAM

He who is born a fool is never cured.

If the old African proverb his grandmother used to discipline him were true, he'd been born the biggest fool of all. Amandi stepped out onto the well-manicured lawns of the American Embassy then popped another antacid into his mouth to calm the fire in his belly. If it wasn't for the roomful of witnesses and guards inside, he'd have considered strangling Dr. Kendall with his own two hands. But acting foolishly would only make things worse. He'd spent far too long getting to this point to have some self-righteous doctor waltz in and destroy everything he'd built. Because no matter what she thought of him, while what he did might line his pockets, it also saved lives. How many patients of his—and hers—would die while waiting for the stuffed suits in the American FDA to approve the new anti-rejection drug?

He fumbled with the cell phone in the front pocket of his tux, not sure who he was more worried about at the moment, Mia Kendall or Hastings. Dr. Kendall might have a handful of shaky evidence, but everything he'd worked for would collapse without his college roommate.

There had to be a way out.

Swallowing any remaining remnants of pride, Amandi dialed the Baltimore number and waited.

"We're in trouble," he blurted out when Hastings finally answered. Even he wasn't against skipping lengthy formalities when his entire career was on the line.

The long-distance connection crackled. "What are you talking about?"

"There is. . ." Amandi swallowed the bile burning his throat. "There's a heart doctor working at the government hospital who has started asking questions. She knows about the drug testing."

"You're certain?"

"Do you think if I was not certain I would waste my time calling you? She flat out asked me why I was using her patients as guinea pigs. . .and she showed me proof, though I did everything I could to convince her she had nothing."

Hastings sucked in a sharp breath. "You promised there'd be no paper trail. No possible way for anyone to find out what was going on. What exactly does she know?"

"For starters, that the Tryoxylate is being replaced with the ZAR242 for her patients."

"You idiot." Hastings' tone exploded. "I entrusted you with this project and promised you a generous percentage of the profits once the drug was approved and on the market, and now you're telling me unauthorized human drug testing will be tomorrow's headlines?"

"Now wait a minute." Amandi felt his knees buckle beneath him, but he was nowhere near ready to take all the blame. "I told you that her patients were dying, and that she was going to start asking why at some point. Which is exactly what she has done."

"Don't you dare try and lay this on me," Hastings shouted into the phone. "You're in as deep as I am."

"I might be able to bribe her." He wouldn't tell him that she'd already ignored his offer, but it might buy him some time.

Hastings' laugh ran hollow. "Forget it. Some humanitarian American doctor trying to save the world isn't going to be swayed by bribery. She'll go straight to the authorities on this one, if she hasn't already."

"I don't think she's done anything yet. If she thought she had enough evidence she would have already gone to them and not wasted her time on me." Amandi stepped into the shadows as a couple meandered onto the lawn, carrying champagne glasses. At least someone had something to celebrate. He lowered his voice. "What would you suggest we do?"

"We? I pay *you* good money to make sure things like this don't happen."

"I realize that, but—"

"No, I don't think you realize exactly what's at stake here. Your American heart patient's grandfather happens to be Tom Bruce, a syndicated radio talk show host who trusted me to find a way to save his granddaughter's life. If this comes out, I promise you he'll find a way to ruin us both."

"The child's rejecting the heart."

"Find another one."

Amandi's ulcer threatened to erupt. "It is not that easy."

"I don't care. Burn any evidence. Make sure your little do-gooder doctor doesn't talk to anyone. Switch that American kid to an oral liquid cyclic polypeptide, then find her another heart before we both hang." Silence weighted the phone line before Hastings spoke again. "And arrange for a chauffeured car to pick me up at the airport. I'll be on a flight out of BWI first thing in the morning."

CHAPTER FORTY-TWO

MONDAY, DECEMBER 16TH, 10:23 PM

DAR ES SALAAM

Mia slipped inside the front door of her apartment, unable to shake the feeling that Amandi was having her watched. Pastor Scott and his wife Brenda, who'd offered to stay with her guests while she went to the Embassy, sat on the couch surrounded by toys they'd brought for Zaina. Mia gave them a distracted little wave of acknowledgement then crossed the room in order to peer through the small hole in her curtain. Her heart told her she should have let Race beat a full confession from Amandi. Her head said Mbui and Kelsey couldn't afford her playing all of her cards before she knew if the sleazy doctor had an unknown ace up his sleeve. But her gut told her there was more at play than an illegal drug. And until she secured enough evidence to connect Amandi's illegal drug testing with Americans coming to Tanzania for possible black market organs, she couldn't allow an altercation to compromise the organ pickups and deliveries.

Mia regretted losing her temper with Race. She'd ended up making him so mad, he hadn't even said good night after walking her to the door. She shouldn't have accused him of being in business with a purveyor of dangerous drugs and ill-gotten organs, but when he'd insinuated that she might have pressed Amandi too far, she'd snapped. If this rugged bush pilot was willing to transport questionable organs, what else was he willing to do?

She knew better than to trust a man with a charming smile.

He'd probably already hopped in his plane and lit out for parts unknown. Why didn't she like how lonely that possibility made her feel? How was she going to handle this on her own and make everything work out before she lost more patients? The overwhelming prospect of it all didn't leave her much hope.

A touch on the shoulder startled her conflicted thoughts back to the one thing she knew for sure: for Jeme and Zaina's sake she couldn't give up now. "Mia, are you all right?"

She turned to face Pastor Scott. "Let's just say I probably don't need to apply for that UN peacekeeping job." She surveyed her cluttered living room. "Looks like a better time was had here."

Brenda hurriedly began picking up the assortment of toys. "They're both finally asleep."

"That Zaina's a real keeper." Pastor Scott stepped around the package of diapers and popped a cartoon DVD out of the player before turning to Mia. "Listen, we don't know everything that's going on here, but if you need something—anything—we're here to help."

She caught the concern in his voice. "I know you are, and I appreciate it."

"I've spent two decades in this country, and in that time I've seen a lot of tragedy and pain." Pastor Scott took the bag of toys from his wife and slung it across his shoulder while she grabbed her purse. "But I've also seen what happens when God's light shines in the darkest of places."

Amandi's self-righteous face flashed before Mia. How could anything good ever come out of the deaths of innocent people? "How do we stop the darkness from taking over?"

"According to scripture, judgment is coming. It might not be delivered today. It might not even arrive tomorrow. But in the end, it'll come. Evil will not win." The pastor put his hand on her shoulder.

"Until then, we're in a battle." He gave her shoulder an encouraging squeeze. "Remember, you're not fighting alone."

Mia forced a smile and nodded. "Thank you."

"Promise you'll call us if you need anything." Pastor Scott opened the front door. "And make sure you lock that extra bolt."

Taking the pastor's advice, Mia checked the lock twice after they left. She pulled off her heels and padded to the bedroom. She cracked the door still thinking of the pastor's words. Because evil couldn't win this round. The hypnotic rhythm of her guests' restful breathing eased some of the tension from her shoulders. At least somebody was getting some sleep, because she probably wouldn't. Amandi's arrogance had lit her temper, and it would take time for her to cool down.

Amandi had left her no choice. It was time to swallow her pride and call her father. By the time America's top transplant surgeon finished with this third-world hack, the African doctor would squeal like a rat in the trap he deserved.

She quietly dropped her shoes in the bathroom and wiggled out of her party dress. Changing into her favorite T-shirt, jeans, and flip-flops would make her feel almost human again. She checked her watch. Nearly three thirty Baltimore time. Her father always finished his Monday surgeries early enough to get in a workout with his personal trainer at the club. If she was really going to go through with calling him, calling while he was stuck in traffic was a perfect time to catch him.

Where had she left her cell phone? She headed for the living room. A loud knock stopped her in the hall.

"Pastor Scott? You forget something?" She glanced around her perfectly restored living room and found nothing belonging to the missionary couple. She could hear the shuffling of feet and the rumble of muffled male voices outside the door. Then another knock. This time insistent and demanding.

"Race? That you?" Her heart rate soared. "I'm sorry—"

A crashing thud hit the door and the flimsy frame holding the hinges in place splintered.

Mia snatched her evening bag containing her phone from the

kitchen table and sprinted back to the bedroom. She slammed the bedroom door, but it had no lock. "Jeme, get up."

Jeme sprang from the pallet, still fully dressed in the shirt and skirt Mia had given her. "The hunters have come." She scooped Zaina into her arms and grabbed her kanga.

Mia pressed her back against the door and frantically dug through her purse for her phone. "We don't know that." She found her phone and crammed it into her pocket. Another crash and Mia heard the front door shatter. "The window. Go—"

Footsteps thundered across the living room. The bedroom door burst open and slammed Mia against the wall. Three men rushed into the room, guns pointing in every direction. Before Mia could get her breath, two of the men had Jeme by the arms.

"An albino." The third man wrenched Zaina free of Jeme's hold and tucked the child under his arm thrilled as if he'd just struck gold. "We will get paid extra for this one."

"Not my baby!"

"No!" Mia flew across the room. "Get your hands off that child." She scratched, clawed, and pounded rock-hard flesh. "Let them go."

Something solid whacked Mia across the back of her knees, dropping her to the floor.

"You want to live?" The man yanking her from the floor was as black as midnight and wore a heavy gold chain around his neck. "Stop fighting." He pushed her toward the bedroom door.

Mia stumbled into the living room just as one of the men clamped a big hand over Jeme's mouth and dragged her, writhing and kicking, outside. "Where are you taking them?"

He ripped the bandana-like headband from his shiny, slick head and thrust it at her. "Cover your mouth."

"No. I won't."

He stuck the barrel of the gun under Mia's nose. "Then I will blow it off."

"What do you want?" Hands trembling, Mia brought the headband to her lips, the soured smell of sweat making her gag. "I can get you money...drugs...anything. Just let her and the baby go."

The intruder rammed the butt of his gun into her unprotected middle and Mia doubled over. "Shut your mouth."

Mia struggled for breath, sure he had broken a rib. She straightened slowly, despite the searing pain, and tied the bandana around her mouth then let him tie her hands behind her back. Next he had Jeme secure Zaina to her chest, then tied Jeme's hands behind her as well. Once he was satisfied his hostages could neither fight or scream, he pushed Mia and Jeme through the demolished front door and out into the dark compound. As far as Mia could tell, the commotion had not stirred a single neighbor to come to their aid.

While shoving her toward a waiting 4X4 truck, the man with the shiny head gave a thumbs-up signal to the driver then wrestled Mia into the back with Jeme and Zaina.

The other abductors piled into the front of the vehicle. The man with the gold chain jumped into the back and sat on the tailgate. Within seconds they were speeding from the compound. Someone must have paid the guards to look the other way.

Mia scooted across the truck bed in the dark. Her hands encountered puddles of something cold and wet while searching for the warm flesh of Zaina's leg. She inched closer to Jeme, then worked to untie her hands. Straining in the darkness, she tried to discern if the man in the back with them could hear her. Convinced the engine would drown out her voice, she spoke through the gag.

"You okay?" she whispered.

"Yes." Jeme's voice barely cleared the roar of the truck's motor.

"Zaina?"

"I think so."

"Don't worry." Mia swallowed the gut-level terror clawing her chest. "We'll be okay. I won't let anything happen to you." She hoped she sounded more convincing than she felt.

For what seemed like hours, they sat in the back of the tarp-covered truck that was ripe with the stench of dead animal decay and gasoline. She felt the stain of whatever was in the truck bed soaking into her jeans.

These men had come prepared to invade her home and to hurt her. Finding an albino had surprised them. She could understand they might not want to mess with managing a baby until they could find a more secluded place to harvest what would sell and that's why they'd taken Jeme, but why had they taken her? Why hadn't they just killed her at the apartment? Someone must want her scared, not dead.

Amandi.

Remembering the anger in his eyes and the threats on his alcohol-tainted breath gave the possibility a mind-stinging validity and turned her cold.

Surely even a blackguard like Amandi would not resort to scaring her into dropping her investigation? If the medical review board ever found out that he'd kidnapped a fellow surgeon, he'd go to prison for life. She'd make sure of it.

But money was at stake, she reminded herself. Lots of it. She'd been a fool to discount the desperation of a man willing to test unproven drugs on the sick and poor for money. If only she could manage to get to her phone, she'd call...who?

Race. He'd know what to do.

In the darkness, all she could see was Zaina's pale legs kicking against her mother and the whites of Jeme's eyes darting back and forth, seeking a way out.

The truck bounced off the road and lurched to a stop, the motor still running. The tarp was ripped away and a flashlight shown in their faces. "Out."

Head ducked to protect her eyes from the glare, Mia caught a glimpse of the truck bed.

Blood.

Everywhere. Some spots black and dried. Some puddles red and wet. Fear caught her breath and held it captive. What had been hauled in this truck?

"Out! Now!" The man with the gold chain shoved them toward the opening.

Mia stayed close to Jeme. Snippets of TV crime shows flashed in her mind. Letting their abductors take them off the road would be a mistake. But it wasn't as if they had a choice. He pushed Mia out. She hit the dirt hard, but managed to scramble to her feet.

He let Jeme climb down from the truck, while Mia tried to get her bearings. They'd made so many turns, she had no idea where they were or how far they'd traveled. Her eyes followed the headlight beams. A wall of dense foliage loomed ahead. *Lord, not the jungle.* Tanzania's forests might not be true jungles, but the dense scrub meant she wouldn't know where she was or how to find help.

She and Jeme huddled together while the man with the gold chain made a phone call. He spoke Swahili while pointing at Zaina.

Jeme's eyes grew wide. She whispered through the gag, "They want Zaina's heart."

Panic thundered through Mia's veins. She searched the darkness for an escape.

The man with the gold chain put his phone in his pocket. "There is no one to hear you scream and nowhere to run." A sly smile spreading across his face, he ripped the gags from their mouths and the ties from their wrists.

Mia wheeled on their captors stalling for time and an idea of how to protect this baby. "We need water."

Laughter ricocheted off the surrounding curtain of tangled vines. "Move." The man with the gold chain jabbed the barrel of his gun into her ribs.

Mia winced. The man poked her again and she willed her legs to catch up to the other two men disappearing into the bush.

Jeme ran back beside her. "Stay close to me." As though equipped with a sixth sense, she slid through the narrow opening one of the abductors had hacked in the thick undergrowth with his machete.

Mia took a deep breath and followed. Immediately, dank darkness swallowed her. Disoriented, she thrashed the tangled air, unable to see anything. The screams of her suffocating panic rivaled the clamor of the hidden nightlife.

Something touched her arm and she jumped.

"Stay close," Jeme whispered. "I am used to walking in the dark."

And threats to her daughter's life, because she appeared calm as the windless night. Heart pounding in her ears, Mia latched on. Allowing Jeme to lead her forward, she tussled with the urge to shout at her to run.

God help us.

Mia blindly stumbled behind Jeme, humbled by the fact that her survival was in the hands of a woman with only one thing left to lose.

Shafts of moonlight pierced the canopy. Slowly Mia's eyes adjusted to the shifting shadows. It would take a miracle for anyone to find them. Something rattled the branches in the thicket to her left. She stretched her stride from one silvery moonlit patch of forest floor to the next.

As they ascended the narrow path, the man with the machete carved through the rough terrain. Each step became more difficult and the pain in her side increased. Mia tripped over every root, fallen limb, and who-knows-what else like a clumsy, slow-motion robot.

The man with the gold chain growled at her in a language Mia couldn't understand. "What did he say, Jeme?"

"You must keep up or they will kill you."

Struggling to keep pace, Mia gasped for breath while Jeme seemed as agile as a jungle cat. Mia's broken rib stabbed as if it could puncture a lung if she wasn't careful. Sweat dripped down her back, and come daylight she'd certainly find her bare arms slashed bloody. Thank God she'd changed into jeans and out of those heels. Whether or not her flip-flops would hold up to this forced march remained to be seen.

If only she knew for sure what these men wanted from her. Then maybe she could offer them some kind of deal and secure Jeme and Zaina's freedom.

Just when she thought her lungs could take no more, their little band broke through the brush. In the small clearing, moonbeams lit the roofs of three crude huts.

The leader grabbed Mia's arm and jerked her toward the middle hut. He opened the door and shoved her inside. She tripped over whatever was littering the floor and crashed into the opposite wall. Head pounding, she slid down the mud wall and landed on a worn patch of hard-packed earth.

She pushed herself upright and shouted, "What do you want?"

He slammed the door without a word. Outside she could hear the laughing jeers of the men, Jeme begging them to leave her alone, and then the shrieking cry of Zaina.

Mia sprang from the floor and barreled toward the door, hitting it full force with her shoulder. It popped open and she landed with a thud at the feet of the man holding Zaina high above his head.

She leapt to her feet. "Get your hands off her." Pummeling her fists into the man's chest did nothing to bring Zaina within her reach.

"Dr. Kendall." The man with the gold chain pulled her off. "You are making it harder to keep you in one piece."

Mia stopped. "How do you know my name?" she panted, her mind too oxygen-deprived to sort things out. "Answer me. Who wants me in one piece?"

He laughed and snatched Zaina from the man twirling her above his head. "Fool. The child must be perfect too." He turned and handed Zaina to Mia. "Tomorrow, Dr. Kendall. Tomorrow all questions will be answered. All debts settled."

He nodded and his two companions shoved Mia and Jeme back into the hut she'd just exited. They closed the door. She tried to shove it open, but something held it firmly shut.

"Don't let them take my baby." Jeme's panting whisper curled around Mia's heart and yanked it out.

CHAPTER FORTY-THREE

TUESDAY, DECEMBER 17TH, 2:52 AM

RACE'S APARTMENT, DAR ES SALAAM

Race flipped onto his back then let out a loud *humph*. The constant whirr of the fan above him grated on his nerves, while doing little to relieve the heat. He'd stared at the ceiling for the past two hours, but was still no closer to falling asleep than when he first went to bed.

Seeing Mia tonight, decked out in that black dress with those long, *long* legs might have temporarily caused him to take leave of his senses, but her final performance had knocked every bit of reality back into him. She actually considered him a suspect in league with Amandi. The very thought made him want to vomit. And to think he'd actually paid good money to rent one of those stupid monkey suits then showed up at her door like some love-struck kid.

He flipped back onto his side and punched the pillow. Of all the ungrateful, unappreciative, and. . . and unbearable people in this world, Dr. Kendall reigned at the top of his list. He'd spent the past week stealing files, breaking into labs, and fishing for answers, until even he, with his "limited morals" as he was certain she saw him, had started to feel guilty.

Apparently, he'd read her wrong. She'd used him then tossed him out like last week's takeout.

Of course, Mia had her daddy to pull her out of trouble, which probably meant that right now she was sleeping like a baby. Amandi wasn't her problem. All she had to do was hand over the pile of evidence she'd collected, smile pretty, and play the role of hero when the truth of what *they'd* discovered came to light.

He kicked his sheet onto the floor. Let her take all the glory and have her photo pasted across CNN's headline news. That was fine with him. He could use a change of pace. Surely there was someone else on this vast continent who could use a hot-tempered, rogue-flying bush pilot—prone to falling for underhanded women—who could ferry rich tourists from one safari camp to the next. That way there'd be no chance of him unknowingly trafficking illegal organs, because no matter what she thought, he didn't need—nor had he ever needed—Amandi to pad his weekly paycheck.

His cell phone rang, jerking him out of bed. He swung his legs over the side of the mattress and answered.

"I have located a heart for the American girl."

"Amandi?"

"Can I count on you to deliver or not?"

Race's gut churned at the idea of working another job for the doctor, but not only was a girl's life at stake, the chance to find out the truth was worth one last flight across the African savannas. This time he was going in with his eyes wide open.

He grabbed a pair of jeans off the floor and tugged them on. "I can be there in a little over an hour."

Twenty minutes later he was airborne. While an emergency flight before dawn was something he preferred to avoid, years of bush flying had left him with a dozen tricks up his sleeve they'd never taught in flying school. And considering some of the conditions he'd had to fly through, tonight would be a snap. Far easier than maneuvering through tight mountain passes or any number of situations most pilots deemed impossible.

Fifty minutes later, Race touched down on a remote landing strip. Leaving the engine running, he exited the plane.

Three men waited for him. His stomach clenched. This was not the typical pickup and delivery protocol.

"Where's the organ?"

"There has been a change of plans. You need to come with us." The tallest man took a step toward him. "We have a few questions for you."

"A change of plans. . .I don't think so." Race swung for the man and let his fist slam into the bridge of his nose.

But the odds were against him, and a second later he felt a crushing impact on the side of his head and fell back onto the packed earth. He looked up at the black African sky, felt another sharp jab to his ribcage then...nothing.

CHAPTER FORTY-FOUR

TUESDAY, DECEMBER 17TH, 10:12 AM

MOROGORO REGION

The aroma of meat cooking over a wood fire prodded Mia from a fitful doze. She opened her eyes to shards of sunlight piercing the lone window of the mud hut. A long night of listening to the throaty calls of wild animals on the prowl had given her plenty of time to regret backing a jackal like Amandi into a corner. The blame for putting Jeme and Zaina in such grave danger belonged squarely on her shoulders. He never would have known about them, if he hadn't come after her.

At least one abductor had stood guard outside their door all night. Even though Race had not been happy with her when he left, she'd swallowed her pride and tried to call him on the cell their kidnappers had somehow missed in her back pocket. But apparently, they'd traveled too deep into the bush to get a decent signal.

Pushing herself up from the worn patch of earth, she took a quick assessment of the physical conditions of her charges. Jeme, sitting cross-legged and leaning against the wall, was nursing Zaina. Although mother and child were filthy, they'd suffered this captivity without a whimper or complaint. She, on the other hand, was scratched, bruised, and fighting mad.

"I'm going to see if I can't get them to give us some breakfast." Mia got to her feet slowly, the pain from her broken rib making it hard to straighten the kinks from her body. She dusted the grime from her bloodstained jeans then rubbed her hands together to remove the caked-on dirt. Rectifying her filthy state would be impossible without soap and water. She gave up and went to the door.

Looking through the slats, she could see three men, their faces black as charred wood, sitting around the campfire. One had the butt of his AK-47 resting on the top of his hiking boot and the gun barrel wedged in the crook of his arm. The other two had their guns within reach.

She picked up a piece of broken pottery and pounded the door. "Hey! We need the toilet."

Three pairs of soot-colored eyes shifted from the pot on the fire to Mia and Jeme's ramshackle prison. Laughter split the smoky air and fanned the flame of indignation that had simmered in her empty belly all night.

She stepped back and hurled the pottery against the door. "Let us out!"

The grinding sound of four-wheel drive chewing through the sticky clay sent the men scurrying for the thick brush and Mia's fears through the thatched roof. A truck with a tarped bed skidded to a halt between the hut and the fire ring. She couldn't be sure, but the vehicle was the same size and make as the one that had transported them out of the city. If their camp could be reached by truck, the forced march through the forest must have been simply another way to terrorize them. Well it had worked.

The driver jumped out and slammed the door. He surveyed the deserted camp then called out in Swahili.

Seconds later, the kidnappers emerged from the dense cover, their guns pointed at the driver. After a hasty conversation, they laughed and clapped each other on the shoulder like long-lost friends, then everyone tramped to the truck's tailgate. The man with the gold chain threw back the tarp, and two of the kidnappers reached in and hauled out a limp body and dropped it on the ground.

"Race!" Mia pounded the door with both fists. "Race!"

Race lifted his beaten and battered head. "Mia?" He tried to push himself up from the dirt.

One of the kidnappers put his foot on Race's back and slammed him to the earth. "Traitor."

Mia peered through the crack in the door slats. "Race, cooperate. We're fine."

The man with the gold chain nodded toward Mia's hut. "Timbo, lock him up."

"With her?" the driver asked.

"Look at him." He nudged Race with the toe of his boot. "Our pilot's not going anywhere." He pointed the barrel of his gun at the hut's door. "And I do not think she is going without him. Haji, help him."

Two muscular men, their black skin gleaming in the morning light, hooked their arms under Race's and dragged him to the hut. They untied the door and tossed him inside.

Mia rushed to check out Race's injuries. "Lie still." She squatted beside his body and carefully turned his bloody face toward hers. He had a gash on his forehead, a fat lip, and what promised to be a doozey of a shiner. "What are you doing here?"

He opened one eye. "Classing up the joint." His lopsided smile slid from his swollen lips as she examined his extremities. "Take it easy."

She ran her hands over the well-defined muscles of his torso, the beat of his heart reassuringly strong and regular considering his blood-soaked shirt. She'd give anything for her medical bag and maybe an x-ray machine to check for internal injuries. "This hurt?"

"Yep."

"Anything broken?"

"Just my heart." His eyes locked with hers. "Do you still believe I had anything to do with this?"

Her head was spinning. He was obviously hurt and their prisoner, same as she, but what if it was all a ruse, a ploy to throw her off his trail? "I don't know." She swallowed the urge to kiss his injured lips. "How did you end up here?"

"I could ask you the same thing."

"You first."

"Amandi called. Said he had a heart for the American girl. I went because I had to know ... where he was getting the hearts."

"And?"

He shook his head. "I didn't get a chance to ask. They jumped me at the plane." He took her hand. "Are you okay?"

"Scraped up a bit. They burst into my apartment and drove us around for hours, then marched us through the bush." Checking the dilation of his pupils as best she could in the inferior light, Mia said, "Jeme, can I use your kanga to clean him up?"

He cupped his hand around her neck and pulled her face close. "Doc, I may need mouth to mouth."

"You will if you don't let me go." She freed his hand from her hair and took the wrap Jeme had silently removed from her waist. "Do you know these guys?"

Race gave a painful nod. "We're not pals, but yeah."

"Who are they?"

He snatched a breath as if the rest of what he had to say would hurt more than any of the injuries he had sustained. "My organ contacts."

"These are the people you've been dealing with?"

"Look—"

"No, you look." She pointed to the cracks in the door. "They're thugs." She dabbed at his forehead. "But why'd they make a punching bag out of you? I'm the one who made that quack mad."

"You're a pistol alright. I guess Amandi's afraid I'm in too deep with you to fly under the radar anymore."

"What are you talking about?"

He jacked up his head and shoulders with his elbows. "Guess what I heard them say they haul in that truck?"

"What?"

The flirtatious twinkle evaporated from his gaze. "They're poachers."

"Elephants?"

He shook his head, his face deadly serious. "Albinos."

Bile rose in Mia's throat. She dropped the kanga and clamped a hand across her mouth. She glanced down at her jeans. The blood staining her clothes belonged to human beings, slaughtered because of the color of their skin.

Terror buried Jeme's calm. "They want my baby's heart. I will not let them take her." She clutched Zaina tight against her breasts, rocking back and forth.

Mia's anger bubbled. "They'd have to kill me to get to Zaina."

Race kicked at a pile of rubble. "We need to find a way out of here."

Mia paced the small space of the hut and started throwing out various escape plans, but Race shot down every one of her ideas with the ease of a military sniper. The heat inside the hut had risen to an almost unbearable level. Mia licked her parched lips. Jeme juggled a fussy Zaina. Race scrounged through the litter strewn across the dirt floor. He found a triangular-shaped piece of pottery on the floor and ran his finger gingerly along the jagged edge.

Mia stopped her pacing to gaze over his shoulder. "What are you doing?"

"Mental diversions." He wiped his brow with the back of his hand. "A little something I took up on the flight line. Calms me down."

She studied the place on the dirt floor where he carved out surprisingly neat rows of letters—six rows across and six down. "So how does your little game work?"

"If I don't have a word search puzzle, I make my own. See how many words I can make out of tossing random letters around."

"Like this." She took the shard from his hand, bent, and circled the letters in her name that cut a diagonal across his square. "A. I. M.—Mia spelled backwards."

She froze, her mind backpedaling to the day she and Race surfed the Internet to track down someone from BPH Technologies.

"What is it?" he asked.

Mia's gaze darted between Race and Jeme. "Makes me think of my father. Whenever I was impulsive, he'd tease me that instead of ready, aim, fire, I had a tendency to ready, fire, aim."

"You never told me about your father."

She cleared her throat, suddenly lost in the past. "I found out a couple years ago that my father was the son of a car mechanic serving time for armed robbery. But he wanted something better for his life. So he worked hard to hone his athletic skills. He ended up going to Harvard on a football scholarship."

"Impressive. Why did he decide to practice medicine?"

"He wanted to make it up to society for his father's failings by helping people. Plus med school seemed the next logical step to prestige and financial security."

She trembled as more memories surfaced. "He eventually made himself into one of the world's most renowned transplant surgeons, with a huge private practice, speaking tours, even a book on a procedure he pioneered. He was my biggest cheerleader...even after..." Mia let her words trail off.

"Even after what, Mia?"

"About five years ago, he had to have my mother committed. It was a pretty dark time for both of us." She raised her eyes to his. "She died from an overdose of painkillers six months later, but no one was ever able to find out how she did it. I think she just stored up her meds and when she thought she had enough, she took them all at once."

"I'm sorry. I know what's it's like to lose someone you love." He began erasing the puzzle with the edge of the pottery.

She stared at the remaining conglomerate of words he'd circled in the dirt. "Who was she?"

He continued scratching lines into the dirt. "Rachel was my wife." He turned away from her, but not before she caught the pain enveloping his expression.

Mia decided to take a chance. "What happened?"

Race smoothed out the dirt and started over with a new puzzle. "Rachel came from a big farm family in Nebraska. We got married right out of college and planned to have a dozen kids together.

"She wanted to grow corn. I wanted to fly planes. She taught school while I worked on my commission as a fighter pilot. Our first assignment was South Georgia. She got a job teaching third grade, and I got sent to Saudi to fly F-16s."

As much as she'd wanted to know what made Race Daniels tick, Mia couldn't help but wonder if she'd gone too far. "You don't have to tell me more. I shouldn't have asked."

His jaw tensed. "I left when she was six weeks pregnant. She was diabetic and the pregnancy took its toll on her kidneys." He swallowed. "The baby died during the last trimester...before the doctors could do anything about it."

"Rachel, too?"

"Yeah." He scratched another line into the dirt with the pottery shard. "She needed a kidney."

"I'm sorry."

He shoved the shard into his pocket and strode to the door, the conversation clearly over for now. "I might have been a perfect match."

CHAPTER FORTY-FIVE

TUESDAY, DECEMBER 17TH, 11:42 AM

SHINWANGA REGIONAL HOSPITAL

Axton darted away from the end of Dryden's sword, but his movements were too slow. His nemesis lunged toward him then thrust his weapon into Axton's ribcage. Axton stumbled across the stone floor, trying to keep his balance. He looked down at the deep wound, but the blood seeping through his coat only intensified his determination to win. He might not survive this final encounter, but he would make certain Dryden would not live to see the dawn of another day. He had been right. They would fight to the death.

Swinging his sword with every bit of remaining strength he could muster, he heaved his weapon through the air. Metal clashed against metal. He thrust the sword again toward his opponent, missing him by inches. Dryden dodged backward to avoid him then knocked over the iron stand holding the burning candles. In an instant, flames devoured the heavy curtain hanging the length of the wall.

Axton took advantage of the diversion and lunged once again at Dryden. This time the tip of his sword met its mark and pierced through the villain's heart. A look of shock registered on Dryden's face as he tottered then crumbled to the ground. Dryden was dead.

The vial tumbled from Dryden's pocket, rolled across the floor, and stopped at Axton's feet. Heat from the flames enveloped him. Gripping the deadly contents in his hand, Axton limped from the entrance of the cathedral, his lungs straining with every breath, before falling to the ground.

"Axton?"

He forced his eyes open. Paige knelt beside him. She grasped the front of his coat, pulled him toward her then offered him water from her carafe. Behind them, the monks fought in vain to save their cathedral, but all he could see was the woman he loved.

"I've been so worried," she began. "When you didn't come to the caves, I thought. . .I thought you were dead."

He choked on the liquid and it ran down his chin. "Dryden is dead, but the virus still must be neutralized."

He handed her the serum from the pouch hanging on his neck. "You know what to do."

"Axton. . .Axton. . ." Her voice shook as she raised her hands, now covered with his blood that stained the ground beneath him. "You're wounded."

He fought to take another breath, knowing he would not live to see their children grow up. "Paige. . .I'm sorry. . .I—"

"You cannot die on me, Axton." Anger laced her words. "You sacrificed everything to save my people and now that victory is ours. We will celebrate together."

"It was a sacrifice well worth my death. They are my people, too, remember."

"I will not let you die."

"Listen to me." He grasped her hand as he felt his life slip away. "With Dryden out of the way and the virus neutralized, your father's troops will be able to contain any remaining rebels on the island."

"No!" Her eyes filled with tears. "Without my father. . .without you. . .They need you to lead them. I need you."

Axton fingered the golden locket around her neck and pulled her toward him until he could feel the warmth of her breath against his face and smell the fragrant perfume she wore. Then he kissed her for the last time.

Someone jolted Harry from behind. Moving aside, he took a deep puff of his inhaler. Waiting for his air passages to clear, he stared down the blue walls of Shinwanga Regional Hospital and tried to gather any remaining threads of courage.

Axton Blade was dead, and he was going to be next if he hung around here.

He staggered toward the nurses' counter and tried not to breathe in the sickly-sweet scent of antiseptic that mingled with the metallic smell of blood. His hatred of hospitals was the very reason he'd never actually practiced medicine. And being a hero was overrated. It was one thing to try and save the world from the comfort of his own lab, but halfway around the world, in a sub-standard hospital where patients were dying of tuberculosis and typhoid . . .well. . .that was a completely different story.

"Can I help you?" A uniformed nurse with rows of neat braids stopped in front of him.

Harry shoved the inhaler into his front pocket then wiped a row of sweat from his brow. "I'm sorry. What?"

"If you need a doctor, you're going to have to wait in line, I'm afraid."

"A doctor?" His head swam. The ebony figure before him disappeared then reappeared. Hallucinations. He must have already contracted some deadly tropical disease. He did need a doctor.

It's time you took a chance, Harry.

He shook his head and pictured Valerie, her hands planted on those cute little hips. He could do this. "I'm looking for a doctor, but not as a patient. I need to see Dr. Kendall as a. . .as a professional colleague from the States." He tugged at his collar. "It's very urgent."

The woman's smile faded. "You are not the only one looking for her. She had surgeries scheduled today, but I have had to cancel them all."

"I don't understand."

"I am sorry. If you can come back tomorrow, perhaps she will be here."

The image of Valerie faded. If Axton, with all his brute strength and courage, had been unable to survive his quest, what hope did he have of surviving Africa? Harry pressed himself against the wall to avoid another nurse trudging down the hall with an empty gurney. People died here.

He noticed the flecks of chipped paint on the cinderblocks. And the suspicious yellowish stain six inches from his head. He was going to be sick. He could name two-dozen deadly African diseases without thinking, and no doubt he'd been exposed to at least half of those in the past five minutes. He wiped the back of his neck. His skin was clammy. Yes. He was definitely running a fever.

Harry stumbled from the building to the parking lot and the car he'd rented. An extra fifteen dollars a day had procured a chauffeur. Still shaky from his car wreck, he reasoned the added expense was worth it if it kept him from having to drive in this foreign city on the wrong side of the road.

He slipped into the seat behind the driver. "George, take me back to the hotel. Immediately."

The locks on the car engaged, and the driver turned around.

Harry swallowed hard. This wasn't George. He yanked on the handle, trying to get out of the car, but the door refused to open. His mouth went dry.

"Where's my chauffeur?" he croaked.

"Plans have changed." The man's hollow laugh filled the car. "George had other. . .business. I will be driving you now."

"Wait a minute. I hired George—"

The man reached over the seat and grasped his arm, his hold nearly cutting off all circulation in Harry's hand. "Like I said. Plans have changed."

Harry's attempts to escape the man's grip proved futile. "Please don't hurt me. I don't have much cash on me, but what I have is yours."

"Shut up." The driver squeezed one more time before sliding on a pair of sunglasses and starting the engine. "Lucky for you, my boss believes you are worth more alive than dead."

CHAPTER FORTY-SIX

TUESDAY, DECEMBER 17TH, 7:03 PM

MOROGORO REGION

Evening shadows crept from the forest and slithered through the cracks in the mud hut. Timbo opened the door and thrust one metal bowl of *ugali* and three bottles of water into Mia's hands. She surveyed the small lump of sticky porridge.

"This isn't enough. We have a nursing mother in here. She hasn't eaten all day."

Anger flashed in the man's eyes. He slammed the door, retied the latch, then walked away without a word.

Mia set their paltry rations in front of Jeme and Race. "Dinner is served." She propped herself against the wall and crossed her arms over the fears that burned a hole in her hollow gut. "You and Zaina eat, Jeme."

Jeme shook her head. At Mia's insistence, she finally pulled off a piece of the gummy mixture. Zaina's mouth flew open like a baby bird waiting on a worm. Watching the child suck down the little bit of sustenance, Mia silently cursed the power of recessive genes.

Race took a bottle of water for himself and tossed one to Mia. "Drink."

The tepid water slid down Mia's parched throat but did not douse the fire in her belly. She could feel her body soaking up the much-needed hydration. She wiped her lips. Finding a way out of their makeshift prison had so far proven elusive.

Race had only drained half his water bottle. "Anybody back at the salt mine that might miss you enough to notify the authorities?"

"Maybe the nurses and Shadrach. But the nurses might think I was out on a medflight house call, and Shadrach's a Congo refugee and very leery of the police."

Race pulled something out of his pocket. "I have a couple ideas."

In the dimming light, she could barely make out the pottery shard he'd used for his word search pen. "Such as?"

"Either flip one of those guys to our side, which doesn't seem very likely, or we try and make a hole in the back of this hut and run. The wall's nothing more than half a foot of hardened mud."

Mia peered through the slats of the door. He was right about their captors. Mbui had better odds of beating a drug-induced heart rejection than they did of winning over one of the sour-faced men camped at the fire ring. But running. . .with a baby. . .

Exhaustion and hunger was about to do her in. "Don't you think they'd hear us? And even if we did get out, then what? We don't even know where we are."

"Do you have a better idea?"

She closed her eyes and let her head rest against the wall. What could she count on? She thought on this a moment. God had not forsaken her. He hadn't miraculously orchestrated their rescue, but he had sent Race. Though counting on Race being able to execute an escape plan with two women, a baby, and a piece of forgotten cookware was enough to make anyone question God's wisdom at this point. And where would they go if they did get free? Her flip-flops were nearly shot, and they hadn't eaten a decent meal in twenty-four hours.

Race scooted closer. "Soon as they fall asleep, we'll bust out of here, then pray we'll come across someone with a car."

Jeme offered Mia a piece of ugali. "I'm good in the dark."

Mia choked down the bland bite. "That you are." She smiled as Jeme scooped Zaina from the pile of pots she was clanging and tucked her into her kanga like she was packing to leave. "And once we have cell phone service again, I'll be able to call the hospital and check on Mbui." She gave Jeme the last unopened water bottle. "Drink some more, then get some rest."

Jeme settled against the opposite wall with Zaina. Mia watched as Jeme gathered her child's pale hand in hers and brought it to her lips. Zaina's puckered mouth broke free of the nipple. She flashed an adoring smile at her mother then hungrily latched on again. In that moment, Mia understood true riches...having someone to love and having that love returned.

Race stroked Mia's arm. "How you holding up?"

"I'm okay."

Slowly, the darkness consumed the last of the hut's light. Mia stewed in silence, listening to Zaina's contented sighs.

Race interrupted her thoughts. "Why'd you do it, Doc?"

"Do what?"

"Come to Africa?"

Had he read her mind? Did he know she blamed herself for the mess they were in? She wished the darkness hadn't made it impossible to make out his face. "Long story."

His hand gripped hers. "We've got nothing but time."

The warmth of his touch melted her resistance. "When I finished med school, I thought I'd be a doctor with a capital D. Different. Better. Able to handle all the pressure."

"Wonder Woman?"

She shrugged. "It was one of those zooish days—no lunch, no dinner, one surgery after another. Early in the day, I operated on this fourteen-year-old cheerleader. Just a simple repair of a hole in the heart. Something I'd done probably twenty times. She did great in surgery. I assumed she'd do fine in recovery, but didn't take the time to make certain. After I finished my last surgery, I ran to Chili's across the street, intending to come back and check on her. While I was eating a salad..."

"The kid was dying."

Vintage regret rose from the depths and lodged in Mia's throat. "The nurses tried to page me, but I'd forgotten to take my pager or my cell." She swallowed hard. "They brought in another doctor to try and save her, but by the time I returned to the hospital, it was too late. She'd thrown a clot." Hot tears, heavy and familiar with well-ripened guilt she might not ever completely shake, streamed down her face. "I had to go tell that waiting mother her little girl had died because I was hungry. The mother started throwing everything at me she could get her hands on."

"And you stood there, letting her give you the stoning you deserved?" He squeezed her hand. "Nobody's perfect, Mia."

"I left the pager on purpose." Confessing the truth out loud sounded far worse than the million times she'd replayed that night in her head. "I just needed a minute to myself." She turned her face to his, grateful he couldn't see the tears streaming down her cheeks. "Have you ever done anything you were so ashamed of, you didn't think you could go on living?"

He let her hand go. "Yes." The buzz of cicadas filled his pause. "I volunteered for an assignment that took me away from my wife and child—" His voice cracked. "And while I was saving the world, they died."

She waited a moment, allowing the sounds of the jungle to absorb the pain he didn't seem to want healed. "So you left the military to work for a nonprofit and ended up flying organs across East Africa."

He shifted his body and she knew she'd struck the right nerve. "I didn't want some other poor jerk to lose his wife because he was stupid." Before she could respond, he changed the subject. "But you're still practicing medicine, Doc, so obviously you didn't completely walk away."

"All the way to Tanzania." Mia felt her heart lunge toward his. "I thought maybe, just maybe, I could find my purpose in life again."

"Have you?"

"It's starting to come back." Mia pointed at Jeme and Zaina curled up together asleep. "Somehow it's wrapped up in making the world a better place. A place where desperate parents wouldn't have to consider exchanging their albino children for money. And where desperate mothers wouldn't have to risk everything to get their children the organs they need." The image of Catherine Taylor clinging to a shoestring of hope flashed in her mind. "The Great Physician's slowly healing me. If good can come from my failure—"

Race let out a skeptical laugh. "Then somehow that makes your pain worth it, right?"

Mia looked at him. "What?"

"My parents might pray for me 24/7, but I don't put a lot of stock in God's interest in this world. Things are the way they are. And bad things happen to even the best of people."

"Like your wife?"

"Where was God when I couldn't be there for my family?" Anger laced his escalating voice. "Where was I?"

"So you're still trying to escape the pain of God's failure to answer your prayers? Or the fact that you weren't able to do anything to save them?"

"I agreed to fly organs from one place to the other because God can't. People that would have died, live because I do what He won't."

"And that's why you didn't question anyone about the organs?"

"Just like you, what I do saves lives. You want to keep everything all lined out in neat little rows like your Sudoku cube. That way you can check your list if something goes south."

"And you need to control the situation by doing everything yourself to ensure justice is done," she said. "But I never said everything is black or white. Sometimes life takes a bit of creative maneuvering."

"Maneuvering?" He laughed. "Doc, bending the rules is bending the rules. I may not be able to put a new heart into someone, but I can sure get it to the folks who can. And if I have to *maneuv*er around the corrupt system so some little girl can live, so be it."

"Race, do you believe one life is more valuable than another?"

He flinched at her question. "No."

"Then you agree that once I cut past the thin layer of skin that defines us all, that everything else—the heart, our feelings, and our fears—are all the same?"

"Of course."

"If I cut you open right now, I'm guessing I'd find a man who's as vulnerable as little Zaina, right?"

"So?"

"So who decides who lives or dies?" She waited for her question to sink in. "I don't have all the answers, but I know that I can never again hold the hearts of Africa in my hands and not wonder from whom they were taken."

CHAPTER FORTY-SEVEN

WEDNESDAY, DECEMBER 18TH, 3:00 AM

KABONI PRIVATE HOSPITAL

Catherine removed the thin pillow from under Kelsey's sweat-drenched head. She folded it like the peanut butter and banana sandwiches Jonathan loved then gently lifted the head full of soppy golden curls. She wedged the dry side of the pillow into place then waited, praying that the increased upper body elevation would give her baby some desperately needed breathing relief. The wheezing stopped.

A gurgling sound escaped Kelsey's lips. Catherine froze, afraid to take her next breath for fear she might miss her daughter's last. Dr. Kendall's new medicine trickled from the IV bag like sand in an hourglass, but it hadn't slowed Kelsey's deterioration. Time was running out. And she could do nothing to stop the clock. Tears leaked from Catherine's eyes as she watched for any movement of the tiny ribcage.

Suddenly, Kelsey's eyes fluttered open. Cloudy-blue and panicked, they darted around the room. Her cracked lips puckered like a goldfish searching the water's surface for air. "Mommy," she whispered.

"Mommy's here, punkin."

Within seconds, Kelsey's eyes closed and the wheezing resumed—

terrifying labored gasps that Catherine had overheard the nurses describing as the death rattle.

"Hang on, punkin." Catherine leaned over and placed her lips to Kelsey's forehead. Still scorching hot to the touch. "Please, hang on for Mommy."

Hands trembling, Catherine pulled her phone from her pocket and checked the messages. Nothing from Brad. Nothing from her father. Nothing from the American doctor. And most frustrating of all, nothing from the African doctor.

A feeling of total aloneness swamped her, drowning her as if her lungs were the ones filling with fluid. She crammed the phone into her pocket. Where was the African doctor who'd performed Kelsey's operation? Didn't surgeons in Africa make rounds? Check on their patients on a regular basis?

She paced the room, wringing her hands, wondering what to do next. She'd called every number both doctors had given her. She'd pointed out to the nurses Kelsey's spiking temperatures and even showed them the swelling in her tiny ankles. She'd done everything but throw herself in front of one of those slow-moving African ambulances, but she'd made no progress in getting anyone to find her a qualified doctor.

Kelsey's legs began to thrash the sheets. Her arms flailed the bed. And then her hands went for the tubes. "It hurts."

Catherine ran to her side. "I know, punkin. Mommy's trying to make it better. Please be still."

"It hurts," she cried, a fine spray of blood shooting from her mouth. "It hurts."

"Oh, my God. Don't move, Kelsey!" Catherine bolted from the room and ran down the hall screaming, "Get me a doctor! Now!" Breathless, she slid to a halt at the nurses' station, blood splattered all over her T-shirt. "Get Dr. Amandi. Now!" She wheeled and raced back to Kelsey's room.

For the next five minutes, Catherine clutched the rail on the side of Kelsey's bed, sopping blood, soothing her daughter as best she could, trying to keep her own anguished screams from escaping and panicking Kelsey even more.

Finally, Dr. Amandi sauntered into the room.

She bit back the tongue lashing he deserved, holding her breath as he eased his stethoscope over the inflamed scar on her daughter's chest.

The man reeked of alcohol and women's perfume. If this gross neglect had happened at Cincinnati Children's she would have marched his shaky butt directly before the hospital administration firing squad.

Instead, she swallowed the desire to punch him and forced a shallow breath. Her tantrum at the nurses' station had finally worked. For now, his lack of professionalism would have to be overlooked. But he wasn't leaving until he made Kelsey well.

Forcing herself to quit wringing her hands, Catherine squared her shoulders and asked, "Have the meds made any progress in reversing her rejection?"

"I'm afraid not." He glanced up from his examination. "Kelsey seems to be in that small percentage that rejects for no apparent reason."

"Has the new medicine slowed it down?"

"New medication?"

"The one Dr. Kendall prescribed."

Dr. Amandi rose from his bent position over Kelsey, looked her in the eye, and shook his head. "Sadly, this child requires another heart."

The thought of another child dying clenched Catherine's stomach. But she'd come too far to turn back now. "And you're getting it, right?"

"I am working every possible connection."

"Don't you think we should call Dr. Kendall?"

His brow furrowed. "She can do nothing to procure another heart."

"But she's a pediatric specialist." Catherine pulled her phone out of her pocket and punched the speed dial number she'd set up for Mia Kendall. "She gave me her cell number. I've tried it several times, but it just goes immediately to her voicemail." The messaging service clicked on and sent panic galloping through Catherine's veins. "I don't understand it. She hasn't been here since Sunday."

"Dr. Kendall has many obligations at her hospital."

"You don't understand. She said she'd help me. Where is she?"

"Mrs. Taylor, calm down." Dr. Amandi draped his stethoscope around his neck. "I am more than capable of performing the operation."

"You screwed up before. What makes you think I'll let you screw up again?" Catherine threw her hands into the air. "How many chances do you think one kid gets?" She waved the phone in his face. "Listen to me, you sorry drunk. My father paid good money to make his granddaughter well. And my father always gets what he pays for." She leveled her glare at him. "Get that heart and get Mia Kendall to put it in." She held her finger threateningly over the cell phone numbers. "Or I'll make sure you never work again."

CHAPTER FORTY-EIGHT

WEDNESDAY, DECEMBER 18TH, 7:19 AM

MOROGORO REGION

Race rolled onto his side and groaned at the sharp pain that shot through his joints. Opening his eyes, he let them attune to the dark shadows enveloping him while his mind adjusted to his surroundings. Reality slashed through him. Exhaustion had finally given way to sleep in the early hours of the morning, but the feeling of helplessness continued haunting his scattered dreams. While the moon rose across the African night sky, he'd questioned his decision for them to run. They'd waited for their captors to let down their guard in order to escape, but at three in the morning, the guards were still wide awake while Jeme and the baby were fast asleep and fatigue registered heavily in Mia's eyes. Even if they did manage to escape the confines of the compound, he was afraid they'd never make it to safety. He'd finally insisted they get some rest and wait for another opportunity.

He licked his swollen lips, tasted the metallic taste of blood, then ran his fingers across the gash on his forehead. His face hurt, his side was bruised, and the lumpy mattress did little to soften the packed dirt beneath him.

Someone grabbed his shoulder. Automatically he swung around to defend himself.

"It's me," Mia whispered.

Her hair brushed against his face. "Mia?"

"Jeme and Zaina are gone!"

"What?" Early morning sunlight now penetrated the east side of the room enough to see Jeme's empty mattress. His hands fisted at his sides. He'd gone to hell and back in the Middle East, but everyone on his team had made it home alive, and he wasn't going to lose anyone this time.

"She's gone, and we've got to go after her." Mia skidded across the dirt floor then slammed her shoulder against the door, but the frame held steady.

"Stop. Maybe they let her use the toilet." Race pulled her away from the door. The doubt in her eyes said he'd better come up with another explanation or she was going to ram that door again. "Even if we were able to escape, we've gone over the risks a hundred times. There are three men out there with AK47s who aren't afraid to use them. Let me have a look. See if she's at the fire." He peered through the door slats and scanned the perimeter.

"Do you see her?"

He shook his head and backed from the door.

Mia slid down the wall and ran her hands through her tangled hair. "They've taken Jeme and Zaina, and I don't even want to imagine what they're doing to them."

Determination flooded through him. "We'll get out of here. . .and we'll find them."

"How?"

"I don't know."

Mia gulped down a breath of air. "If they want money, Zaina's the one they need, but if they kill her. . ."

Race grasped her shoulders. "Stop it. We don't know what's happened. Stop borrowing trouble. Not yet, anyway." He plastered his face against the thin crack in the door. "I only see two guards."

She joined him at the door. "Where's the other one?"

"He could be anywhere."

"Maybe he took Jeme."

Which would help even out the odds. Race started pacing. Following through with any plan, no matter how risky, was still better than sitting and doing nothing. Adrenaline pumped through his veins. He'd had enough. "You call Timbo and Haji, tell them you need the toilet, or something, and I'll ambush them—"

Before Race could finish his sentence, the door flung open and slammed against the wall. Sunlight blinded him. Race held up his hand to block the light then lunged toward the towering silhouette in front of him.

Haji was quicker. One hard strike with the butt of the gun knocked Race to the ground. Haji grabbed Mia's arm and dragged her from the hut.

CHAPTER FORTY-NINE

WEDNESDAY, DECEMBER 18TH, 7:26 AM

MOROGORO REGION

Face down in the muddy clay, Mia struggled against the guard's foot planted in the middle of her back. She didn't know what had happened to Jeme, but she wasn't about to roll over and let it happen to her. *God help me.*

Haji removed his foot and yanked her up. "Come."

She spat red mud from her mouth then lifted her chin. "No." Squinting against the early morning sun, she straightened against the rib piercing her side. "I'm not going anywhere until you tell me what you've done with Jeme and her baby."

"You will help." His grip tightened on her arm. He waved a bloody knife in front of her face. "Or I will kill your pilot friend."

Mia gasped. She jerked free and sprinted toward the sound of Race's boot kicking the inside of the hut's locked door. "Where are Jeme and Zaina?"

The guard thundered after her. He tackled her before she reached the hut. They rolled around on the hard-packed earth, the flash of his blade passing before her eyes. Adrenaline numbed the pain in her side and pumped angry power to her extremities. She pounded his back and clawed at his face. Wiry and strong, he flipped her over and pinned her beneath him, his quick breaths hot and furious on her neck.

"You will come." Grasping her arm, he stood and wrestled her to her feet. He dragged her across the compound, the stranglehold on her bicep sending tormenting jolts to her stiff muscles and empty belly. Her feet scrambled for solid ground while her eyes searched the edge of the clearing for a way of escape.

"He needs a doctor." Haji shoved her toward the fire ring where Timbo slumped on a log. Blood dripping from the palm of his outstretched hand hissed in the tiny flames.

Mia froze. "What happened?"

"Snake."

She immediately checked the ground around her. "Where?"

"Dead." The guard pointed to the thick coils at Timbo's feet. "You are a doctor. Help him."

Mia's skin crawled. She'd rather work a car wreck than deal with the damage caused by anything that slithered. Maybe Timbo's bite had been inflicted by a non-venomous serpent. She eased forward slowly to get a better look at the slain perpetrator. Its triangular head had been cleanly severed from a stout dusty-brown body branded with the chevron-shaped black bands of a puff adder—one of Africa's deadliest snakes. Shivers ran up her spine.

A quick glance at Timbo's face told her that shock had already begun to set in. She turned to the guard standing beside her. "Your friend's going to die."

He pressed the point of his knife against her side. "You are a doctor," he repeated. "Make him well."

Mia flinched, but didn't budge from her stance. "That particular species of viper is responsible for more fatalities than any other African snake. Timbo needs to be taken to the nearest hospital immediately."

"We have no truck."

She glanced around the godforsaken campsite. "Then you better get on that radio thing you've got rigged up over there and call for some transportation. And while you're at it, you can tell whoever took Jeme that I'm coming to get her."

Timbo hoisted the barrel of his AK47 with his good arm. "Haji calls when I say." Tremors ripped through his arm. He dropped the gun and vomited.

"Then you better make up your mind really quick." Mia turned to Haji. "How long before your friends return with the truck?"

Haji shrugged. "One day, maybe two."

"That's too long." She turned back to the man with his head between his legs. "You're a sick man, Timbo." Mia fought the urge to run to his side. "The pain will just get worse. Ten minutes from now your hand will be so swollen you won't be able to close it. Pretty soon, your arm will be twice its normal size and purple as a grape. Blood will start oozing from every major orifice in your body. Next thing you know, you won't be able to breathe. Your stomach will cramp worse than a woman in labor. Then you'll go into shock, and eventually organ failure."

She put her hands on her hips, waiting for Timbo to finish his retching. Once he sat up and wiped his mouth with the back of his hand, she continued. "Here's the worst part. It could take up to twenty-four hours for you to die." Pleased that her step-by-step medical guide to his possible demise had gotten his wide-eyed attention, she took a step forward. "Tell me what you've done with Jeme and I'll help you."

Haji waved his bloody knife. "You help or I kill you."

Mia wheeled on him. "Did you cut the bite puncture?"

Haji lowered his knife from her face, but kept it aimed at her chest. "I tried to bleed out the poison."

"Fool." She pushed the knife away and went to Timbo. "I'll try to limit the damage that idiot may have caused, but I'm going to need a few things. And an assistant."

Timbo gave a quick nod toward the hut. "Get the pilot."

Haji scurried to the hut. Mia tried to recall the details of the brief snakebite training she'd received when she arrived at the government hospital. Antivenom was so expensive, Shinwanga Regional didn't keep any in stock. She always thought her first course of action would be to refer any snakebite victim directly to Kaboni Private rather than treat it herself. She'd thought wrong.

The moment Haji freed the rope lock, Race shot from the hut and made a beeline for her. "Mia, you all right?"

She nodded and pointed at the dead snake. "Puff adder."

"They're a bad-tempered lot."

"Like someone I know." She returned Race's smile, doubly aware that she appreciated his steady presence more than a good scrub nurse. "He's got less than twenty-four hours. Help me get him to some shade."

Race came around and slid his arms under Timbo's. He lifted the good-sized black man off the log and dragged him toward the forest shadows. "Whew, Timbo, you're a big boy. You need to lay off the seconds on *ugali*."

Mia kept a close eye out for the possibility that the dead puff adder had been traveling with a companion.

Praying the area was free of the well-camouflaged reptiles, she told Race, "Put him here." She squatted beside her patient, her eyes double-checking every stick or clump of grass for movement.

Timbo moaned.

She examined his hand, checking for additional strikes. "Try to stay calm, Timbo." She made certain to keep her worry from his darting eyes. No sense riling him more than he already was. "Race, we have to keep him as flat as possible, but I need to elevate his torso a little bit so that his wound will be lower than his heart. Can you bring me that blanket from the hut? And see if you can find something I can use to splint his arm."

"Sure." Race sprinted toward the hut then stopped. "Hey, I've got an idea." He scooped up the radio and the battery attached to it.

"Put that down." Haji raised his knife. "No one calls until Timbo says."

Race clutched the primitive communication device in one hand and raised his other in surrender. "Look man, I'm just trying to help."

"It's no use," Mia said. "Even if you called, we're too far out to expect any emergency assistance."

Race inched toward her. "When I was in Iran, I saw a guy treat a snake bite with a battery."

"What?"

"He claimed the electric shock deactivated the venom. I don't know how it works, but the victim lived."

"I remember reading about some crazy Ecuadorian theory that claimed electric shock changed the three-dimensional structure of the toxin and converted the venom into an inert material, but. . ." Mia hesitated, weighing her options. "I'd feel better if we used a more traditional standard of care." She slid her knee under Timbo's head. "We need to bind his arm as tight as we dare and then get him to the nearest available antivenom."

"Well, Doc, in case you haven't noticed, we don't have a ride out of this hellhole. And like you said, the cavalry can't get here in time to save your patient."

Haji waved his knife. "If Timbo dies, you die."

He had her over a barrel. She couldn't die and let Jeme down. If only she could be sure where they were or how far into the bush they'd been taken. Maybe Haji would allow Race to go for help because Timbo weighed too much for them to carry. But from the set of Haji's jaw, unless the truck came back sooner than their captors expected, they had no guarantee of getting Timbo out of this alive.

Her eyes roamed the compound for another option. When she came up empty-handed, she allowed her gaze to return to Race's impatient one. "Fine, electrocute the man. But you better hope your medical malpractice insurance is paid up."

Race grinned as he lugged the radio equipment across the compound and plopped it down beside her. "Sometimes things don't fit into nice, neat little *standards*." He looked at her, his eyes deep calming pools. "Sometimes you gotta go for it." He started messing with the wires connected to the battery. "All I need is a solid connection to the wound and a strong DC pulsating electrical current."

Mia dragged her gaze from Race. The man had guts. "Mind if I check my patient before you blow him to kingdom come?"

Race stepped aside. "Be my guest."

Timbo's breathing was labored and watery blood oozed from the wound site. She ran her hand along the inside of his arm. His lymph nodes were swelling. She didn't have a better idea or the time to conjure one. And she wasn't sure Race could take Haji if it came down to it.

She sighed. "What can I do to help?"

Pleasure at her willingness to trust him tugged at the corners of Race's lips. "See if they have any bottled water left and wash the site then dry it completely."

Mia shouted an order at Haji, "Water."

He ran and fetched a bottle from near the fire ring. While she rinsed Timbo's wound and patted the area dry with the hem of her shirt, Haji paced.

"Now what?" Mia asked.

Race ripped his belt from his pants. "Place his arm on the ground and tie these wires so that the tips make direct contact with the wound."

Mia worked quickly, her nimble fingers expertly obeying his commands despite the trembling in her heart. If this unorthodox treatment didn't work, this man would die. "Done. Now what?"

"Good." Race held the opposite end of the two wires attached to Timbo's quivering hand. "Stand back." He held the free end of the wires over the battery posts. "Timbo, my friend, I'm going to save your life today. But I'm gonna hold off until you tell me which way to my plane."

Timbo tightened the grip on his weapon. "I will die then."

Mia jumped to Race's aid. "Haji, maybe you ought to explain to your friend how close he is to having a painful heart attack."

Haji looked at his perspiring friend, then pointed toward the two ruts cutting a narrow swath through the forest. "It's about fifteen kilometers from here."

Race smiled. "I think we can hike that, Doc. Don't you? If you're lucky, Timbo, we might even send someone to fetch your sorry hide."

"Except you are not going anywhere," Haji said.

Race moved the wires toward the battery then grabbed Timbo's gun in one swift move and aimed it at Haji. "That's where you're wrong. The two of us will be walking out of here."

"Never." Haji aimed his weapon at Race.

"Drop your weapon, Haji, and we'll save your friend before we leave."

Haji glanced at Timbo, then back to Race before finally setting his weapon down beside him.

"Mia?" Race pointed at the gun.

Mia's heart quickened as she picked up the weapon then stepped back again. She never should have questioned Race's ability to find a way out of this.

"Oh, one more thing, Haji, my friend," Race said. "I wanna hear all about who has that mother and baby."

Haji shook his head.

Anger flashed through Mia like a grease fire. The horrible images of Numa's mutilated body scorched her mind. If they'd taken Jeme so that they could sell Zaina's body parts, she'd kill the man herself. She sprang toward Timbo. "I'll make sure you rot right here if you don't answer him." She used the toe of her flip-flop and nudged his arm.

Timbo screamed at the pain. "Amandi."

Mia's mouth went slack. She dropped down beside him. "What about Amandi?"

He caught his breath then spit out, "He has the cursed one."

"Amandi has Zaina?"

Closing his eyes against the pain, Timbo nodded.

Mia's mind kicked into overdrive, worst case scenarios presenting themselves one after another. She'd seen what these men were capable of when it came to albinos, but why would a well-known surgeon want an albino? "Why would Amandi want the child?" She grabbed Timbo's shoulder. "Answer me."

Timbo's eyes slowly opened. "He needs a heart."

Mia fell to the ground, her heart twisting with a pain she'd never felt before. "Zaina's going to die so Kelsey can live."

CHAPTER FIFTY

WEDNESDAY, DECEMBER 18TH, 7:11 AM

DAR ES SALAAM

They'd taken her. Just as Jeme feared they would from the day Zaina was born. She'd been snatched from the safety of Dr. Kendall's home and then from the prison hut where they'd threatened her to keep silent. Now she and Zaina were alone and trapped in the backseat of a vehicle whizzing through the outskirts of Dar es Salaam.

Jeme glanced out the closed window at the sun that had just begun to peek over the city skyline. In the hazy morning light, people were already lined up along the sides of the road, waiting for a *dala-dala* to take them into the city. But the yellow rays of a new day did little to alleviate the terror swelling within her.

She glanced down at Zaina's sleeping form, her pale skin color lost in the still-dark shadows of the car. Born black in white skin. A curse to her people, yet one possessing mythical powers. How had a legend grown into this horrid reality that had brought her child to this point with no escape?

Jeme closed her eyes and replayed Dr. Kendall's conversation with the pilot the night before. Their words had tugged at the recesses of her soul and refused to quiet. Never before had she heard anyone speak about the worth of her child. Or about a God who didn't look at the color of skin. Powerful spirits manipulated her world by their own whims and fancy.

Jeme ran her finger across Zaina's soft cheek and breathed in the child's presence. As much as she longed to believe their words, how could their God, a God they claimed loved everyone, form a child then allow it to be taunted and murdered by others he'd created?

She moved her hand to the beaded band circling her waist. The amulets worn for protection had failed to heal Mbui or ensure the delivery of a normal child. Neither was her fierce love enough to protect those she loved.

The vehicle hit a pothole, and a sense of vulnerability washed over her. Her father wanted to kill Zaina. Her sister Patience had failed to defend her. In her family's minds, the fire that had ravaged her father's hut was simply another sign of the curse of her daughter's birth on the village. While she had never wanted to believe her daughter carried the legendary curse, neither could she believe that Zaina would grow up untouched.

The sound of murmuring voices snapped her attention to the front seat of the vehicle. She pulled Zaina tight against her, forbidding even the slightest breath to escape her lips and draw their attention to her.

The driver turned a sharp corner, slamming Jeme's shoulder into the door. She sat still, contemplating escape as the car stopped in the middle of a circular driveway. Her heart ached for the familiar cackling of her chickens, clothes blowing in the wind, and Mbui's presence in her own compound, but nothing about the scene before her was familiar.

"Where are we?" she asked.

"Shut up."

Rough hands dragged her from the vehicle, dashing any hopes of escape from the walled compound. She tripped up the stairs of a large house and tightened her grip on Zaina. She wanted to run, but these men smelled of blood. They would kill Zaina, and no loving God or spirits would be able to stop them. It was just a matter of time.

CHAPTER FIFTY-ONE

WEDNESDAY, DECEMBER 18TH, 9:49 AM

MOROGORO DISTRICT

Race trailed Mia in the direction Haji had assured them was the way to the nearest town and his plane. Their abductors might have had no choice in letting them go, but part of him still believed that he should have fried Timbo instead of trying to save his life. Of course, Mia wouldn't have agreed with him, but he still wasn't convinced her lofty ideals of doing good would ever make up for the evil in this world.

Mia picked up her pace a good twenty feet ahead of him. If she continued at this clip, with one water bottle between them and nothing to eat, she'd never outlast the heat.

She skittered to the right then froze.

"What is it?"

She jutted her chin toward the undergrowth. While he knew that the more forested areas of this area contained wildlife like monkeys, baboons, and antelopes, he figured they were far enough from any of the game reserves to be safe. Or so he hoped.

"I guess it's nothing." She leaned over and rested her hands against her thighs to catch her breath. "I thought I saw a snake."

He glanced again where she'd pointed, glad he'd kept the knife but thinking that the AK47 he tossed into the foliage a mile back might have come in handy. "Your chances of getting bit by a snake are actually quite slim unless you're tramping through the thick grass."

"Tell that to Timbo."

Race wiped the beads of perspiration from his face with the bottom of his shirt and ignored throwing out a comeback. He knew her well enough by now to know that arguing with her was a waste of time. She attacked the narrow tire ruts at a fast-paced jog.

He took off after her. "Mia, you've got to slow down."

"I can't." The sound of her voice was drowned out by the shrill call of one of the dozen or so birds he'd seen so far.

He lengthened his stride. "You'll never make it another five miles at this pace."

"Says who?"

"You've hardly eaten or slept for the past thirty-six hours, you have a broken rib, and now you're going to run a marathon in this heat?"

She spun around to face him. "Then tell me what to do. We hit this godforsaken road forty-five minutes ago and we still haven't seen a soul. We're not sure where your plane is, let alone the nearest town, and if Amandi has his way, he's at the hospital right now putting Zaina's heart into Kelsey's body."

He grabbed her by the wrist. "We're going to stop him."

"Not by standing here arguing."

The grinding clatter of a motorcycle coming toward them ended their bickering. The engine obviously needed a major overhaul, but the bike was running. . .Race didn't have to think twice about the harebrained idea that surfaced. He'd just found their ticket out of here.

Race let go of her wrist. "You don't happen to have any money on you, do you?"

"Why?" She eyed the oncoming heap. "Don't even tell me you're thinking about buying that jumble of metal. I could walk to Dar faster."

"Don't be too hasty with your evaluation of the situation. Watch and learn." He winked at her before he moved into the center of the road and flagged down the young driver wearing a ratty New York Giants T-shirt. "Jambo, Bwana."

The man reined the two-wheeled bucket of bolts to a jerky halt. Straddling the vibrating seat, he gave Race and Mia a wary once-over. "Jambo."

"What's your name?" Race shouted in Swahili over the chainsaw roar of the engine.

"Cigarette."

"Cigarette." Race's brow rose, wondering if this man's mother knew exactly what kind of heritage she'd passed on to her son when she'd named him. "You seem to be having problems with your motorcycle, my friend."

The engine sputtered and a plume of black smoke erupted from the back. "It's old and needs a few new parts, but it still runs." Cigarette grinned, displaying several missing teeth.

"How about I make you a deal and take this problem off your hands."

Cigarette looked more suspicious then interested. And who could blame him. Two *wazungu* in the middle of nowhere trying to wheel and deal him was enough to make any local nervous.

"What kind of deal?" he asked.

Race slipped off his watch and held it out. "This is a genuine Seiko."

"Or a cheap imitation," Mia whispered beside him.

"You are so not helping." He turned back to Cigarette. "It's worth at least a hundred American dollars."

The man rubbed his chin. "And you want to make a trade for my motorcycle?"

"You'd never sell this bike for that much."

The man shook his head. "Give me two hundred US dollars and you have a deal."

Race squirmed. "Well, here's the problem, Cigarette. Normally, I'd jump at a fair offer like that, but you see. . .I don't have any cash on me."

The man's chin dipped. "What about your shoes?"

"My shoes?" Race looked down at his Reeboks. They were now at a hundred and fifty bucks for a piece of junk?

"Your shoes and the watch. . .and your sunglasses." Cigarette smiled.

"Now wait a minute—"

"Watch and learn? Right." Mia chuckled under her breath.

He glared back. "I don't see you offering anything."

Mia shrugged. "You're the master."

Cigarette punched the gas. "Do you want the bike or not?"

Race reached down and yanked off his shoes. "Fine, we want the bike."

The man got off the bike and handed him the pair of sandals made from tire treads he'd been wearing. "I would not want you to get a bad deal."

You've got to be kidding. Race forced a smile. "Thanks."

The man laced up his new shoes, slipped on the watch and glasses, and headed down the road whistling.

Of all the dirty rotten. . .Race climbed onto the bike, which promptly sputtered and died. What else could go wrong? "Now I've officially been stripped of everything I have of value, including my pride."

He restarted the engine, gave it some gas, and prayed. Mia climbed on behind him and wrapped her arms around his waist.

Oh, boy. Now he was really in trouble.

Race eased on the throttle and took off, feeling every jolt in the bumpy road *and* every breath Mia took on the back of his neck. Leave it to him to have zero immunity to the most exasperating—and exhilarating—woman this side of the Sahara.

Forty-five minutes later, past dozens of potholes, overloaded bicycles, and faded Coke signs, the motorcycle shook, sputtered, then breathed its last on the outskirts of a small town.

But they'd made it back to civilization.

Race inhaled the smoky scent of cooking fires that filled the air. He took a moment to get his bearings, then spotted the landing strip just beyond a poorly constructed structure where a group of men lounged and shot pool.

"My plane's just across that field." He signaled for Mia to follow him. "We can be out of here in ten minutes."

Twenty minutes later, with grease up to his elbows, Race spun the unresponsive propeller and admitted defeat. Apparently, his captors had gone out of their way to ensure the plane was grounded. He was out of commission until he had time to scrounge up a few spare parts.

Race kicked the flat tire then squatted down beneath the wing.

What now, God? Don't tell me you're going to let that baby die because I was stupid enough to let Amandi win the last round. Don't tell me that.

Mia stood over him, her eyes rimmed with tears. "It won't fly, will it?"

"I could fix it if I had the parts and a day or two."

"We're still a couple hours from Dar, in the middle of nowhere, with no money, a dead phone battery, and Kelsey and Zaina don't have a day or two."

"I know." Race scanned the far side of the landing strip where a group of women, in their brightly colored African dresses, walked along the side of the road balancing plastic water containers on their heads. "Follow me."

"Where?"

"Back to town. I know a couple people who might be willing to help."

She shot him a guarded look. "People who will cough up enough cash for a taxi ride to the city?"

"Yeah. Maybe."

She folded her arms across her chest. "Do your contacts in town have anything to do with your organ jockeying?"

"There's a nun who works at the local clinic. I bring her food and medicines once a month and she distributes it." He brushed off his pants and started up the path, ignoring her guilty look. "There's a solar charging station two blocks away. Use some of your charm to charge your battery, then see if you can phone someone for help while I find us a ride back to the city."

She was washing off two-day's worth of dirt at the town pump, while letting her phone charge when he finished his second round of negotiations for the day.

"What'd you find out?" He started scrubbing his own hands, wishing he didn't notice how Mia's freshly scrubbed face glowed.

"Besides the dozen messages from people wondering where I am, there was a message from Harry Spence claiming to be in Dar."

"Spence? The researcher? He came?"

She nodded. "He says he needs to talk to me, but when I tried to call him, his phone went straight to voicemail." She twisted her hair into a knot and stuck a stick through the thick coil to keep it in place. "I spoke to someone at the American Embassy. They're going to need some proof before they start accusing one of this country's leading doctors of wrongdoing, but one of their officers has agreed to go Kaboni Private and talk to him. And they will search for Jeme while they are there, but I don't think he'll take her back there." She caught his gaze. "But you did find us a ride. Right?"

"Everything's under control." He ushered her down the street.

"In what universe?" Mia's voice had reached a frantic decibel. "If we don't find Zaina, she'll pay with her life."

"Do you think I don't know that? That's why I've found us a miracle. We'll be in the city in two hours."

"You've found us a miracle?" She skittered around a little boy chewing on a piece of sugar cane. "If it's anything like your motorcycle miracle, I still think I'd rather walk back to Dar."

Race pulled her in front of a dilapidated *dala-dala*. The small taxi van was loaded down with people, luggage, and half a dozen chickens. A two-liter Coke bottle filled with dirty water hung in the place of a fire extinguisher, and the front passenger door was missing.

Mia glanced up at the goat tied on top then back to Race. "You've got to be kidding. This will never make it out of town, let alone all the way to Dar."

A tall, wiry man stepped out from behind the taxi, his grin showing off his front pair of gold teeth. "We are set to go, Mr. Daniels."

"Dr. Mia Kendall, I'd like you to meet Moses."

Moses held out his hand. "I am pleased to meet you, doctor."

Race slung his arm around Mia, who stood beside him, speechless. "Moses here has two seats left and has agreed to take us to the Promised Land."

CHAPTER FIFTY-TWO

WEDNESDAY, DECEMBER 18TH, 11:32 AM

DAR ES SALAAM

Jeme rose from the thin mattress where Zaina slept unaware of the horror awaiting her. Once more she tried to open the door of the small room, but it remained locked. She glanced around the stuffy space and landed on the barred window. Rising on her tiptoes, she stretched as far as she could. But the tiny opening remained out of her reach.

She was trapped. And with no one to help her stop the man with the white coat. When he returned, he would take what he wanted. She would fight with all her might, but he had the gun. Like it or not, her Zaina would die.

Fear snaked through her body, hissing at the questions she could no longer ignore. Was the legend true? Would Zaina live forever? An albino's body may be killed, but according to the stories her father's wives told around the cooking fires, the spirit of the zeruzeru never died.

Jeme sank onto the mattress and stroked Zaina's snowy head. She wrapped a strand of her daughter's tight little curls around her black finger. This child was bone of her bone, no matter the difference in the color of their flesh. She scooped the sleeping child into her arms, unable to bear the thought of her baby floating over the grassy plains, a spirit forced to forever wander the savannas alone.

Fingering the beaded cord cinched at her waist, Jeme prayed to the spirits, but heard no response. Only the slumbering rise and fall of Zaina's chest. Her village had turned against her. Her family had deserted her. Even the ancestors had turned their backs on the cursed child and the mother who loved her.

What if Dr. Kendall was right? She cradled Zaina to the ache in her breast, careful not to wake her. What if the American really knew a God who didn't see Zaina's soft pinkish feet that would one day turn thick and leathery? What if it was true that the doctor's God could look at Zaina and see into the very depths of her heart? A God who believed that her child deserved a future because she was a human being?

Her mind tried to wrap itself around the strange notion. What kind of God loved unconditionally? What kind of God didn't see what everyone else saw, or valued life no matter the color of the skin? Was such a thing even possible?

Jeme fumbled with the beaded amulet band cutting her in two and tried to comprehend what it would mean if Dr. Kendall's words were true. Something within her stirred. Her friend had spoken to her about how her God had created the night stars, the vast savanna, and made the corn to grow in its season. If Dr. Kendall's God had created such wonders, then he must have created Zaina as well. Jeme's fingers yanked on the band around her waist. The beads scattered across the floor like tiny pebbles.

Zaina stirred and began to cry.

Jeme offered the child her breast and began to pray to the only God who could help her.

CHAPTER FIFTY-THREE

WEDNESDAY, DECEMBER 18TH, 11:40 AM

DAR ES SALAAM

The barred windows of the makeshift lab enclosed Harry like a prison. All he could see was a long, green lawn framed by palm trees that finally ended at a high, stone wall. Mia's cell phone number spun around and around in his head. He needed to call her, or the police, or anyone who could help, but that meant he needed a phone. And the man who'd taken him had confiscated his the moment he'd arrived.

Harry flipped through the stack of notes that had been left for him on the long table. His instructions had been clear: make ZAR242 work and make it work now. But how could he modify a faulty drug in such a short amount of time when he wasn't sure what needed to be altered? Everyone at BPH knew he'd been at least six months away from human testing. Throwing him into some third-world lab with a fraction of the equipment he needed wasn't going to change that timeline. All the notes had managed to confirm were his fears that someone had begun human testing with his unfinished anti-rejection drug. And that Dr. Kendall had been right. The files she'd sent him had convinced him that the increased rejection in her patients had been due to ZAR242.

He eyed the box sitting on the table. It had an American postmark. He picked it up and looked more closely. A Baltimore, Maryland overnight postmark. And the return address was BPH Technologies. He ripped away the clear packing tape and peered inside.

Copies of his research notes, a vial of ZAR242, and a note.

Make this count. If he can't make this work, kill him.

Billings

Hands trembling, Harry removed his glasses and wiped away the sweat. He'd been set up by his own boss. But how did Billings know he'd come to Africa when he'd only made the decision on a dare from Valerie?

Harry's body began to quiver with rage. Was she in on the whole sorry deal? Was she sent in as a spy, a decoy to keep an eye on him?

He slammed the paper on the table and studied the walls of the cinderblock room for the hundredth time. Two small windows were covered with iron bars and the only door was locked from the outside with a heavy bolt. He eyed the wooden structure and weighed his options. His doom would be sealed once his captors realized he wasn't going to produce some magic formula anytime soon. He'd become a liability. Which would leave him no better off than Axton. Dead. And he wouldn't even have the luxury of dying in the arms of the woman he loved...had loved.

Harry closed his eyes and pictured Valerie's red hair, blue eyes, and the sweet scent of gardenias that followed her. If she were here, she'd have him doing more than just studying cracks in the yellowed walls. Wait a minute. What was he thinking? She was the reason he was here.

But he was no dummy. Surely his stack of advanced degrees was worth more than the pieces of paper they were printed on. All he needed was a quick exit out of this sweltering prison.

He took a deep breath and tried to relax. "Think, Harry. Think. All you have to do is get the guard back into the room, then come up with some kind of distraction so you can escape. A chemical explosion, or a smoke bomb."

Harry smiled. At the age of fifteen he'd been competing in science fairs on an international level in biophysics. A smoke bomb was nothing.

But an explosion required some sort of a chain reaction. He started digging through the drawers of the large metal cabinet, looking for anything he could mix together. He'd seen only one other person since his arrival. Someone had brought him breakfast this morning after a restless night on the lumpy cot in the corner. He glanced down at his flabby gut, wishing suddenly he'd opted for hours at the gym instead of sitting in his lab chair. The odds of him throwing a punch hard enough to knock the man down were slim to none. But if he could get the guard to open the door, he might just be able to even out the odds.

He thrust his hand into the next drawer and sifted through the contents, looking for anything he could use. Matches, alcohol. . .Three drawers down, his hands closed around a ring of keys. He paused. Maybe he didn't have to blow his way out after all.

With shaky hands, he moved to the door and tried the first key. Nothing. The second and third were too big. The fourth. . .a perfect fit.

Harry reached for his inhaler then remembered they'd confiscated it along with his cell phone. He sucked in a calming breath and tried to relax. Maybe it was just as well he hadn't gone ahead with his smoke bomb plan.

Slowly, he cracked open the door and peeked into the hall. No one in sight. He stole through the door then paused again to listen for voices, but all he could hear was the faint cry of a baby. Strange. Easing down the hall, Harry followed the baby's whimpering, his heart threatening to burst from his chest. His fictional pages crawled with villains and scoundrels, and he'd equipped Axton with everything he needed to defend himself. He glanced down at the key ring and the water bottle he'd grabbed from the counter before leaving the lab. Some hero he made.

He listened for the sound again and finally decided on one of the locked doors. His key undid that lock as well. He cautiously pushed open the door. A young woman and a small child lay huddled in the corner of the room on a mattress.

She pulled further into the shadows. "Please do not hurt us."

"Hurt you? No, of course not." He eyed the terrified mother. Whatever was going on, the stakes had just multiplied.

She inched forward on the mattress. "Then help me, please. They are going to kill my baby."

"I don't understand." Harry forced back the seeds of panic. Surely Axton wasn't the only one who could play hero. "Who's going to kill you?"

"The human hunters."

"*Human* hunters?" Harry took a step backwards as his lungs constricted.

The woman held her pale child closer. "They will take our hearts."

Harry gasped for breath, the loss of oxygen draining his much-needed brain-cell power. What would Axton do? What he wouldn't do was drop over from an asthma attack and let a woman and child die.

Harry snatched a breath and forced it down his narrowed throat. "Don't worry." He tossed her his water bottle. "I'll figure out a way to get all of us out of here."

CHAPTER FIFTY-FOUR

WEDNESDAY, DECEMBER 18TH, 12:11 PM

MOROGORO DISTRICT

As the multi-colored van bounced toward Dar es Salaam, Mia closed her eyes so that she wouldn't have to watch Moses swivel in the driver's seat, completely taking his hands off the wheel and his eyes off the narrow mountain road. Try as she might to block out his near miss of every large tree or the occasional unsuspecting pedestrian, she couldn't shake the feeling that she'd completely lost her better judgment.

Maybe she was going insane. Same as her mother. What other explanation could possibly account for her willingness to squeeze into an overloaded vehicle that stank of wild onions, unwashed bodies, and dirty diapers?

Dirty diapers? She lifted the chocolate-brown infant Moses had stuffed into her arms and checked the dingy cloth wrapped around his tiny bottom. Stained and well-worn, but clean and dry. Cradling him close, she gazed into his black-button eyes. His puckered lips curved into a toothless smile that tugged at her heart. She couldn't resist pressing two fingers to his bare chest, secretly counting each strong beat. Steady and healthy. So different than the rhythm in Kelsey's...so much like Zaina's.

Mia blinked back tears and pulled her hand away. What if she didn't get to the hospital before Amandi... she could not allow the image of Amandi committing murder in his operating room to form in her head. Until they reached Dar, all she could do was pray that the woman she'd spoken to at the Embassy would follow through with her promise to send someone to the hospital. This horror had to be stopped.

Moses stomped the gas and goaded his ancient *dala-dala* around a hairpin curve and up a small incline. Coughing and chugging, the van crested the hill. Through the dirty windshield, Mia could see the city of Dar es Salaam shimmering in the afternoon heat. Her heart raced while her mind braked at the stampeding fear of blowing a tire and careening off the road before they reached the hospital. If that happened, who would save Kelsey and Zaina?

"Can't he go faster?" she shouted to Race over the noise of the engine.

He shifted the chicken crate on his lap. "Can't you scoot over, Doc?"

"Just where do you think we can go?" She transferred the baby from one arm to the other. "We're wedged in tighter than sardines."

"My point exactly. Moses is doin' the best he can."

Mia reached over and plucked a downy feather from his hair. "Guess you get what you pay for."

His lopsided smile was meant to reassure her, but it was nearly impossible for her to breathe.

About three blocks from Kaboni Private the taxi stalled in traffic. Horns blared and venders pounded the vehicle vying for attention. Sweat dripped down Mia's back. She could walk faster. Just as she was about to suggest she and Race make a run for it, she felt her phone vibrate in her pocket.

"I'm getting a call." She handed the baby to Race. He balanced the little fellow on top of the chicken crate while she squirmed to fish the phone from her pocket. A quick glimpse at the caller ID sent her heart to the pit of her stomach. "It's Shadrach." She swiped the screen. "Shadrach, how's Mbui?"

"Dr. Kendall." He sounded frantic. "I'm sorry I missed your call. Where have you been?"

"It's a long story, but I'm okay. Update me on Mbui."

Shadrach said nothing for a moment, then cleared his throat. "Your patient is dead."

The news knocked the last of the breath from her lungs. "When?" she gasped, trying to force air into passages that had constricted with a crushing grief. If she could have called earlier, maybe she could she have saved him.

"Early this morning."

"What is it?" Race demanded.

Mia waved him off, afraid she'd cry if she tried to explain. "Shadrach, I'm on my way to Kaboni Private. Call Pastor Scott to help you with the funeral arrangements." She turned off her phone and looked at Race. "Mbui didn't make it."

"Oh, Mia. I'm sorry."

She reached for the infant, desperate to feel life in her arms. "What if—"

"Don't even think it. Somehow, someway, we're gonna save those girls." He passed the chicken crate to the man behind him. "Let's go."

Mia handed the baby back to its mother and followed Race as he stepped over children and market goods blocking the aisle. He clamored out of the van and waited. Mia fought her way to the door then she jumped into his arms. He set her on the ground and they both took off at a dead run.

Dodging coffee salesmen and women weaving colorful mats, they galloped the last three blocks to Kaboni Private. Less than five minutes after leaving Moses and his tribe, they bolted through the hospital doors. The sanitized smells of sickness and death hit Mia in the face. She raced toward the reception area and the woman typing on an older model computer.

Breathless, she gripped the counter's worn edges. "Where's Amandi?"

"Dr. Kendall? Dr. Amandi is not here."

Mia wheeled. The same woman who'd had her removed from the hospital stood in the hall.

"Where is he? Don't even think about lying to me. Is he in OR one or two?"

"Neither." She clutched a medical chart. Her eyes surveyed Race, who stood next to Mia. "I have no idea where the doctor is. His American patient is dying and I can't find him anywhere. I've called and paged, but he doesn't answer."

"Excuse me." A woman tapped Mia on the shoulder. "Dr. Kendall, I'm Juliet Stevens. I'm with the Embassy."

"Thank God. Dr. Amandi has got to be arrested. One little girl's dying and another—"

"Dr. Kendall. We don't have the authority to make arrests, but I have taken your statement and notified the proper authorities. And if they determine your allegations have merit—"

"Merit? Are you kidding me?" Mia's anger ricocheted off the cinderblock walls and echoed down the halls. "How many dead bodies do we have to have before you'll decide this situation has merit?"

"Dr. Kendall, we have international guidelines and rules that prevent us from—"

"Two little girls are going to die if they have to wait on a mountain of bureaucratic red-tape to clear. For their sakes, I'm begging you to bend the rules."

Race took hold of Mia's elbow. "Mia, let's check Kelsey's room."

Mia shot off toward the ICU. She burst through the door.

Catherine Taylor, who was leaning over Kelsey's bed, jumped. "Dr. Kendall. Where have you been?" Her shirt was covered in blood spatter.

"Oh, God no. . ." Mia pushed past her for a good look at Kelsey. She grabbed the child's tiny wrist and felt for a pulse, checking the machine on the wall at the same time. "She's still alive."

Catherine nodded. "Dr. Amandi said he had a heart."

"Where is he?"

"I don't know. My father just called and told me that the replacement heart would be here today."

Mia looked at Race standing in the doorway, the color drained from his face. "What are we going to do?" She clamped her hand over her mouth to keep from vomiting.

Race pointed at her vibrating pocket. "Is that your phone?"

She looked at him, trying to decipher a question that didn't make sense. "What?"

"I hear a cell. Is it yours?"

She dug her phone out of her pocket. Amandi's residential number was on the caller ID. She flipped it open. "Amandi! You sorry—"

"Dr. Kendall." She could barely make out the whispered voice. "This is Harry Spence."

"Who?"

"The researcher from BPH."

"What—"

"Please, Dr. Kendall. Just listen. I can't talk long. I'm afraid they'll catch me using the phone. I'm in Africa and I've been kidnapped. I'm being held in a below-par lab and expected to fix ZAR242. I can't work in these conditions. Besides, ZAR242 is six months away from being ready. But they won't listen to me. I'm afraid they're going to kill me if I don't come up with something. And not too long ago they brought in a black woman and her albino child. I don't know where we are—"

"I know where they are," Mia said to Race before she turned to the Embassy worker who crowded into Kelsey's tiny ICU room. "Juliet, if it's not too much trouble for the American government, we need a ride."

CHAPTER FIFTY-FIVE

WEDNESDAY, DECEMBER 18TH, 2:52 PM

DAR ES SALAAM

Mia and Race bolted from the Embassy liaison's small government-issued car. They left Miss Stevens sitting behind the wheel and stewing in her insistence that they produce hard evidence before she initiated U.S. involvement.

They sprinted across Amandi's fancy drive, toward the white stucco bungalow tucked beneath the shade of lofty banana trees and lush leafy palms.

Mia reached the cool of Amandi's shady porch a split-second before Race. "If BPH Technologies gets away with their backwoods-testing program. . ." She pounded on the thick slab of shellacked hardwood, not willing to think about that now.

"Stand back." Race raised his leg and kicked at the door. It didn't budge. He kicked it again, this time breaking the frame loose. He pulled at the splintered pieces, prying the door from the frame enough for her to squeeze through. "Get going."

Mia wedged herself through the fractured opening and landed with a thud in the tiled entryway. She sprang to her feet then froze. Three different halls led in three different directions. Behind her, Race alternated between kicking and prying, trying to make a gap big enough for his broad-shouldered body to squeeze through.

Suddenly the entire frame gave way and he burst into the foyer. He stumbled to her side, listened for a moment, then said, "Follow me."

They tore toward the angry voices coming from the end of the middle hallway. Mia's flip-flops smacked each tile. Simultaneously, they burst into the room and halted.

The heated conversation abruptly stopped.

Mia's eyes swept the large living room. To her left, Amandi held a gun. He had it pointed in her direction. Opposite her, Jeme and Zaina huddled on one end of a leather couch and a frazzled man with thick glasses and a nose splint hugged the opposite arm of the couch. Her gaze continued to the right, as if her eyes were instinctively drawn to the tall, distinguished man wearing a baby-blue golf shirt that accentuated his healthy tan.

"Dad?"

"Mia?" Her father turned to her and opened his arms. "Thank God you're all right."

"What are you doing here?" She wanted to run to him and melt into his embrace like the little girl who used to wait up way past her bedtime. But something wasn't right.

"Yes, Dr. Hastings, why don't you explain to your daughter how you—"

"Shut up, Amandi." Her father snapped.

"Hastings?" Race turned to Mia. "I thought your last name was Kendall?"

Mia's eyes flicked from her father to Race and his confused face, then to Doctor Amandi, and back to her father. "I've been using my mother's maiden name."

"Why?" Race asked.

"To protect me and my reputation. Though you never needed to do that." He strode toward her. "I've missed you, Mia."

"And I'm sure this is how you envisioned your family reunion," Amandi said. "Though be careful, Dr. Kendall. When Miranda discovered the truth, it killed her."

Mia wheeled. "What are you talking about?"

The African doctor's position under the polished ivory tusk mounted on the wall made it appear he had a shiny horn protruding from his head. "Everyone on campus had a crush on the beautiful Miranda Kendall...but my good friend and roommate, Charles Hastings, was the one who managed to win her heart."

"You knew my mother?" she asked, trying to make the pieces of the puzzle fall into place.

Amandi's smile stretched across his face, his gold eyetooth glinting in the antler-chandelier's light. "Of course I did. And let me tell you, when the son of a death row inmate manages to marry the daughter of a prominent East Coast banker, he has arrived." His obvious pleasure at dragging up her family tree rippled across his potbelly.

"Death row? You told me he'd gone to prison, but never that he was on death row." What else had her father lied about?

Her father's jaw tensed. "Mia, all I ever wanted was to make a difference in this world."

"Maybe at first." Amandi kept the gun level. "Until your wife got sick, and the bills began to pile up faster than the hours you worked."

Her father smiled that same gracious, placating smile she'd seen him give his patients right before he split them open from stem to stern. "Dr. Amandi has had too much to drink. Again." He stepped toward her. "Obviously, he's been up to no good, and now that you've found him out, he's determined to turn you against me."

"That's because you're in just as deep as I am," Amandi spouted.

Mia held up her hand, the things her mother used to mumble tumbling into her head. "What did you do to my mother?"

"I loved your mother, but she was sick. You know that."

She backed toward Race.

"Sweetheart, I'm so sorry. It never should have come to this—"

"Just tell me what's going on?"

"Mental illness is a horrible disease. And when your mother got sick I needed a way to make some extra money. All I wanted to do was help her."

"So you what? Got involved in some unscrupulous drug company?"

"Of course not, sweetheart."

"Well, actually, if I could interject something here..." The frazzled man with thick glasses had his hand raised as if he awaited a teacher's permission to continue. "I'm Dr. Harry Spence, and your father is a silent partner at BPH." He pushed his glasses up over the splint. "Who I'm sure was part of setting me up and illegally pushing for FDA approval."

"Shut up, Spence," Mia's father snapped.

"So that's it?" Mia took a step toward her father. "This is all about money. People are dying."

"Mia, I didn't know—"

Harry cleared his throat. "Excuse me, doctor. I just think it important that if we're clearing the air, so to speak, that Dr. Kendall have all the facts, especially the ones that relate to the organ rejection problem that seems to be at the root of this whole mess."

Mia stared at this strange man, her mouth hanging open.

Dr. Spence scooted forward on the couch, his forearms resting on his thighs, his steepled fingertips tapping a nervous rhythm. "BPH Technologies originally hired me to perfect Tryoxylate. But the formula is hopelessly flawed." He cleared his throat again. "So I began working on a replacement drug, ZAR242. That way, if the FDA pulls Tryoxylate, which I know they will, BPH Technologies' losses will be minimized." He let out a sigh, seemingly relieved to have all of that off his chest.

"And to speed up the process, you needed test subjects," Mia snapped, horrified that her father was somehow involved in this.

Harry stopped fidgeting. "Oh, my. No." He sat very still, his bug eyes darting from Amandi to her father. "ZAR242 is not ready for human trials."

Mia's father smiled. "Now, Harry, I'm sure you've underestimated the extent of your talents."

The change in her father's tone set off alarm bells in Mia's head. This was the same voice he'd used when he talked to her mother, cajoling her, convincing her everything would be fine.

"No." Harry smoothed his rumpled shirt. "At this point administering ZAR242 would be extremely dangerous. Most patients wouldn't survive."

Anger surged through Mia's limbs. She'd been right. A drug *was* killing her patients. Her father's greed had killed Mbui and her other patients. "The game is over, Dad. Real people have died."

"You have to believe me, Mia. I never meant for this to happen."

"Using patients as a testing ground? And where did you think Amandi was getting his seemingly unlimited supply of organs? Neiman Marcus?"

"I swear I didn't know."

"You play so innocent, but you are just as guilty as I am," Amandi said. "Go get the child and let's be done with this."

Jeme handed Zaina to Harry, then flew from her perch and dropped to her knees before Mia's father. "Please, do not hurt my baby. Take me. Take my heart." Tears glistened on her upturned face.

Mia's father hesitated.

"Get the child, Hastings," Amandi waved his gun. "If that American girl dies, it's over for both of us."

Jeme moved in front of her screaming baby.

Amandi raised his gun. "Stop right there."

Mia stepped up in front of her father. "I'm not going to let you harvest a heart from a living donor. You kill this little girl, and you'll never be able to drink enough to wash the guilt away." She turned to her Amandi. "Both of you."

Her father watched the flailing child, his eyes weighing his choices as Amandi took a step and shifted his aim toward Zaina.

"Don't do it, Amandi," Race said.

"He's right," Mia's father said. "There has to be another way."

"You never did like getting your hands dirty." Amandi cocked the hammer on the revolver. "But you owe me way too much to back out now."

"Sorry," Mia's father said, "but if you want this heart, Amandi, you'll have to take it out yourself."

A shot ripped through the tense air.

Mia felt her breath leave her body in hot, jagged gasps. Her father's body slumped against hers. She managed to shift her torso and the surgeon she'd always wanted to emulate dropped face-first to the floor. A pool of blood blossomed from under his head. "Dad!"

Nausea bent Mia over. She squatted and put her finger on her father's neck, checking for a pulse. But she knew by the pool of blood spreading beneath his head she would not find one. Her gaze tore to Amandi. "What have you done?"

"What I should have done the moment you arrived in Africa." Amandi pinched the bridge of his nose as if this whole ordeal had given him a tremendous headache, then raised his steel-gray eyes to hers. "You're a smart girl, Mia. Smarter than your mother. And a very talented surgeon. I should have known that anyone who'd walk away from a million-dollar-a-year practice because a little cheerleader had died on her table would question unexplained rejections."

"You knew who I was?"

"The medical community is a small world."

Race started for her.

"Stay where you are," Amandi ordered, waving the gun at Race and then at Zaina. "This albino will die of melanoma or at the hand of a witch doctor before she's thirty. Why not use her heart now to save a child who can have a real life?"

Jeme leapt from her kneeling position. "You cannot have my Zaina. She is the daughter of Mbui. A great man. A better man than you."

Amandi took a step closer, the gun raised above Jeme's head. "You're letting this useless woman waste valuable time here, Mia. You and I both know that little Kelsey Taylor doesn't have long to live. We're in the business of saving lives. Help me out here."

"I'm in the business of saving lives." Mia snatched Zaina from Harry, hiding the child in the crook of her body and shielding her with her hands. "You're in the business of saving yourself. Making more and more money, and a bigger and bigger name for yourself!"

"My unconventional methods may not fit into your interpretation of the Hippocratic Oath, but because of me, that American child will live."

"And to hell with anyone who gets in your way, right? Even if it's a beautiful little girl who just happened to be born in Africa instead of Cincinnati's upper eastside?"

"That's what the Americans pay me for."

"No!" Harry lunged from the couch and tackled Amandi.

The gun spun across the room.

End over end, the two men tussled across the floor, knocking a vase from the coffee table, crashing into a chair, and then grabbing for the gun that was now underneath both of them. Race jumped into the fray and the three of them spun like a snowball being rolled around a yard to make a giant snowman.

A shot rang out.

The snowball fell apart. Race going right. Harry going left. Amandi coming up in the middle with the gun.

A scream started in Mia's gut, traveled up her throat, and ripped her vocal chords on its way out of her mouth. "Jeme!"

Jeme wavered for a moment. Then, like a reedy stalk of brown grass being rustled by a soft savanna wind, she sank to the floor.

CHAPTER FIFTY-SIX

WEDNESDAY, DECEMBER 18TH, 3:00 PM

DAR ES SALAAM

"Stay down." The impact of Race's sudden pounce slammed Mia and Zaina against the cool terrazzo. He rolled off them and scrambled to his feet.

Mia lifted her head. "Race, no!"

Another gunshot sounded just as Dr. Spence did a swan dive between her and Race, slamming Mia to the tiles again.

Dr. Spence landed in a groaning heap on top of her. Frantic, she scooted out from under him. Blood gushed from his shoulder. "Hang on, Dr. Spence." She pressed her hand to his wound to staunch the flow.

"Halt!"

Mia jerked up her head to locate the commanding voice. A visual sweep of the door produced a pale-faced Miss Stevens, her eyes wide with horror, and two police officers standing on either side of her with their weapons drawn.

"You'll have to kill me." Amandi fired at the policemen.

Bullets whizzed through the air in rapid, machine-gun succession.

Race dove for cover on the other side of the room. Mia flung her body over Jeme's child.

The loud ringing lacerated her ears and split her heart. Plate-glass windows shattered and priceless pieces of native art exploded into tiny pieces that showered the zebra rug with wood shavings.

Then suddenly there was quiet. Deathly quiet.

As quickly as the chaos had started, it ended, but the smell of gunpowder lingered in the air and splintered shards of debris slowly tinkled to the floor like falling stars.

Heart beating through her skin, Mia peered over her arm. The alert eyes of the two policemen surveyed the living room, then on the count of three they stormed into the shot-riddled melee. Mia pushed herself upright on shaky limbs. She spotted their suspect target before they reached him.

Amandi lay sprawled on the floor, dead, next to her father.

It was over.

All of it. BPH Technologies. Tryoxylate. ZAR242. Their involvement in black market organs ripped from albinos and other unsuspecting victims. New drug-therapy hopes for transplant recipients. And her family. But, in truth, the family she thought she'd had was taken from her long before her father squeezed the trigger. Charles Hastings had made a deal with the devil. And in the end, his greed had cost him his soul.

The policemen approached him with their arms extended and weapons braced.

Mia's emergency training snapped her shaky legs into gear. "Race, get Zaina." She turned to the officers. "I'm a doctor. I need to tend to this woman." She hesitated at the sight of her father's gunshot-laced torso then raced to Jeme. She turned and squatted beside Jeme and placed two fingers against her slender neck. And found a pulse.

Jeme fastened her eyes on Zaina and the child wrapped in Race's arms. "Now you will live my little one." She cupped her hand to her bloody abdomen. "Give my heart to Kelsey."

Amandi's head scrub nurse dabbed at the sweat trickling from Mia's forehead.

Her shoulders ached with the frightened tension she'd banished from the daunting task before her. This was a routine transplant, she told herself again. Allowing emotions to shake her ability to keep a steady hand on the suture threads would not do this little girl one bit of good. Mia stared over her surgical mask, afraid to blink lest she break her concentration. She'd deal with all she'd lost another time.

She cinched the last of her precise and tidy knots that would forever bind these two strangers. "Cut." The nurse clipped the line and Mia treated herself to a tiny relieved step back. "Let's take her off bypass."

As her staff fluttered around the operating room tending to their assigned jobs, she surveyed the purplish organ lying dormant in Kelsey's open chest. The ancient Greeks believed that a person's soul resided in the heart rather than in the brain. For this moment, her mind would willingly forsake modern science if believing that folly could make the theory true for this heart.

The donor organ had been a snug fit for the child's small torso, but the blood and tissue match had been perfect, as if this particular heart had been divinely ordered ahead of time for this sick little girl. Even though the child's immature immunity system gave her a little more leeway than an adult donor-host consideration, Mia always preferred giving her patients the advantage of matched compatibility and optimal size. This time, she'd been blessed with both.

Every step of the intense harvest and subsequent transplant had gone without a hitch. Textbook by every medical standard.

Yet, until she saw a definitive blip on the monitor, or that surging quiver of life that jolted lethargic organs from hibernation, she knew better than to take a breath.

"Doctor, the heart is not beating," Shadrach reported solemnly.

God, please.

Mia leaned over Kelsey and checked inside the open chest cavity to make sure that every suture was still holding. Convinced she'd done everything right, but unwilling to leave anything to chance, she gently massaged the exposed organ as precious seconds ticked away the odds of this child coming out of surgery alive.

Please, God. Let her live. For the sake of the mothers, let her live.

Catherine perched on the edge of the plastic chair in the surgical waiting niche. She checked her watch again. Four hours had passed since the crazy invasion of ambulance sirens transformed Kaboni Private's quiet halls into a war zone.

When she'd heard Dr. Kendall shouting, "We've got a heart. Prep the Taylor girl," she'd burst from the ICU and came running. Medical personnel streamed through the doors of the lobby hurriedly pushing three bloody bodies strapped to squeaky gurneys.

God had provided the second chance she'd begged him to give her Kelsey.

Yet, when the final moment came to part with her baby, Catherine had wanted time to stand still. She'd pled for one more opportunity to feel her lips against Kelsey's velvety-soft cheek. But all too quickly, the nurses had whisked her daughter from the ICU. Dr. Kendall's solemn face had not given her much hope that she'd ever kiss Kelsey's sweet cheeks again.

Hands trembling, Catherine pulled her cell from her pocket. No messages. None. She'd called Brad, but when he didn't answer, she left a voicemail that they'd taken Kelsey in for the second transplant. In her panic, she'd even phoned her father, but she'd failed to locate him, too.

Fingers of fear clawed at her breaking heart. She crammed the phone into her pocket. Alone and scared to death, her eyes focused on the closed operating room door. How much longer before she knew something? How much time did she have before she had to face life without her little girl? She buried her face in her hands and let the tears flow.

"Mommy?"

Catherine raised her head. "Jonathan?" She opened her arms and sucked her son to her. She squeezed him tight. "What are you doing here, buddy?" She held him out at arm's length, blinking back the tears to make sure he wasn't a figment of her imagination. "My precious boy." She kissed his face over and over, weeping and laughing at the same time.

"Cat?"

Her eyes grazed the top of Jonathan's curls. "Brad?" She released their son and stood. "Oh, Brad." Sobs closed her throat. "I'm so sorry. I should've listened. I don't know if Kelsey's going to live."

"Shhhh." He held out his arms and she buried her shame in his embrace. "I should have listened." He held her tight, kissing the top of her head as all of their exhaustion and emotion of the past five years combined to generate racking, gut-wrenching sobs. "We did the best we could, Cat. We did the best anyone could do."

"Mommy?" Jonathan tugged on her shirt. "Grandpa let me sit by the window."

She lifted her head from Brad's chest. "What, buddy?"

"Grandpa let me sit by the window so I could see the ocean."

Catherine turned. Her tear-blurred vision landed on her father, his pleased grin taking years off his lined face. "Dad?" Her confusion flicked from Brad to her father and back to Brad. "What's going on?"

"Grandpa says Daddy beat some sense into his hard head."

"Actually it was the jab above the belt that humbled me." Her father's grin had spread into his trademark, full-fledged chuckle.

"The Deuce and I have come to an. . .understanding." The twinkle in Brad's eyes melted the ice between all of them.

Salty tears wet Catherine's expanding smile. "But what about the divorce?"

Her father reached into his pocket, pulled out an envelope, and ripped it in two. "What divorce?" He stuffed the pieces into a nearby trashcan. "My grandkids deserve a mom...and a dad."

Mia cleared the operating room, determined to do this one last thing alone. She should go out and speak to Mrs. Taylor, explain to her what had happened, but that task would have to wait.

Blinking back tears, Mia turned her attention to the still body on the gurney. She took hold of the sterile drape and carefully folded it back.

Tight cornrow braids framed the peaceful ebony face. She gently closed Jeme's eyelids, remembering the joy she'd seen in those eyes as this mother watched her baby play.

She exposed the hurried gash between the tiny breasts that had nursed Zaina. Mia picked up her needle. Stitch after meticulous stitch, she closed the hollow cavity made empty by the selfless gift of a mother's love.

CHAPTER FIFTY-SEVEN

FRIDAY, DECEMBER 20TH, 4:00 PM

DAR ES SALAAM, KABONI PRIVATE HOSPITAL

Kelsey giggled and squirmed away from Catherine in an attempt to intercept the matchbox-sized Batmobile her brother pushed across the metal rail of her hospital bed.

"Hold still, punkin." Catherine secured the ends of the leather cord Kelsey had insisted Catherine return to her neck after her spit bath. "You don't want to lose the pretty charm, do you?"

Kelsey's cherub face scrunched into serious consideration. She thought for a moment, and then with a decided shake of her blond curls declared, "No. Never."

The appreciation her daughter was developing for a stranger's token of love brought a smile to Catherine's lips. As a mother, she understood the significance of Jeme's gift, but how a five-year-old could acquire such a strong attachment and innate understanding of the sacrifice was a mystery. She had to admit Dr. Kendall's explanation made the most sense. Organ transplantation melded bodies, but God united spirits.

From the moment Kelsey aroused from the anesthesia, she could tell Jeme's heart was doing far more than pumping physical strength into her baby. Wisdom and compassion seemed to be transfused into Kelsey with each steady beat.

Catherine glanced at the two men sitting side by side at the foot of Kelsey's bed. Brad and her father had their attention glued to the snowy figures on the TV set bolted to the wall. Kelsey's had not been the only heart healed by Jeme's gift.

"Can Zaina watch cartoons with me and Bubby?" Kelsey's tug on Catherine's T-shirt yanked her from her thoughts. "I made room for her right here." She patted her pillow, her eyes bubbling with newly-acquired vitality.

Catherine laughed. She could drink from the sparkling blue wells and never get enough. Cupping Kelsey's rosy cheeks between her hands, she pulled her daughter close and kissed her pink lips. "Daddy and Grandpa are catching up on the news. Soon as it's over, we'll see about finding Zaina."

Catherine's father swiveled in his plastic chair. "Oh, let her watch what she wants."

"Dad, she has to learn that her every wish isn't a command." She slid a clean gown over Kelsey's shiny curls then began threading the IV line through the armhole.

"Well, it is while her Grandpa's here." The Duece pushed up out of his chair. "You want Zaina, doll baby?"

Kelsey's smile crinkled the corners of her eyes. "Zaina wants me." She pointed at her chest. "I feel it here."

Catherine and her father exchanged surprised looks across the bed.

Her father was the first to recover. "Well, when a woman knows her heart, a smart man does what he can to help or gets out of her way." He looked at Catherine and she knew this admission was an apology to her. "I'll see what I can do about finding Zaina."

"Before she cries," Kelsey added, her face gravely serious.

"Causing a woman to cry wouldn't do my ratings a bit of good, so I'm going to get right on this."

"Dad. You'll spoil her rotten."

"Are there any other reasons to have grandkids?" He took

Jonathan's hand. "Come on, buddy. Let's see if we can't scare up a cold Coca Cola along the way."

"Dad, you'll ruin his dinner."

"Fully intend to." He winked at her. "Ruined yours many times," He paused and smiled the Deuce dazzler. "And you turned out just fine."

"Dad—"

"Let 'em go, Cat." Brad stood and shooed them out the door. "Jonathan expended so much energy trying to get me to do the right thing, he probably could use the extra sugar. And I know he's eating up the attention your dad is showering on him."

Catherine looked up and saw the young assistant district attorney that she'd interviewed years ago. The man she'd fallen in love with the moment she saw how much he cared about obtaining justice for people who couldn't defend themselves.

"Need some help?" he asked her.

Catherine's heart ached to be one with his again, to know the strength that comes from having someone in your corner. "I could use a hug."

"That I can do." He came around behind her and slipped his arms around her waist. She melted into his embrace as he nuzzled her neck. His touch sent goose bumps down her back. He rested his chin on her shoulder and they both stared at their daughter.

Kelsey beamed at them, as if this moment of reconnection had been the result of her own orchestration. "Daddy's kissing Mommy."

Brad snuggled Catherine tight against him. "She's a totally different kid, isn't she?" The pleasure in his voice was as warm as his breath on her neck.

"We all came out of this different." Catherine turned and wrapped her arms around his neck. "And I, for one, am glad." She kissed him, letting Brad's strength infuse her rather than pushing it away like before. She needed his help. No, she wanted his help. And, Lord willing, she'd never charge through another minute of this precious life without him.

While she drank her fill of Brad's support, she could hear Kelsey clapping and chanting. "Daddy's kissing Mommy."

A satisfied tingle running through her body, Catherine pulled away to check on their little cheerleader. "Wanna see if you can get her settled down before she has a heart attack?"

Brad's grin stretched from ear to ear. "Not funny." He gave Catherine another quick peck, then released her and stepped up to the bed. "All right, punkin. Nap time."

Kelsey flashed an impish grin, showing perfect little teeth that had previously only been seen when her mouth had to be pried open for meds. "I not tired."

"She's not tired," Catherine whispered. "For the first time ever."

Brad and Catherine couldn't contain their joy. The dam that suffering had built between them broke, and they laughed until tears cascaded down their faces, the salty streams washing away years of stress and tension.

Swiping at his cheeks, Brad did his best to get his emotions under control and put on a stern parent face. "You may not be tired, little lady. But we are." Careful to avoid the scar on Kelsey's chest, he gently fished the necklace out from under her gown so that the tiny charm glowed in the afternoon light.

He handed Kelsey her pink night-night. "Here you go." So he *had* been paying attention to his daughter's care all those years. Catherine had just been too exhausted and single-minded to see it. "You need to take a little rest before dinner."

To Catherine's surprise, Kelsey quickly and happily obeyed. She settled back on her pillow. "You promised I'd see a monkey, Mommy."

"We'll do our best," Catherine reassured.

Immediately Kelsey's eyes grew heavy.

As she drifted off, she murmured, "I want Zaina, Daddy."

"And I want you to get well. Sleep, my little one." Brad leaned over the rail, and before he could kiss her she was sound asleep.

The door opened and Catherine's father and Jonathan blustered into the room with Dr. Kendall and Zaina in tow. "Look who we found," her father shouted.

"Shhhh," Catherine and Brad said together.

"Sorry." With a sheepish grin, The Deuce and Jonathan quietly stepped aside and allowed Dr. Kendall and Zaina to approach Kelsey's bed.

Zaina lunged for Kelsey. "No, sweetie. Kelsey can't play right now." Dr. Kendall shifted Zaina to her other hip. "How's our patient?"

"She's doing great." Catherine thought the word far too inadequate to express the urge she had to offer herself as an indentured servant to Dr. Kendall for the rest of her life. "She's the daughter we never thought we'd have."

"We can't begin to thank you..." Brad choked up and couldn't finish.

Dr. Kendall waved off their gratitude. "Mind if I take a look? I'll try not to wake her."

"She's been going at bat-speed since lunch," Catherine said. "But I think she's out for a bit."

"Will you hold Zaina for me?"

"I'd love to." Catherine extended her hands and Zaina smiled and reached for her. The instant their flesh connected, Catherine felt the same tug she had the day Jeme had trusted her with her most prized possession. "What's going to happen to this baby now?"

"Not sure." Dr. Kendall lifted the stethoscope draped around her neck. "There are some orphanage options here in Dar where she would be safe. Nothing close to her own people." She hesitated. "I've even thought of raising her myself, but my schedule is crazy."

"Can't you find a family who'd take her in? Adopt her or something?" Brad's legal wheels were spinning. Catherine could see them careening way ahead of the conversation.

Dr. Kendall shook her head. "Zaina is zeruzeru. A ghost. A curse. A child no one will want for fear she will bring bad luck and death to their family."

Catherine had explained Zaina's predicament to Brad. The unfathomable idea that anyone could allow the slaughter of a people group simply because of their skin color had raised every hair on his defending-the-defenseless neck. Now, it seemed to stir the passion she'd long admired in him.

"But now that the government knows about the albino slaughter and the transplant tourism thing Amandi had going on with your—" Brad cut himself off.

Catherine could see that the near mention of Mia's father was very painful for the doctor, but the woman did her best to cover it up. "High-ranking government officials have promised me they'll step up their efforts to protect the albinos." The doctor didn't look as confident as she was trying to sound. "They've even put an albino woman into parliament in an attempt to debunk the myths, but freeing people from a legend that has them by the throat takes time. I'll continue working toward that end, but Tanzania is a big country with not enough—"

Jonathan tugged on Catherine's T-shirt. He pointed at the TV. "Mommy, isn't that the doctor who's going to make Sissy some new medicine?"

Everyone turned their attention to the TV. A CNN reporter, decked in a winter scarf and hat, was standing in the snow piled beside a BPH Technologies sign. Dr. Harry Spence stood next to a striking redhead, his arm still in a sling, as he shivered behind the reporter's microphone.

"Turn it up, Dad." Catherine laid Zaina down beside Kelsey, gave her a night-night, and moved closer to the TV.

The reporter shoved the microphone into the scientist's face and asked, "Dr. Spence, is it true that you single-handedly stopped the illegal human drug trials conducted by BPH Technologies on the unsuspecting impoverished in Africa?"

Dr. Spence pushed his glasses over his nose splint. "Well, actually—"

The redheaded woman grabbed hold of the reporter's mike. "Harry Spence is a hero." Her breath came out in big, foggy puffs. "And someday the world will thank him for the way he put his very life on the line for the sake of mankind."

The picture went fuzzy and they lost the connection. The room was silent, no one knowing whether to pray Harry Spence would indeed save the world, especially Kelsey's future, or that BPH Technologies would burn to the ground for all the harm it had caused.

"Mommy, can I watch TV?"

Jonathan's question was a welcome relief. "Sure, buddy. Let me get Zaina out of your way." Catherine turned to retrieve the child from

Kelsey's bed. Jeme's baby was curled beside Kelsey, sound asleep, her pale little hand clasping the charm.

"I'll move her as soon as I examine Kelsey."

"No. She knows where she belongs." Catherine looked to Brad. Full agreement passed between them. "And so do we."

EPILOGUE

MONDAY, JANUARY 11TH, 1:00 PM

DAR ES SALAAM

Rain dripped like tears from Mia's umbrella as she and Race stood outside the chain link fence watching the Taylors' chartered plane disappear into the dark clouds. She'd known with each passing day that eventually Kelsey's health would improve enough for them to take her home. Two weeks after Christmas, she could think of no more reasons to put off signing the thriving child's discharge papers. But nothing, not even the conjoining of Kelsey and Zaina or their refusal to be separated, had prepared her for this day and the intense pain breaking her heart.

Race put his arm around her shoulder. "Zaina has a much better shot at a future in the States," he soothed.

"I know she would have died here. If not from melanoma, then maybe at the hands of the albino butchers still eluding the authorities. But..."

"You love her."

Mia nodded, swallowing the lump of sorrow wedged in her throat. Once the high-profile case had hit headlines across the globe, the

Tanzanian government—intent on shedding a good light on their country and proving they were intent on combatting crimes against albinos—had made an unprecedented exception and fast-tracked the Taylor's adoption of Zaina.

But that wasn't all that had happened since Jeme's death. One of Amandi's nurses had come forward, confessing she was the one who'd left the BPH clue on Mia's car. Once taken into protective custody, she'd gone ahead to provide further information into Dr. Amandi's illegal operations. As a result, local authorities—along with help from the World Health Organization—had worked quickly to track down those involved in Amandi's illegal schemes. In the following days, Mia's secretary Sarah, who had turned out to be the leak between the two hospitals, was arrested, along with seven other people, including three from Shinwanga Regional, Amandi's secretary, and a doctor running a mobile clinic that had been used to identify potential donors. In the U.S., not only had Billings been arrested, but a full investigation into BPH Technologies had begun with assurances of more indictments to come.

Judgement might not be delivered today. . .It might not even arrive tomorrow. . .but in the end, evil will not win.

"I was wrong about something," Race said, interrupting her thoughts. "Wrong about God."

"What do you mean?" She looked up at him, waiting for him to elaborate.

"Things haven't always turned out the way I wanted them, but I'm realizing that God was never the one who failed me." He brushed back a strand of hair from her face. "And I don't know about you, but I'm ready to stop running."

She smiled up at him and let him kiss her while the rain fell softly around them.

He turned her from the fence and took her hand. "Come with me."

Fifteen minutes later they were strapped into Race's yellow Piper Cub. The rain had stopped, leaving the air sticky and the sandy runway steamy. Race hit the throttle and his little plane sped toward the end of the strip. They lifted through the muggy atmosphere and veered toward the western sky.

A bank of clouds, swathed in brilliant purples and various shades of blue streaked with pink, filled the horizon. The stunning picture was outlined in a vibrant orange glow. The kaleidoscope of color reminded Mia of the finger painting Kelsey had made for her office. Each family member was a stick figure drawn in a different color. Zaina, in rosy pink, had been placed in the very center. When Mia asked Kelsey why she'd made everyone a different color, she'd considered the question for a moment and then said, "If we were all the same, the picture would be boring." If only adults had the accepting vision of a child, a vision that saw the merit of a world that was neither black nor white.

Mia clutched the package Race had placed in her lap before take-off. She and Race rode in silence. Their shoulders touching. Their hearts bent on the same mission.

"There it is." Race pointed at the barren expanse of black volcanic ash that covered Mt. Meru's jagged peak. He patted her leg. "Ready?"

She hugged the small wooden box to her chest and nodded. Race circled the mountain, skimming low over the horseshoe-shaped crater that looked like God himself had left his thumbprint amongst the huge cliffs and spectacular waterfalls.

Mia slid open the window. Ocean breezes that had traveled inland to dance upon one of Tanzania's highest peaks ruffled her hair. Hands trembling, she lifted the lid and gazed at the powdery gray contents. The physical lives of Jeme and Mbui had been reduced to ashes, but their spirits would live forever in two precious little girls. She held the box out the window and wept as the African winds scattered the remnants of unconditional love to the four corners of the earth.

"It's finally over." Race squeezed her knee.

"No." She pulled the empty box back into the plane. "It's just beginning."

ACKNOWLEDGMENTS

Stories this complicated to tell require a bevy of expert help. We are grateful for the many people who shared their expertise or pointed us in the right direction. Dr. Megan Maxwell, Don Crum, Jody Dean and the KLUV Morning Team, Ellen Tarver, Lonnie Gentry, Scott Harris, and Janet Johnson. A special thanks to all our beta readers as well as our influencer team's enthusiastic support.

It truly does take a village.

DISCUSSION QUESTIONS

1. While Ghost Heart explores the prejudices that separate us, what are some of the things you believe unify us?

2. Caring for a critically ill child, as the Taylors had to do in Kelsey's case, can be financially, physically, and emotionally taxing. Share your ideas of how to relieve the burden of a family under this kind of stress.

3. In many ways, the racial targeting of albinos mimics the attempted Jewish genocide of World War II. Discuss the dangers of a movement driven by fear and suspicion. How can the walls we build around our preconceived notions be brought down?

4. Of all the issues addressed in this story, what surprised you the most? Prejudice? Transplant tourism? The slaughter of a minority people group? Unethical practices in pharmaceutical testing? Struggles of the uninsured? Which one terrifies you the most and why?

5. How can we make a difference in a world that judges people by their appearance, financial status or their physical health?

ABOUT LISA & LYNNE

LISA HARRIS is a Christy Award finalist for Blood Ransom and Vendetta, Christy Award winner for Dangerous Passage, and the winner of the Best Inspirational Suspense Novel for 2011 (Blood Covenant) and 2015 (Vendetta) from Romantic Times. She has over thirty novels and novellas in print. She and her family work as missionaries in southern Africa. Lisa loves hanging out with her family, cooking different ethnic dishes, photography, and heading into the African bush on safari. Visit Lisa's website at www.lisaharriswrites.com to learn more. You can also find out more about her ministry at http://africanoutreachministries.org

LYNNE GENTRY is an actor/director turned fiction author who loves using her crazy imagination to entertain audiences with her books. Her varied works range from the highly-praised time travel series (Carthage Chronicles) to a laugh-out-loud romantic comedy series (Mt. Hope Southern Adventures). Romantic Times calls this Top Pick author "one to watch." Readers say her writing is extraordinary and her stories exceptional. When Lynne is not creating enchanting new worlds, she's laughing with her family or working with her medical therapy dog. Find out more about Lynne on her website at www.lynnegentry.com.

Sign up at http://bit.ly/2uXpHIQ **for BOTH Lisa and Lynne's**

Newsletter and receive a complimentary ebook copy of Blood Ransom & Walking Shoes!

INSIDER CHAT WITH THE AUTHORS

Where did you get the idea for this story?

LYNNE: Just over a decade ago, a newspaper picture of a terrified albino caught my attention. As I read about the horrors these fragile people face, I couldn't believe such evil existed in the world. I contacted Lisa, who lives in Mozambique, and asked her to find out if what I'd read was true.

LISA: Until Lynne wrote to me about the article she'd read, I'd never heard of these barbaric crimes. But after doing some further research, I discovered that what she'd read was true. Once we learned that the witch doctors use the pale skin and hair of these fragile people to make good luck charms and potions, we knew we had to tell their story.

Is the plight of albinos real or something you made up for this story?

LYNNE: Sadly, the atrocities committed against those born with this rare genetic mutation is very real. Less than two percent of Tanzanian albinos survive beyond their 40th birthday.

Why did you feel that writing about the atrocities happening to albinos was a story that needed to be told?

LYNNE: We both have a heart for those suffering prejudice and discrimination. People with albinism are not ghosts. They are human beings.

LISA: And this issue goes far beyond the horrors facing albinos. All around the world people are discriminated against. Sometimes it's for the color of their skin. Other times it's for their faith or beliefs. But in the end, we are all human beings and we all bleed the same color.

What is happening to stop this practice?

LYNNE: Superstition still has a strong hold in Africa. It is a widely-held belief that the body parts of an albino can bring healing to the sick, fertility to the infertile, and wealth to those who possess a charm made from albinos. According to Amnesty International, the macabre trade is also fueled by a belief that bones of people with albinism contain gold and that sex with a person with albinism can cure HIV. For years, the attacks against these people have been met with social indifference and are seldom followed up by investigation or prosecution.

According to the United Nations Human Rights Office of the High Commissioner, international and regional human rights mechanisms have only "sporadically addressed the needs of persons with albinism. Since June 2013, because of the recrudescence of attacks against them these bodies have given more attention to persons with albinism."

LISA: The United Nations Human Rights Council has passed a mandate of Independent Expert on the enjoyment of human rights of persons with albinism. This will help to give a voice to people with albinism and create a greater awareness of what they are suffering.

For those interested in exploring more about what is happening to albinos, where can they start?

Here are three ideas.

1. Visit United Nations Human Rights Office of the High Commissioner: http://www.ohchr.org/EN/Pages/Home.aspx Tweet your support to persons living with albinism *#notghosts*
2. Ask your leaders to protect and promote the rights of persons with albinism
3. Report human rights abuses against persons with albinism through a local non-governmental organization, the UN Human Rights Office Headquarters, or a UN Human Rights office near you.

Besides giving readers a fast-paced thriller, what do you want people to get out of this story?

LYNNE: Beneath the color of our skin we are all alike. Because my novels always speak to the intrinsic worth of each of us, I long for the day we can all learn to look past outward appearances.

LISA: In most of my suspense novels, I turn to real life events that affect our world today. In highlighting things—like the issues facing albinos today, I hope that people will step up and get involved in their own communities and make a difference.

How does co-writing a book differ from writing your own story?

LYNNE: There is a creative give and take that makes the storytelling process more difficult, but in the end, we believe also makes the story more powerful.

LISA: This was the first time I'd ever done anything like this, but while it was challenging, it was also a huge blessing to me. It allowed us to each take our strengths and put them together, while also learning from each other.

Can you tell us some about the brainstorming process of this book?

LYNNE: Since we live on different continents and in different time zones, we did a lot of the work via email. The skeleton of the story went back and forth between us many times. However, when we really needed to solve a plot point we would set up a Skype call, which also gave us a chance to visit and reconnect. And since we really do enjoy each other, those calls were a treat for both of us.

LISA: A project like this definitely was something I loved doing since I don't have a lot of contact with other writers on a day-to-day basis. And having two people brainstorm ideas for a book is always a win-win situation.

As co-authors, how did you do the actual writing of the book?

LYNNE: First, we decided we wanted our hero and heroine to each have a distinctive voice. The easiest way to achieve their separate voices was for each of us to choose which one we wanted to write. Next, it made sense for Lisa to write the scenes involving African characters since she lives there. Because of my connections to the medical world through my daughter and husband, I did the research and writing for those scenes.

LISA: Once we decided on who was going to write which characters, it allowed us to focus on that part of the story line, and on each specific character's backstory and personalities. Watching the story then come together was really exciting.

What was the hardest part of writing this book?

LYNNE: It is never easy to examine your own assumptions and prejudices. Even while writing this story, I had to come face to face with erroneous ideas I had about Africa and the people who live there. Lisa was forever pointing out those errors. I'm grateful for the deeper understanding I have of these beautiful people and believe taking time to get to know another culture removes the barriers caused from ignorance and fear.

LISA: For me, just the reality that what we were writing about might be fiction, but the story behind the story is real. It's given me more of a heart to listening to others in their difficult circumstances.

How long have you been writing?

LYNNE: I've always been a storyteller, focusing on dramatic works, but I didn't start novel writing until 2002.

LISA: I began writing after my husband and I adopted our oldest son back in 1997. Six years later, I had my first novella published and I've been writing ever since.

What is your writing process like?

LYNNE: My inspiration usually comes from a small tidbit or interesting historical fact that I stumble across in my reading. I love to take unusual events or circumstances or characters and spin them into tall tales. I will then allow a seed of an idea to germinate, sometimes for years, and then it seems something will happen that magically waters the idea and suddenly a story sprouts. I'm more of a seat-of-the-pants writer than Lisa. Working with her has taught me so much about the value of planning and plotting ahead.

LISA: Since I write romantic suspense, I often get inspiration from a movie, TV show, or real life situations like with *Ghost Heart*. I spend a lot of time upfront brainstorming to get a framework for the story. I also don't write chronologically, but often will write through different threads. For me, that can really help me get to know my characters better, something that Lynne taught me.

What other books have you written?

LYNNE: I've written ten books including, The Carthage Chronicles, a time travel series, and the Mt. Hope Southern Adventures, a humorous small town series. Learn more at www.lynnegentry.com.

LISA: I've written around thirty books. While I started off writing romance novels for the Christian market, I now write romantic suspense. You can check out my books at www.lisaharriswrites.com.

What projects are you working on right now?

LYNNE: I'm finishing up my Southern Adventures series and starting an exciting young adult time travel series.

LISA: I'm currently writing a stand-alone novel for my publisher Revell that will come out next year, as well as one for Love Inspired Suspense set in Brazil and the Amazon.

Are you planning on co-writing another story together?

LYNNE: Lord willing and the creek don't rise.

LISA: We do have another story line worked out that I'm itching to write.

Visit
Harris-Gentry Suspense Blog @
harrisgentrysuspense.blogspot.com
to learn more!

ALSO BY LISA HARRIS

SOUTHERN CRIMES

Dangerous Passage

Fatal Exchange

Hidden Agenda

THE NIKKI BOYD FILES

Vendetta

Missing

Pursued

A NIKKI BOYD NOVEL

Vanishing Point

MISSION HOPE

Blood Ransom

Blood Covenant

LOVE INSPIRED SUSPENSE

Deadly Safari

Desperate Escape

Taken

Stolen Identity

Desert Secrets

Fatal Cover-Up

Deadly Exchange

MEDICAL THRILLER

Ghost Heart

ALSO BY LYNNE GENTRY

THE CARTHAGE CHRONICLES

A Perfect Fit (eShort Prequel)

Healer of Carthage

Shades of Surrender (eShort Prequel)

Return to Exile

Valley of Decision

MT. HOPE SOUTHERN ADVENTURES

Walking Shoes

Shoes to Fill

Dancing Shoes

Baby Shoes

MEDICAL THRILLER

Ghost Heart

Sign up for Lynne's newsletters @ https://www.lynnegentry.com/landing-1/
and keep up with her latest news and book releases!

MISSING
LISA
HARRIS
THE NIKKI BOYD FILES
Best-selling Romantic Suspense
The Nikki Boyd Files